NIGHTMARE

NIGHTMARE

STEPHEN LEATHER

ISIS
LARGE PRINT
Oxford

First published in Great Britain 2012
by
Hodder & Stoughton

Published in Large Print 2012 by ISIS Publishing Ltd.,
7 Centremead, Osney Mead, Oxford OX2 0ES
by arrangement with
Hodder & Stoughton
An Hachette UK Company

British Library Cataloguing in Publication Data
Leather, Stephen.
   Nightmare.
   1. Nightingale, Jack (Fictitious character) - -
   Fiction.
   2. Demonology - - Fiction.
   3. Suspense fiction.
   4. Large type books.
   I. Title
   823.9'2–dc23

ISBN 978–0–7531–9034–0 (hb)
ISBN 978–0–7531–9035–7 (pb)

Printed and bound in Great Britain by
T. J. International Ltd., Padstow, Cornwall

CHAPTER
ONE

Jack Nightingale opened his eyes to find the barrel of a police-issue Heckler & Koch MP5 carbine about an inch from the end of his nose.

"If that's anything other than your dick in your hand I'm pulling the trigger," growled the police marksman holding the weapon. He was wearing a Kevlar helmet and protective goggles.

"That's not the official police warning, is it?" said Nightingale. Two more armed police appeared at the end of the bed and their weapons were also aimed at his head. "What the hell's going on?"

The marksman stared at Nightingale with unblinking grey eyes. "Move your hands very slowly from under the quilt," he said, saying the words slowly and clearly.

"I don't have a gun and I'm stark bollock naked," said Nightingale.

"Just show us your hands, nice and slowly," said the marksman.

Nightingale did as he was told, sliding his arms from under the quilt and raising them. A fourth officer appeared and grabbed Nightingale's wrists, quickly fastening them together with a plastic tie.

"Are there any weapons in the flat, Nightingale?" asked a voice from the end of the bed. Nightingale squinted at the man. He was wearing a bulletproof vest over a dark blue suit. It was Superintendent Ronald Chalmers. Tall with greying hair and flecks of dandruff on his shoulders.

"What the hell's going on, Chalmers?"

"We're going to be searching your flat from top to bottom so you might as well tell us now," said the superintendent. "Do you have any weapons here?"

"Of course not."

Chalmers nodded at the door. "Take him through there and start on this room."

The officer who'd tied Nightingale's hands pulled him out of the bed.

"At least let me hide my modesty," protested Nightingale.

The superintendent picked up a sheet and threw it at Nightingale. Nightingale caught it and the officer pushed him through the door to the sitting room. Two more armed officers in black overalls and bulletproof vests and helmets stood by his dining table, cradling their weapons.

Nightingale wrapped the sheet around himself and sat down on his sofa. A portly man in dark blue overalls was kneeling next to a plastic toolbox by the front door. "Did you pick my lock?" asked Nightingale.

"I'm just doing my job," said the man. He was in his sixties, his bald head spotted with dark brown liver spots.

"Yeah, well, I hope they're paying you overtime," said Nightingale, looking at his watch. It was five o'clock in the morning and still dark outside.

Chalmers walked out of the bedroom and glared at Nightingale. "Where's the gun, Nightingale?"

"What gun?"

"We'll tear this place apart, if we have to," said the superintendent.

"Yeah? Well, you'd better have a warrant."

Chalmers reached inside his jacket and pulled out a sheet of paper. He tossed it onto the coffee table.

"Warrant or not, the Met's going to be paying for any damage," said Nightingale.

A uniformed sergeant appeared at the door. Chalmers turned around to look at him and the sergeant shook his head. "Kitchen and bathroom," said Chalmers. "Then the spare bedroom." The sergeant went back into the bedroom to speak to his men. Chalmers pointed at Nightingale. "Get some clothes on," he said.

"Are you arresting me?"

"I will if you don't get in there and get dressed," said the superintendent.

Nightingale held up his hands. "How am I supposed to get dressed like this?"

Chalmers sighed and took a Swiss Army knife from his pocket. He pulled out a small blade and cut the plastic tie. It fell to the floor and Nightingale rubbed his wrists. "What's this about, Chalmers?" he asked.

"Get dressed. You'll find out soon enough."

3

CHAPTER
TWO

Nightingale was taken down the stairs to the street handcuffed to a burly constable wearing a bright yellow fluorescent jacket over a bulletproof vest. Nightingale had pulled on black jeans, a blue pullover and a leather jacket but had forgotten to pick up his cigarettes and lighter from the bedside table. "Don't suppose you've got a cigarette on you?" he asked the cop.

"Filthy habit," grinned the man, pulling open the side door of the police van. It was a grey Mercedes Sprinter van with TSG markings. The Territorial Support Group. The Met's heavy mob. Behind it were two blue saloons. Armed cops were stowing their gear into the boots.

"Yeah, well, it's not as disgusting as breaking into people's homes at the crack of dawn," said Nightingale.

The cop climbed into the van and jerked the handcuffs to pull Nightingale inside. There were two armed police officers in black overalls, bulletproof vests and Kevlar helmets sitting at the back, cradling MP5s. Nightingale grinned and waved with his free hand. "Expecting trouble, boys?" he said as he sat down.

The two men stared at him impassively.

More armed officers were piling into the back of a Volvo V70 Armed Response Vehicle as the driver turned on the siren and flashing lights. Curtains and blinds all the way down the street began to twitch.

Nightingale looked at the cop sitting next to him. "This isn't going to win you friends, you know that," he said. "Most people have got jobs to go to."

Chalmers walked out of Nightingale's building and nodded at the driver of the van as he got into the back of a black Vauxhall Vectra.

The driver put the van in gear and followed the ARV down the street; Chalmers pulled out behind them. They drove in convoy south to the Thames and over Vauxhall Bridge towards Stockwell. Eventually they pulled up in front of the main entrance of Lambeth Hospital.

Chalmers got out of the Vauxhall and went over to talk to the men in the ARV, then the Volvo peeled away from the kerb and sped off back to north London. Chalmers walked over to the van. A stick-thin cop with ginger hair and freckles across his nose and cheeks pulled open the side door. "Out you get," he growled at Nightingale.

Nightingale and the constable climbed out. Nightingale held up his handcuffed wrist. "There's no need for this, Chalmers. I'm hardly likely to do a runner, am I?"

Chalmers said nothing. He turned on his heel and walked inside the hospital. Nightingale and the cop followed him. Heads turned to look at them as they strode across the reception area to a bank of lifts. They

5

rode up in silence to the fourth floor. The Intensive Care Unit. They walked down a corridor lined with glass panels that looked into small rooms where patients, mainly elderly, were attached to machines that were either monitoring them or keeping them alive. The doctors and nurses paid the police no attention and there was a purposeful buzz of conversation overlaid with the beeping of sensors.

"Are you going to tell me what's going on, Chalmers?" asked Nightingale, but the superintendent ignored him. Nightingale grinned at the cop. "Maybe his wife's giving birth and he wants me to be the godfather," he said. The cop scowled but said nothing.

At the far end of the corridor was a young constable sitting on a chair reading a newspaper. He looked up, saw Chalmers approaching and hurriedly got to his feet, hiding the paper behind his back. Chalmers brushed past the man and opened the door to the room. He walked in and jerked his thumb at Nightingale. "In," he said.

Nightingale went through first, followed by the cop he was handcuffed to. The man lying on the hospital bed in front of him was Afro-Caribbean and in his late twenties. There were wires leading from his chest to a heart monitor that was beeping softly at the side of the bed. His head was bandaged, covering his skull and one eye. The uncovered eye was shut.

"You know him?" asked Chalmers.

Nightingale shrugged. "Hard to say, looking like that."

"Dwayne Robinson," said Chalmers. "Gangbanger from Brixton. Someone shot him in the back of the head six months ago; he's been in a coma ever since."

"And this concerns me how?"

"Where were you on July the twentieth?"

Nightingale laughed. "Are you serious? How would I know? Who knows what they were doing six months ago?"

"So it could have been you who blew his brains across the pavement?"

Nightingale sneered at the superintendent. "This is what passes for interrogation these days, is it? Look, Chalmers, I know you're not the sharpest knife in the drawer but what makes you think I had anything to do with this? I'm not generally the first person that Trident calls on to help with their investigations."

"We don't think this was black on black. There was a white male seen running from the scene."

"I'm not a great runner, for one," said Nightingale. "And I don't often go south of the river, for two. And for three, I don't go around shooting people."

"But a lot of people around you have been dying lately, haven't they?" said Chalmers. "Starting with your father."

"My biological father. And he killed himself, remember?" Nightingale pointed at the man in the bed. "What's this about? I've never seen him before and I certainly didn't shoot him."

The door opened and an Indian doctor walked in. He nodded at Chalmers. "I hope this isn't going to take long, Superintendent. I'm not happy about having this many people in the ICU."

"A few minutes, Dr Patel. Has there been any change since last night?"

The doctor picked up a clipboard from the bottom of the bed, looked at it, then shook his head.

"Robinson has been in a coma since he was shot," Chalmers said to Nightingale. "There's minimal brain activity. He's never going to wake up. That's what they thought, anyway. Until yesterday." Chalmers stared at the beeping monitor and folded his arms.

"All right, Chalmers, I'll bite," said Nightingale testily. "What happened yesterday?"

"You'll see," said Chalmers. He looked at the doctor. "How often?" he asked.

"Still every half hour or so," said the doctor. "Any moment now." He put the chart back on the end of the bed and stood next to Chalmers, his hands deep in the pockets of his white coat.

"Will somebody please tell me what's going on?" said Nightingale. Just as he finished speaking, Robinson's whole body shuddered as if he was having an epileptic fit. His arms trembled, his heels drummed against the mattress, his back arched and the heart monitor began to beep rapidly.

"You're sure he's okay like this?" Chalmers asked the doctor.

"Nothing we do has any effect. We've tried anti-convulsion drugs, all the epilepsy treatments, painkillers, muscle relaxants. Nothing works. And it's a

8

purely physical reaction; his brain activity isn't affected at all."

Robinson went suddenly still. Then he took a long, slow, deep breath. "Jack," he said as he exhaled. Then he took another deep breath. "Jack Nightingale."

Nightingale froze.

Chalmers grinned at him. "So you never met the man, huh? Why's he saying your name?"

"I've no idea."

"He's identifying the man who shot him, that's what he's doing. What we've got here is a deathbed statement and that carries a lot of weight in court."

"He's not dead, he's in a coma," said Nightingale.

"Same thing," said Chalmers.

"How's it the same thing?" asked Nightingale. "If he knew he was dying and named me as his attacker then that would be a deathbed statement. But he's in a coma and hasn't accused me of anything."

"I wouldn't categorise it as a coma," said the doctor. "With the sort of damage he has experienced, I wouldn't expect there to be any hope of recovering any brain function. Frankly, under more normal circumstances, we'd have already started looking into the possibility of harvesting his organs. Other than the head wound, Mr Robinson is actually in very good physical condition. He's breathing without assistance, his heart is strong, all his metabolic signs are positive. He could live for ten or twenty years like this. But it's not as if he's in a coma that he might one day recover from."

Chalmers put up a hand to silence the doctor. "I'm talking legally rather than medically," he said. "Mr

Robinson is clearly identifying Nightingale as his attacker."

"He's saying my name, that's all," said Nightingale.

"And you said that you don't know him," said Chalmers. "If that's true, why is he saying your name?"

Nightingale took a step towards the bed but the cop he was handcuffed to didn't move.

"Take the cuffs off," said Chalmers.

The cop took a key from his pocket and unlocked the cuffs. Nightingale moved closer to the bed, massaging his right wrist.

"Jack," mumbled the man again. "Jack Nightingale."

Nightingale looked over at the doctor. "No brain activity, is that what you said?"

The doctor nodded and pointed at a green monitor. "See the flat lines there? That's the neural activity. There's some movement occasionally and we can get a reaction with loud noise or light but that's almost certainly at the autonomic level. He's lost a big chunk of his brain."

"So what's happening?" asked Nightingale. "Why's he talking now?"

"Because he's telling us who shot him," said Chalmers. He leaned over the bed. "Mr Robinson, can you hear me? My name is Superintendent Chalmers. Can you tell me what happened the night you were shot?"

"You're wasting your time, Superintendent," said the doctor. "He's totally non-communicative."

"I'll be the judge of that, if you don't mind," said Chalmers. He wagged his finger at Nightingale. "Say something to him," he said.

"What do you mean?"

"It might get a reaction. Coma patients sometimes come out of their comas when they hear a voice they recognise."

"Superintendent, he isn't in a —" began the doctor, but Chalmers silenced him with an icy stare.

"Fine, have it your own way," said the doctor, and he walked out of the room muttering to himself.

"Say something to him," Chalmers said to Nightingale, nodding at the man in the bed.

"Like what?"

"Say you're here. Tell him your name."

"This is ridiculous. Didn't you hear what the doctor said?"

"Just do it, Nightingale. Unless you've got something to hide."

Nightingale stared at the superintendent with contempt, then turned back to the bed. He bent down over Robinson, close enough to see a rash of small spots across his cheeks and the tufts of hair protruding from his nostrils. "I'm Jack Nightingale," he whispered.

"Louder," said Chalmers.

Nightingale sighed. "This is Jack Nightingale. I'm here."

Robinson took a deep breath and exhaled slowly. Nightingale's stomach lurched at the fetid stench and he backed away.

"This is a waste of time," said Nightingale. "I've never seen him before and I certainly had nothing to do with shooting him."

"Jack?" murmured Robinson. "Are you there?"

Chalmers waved for Nightingale to get closer to the bed. "I'm here," said Nightingale. He frowned. He was sure he didn't know Robinson, and equally sure that Robinson didn't know him.

"Why won't you help me, Jack?" His voice was a hoarse whisper, barely audible.

Nightingale moved closer. "What?"

"I don't like it here. I want to go home." Robinson took a long, deep breath and then slowly exhaled.

"What did he say?" asked Chalmers.

Nightingale didn't bother to reply. "Where are you?" he asked the man in the bed.

Robinson took another long breath. "I don't know," he said. His voice was a faint rattle and his lips were barely moving. "I'm scared."

Nightingale shivered.

"Please help me, Jack. Don't leave me here."

Chalmers pushed Nightingale to the side. "Mr Robinson, can you confirm that it was Mr Nightingale who shot you?"

Robinson's chest rose and fell slowly.

"That's not him talking," said Nightingale quietly.

"Bollocks," said Chalmers. "What do you think, that someone's playing ventriloquist?"

Nightingale held Robinson's left hand. It was warm and dry. "Sophie, is that you?" he said.

"Who the hell's Sophie?" said Chalmers.

Nightingale ignored Chalmers. He gently squeezed Robinson's hand. "It's me, Sophie. Jack."

"Jack?" said Robinson, his voice a dry rasp.

"I'm here, Sophie."

12

"I want to go home," said Robinson. "Please help me, Jack."

"I don't know what to do, Sophie. I don't know how to help you."

Robinson's chest stopped moving. Nightingale looked over at the vital signs monitor. Nothing had changed.

"Sophie?"

Nightingale flinched as Chalmers grabbed his shoulder. "What are you playing at, Nightingale?"

Nightingale shook the superintendent's hand away. "Sophie?"

Robinson was lying perfectly still.

Chalmers gestured with his chin at the policeman at the end of the bed. "Get the doc back here now," he said. The cop hurried out of the room. "All right, Nightingale, that's enough of that. Get away from him."

Nightingale let go of Robinson's hand. Just as his fingers fell onto the mattress, Robinson sat bolt upright. He opened his uncovered eye wide and then screamed. Chalmers took a step backwards and tripped over a power cord, his arms flailing as he tried to regain his balance. He stumbled against a chair and fell to the floor, cursing.

Nightingale didn't flinch. He looked straight at Robinson, who continued to scream at the top of his voice as he stared ahead. Then, just as suddenly as it started, the scream stopped and Robinson fell back on the bed. The monitors started buzzing and an alarm sounded in the corridor. The doctor burst into the ICU followed by two nurses. "Get out of here now," he shouted at Chalmers. "Where the hell's the crash trolley?"

CHAPTER
THREE

Nightingale stretched out his legs and groaned. He was sitting in an interview room in Charing Cross Police Station. There were fluorescent lights set behind protective glass in the ceiling and high up in one wall there was a window made of glass blocks. Around the middle of the wall at waist height ran a metal alarm strip which, if pressed, would summon assistance within seconds. "Any chance of a coffee?" asked Nightingale.

"About as much chance as there is of hell freezing over," said Superintendent Chalmers. He looked across at his colleague, who was unwrapping two brand-new cassette tapes. "Sometime today, Inspector Evans," he said.

"Sorry, sir, the wrapping's a pain to get off."

Nightingale had worked with Dan Evans a few times when he'd been with CO19, the Met's firearms unit. In the two years that Nightingale had been out of the job, Evans had put on several pounds and his hair was now streaked with grey. He was in his late thirties but he looked a good ten years older.

Evans managed to get the plastic wrapping off the cassettes and slotted them into the recorder, which was on a metal shelf fixed to the wall above the table. Chalmers nodded at him and Evans pressed "record". Chalmers looked up at the clock on the wall by the door and checked his wristwatch. "It is now seven forty-five on Tuesday January the fourth. I am Superintendent Ronald Chalmers, interviewing Jack Nightingale." He looked at Nightingale, expectantly. Nightingale smiled but didn't say anything. Chalmers glared at him. "Come on, you know the procedure by now," he said. "Say your name for the tape."

"I think I'll exercise my right to silence," said Nightingale. "Other than to point out that as yet I haven't been read my rights."

"You haven't been read your rights because you haven't been charged yet," said Chalmers. "Now give your name for the tape."

"Say please."

"You're trying my patience," said Chalmers, leaning across the table towards Nightingale.

"I've not been charged, I'm not under arrest, so I can walk out of here whenever I want," said Nightingale. "So if you want me to stay, you're going to have to get me a coffee and if you want me to say my name for the recording then you're going to have to ask me nicely."

Chalmers nodded at Evans and the inspector switched off the recorder. "Do you mind?" Chalmers asked Evans.

The inspector stood up.

"Milk, no sugar," said Nightingale. "And I need a cigarette."

"You can't smoke in here," said Chalmers.

Nightingale smiled sarcastically. "You dragged me out of my flat before I had time to pick up my smokes," he said. "I need a pack of Marlboro and a lighter."

"We're not buying you cigarettes, Nightingale."

Nightingale shrugged. "Then I'm out of here." He started to stand up but Chalmers waved him back down.

"Okay, we'll get you cigarettes."

"And a bacon sandwich," said Nightingale. "PACE says you have to keep me well fed."

"The Police and Criminal Evidence Act says nothing about bacon sandwiches. We'll see what's going in the canteen." He looked over at Evans. "Three coffees, and a pack of cigarettes for Mr Nightingale. And a sandwich — bacon, if it's available."

"Marlboro," said Nightingale brightly. "The red pack."

"I'll have to go out for them," Evans said to the superintendent.

Chalmers waved his hand dismissively. "Just get them," he said. Evans flashed the superintendent a tight smile as he let himself out.

Nightingale folded his arms and settled back in his chair. "Fancy a game of charades while we wait?" he asked.

"You think this is a game, do you?"

"I think you're wasting your time and mine," said Nightingale.

The superintendent stood up and pointed a finger at Nightingale. "We'll see who has the last laugh," he said.

Nightingale yawned and stretched.

16

"I'll tell you something you don't know, Nightingale. Just after we left the hospital Dwayne Robinson died. This is now a murder enquiry." He grinned when he saw Nightingale's reaction. "I thought that would wipe the smile off your face."

CHAPTER
FOUR

Nightingale finished his bacon roll, took a sip of coffee and smiled at Chalmers. "Right, ready when you are," he said.

Chalmers scowled at him. "If you piss me around one more time I'll have you charged and processed and make sure that all your clothes are taken away for forensic analysis," he said. "You can sit in a cell for twenty-four hours in a paper suit and you can whistle for your cigarettes."

Nightingale stared stonily at the superintendent but said nothing.

Chalmers nodded at Evans and the inspector pressed "record". "It is now eight fifty-two on Tuesday January the fourth and I am Superintendent Ronald Chalmers. The tape has been switched off while we fetched Mr Nightingale food and a beverage. Say your name for the recording, please."

"Jack Nightingale. And can I just say for the record that the bacon was a tad fatty."

Evans smirked and looked down at his notebook and Chalmers glared at Nightingale. "And with me is . . ." Chalmers looked over at Evans.

"Detective Inspector Dan Evans."

"Mr Nightingale has been informed that Dwayne Robinson has succumbed to his injuries and that this is now a murder enquiry," continued Chalmers, taking a slim gold Cross pen from his pocket.

"And can I point out that I am here helping you with your enquiries," said Nightingale. "I haven't been charged and I haven't requested legal representation."

"Duly noted," said Chalmers. "Earlier this morning we took you to see Mr Robinson in the intensive care unit at Lambeth Hospital."

"After dragging me out of bed at gunpoint," said Nightingale.

Chalmers ignored the interruption but his fingers tightened on his pen. "Mr Robinson was shot on July the twentieth last year. Can you tell me where you were on that date?"

"No," said Nightingale.

"No?"

"That was almost six months ago. How am I supposed to know what I was doing? Can you tell me what you did on the twentieth of that month? What did you have for breakfast? What time did you get home? What position did you use to satisfy your wife sexually —"

"Nightingale —"

"Mr Nightingale to you. Let's not forget that I haven't been charged."

Chalmers took a deep breath that reminded Nightingale of the way that Robinson had inhaled just before he started talking. "So you are unwilling to account for your whereabouts on July the twentieth last year?"

"Not unwilling. Unable. What day of the week was the twentieth?"

"It was a Tuesday. Same as today."

"Then I'd have been at work during the day. Probably in the office. But I could have been out on a job. I'd have to check with my assistant. She keeps my diary."

"So it is possible that you were in Brixton on July the twentieth?"

"I don't remember being in Brixton during the summer; but, like I said, the diary will tell you. Or you can check my phone records."

"Phone records?"

"My phone has got GPS. If I was in Brixton on July the twentieth the phone company would be able to tell you."

"Unless you left your phone at home that night. Or gave it to someone else."

"Now you're being ridiculous," said Nightingale.

"I'm simply asking you to account for your whereabouts on the night of July the twentieth. And you seem unwilling to do that."

"Talk to my assistant, Jenny McLean. She'll confirm where I was. But sitting here, no, I don't know where I was that night. But I'm damn sure that I didn't have a gun and just as sure that I didn't shoot Robinson."

Chalmers put down his pen and linked his fingers on the table as he looked at Nightingale without saying anything. Nightingale looked back at him. It was a standard interrogation technique, he knew. The idea was to leave a long silence in the hope that the suspect would start talking. It often worked. People didn't like sitting in silence and nerves kicked in; they'd start to talk and hopefully they'd trip themselves up. Nightingale settled back in his chair and folded his arms.

Chalmers's eyes hardened as he realised that Nightingale was playing him at his own game. Nightingale saw the man's knuckles whiten and he smiled.

"Do you think this is funny?" asked Chalmers.

"Ridiculous rather than funny," said Nightingale. "Exactly what evidence have you got to tie me in with Robinson's shooting?"

Chalmers tilted his head back and glared at Nightingale. "You were there in the hospital, you heard him yourself. Several times Mr Robinson identified you as his killer."

"That's not what happened and you know it," said Nightingale. "For a start, when we were there he wasn't dead, so being a killer doesn't come into it."

"Attacker, then," said Chalmers, picking up the gold pen. "If you want to split hairs, he identified you as his attacker before he died." He tapped the pen on an open notepad as he stared at Nightingale.

Nightingale stared back. The intimidating stare and the long silences were both techniques taught on the Basic Interrogation Course at the Hendon Police College in north-west London. The simplest way to counter either method was simply to say nothing.

"Cat got your tongue, Nightingale?" said Chalmers.

"I need a cigarette," said Nightingale. Evans had brought a pack of Marlboro and a yellow disposable lighter into the interview room along with the bacon roll and coffee.

"Your smokes can wait," said Chalmers.

Nightingale looked pointedly at his watch. "It's been almost twelve hours since I last had a cigarette and I usually smoke forty a day," he said. "So I am now suffering from the symptoms of nicotine withdrawal, which means that anything I say during this interview can be treated with suspicion."

"What the hell are you talking about, Nightingale?"

"The lack of nicotine in my system will produce medical side effects that will invalidate anything I say. Plus, deliberately depriving me of nicotine could be deemed to be a form of torture and is almost certainly a violation of my human rights." He smiled amiably. "Easiest option would be just to let me go outside for a smoke." He jerked his thumb at Evans. "Dan here's a smoker; he can keep me company."

"I don't smoke," protested the inspector. He looked over at Chalmers. "I'm not a smoker, sir."

CHAPTER
FIVE

Nightingale caught Evans looking wistfully at his cigarette and he offered him the pack.

"The wife'll kill me," Evans said.

"Your secret's safe with me," said Nightingale. They were standing in the car park at the rear of the building, hidden from the street by a high brick wall topped by razor wire. A blue metal gate rattled open to allow two detectives to leave in an unmarked Vauxhall Vectra.

Evans grinned and took a cigarette. Nightingale lit it for him and Evans inhaled with relish and then slowly blew smoke up at the sky. "You know, if it wasn't for bronchitis, cancer and heart disease, cigarettes would be great."

"All that stuff is down to your genes more than the ciggies," said Nightingale. The metal gate rattled shut.

"You believe that?"

Nightingale took a long drag on his cigarette and blew smoke before replying. "If cigarettes caused cancer, everyone who smoked would get cancer. And they don't. Less than fifteen per cent of smokers get lung cancer. Eighty-five per cent don't. So how can they say that cigarettes cause cancer?"

"Because the incidence of lung cancer is greater among smokers."

"Everybody dies, mate," said Nightingale.

"That's certainly true." Evans grinned at Nightingale. "And it feels good, doesn't it? Smoking?"

"We wouldn't do it if it didn't," agreed Nightingale. He took another long pull on the cigarette and held the smoke deep in his lungs. He could almost feel the nicotine leaching into his blood, coursing through his veins, revitalising him. Evans was right. Smoking did feel good. He exhaled slowly and watched the smoke gradually dissipate. He looked over at Evans, who was doing the same, and they giggled like naughty schoolboys. "When was your first ciggie?" asked Nightingale.

"At school, where else? The proverbial bike sheds. I was thirteen. Benson & Hedges. Coughed like nobody's business and I was nearly sick but I was hooked. You?"

"I was a late starter," said Nightingale. "Sixteen. Down at the pub. Back in the days when they didn't throw you in prison for smoking in a bar."

"Strictly speaking, it's only a fine," said Evans. He flicked ash onto the ground. "First brand?"

Nightingale held up his cigarette. "Marlboro," he said. "Red pack. It's the only brand I smoke."

"I'll take whatever I'm given," said Evans. "I figure if I don't actually buy any then I can say that I've given up." He chuckled. "Wife hates the smell. I'll have to chew a pack of gum before I go home." He sighed and put the cigarette between his lips again.

They smoked in silence for a while. A TSG van drove into the car park and a group of officers piled out and headed for the canteen, laughing and joking. Two uniformed constables in fluorescent jackets came out of the station, nodded at Evans and walked over to the wall, where they began smoking.

"Is Chalmers serious about this Robinson thing?" asked Nightingale.

Evans shrugged. "He wants you for something," he said. "Robinson will do."

"He's clutching at straws. Why would I want to shoot a Brixton gangbanger?"

"I guess he figures that if he keeps on throwing shit at you, something's going to stick eventually. He hated you when you were a cop and he hates you even more now that you're a private eye."

"But he's got nothing. Just Robinson saying my name."

"But that's the thing, isn't it?" said Evans. "If you've never met Robinson, why would he do that? He's brain dead, right, so why's he going to say your name?"

Nightingale blew smoke. "It's a mystery," he said.

"But you say you never met him," pressed Evans. "Presumably he didn't pluck your name out of the air."

"You weren't there."

"No, but I was there last night when we were called in."

"What happened?"

"Robinson started talking. No brain activity, but the words were coming out of his mouth. Your name. Jack Nightingale. The doctor told the woodentop sitting outside and he called his boss; his boss ran your name through the computer and Chalmers got a call." He smiled ruefully. "Which is when I got dragged out of bed just as the missus was about to give me my weekly treat."

"Sorry about that," said Nightingale.

"Yeah, not as sorry as I was," said Evans. "Anyway, Chalmers drags me down to Lambeth and we go into the ICU and, sure enough, there's Robinson saying your name. Chalmers gets all excited and books an armed response team for first thing this morning."

"You know, with the way the Met's budget has been cut you'd think he'd have better things to spend his money on."

"Yeah, well, with you it's personal, I think. And you can understand why, can't you? Just look at the body count racking up around you. That's just a coincidence, is it?"

"Chalmers doesn't seem to think so."

"He's got a point, though, hasn't he? People close to you seem to have a nasty habit of either killing themselves or being killed. So what's going on? Are you cursed, is that it? Some sort of Jonah." He laughed but stopped when he saw the frown on Nightingale's face. "You do know what's happening, don't you? It's not a coincidence, right?"

"Dan, you don't want to know. And even if I told you, you wouldn't believe me."

"Try me."

Nightingale sighed. The officers in fluorescent jackets started laughing and one of them looked over in his

26

direction. Nightingale sensed that they were laughing about him and he turned his back on them. He looked at Evans and smiled. "Okay, you want to know, so I'll tell you." He took a drag on his cigarette, blew smoke, and then shrugged. "You know that my biological father killed himself. But what you don't know is that Ainsley Gosling was a Satanist. A devil-worshipper. And he sold my soul to a devil, a bitch by the name of Proserpine. I managed to get my soul back from her but then it turns out that Gosling also sold the soul of the sister I never knew I had, so then I had to negotiate with another demon from Hell and as part of that deal Proserpine sent three of her minions to kill me. And pretty much everyone who might be able to help me dies violently before I can talk to them. I think that pretty much sums up the state of play, Dan. Happy now?"

Evans shook his head sadly. "You're a bastard, Nightingale. I was only trying to help." He took a last drag on his cigarette, dropped the butt onto the ground and stamped on it. "You should remember who your friends are." He gestured at the door. "Get your arse back inside."

CHAPTER
SIX

Nightingale sat down and toyed with his pack of cigarettes as Evans pressed "record" and nodded at the superintendent. Chalmers looked up at the clock on the wall. "It is now nine twenty on Tuesday January the fourth and this is Superintendent Ronald Chalmers and Inspector Dan Evans recommencing our interview with Jack Nightingale. So, Mr Nightingale, we were talking about what happened at Lambeth Hospital this morning."

"If you say so," said Nightingale.

"You heard Mr Robinson say your name several times, did you not?"

"That wasn't him," said Nightingale.

Chalmers snorted dismissively. "I can assure you that it was most definitely Dwayne Robinson that we saw in the ICU."

"His body, yes. But it wasn't him speaking."

Evans grunted and shifted in his chair. Chalmers looked across at the inspector and then shook his head slowly. "We both heard him speak. We both heard him say your name. He was identifying you as his killer."

"As I said before, at the time he wasn't dead. Brain dead, maybe, but that's not the same as dead dead."

"But he is dead now. Dead dead. And this morning, before he passed away, he identified you as his assailant."

"That's not what happened."

"Mr Nightingale, I put it to you that on the evening of July the twentieth last year you shot Dwayne Robinson in the head and that this morning he identified you to that effect."

"It wasn't Robinson talking," said Nightingale.

"Who was it, then? Because I'll be swearing in a court of law that it was Dwayne Robinson lying in that hospital bed."

"You know who it was," said Nightingale. "It was Sophie."

Chalmers looked down at his notebook and clicked his pen. "You said the name Sophie while you were in the ICU. Who were you referring to?"

Nightingale folded his arms. "What are you trying to do here, Chalmers?" he asked.

"What I'm trying to do, Mr Nightingale, as you well know, is to find out who killed Dwayne Robinson. And so as far as I am concerned, you are the prime suspect. Now, who was the Sophie that you kept referring to at the hospital?"

"You've forgotten already, have you?" Nightingale sneered.

"What do you mean?"

"You know full well who she is." Nightingale took a deep breath. "Sophie Underwood."

Chalmers frowned. "Sophie Underwood? Why do I know that name?"

Evans jutted his chin at the superintendent. "That was the little girl who died at Chelsea Harbour two years ago," he said. He nodded at Nightingale. "The one that . . ." He left the sentence unfinished.

Chalmers looked back at Nightingale. "The girl whose father you threw out of the window?"

"Allegedly," said Nightingale.

"And what made you start talking about her? Is she connected with Dwayne Robinson in some way?"

"You just don't get it, do you?" said Nightingale. "It wasn't Robinson talking. It was Sophie."

Chalmers sneered. "What the hell are you talking about?"

Nightingale clasped his hands together and leaned across the table towards the superintendent. "It was her. She was asking me to help her. You heard that, didn't you? She wants my help."

Chalmers looked across at Evans, then back to Nightingale. "Are you seriously telling me that a girl who died two years ago was talking to you through Dwayne Robinson?" Chalmers sat back and tapped his pen on his notepad. "Are you planning some sort of insanity defence, Nightingale? Because I'll tell you now that's not going to wash."

"You heard what she said," said Nightingale. "You were there."

"I heard Dwayne Robinson say your name several times, and as far as I'm concerned that was because he was identifying you as his killer."

"It wasn't him. How could it be? You heard what the doctor said. Dwayne Robinson was brain dead. It couldn't have been him speaking."

"So what are you saying, Nightingale? That a dead girl has a message for you from beyond the grave?"

Nightingale ran a hand through his hair and then rubbed the back of his neck. He could feel the tendons there, as taut as steel wire.

"Cat got your tongue again, Nightingale?"

"I don't know what was going on," said Nightingale. "But it was her."

Chalmers nodded slowly. "I see what's going on here," he said. "That was the day your life turned to shit, wasn't it? You screwed up with the little girl; you threw her father out of his office window and your career with it. And don't think we've forgotten about the father. That case is still open."

Nightingale shrugged.

"Just because he'd been fiddling with his daughter didn't give you the right to kill him," said Chalmers.

Nightingale shrugged again.

"No comment?"

"It sounds like you've already made your mind up," said Nightingale.

"This Sophie, how old was she?"

"Nine when she died. She'd be eleven now." Nightingale picked up his pack of Marlboro and toyed with it.

"And why do you think she'd want to talk to you?"

"I don't know."

"Do you think she blames you for her death?"

Nightingale's eyes narrowed. "What do you mean?"

"I mean that maybe this is just your guilty conscience at work. Maybe you feel that you're responsible for her death and for the death of her father. That's a lot of guilt for a man to bear, and in my experience sooner or later guilt manifests itself."

"You were there this morning, Chalmers. You heard her."

"I heard Dwayne Robinson say your name shortly before he died."

"Sophie was talking through him. She wants me to help her."

"She's beyond help. She's dead."

Nightingale sighed and looked at his watch pointedly. "I've got a business to run," he said.

"You're a self-employed private detective," said Chalmers.

"Look, Chalmers, I didn't kill Dwayne Robinson, and you haven't got any evidence that says I did. All you've got is Robinson saying my name and I've explained that."

"By telling me that a dead nine-year-old girl was using him as a ventriloquist's dummy? You think I'm going to buy that?"

"Buy, sell, steal, I don't give a toss." Nightingale stood up. "I'm out of here. The only way you can keep me here is to charge me and if you do that I'll sue you for false arrest faster than you can say 'Colin Stagg'."

Chalmers glared at Nightingale but didn't say anything. Nightingale pulled open the door and walked out.

CHAPTER
SEVEN

Jenny McLean was sitting at her desk sipping a mug of coffee and reading the *Guardian* when Nightingale walked in. She was wearing a dark blue dress that ended just above the knee and had her blonde hair tied back in a ponytail. She put down her mug and looked at him quizzically. "You haven't shaved," she said.

"Or showered. Or had breakfast. I was hauled in by the cops first thing this morning. I've come straight from the station."

"Now what have you done?" asked Jenny.

"Shot a drug dealer in Brixton," said Nightingale. "Allegedly." He hung his jacket on a rack by the side of the door and went through into his own office, which overlooked the street. "Any chance of a coffee?" There were two old Starbucks cups next to his computer and he tossed them into the wastepaper bin.

Jenny got up from her desk and followed him into his office. "You shot a drug dealer?"

"Allegedly," said Nightingale again. He dropped down into his chair and swung his feet up onto the desk. "Of course I didn't shoot a drug dealer," he said. "And when was the last time I was in Brixton?" He rubbed his hand across his chin. "Do you think I need to shave? Have I got any meetings today?"

"You've got a three o'clock and after that you're supposed to be pitching your services to that solicitor in St John's Wood, and you look like shit so, yes, you need a shave. And a shower."

"But coffee first, yeah?"

Jenny sighed and went over to the coffee-maker. "Why do they think it was you?" she called as she poured coffee into a mug.

"It's complicated," said Nightingale, picking up a copy of the *Sun*. "But there's no hard evidence. No evidence at all, as it happens." He looked up as she brought over his coffee. "I don't suppose you can tell me what I was doing on July the twentieth last year, can you?"

"Are you serious?"

Nightingale picked up his mug. "They might be asking for proof, down the line."

Jenny walked behind his desk and clicked on the mouse of his computer. "You know how this works, right?"

Nightingale looked pained. "I can never find the diary," he said.

"You click on this icon," she said. "The one that says 'Diary'. Really, Jack, it's time you joined the rest of us in the third millennium." She tapped on the computer keyboard and peered at a spreadsheet that filled the screen. "Tuesday?" she said. "Tuesday the twentieth?"

"Yeah, that's what the cops said."

"You had a six o'clock meeting with a Mr Winters. Divorce case. He came after work, remember? Wanted you to follow his wife while she was at a conference in Brighton."

Nightingale shrugged. "Doesn't ring a bell," he said.

"Jack, come on. You spent two days in the Metropole and ran up a ninety-quid bar bill."

"I remember Brighton and I remember Mrs Winters and the guy she was shagging but I don't remember Mr Winters. Were you here?"

"I let him in and then left you to it. He was a big guy, balding, had a sovereign ring and a big gold chain on his wrist. Called me 'darling', which I didn't care for much. When did the drug dealer get shot?"

"Evening. I didn't ask when exactly. Do you have any idea what I did after the meeting with Winters?"

Jenny grinned. "United were playing Liverpool," she said.

Nightingale laughed out loud. "Why didn't you say so?" he said. "I was in the pub with Robbie, watching the game. United won two — nil and I won twenty quid off Robbie." His smile slowly faded as the memory flooded back: Robbie handing over · the money but insisting that Nightingale spend the cash on a decent bottle of red wine that they drank there and then. Four months later Robbie had died, run over by a black cab as he crossed the road. A stupid, senseless accident. "They'll remember me in the pub," said Nightingale. "The landlord knows me. Do me a favour and call Winters sometime, just ask him if he recalls being here and what time he left. I'll talk to the landlord. I'm pretty sure there won't be a window of opportunity for me to have gone south of the river to shoot anyone."

"Do you know the guy? The guy that was shot?"

"Drugs was never my brief when I was a cop," said Nightingale. "And I rarely went south of the river."

Jenny sat down on the edge of his desk. "What happened, Jack?" She took the newspaper from him and dropped it on the desk. "The police generally don't arrest people for shooting drug dealers unless they have reasonable grounds for believing it."

"First, it was Chalmers, so reasonable doesn't enter into the equation," said Nightingale. "And second of all . . ." He shrugged but didn't finish the sentence.

"What? What aren't you telling me?"

"You'll think I'm crazy."

"I think that horse has already bolted," she said.

Nightingale looked up at her. She was smiling but he could see from the look on her face that she was genuinely concerned. He explained to her what had happened in the ICU. Her expression gradually changed from concern to dismay. "See, I knew you'd think that I was crazy," he said.

"It was her voice?"

"No. It sounded like a twenty-something gangbanger from Brixton. But there's no way that it could have been him talking. The bullet blew away a big chunk of his brain. He was brain dead according to the doctor."

"So you think Sophie's talking to you from beyond the grave? That makes more sense, does it?"

Nightingale shrugged. "When I told Chalmers he suggested that I was on some sort of guilt trip. That I was imagining it because I feel responsible."

"And do you?"

"Feel responsible? Come on, Jenny, what do you think? I was there when she jumped. If I'd handled things differently maybe . . ." He shook his head. "Who knows, yeah? Maybe I should have tried to grab her, maybe there was something I could have said that would have got her down off the balcony, maybe if someone else had gone up to talk to her . . . Could have, would have, should have, right?"

"You were there to help. That was your job."

"Yeah, I was there to help but I didn't, did I? Not unless the dictionary definition of 'help' has changed recently. She jumped and she died and the answer to your question is yes, I do feel responsible. But that doesn't mean I was hearing things."

"But it wasn't her voice, was it? You said it was the man's voice. So why do you think it was her?"

"Why would a drug dealer be asking me for help?"

"The better question is why would Sophie? She's dead, Jack. So what are you going to do?"

"I'm going to read the *Sun*, drink my coffee, and then go back home to shower and change before heading back here all bright-eyed and bushy-tailed for my three o'clock meeting."

"And that's it?"

"That's my plan." He picked up his coffee mug.

"And what about Sophie?"

Nightingale grinned. "If it's important, she'll call back."

Jenny stared at him for several seconds, then sighed exasperatedly and went back to her desk. Nightingale sipped his coffee, wishing that he felt half as relaxed as he'd pretended to be. It had been Sophie trying to talk to him in the ICU, he was sure of that. And he was equally certain that whatever she wanted, she'd try to contact him again.

CHAPTER
EIGHT

Mrs Chan was the lady who owned and ran the small Chinese restaurant on the ground floor of the building where Nightingale lived. She waved at him as he walked by her window and he waited for her on the pavement as she bustled out of the door. She was barely five feet tall with a round face and thick-lensed spectacles that gave her the look of a mole that had just emerged from its lair. "Mr Jack, is everything okay?" she asked. She had arrived from Hong Kong with her husband thirty years earlier but she still spoke English as if she had just stepped off the plane. Her husband had died five years earlier and now she ran the restaurant with her two daughters while her son was back in Hong Kong running a very successful property company.

"Everything's fine, Mrs Chan."

"The neighbours said police take you away."

"It was a misunderstanding."

"You look terrible."

"Thank you for your honesty," he said, but Mrs Chan had no sense of humour and she nodded seriously.

"You not shave. And you smell bad."

"I've just come home to shower," he said.

She waved at her restaurant. "Come in, sit down, I will make duck noodles for you." Nightingale hesitated but Mrs Chan grabbed him by the arm. She had a child's hands but her grip was like a steel vice. "I make for you special, Mr Jack."

Nightingale allowed himself to be led into the restaurant and over to a corner table. He actually didn't need much persuading because Mrs Chan served the best duck noodles in London. There was a line of ten roast ducks hanging by their necks from a stainless-steel bar in the window. Mrs Chan selected one and then disappeared into the kitchen. A few seconds later he heard the dull thud of a cleaver chopping through meat.

One of Mrs Chan's daughters came over wearing her usual bright red cheongsam. The bottle of Corona she was carrying on a tray was already opened, with a slice of lemon in the neck. "When are you going to start drinking Chinese beer, Jack?" she said as she put down the bottle in front of him. "Tsingtao is better than Corona."

"I'm a creature of habit, Sue-lee," he said, pushing the lemon down into the bottle. "I've been drinking the same beer and smoking the same cigarettes for as long as I can remember." He raised the bottle in salute and then drank. Mrs Chan returned from the kitchen with a big bowl of flat white noodles in a broth that she made herself, with half a dozen thick slices of roast duck on top.

"On the house, Mr Jack," she said.

"You spoil me, Mrs Chan," said Nightingale, picking up a fork and a spoon. Despite being a big fan of Chinese food he'd never managed to master chopsticks.

"When they tell me the police take you away this morning, I think I lose good customer," she said.

"Like I said, it was just a misunderstanding."

Mrs Chan reached over and grabbed his wrist, her nails biting into his flesh so hard that he winced. He tried to pull his hand away but her grip was unbreakable. She stared at him, her face a blank mask. "Please help me, Jack," she said, though her thin lips barely moved.

"What do you mean?"

"Please help me, Jack," she repeated, her voice robotic, her eyes staring through him.

"Mrs Chan, what's wrong?" Her grip tightened and the nail of her index finger pierced his skin. Blood dribbled down his wrist.

Mrs Chan's jaw was clamped shut and she was breathing through her nose so hard that her nostrils flared with each breath.

"Mrs Chan, are you all right? You're hurting me."

"Please help me, Jack." The hand tightened and now all the nails were deep in Nightingale's flesh and a drop of blood plopped onto the table. Nightingale stood up and tried to twist out of her grasp. Mrs Chan held on and he dragged her across the table. Her left arm sent the bowl of noodles and his bottle of beer crashing to the floor.

Sue-lee came running and one of the cooks appeared at the kitchen door, a cleaver in his hand. He was wearing baggy grey shorts and a stained vest and he stared open-mouthed at Mrs Chan, who was sprawled across the table, still gripping Nightingale's wrist.

"Jack, what are you doing?" shouted Sue-lee, grabbing her mother around the waist. Mrs Chan released her grip on Nightingale's arm and staggered backwards. Her daughter held her and then Mrs Chan turned and sobbed into Sue-lee's shoulder.

"I didn't do anything," said Nightingale. "Your mum grabbed me." He held up his hand and showed her the wounds on his wrist. "Look what she did."

"Just go," said Sue-lee, stroking her mother's hair.

"Sue-lee, I was just sitting here." The cook stepped towards Nightingale, the cleaver held high. Nightingale raised his hands and backed towards the door. There were only a few customers in the restaurant but they had all stopped eating and were watching Nightingale in horror. "Okay, I'm going," said Nightingale.

"And don't come back," said Sue-lee emphatically as her mother continued to sob.

CHAPTER
NINE

She was wearing a white sweatshirt, a blue cotton skirt and silver trainers with blue stars on them. She was sitting on the wall of the balcony, her legs under the metal rail, her arms on top of it. Her name was Sophie Underwood, she was nine years old, and Jack Nightingale was the only person in the world who could stop her falling to her death.

He took his pack of Marlboro and lighter from his pocket. He was on the balcony of the adjoining flat and there was a gap of about six feet between the terrace where he was standing and the one where Sophie was sitting, whispering to her Barbie doll.

Nightingale lit a cigarette and inhaled as he tried to work out what he should say to the little girl. There had to be something, some combination of words said in the right way that would change her mind. He blew smoke and tried not to look at her. The words that would save her were just out of reach, at the edge of his consciousness. If he could just focus he'd come up with the right words and then everything would be okay.

He was alone on the balcony and he knew that was wrong. Negotiators always worked in threes. Always. So why was he alone? He couldn't remember how he'd got onto the balcony or why he didn't have any back-up, all he knew was that he needed to find the right words to say to stop Sophie Underwood from falling to her death. Nightingale was on the balcony which meant that he was the Primary. Number One. It was the Primary's job to communicate with the subject. That was what Sophie was. The subject. The person in crisis. The little girl who was about to fall thirteen storeys to her death unless Nightingale came up with the words that would stop her. Nightingale looked over his shoulder at the room behind him. That was where the Number Two would be, if he had a Number Two. The Secondary. It was the Secondary's job to monitor the situation, keep notes and offer advice. The Primary was often caught up in the moment and had to think on his feet but the Secondary was able to supply a dispassionate perspective. The third member of the team was the Intelligence Negotiator. Number Three. He would be down on the ground talking to anyone who knew the person in crisis, friends and relatives, anyone who might be able to provide information that could be useful for the Primary. That information would be relayed to the Number Two who would pass it on to the Number One. Except that there was no Number Two and no Number Three. There was just Nightingale and the nine-year-old girl who was sitting on the balcony swinging her legs and whispering to her doll and preparing to fall to her death.

Nightingale looked across at the balcony where the girl was. She was still whispering to her doll. She had long blonde hair that she'd tucked behind her ears and skin as white and smooth as porcelain. He could see dark patches under her eyes as if she had trouble sleeping. He took another long drag on his cigarette. He had to find some way of initiating a conversation because so long as she was talking she wasn't falling. He couldn't talk about her family because it was her father who was abusing her and her mother knew but wasn't doing anything to stop him. School, maybe. Maybe she was happier at school so if they talked about that then she'd realise that there were people who loved her and wanted to protect her. He didn't know if she had a pet. Pets were good because pets loved unconditionally. She lived in an apartment so that probably meant she didn't have a dog but there could be a cat or a gerbil, something that depended on her. That was always a good way of reaching a person in crisis: appeal to their caring side, show that the world was a better place because they were in it. That's why he needed a Number Two and Number Three because then he'd know for sure and he wouldn't say anything that would provoke a negative response. All the responses had to be positive because she was sitting on the edge of a wall with nothing other than a rail between her and the ground thirteen storeys below. He looked over his shoulder again but there was no one there. No back-up. No support. Just Jack Nightingale and a nine-year-old girl. And for the life of him he had no idea what to say.

He took a quick look to his right. She had stopped whispering to the doll and was staring out over the

Thames. Seagulls were gliding over the river, searching out the updrafts so that they didn't have to flap their wings. Nightingale smiled. The birds. He could talk about the birds. All kids liked birds and she must have seen them every day from her apartment. Perfect. He took a final pull on his cigarette and flicked it away, watching it spin through the air, sparks scattering from the lit end as it fell. He flinched, realising that had been a mistake.

He turned to look at her, smiling to show that he was on her side, but just as he opened his mouth to speak she slid off the balcony, her eyes tightly closed, the doll clutched to her chest.

Nightingale screamed and that was when he woke up, bathed in sweat. His heart was pounding. He padded to the kitchen and took a bottle of Russian vodka from the icebox of his fridge, where it had been since the Christmas before last. He unscrewed the top and drank from the bottle. The warmth spread across his chest but it didn't make him feel any better. He paced up and down as he drank, trying to blot out the image of Sophie falling to her death, her blonde hair whipping around in the wind, the doll in her arms. He shivered as he remembered the dull wet sound she'd made as she hit the ground. He took another drink and wiped his mouth with his arm, then went through to his sitting room and sat down on the sofa.

He looked at his watch. It was three o'clock. He knew that it wasn't a good idea to be drinking vodka at that time of the morning but he didn't care. He just wanted to stop thinking about Sophie and the way that she'd died. And the fact that he hadn't stopped her. He lay back on the sofa and stared up at the ceiling. Tears welled in his eyes. "I'm so sorry, Sophie," he said. "I'm so, so, sorry."

CHAPTER
TEN

Nightingale woke up with a thumping headache and a bad taste in his mouth as if something had crawled in there and died. He turned on his side and squinted at the clock on the bedside table. It was just after nine thirty. Next to the clock was an empty bottle of vodka that he only half-remembered finishing. He rolled out of bed, staggered to the bathroom and drank from the cold tap. He walked unsteadily back to his bed, sat down and lit a cigarette, then lay back and blew smoke up at the ceiling.

He heard his mobile phone ringing in the sitting room. Nightingale groaned before pushing himself off the bed, stubbing out the remains of his cigarette in a glass ashtray and retrieving the phone from the pocket of his raincoat. It was Jenny.

"Are you okay?" she asked.

Nightingale sat down and ran his hand through his hair. His stomach lurched and he had to fight the urge to vomit.

"Jack?"

"Yeah, I'm okay. What's up?"

"I was just checking to see if you were going to be in the office this morning," said Jenny. "There're papers here that need signing."

"Can't you do it?"

"Your accountant sent them. Inland Revenue. I'm not putting my signature on anything that could get me put behind bars."

"I'm up to date with my taxes."

"Not with VAT you're not," said Jenny. "And I found these forms in your desk. You got them well before Christmas and your accountant called me to say he really needed them before the year end."

"You know the last few weeks have been crazy, kid."

"Yes, well, I don't think that the Revenue accept that as a valid excuse."

"I'm on my way in," said Nightingale. His stomach lurched again and he lay back and concentrated on not throwing up.

"Don't forget you've got that surveillance thing at lunch-time," said Jenny.

Nightingale screwed up his face. He had forgotten. He tried to remember where he'd left his camera.

"You've got your camera and stuff, haven't you? Mr Stevens wants photographs."

"Yeah. Sure. Somewhere." He closed his eyes and took a deep breath.

"Are you sure you're okay? You sound a bit strange."

"I'm not feeling so good," said Nightingale. "Tell you what, I'll go straight to the surveillance job. I'll do the forms this afternoon." He ended the call, took another deep breath to steady himself, then went through to the kitchen to switch on the kettle. He grinned as he saw his black holdall containing his camera equipment on the table by the fridge.

He shaved and showered then put on a suit that he'd just had back from the dry cleaners, selecting a blue tie with boomerangs on it that his aunt and uncle had given him for his birthday three years ago. They'd been on holiday in Australia and had obviously been browsing in the duty-free shop in Sydney Airport on their way back; the tie had still had the price sticker on it when they gave it to him. "Many happy returns," his aunt had said when he opened the package, and then his uncle repeated it, just in case he missed the boomerang reference. He stared at his reflection as he fastened the tie, remembering the last time he'd seen his aunt. She had been lying on the kitchen floor of her house in Altrincham, to the south of Manchester, her head smashed open, blood and brains congealing on the lino. He shuddered as he remembered walking up the stairs and finding his uncle hanging from the trapdoor that led to the attic. Murder-suicide, according to the Manchester Coroner, but Nightingale knew there was more to it than that. He stared at the tie, shuddered again and took it off. He tossed it in a drawer and put on a tie with alternating dark and pale blue stripes, then went back to the kitchen and made himself a cup of coffee. He didn't feel like eating but figured that a bowl of porridge would settle his stomach, so he microwaved a bowl of instant Quaker Oats and ate it while he watched a bleached blonde on Sky News explain why house prices were going to drop by ten per cent over the next year, her report complete with computer graphics and interviews with householders facing bankruptcy because they were being forced to sell their homes for less than they'd paid for them.

When he'd finished he put his bowl and coffee mug in the sink, picked up the holdall and his raincoat and headed out of his apartment. His MGB was in a lock-up a short walk from his flat, but there was no point in taking the car: the woman he was supposed to be photographing worked in Chelsea and usually took the Tube to the hotel in Battersea where she met her lover. Mr Stevens had known about his wife's affair for more than a month and he wanted pictures of his wife and lover entering and leaving the hotel as ammunition in a very nasty custody battle that he knew was heading his way. There were no children involved — Mrs Stevens had never wanted kids — but the couple owned three pedigree Red Setters that between them had won more than a dozen Crufts titles and whose offspring sold for thousands of pounds. Nightingale wasn't sure why his wife's infidelity gave Mr Stevens more of a chance of keeping the dogs, but he was paying well so Nightingale simply applied the philosophy that the client was always right, even when he clearly wasn't.

As he pulled the front door closed behind him, a black Range Rover went by and he caught a glimpse of sullen black faces staring at him from the half-opened windows. Keeping his eye on the vehicle Nightingale watched it drive along the road then go down a side street. He turned to the right so that he didn't have to walk by the window of Mrs Chan's restaurant, and lit a cigarette as he walked to Queensway Tube station. The sky overhead was gunmetal grey and the weather forecast had warned of snow showers.

He was about a hundred feet from the Tube station when he saw the Range Rover again, this time driving towards him. He looked down at the registration plate and made a conscious effort to remember it. As he stared at the plate the car stopped and the rear doors opened; two men got out, one from either side. They slammed the doors shut and the car drove off. As it went by him Nightingale saw his reflection in the darkened windows.

Two motorcycles turned into Queensway close to Whiteleys Shopping Centre. They were trail bikes with riders dressed in black leather and white helmets, their faces hidden behind tinted visors. They pulled up at the side of the road and gunned their engines. Nightingale stopped and felt a shiver run up his spine. Something was wrong; he could feel it on a subconscious level, his animal instincts sending his adrenal glands into overdrive. The hairs on the back of his neck stood up and he looked over his shoulder.

Standing in a shop doorway was a young girl dressed from head to foot in black. Tight black jeans, a long black coat over a black leather waistcoat and around her neck was a heavy silver chain with an upside-down silver cross hanging from it. She smiled, showing perfect teeth. Her eyes were as black as coal, her lashes were coated with thick mascara and her lips glistened with black lipstick. Standing next to her was a black and white dog, a collie, its tail swishing from side to side. The dog's eyes were as black as those of its mistress. Her jet-black hair was cut jaggedly, with a fringe hanging over her forehead. The hairstyle had changed since the last time Nightingale had seen her. Proserpine. Her smile widened.

"They're coming for you, Nightingale," she said.

Nightingale looked over at the two men who'd climbed out of the Range Rover and realised that they were both wearing ski masks and had their right hands concealed beneath dark Puffa jackets. He stepped back from the road. He heard raised voices behind him and turned to see an Indian shopkeeper shouting at two teenagers, accusing them of stealing. He heard a horn pound and flinched as a black cab drove by. The two men were walking purposefully towards him, their right hands still under their jackets, their hoods up over their masks. They moved apart, one stepping onto the pavement.

Behind him the two teenagers were shouting racist abuse at the shopkeeper. Two pensioners in long coats and pulling shopping trolleys stopped to listen to the argument but Nightingale's attention was focused on the two men in ski masks. They were both on the pavement now, moving towards him, carving through the pedestrians like sharks cutting through a shoal of fish. No one seemed to notice that under their hoods they were wearing ski masks.

Nightingale took a quick look, left and right. One of the men pulled out a gun. A MAC-10. Nightingale's heart pounded. He moved until his back was against a shop window. The second man pulled out his weapon. Another MAC-10. He pulled the trigger and the gun kicked in his hands. The window behind Nightingale shattered. Pedestrians screamed and ran for cover as glass crashed down onto the pavement.

One of the black teenagers fell to the ground, yelling in pain. The shopkeeper stood with his mouth wide open, too shocked to move.

The first gunman seemed to be having trouble getting his gun to work. He was cursing and banging the magazine. The gunman who'd fired looked over at him. "What's your fucking problem?" he shouted.

"It's jammed. It's fucking jammed."

Nightingale started to run. The second gunman turned and fired but Nightingale was a moving target now and the shots went high, slamming into the brickwork above his head. Nightingale crouched low and ran down the road, zig-zagging. The first gunman finally let rip with his gun and bullets whizzed around, smashing the windows of a Chinese restaurant. Pedestrians were screaming and running away from the gunmen, towards Hyde Park. A car veered to the right and collided with a taxi and a white van slammed into the back of them both.

The first gunman fired again and bullets screeched off the road, this time missing Nightingale's feet by inches. A Muslim woman completely covered in a black hijab threw herself to the ground, wailing. A young father clutched his baby son to his chest and ran into a coffee shop, barging past a middle-aged couple laden down with carrier bags who were staring wide-eyed at the mayhem.

54

Nightingale ducked behind the taxi as bullets thudded against the side of the vehicle. He was breathing hard and fast, trying to work out how many rounds they still had in their weapons. Nightingale knew that the MAC-10 came with two types of box magazine: a regular version holding twenty rounds and an extended version that held thirty-two. The fact that the guns were hidden under the shooters' jackets suggested that they'd used the smaller magazine, which meant that they could be emptied in two seconds. And the fact that they'd both fired three short bursts meant that they'd be running low. So either it would all be over soon or they'd stop to slot in fresh magazines.

He risked a look over the wing of the taxi. The two men were walking towards him, their guns held out at arm's length. They were both firing one-handed, which accounted for the terrible marksmanship. They must have fired more than twenty rounds between them and so far they'd not managed to hit him. But the closer they got the more likely they were to hit home so he had to move and he had to move fast. One of the men fired a quick burst but it went high and shattered the windows of the shop behind him. Nightingale bent low and scuttled behind the white van. The driver's door burst open and the driver, a West Indian in his twenties, fell out onto the pavement. He scrambled to his feet but Nightingale pushed him back down. "Stay low," he hissed. A siren started to blare at the far end of Queensway. It was a paramedic's vehicle, trying to clear the traffic ahead of it.

More bullets thudded into the side of the taxi. Nightingale looked around for something to use as a weapon but there was nothing at hand. All he had in his holdall was camera equipment, and he doubted that his attackers would be deterred by his telephoto lens.

One of the gunmen stepped from behind the rear of the taxi and onto the pavement. He raised the gun and pointed it at Nightingale's chest. Nightingale crouched down, making himself as small a target as he could, and he held the holdall up in front of his face, bracing himself against the hail of bullets that he was certain was about to be heading in his direction. He heard a metallic click followed by a curse. He moved the bag and saw the shooter staring at the side of his gun. The shooter cursed again and Nightingale realised that he was out of ammunition. Nightingale roared and got to his feet. He started towards the shooter, but as he did so the other gunman appeared and fired. The shots went low and smacked into the wing of the white van. Nightingale spun around and began running down the pavement, towards the Tube station.

The two trail bikes had started to move down Queensway, the riders clearly panicked by the siren. The bikes braked hard and squealed to a halt close to the white van. The two shooters jumped on the pillions and the bikes roared off.

Onlookers were still screaming and crying and running for cover. Nightingale looked across the road. The black teenager that had been shot was sitting in the doorway of the gift shop, holding his hand to his shoulder. His friend had run off but the Indian

56

shopkeeper was kneeling down next to the injured boy and talking into a mobile phone.

Nightingale slowed as he reached the entrance to the station. The people walking away from the escalators towards the exit had no idea of the mayhem that had just taken place outside and they had the blank bored faces of seasoned commuters. Nightingale forced himself to relax and tried to blend in, but his hand was shaking as he pressed his Oyster card against the reader to open the barrier.

CHAPTER
ELEVEN

Nightingale walked into the office and grinned when he saw Jenny at the coffee machine. "Perfect timing," he said. He took the camera from his holdall and put it on her desk. "Loads of pictures of Mrs Stevens with her gentleman friend entering and leaving the hotel, including a couple where they're very lovey-dovey."

"Well done you," she said, picking up his mug and filling it full of coffee. "Any problems?"

"Two guys tried to kill me with automatic weapons in Queensway. Does that count?" He took the mug from her.

Jenny's jaw dropped. "Please tell me you're joking," she said.

"I wish I was. They had machine pistols and tried to mow me down on the way to the Tube station."

"Are you okay?"

Nightingale shrugged. "Ran like the wind," he said. "Might need a change of underwear."

"Are you serious?"

"About the underwear? No. Not really."

"Jack, I'm never sure whether you're joking or not these days. Did someone try to shoot you or not?"

"I'm just trying to lighten the moment, kid," he said. "Yes, two black guys, gangbangers, with what looked like MAC-10s. They got out of a Range Rover and escaped on bikes. The only reason they didn't stay and finish the job was because a paramedic hit his siren and they panicked."

"And this happened in Queensway?"

"Just near the Tube station. Innocent bystander got shot. A teenager." He sipped his coffee and then went through to his office.

Jenny followed him. "Come on, Jack. Details."

"It's no biggie," he said, sitting down at his desk.

"Like hell it's no biggie. You said someone got hurt."

"That tends to happen when bullets are flying around."

"Damn you, Jack, how can you be so blasé about what happened?"

"I guess I'm just getting used to people trying to kill me. Anyway, it all happened so fast, it was over in seconds."

"And you just went on to the surveillance job?"

Nightingale forced a smile. "There wasn't much I could do."

"You could have talked to the police, for a start."

"And get hauled in by Chalmers again?"

"Did you get a look at them?"

"They were wearing ski masks but I saw them go by in their car before they started shooting." He sipped his coffee.

"Then you have to go to the police. You can't just walk away from something like that."

Nightingale laughed. "Walked? Do me a favour! I ran. My feet hardly touched the ground."

"And nobody stopped you?"

"Everyone was pretty much down on the ground or hiding," said Nightingale. "There was one hell of a lot of lead flying around."

"And they still missed you?"

Nightingale looked at her in astonishment. "You sound disappointed."

"Idiot. I'm just saying that you were lucky, there's not a mark on you."

"MAC-10s are difficult to control," said Nightingale. "Gangbangers love them because they look the business, but they're a bugger to aim and the recoil is fierce. In a street fight it comes down to spray and pray."

"You prayed? Is that what you mean?"

Nightingale grinned and shook his head. "They pray is what I meant. Spray and pray. They point the gun in the general direction of the target, pull the trigger and hope for the best."

"In Queensway? They didn't care about passers-by?"

"The days of worrying about innocent bystanders are long gone, kid. It's like the Wild West in parts of London. They hit a young lad but he seemed okay."

"But Bayswater? It's hardly Brixton, is it?"

"Yeah, well, I think it was a case of Mohammed coming to the mountain. They were outside my flat first; they were waiting for me."

"But who, Jack? Who would want to shoot you in broad daylight?" Her eyes widened. "You don't think it was Proserpine, do you? Were they working for her?"

"That's the sixty-four-thousand-dollar question, isn't it?"

Jenny frowned. "I've never understood that. What does it mean? Sixty-four-thousand-dollar question?"

"It was an American game show in the fifties. Like *Who Wants To Be a Millionaire?* Back then, sixty-four thousand dollars was a lot of money."

"You don't seem particularly upset about what happened. They tried to kill you, right?"

"What do you want me to do, Jenny? Lock myself in the bathroom? Hide under the bed? I was in an armed response unit when I was with the Met, remember? I'm used to facing bad guys with guns."

"Sure, but when you were a cop you'd have been wearing a bulletproof vest and not a raincoat. And you've have had an MP3 to fire back with."

Nightingale laughed. "I bloody hope not," he said. "An MP3's a music player. You mean a Heckler & Koch MP5."

"Whatever I mean, you'd have had a gun and protection. Why are you being so bloody calm about this?"

"Because it's over and I'm alive and all's well that ends well," he said.

"Except for the teenager who got caught in the crossfire." Her eyes narrowed. "You're avoiding my question, aren't you?"

"What question?"

"I asked you about Proserpine and you did that clever thing you do of making a joke to get out of answering. Jack, could she be behind this? She said she'd send three people to kill you. Two have already tried, right? Maybe this is the third attempt."

Nightingale finished his coffee, put down his mug and reached for his cigarettes.

"Jack, talk to me. Is it possible that Proserpine sent them?"

"I'm not being evasive, kid. I just don't know. I suppose it's possible." He didn't want to tell her that he'd seen Proserpine just before the shooting. Or that she'd said they were coming for him. Maybe Jenny was right, though. Maybe they had been working for her and maybe she had been there to watch.

"Suppose isn't really good enough, is it? Not when your life's on the line."

"What do you think I should have done? Interrogated them as the lead was flying?"

"You make a joke of everything, don't you? Look, you did a deal with a devil. She gave you the information you needed to find your sister and help get her out of prison. But for every question of yours that she answered she said she'd send someone to kill you."

"To try to kill me," corrected Nightingale. "She hasn't had much luck so far."

"Yes, well, maybe she's saving the best until last. Men with guns shooting at you in broad daylight? That sounds like she's getting desperate. Like she's annoyed that the first two failed and this time she wanted to make sure."

"But doesn't the fact that they made such a mess of it show that it wasn't her behind it?"

"I don't know, Jack. That's why I'm asking you. You're the one who summons her, not me."

"I don't know, kid, I really don't know. I can't help thinking that Proserpine's minions would be more creative. This just seemed like a gang thing."

"So it's connected with the drug dealer you're supposed to have shot?"

Nightingale slid a cigarette out and slipped it between his lips. "That seems more likely," he said as he took his lighter from his pocket.

"You need to find out for sure," said Jenny.

"I will," said Nightingale. He lit his cigarette. "And I know just the person to ask."

"Please don't tell me you're going to start summoning up devils again," said Jenny. "You know that always ends in tears."

"I was thinking of someone closer at hand, actually," said Nightingale. He handed her his empty coffee mug. "Couldn't have a refill, could I?"

CHAPTER
TWELVE

Nightingale pushed open the door to the pub, stepped inside and looked around. Evans was standing at the corner of the bar from where he could watch the door and the flatscreen television that was showing a Chelsea-Liverpool game. Evans nodded when he saw Nightingale, then raised his glass to his lips as he watched the football. It was stiflingly hot in the pub and Nightingale took off his raincoat and slipped it over his arm on his way to the bar.

"If Chalmers finds out that I'm drinking with you, he'll blow a fuse," said Evans as Nightingale joined him.

"That ship has already sailed, I think." He waved over at the barmaid, a redhead with shoulder-length hair and a sprinkling of freckles across her upturned nose. "What are you on, lager?" he asked.

Evans nodded and Nightingale ordered a pint of Fosters and a bottle of Corona.

"So what do you want, Jack?" asked Evans, putting down his glass. "I'm assuming you're not going to confess to shooting Dwayne Robinson."

"You know full well that what happened to Dwayne Robinson has got nothing to do with me. Chalmers is clutching at straws."

"He's got you in his sights, that's for sure," said Evans. "He's trying to get funding to put together a full Tango team and really put you under the microscope."

"Great," said Nightingale. The drinks arrived and Nightingale paid for them. There was a group of Chelsea fans within earshot so Nightingale nodded at the fruit machine and the two of them went over to stand by it. "I need a favour," said Nightingale.

Evans chuckled. "And in the whole of the Metropolitan Police I'm the only cop you can ask? You really don't have any friends, do you?" He sipped his lager.

"You're the only one that can help me, Dan."

"You mean everyone else has told you to go screw yourself? I'm your last resort?"

"It's more complicated than that," said Nightingale. "Did you hear about a shooting in Bayswater this morning?"

"Sure. Trident are on the case. Black on black. Black teenager took a bullet in the shoulder but it's not life-threatening. Looks like a turf war."

"Yeah, well, that's not what happened."

"Says who?"

"Says the guy they were shooting at." He raised his bottle in salute. "Here's to dodging bullets," he said.

"Please don't tell me that you're withholding information," scowled the detective. "A teenager got shot."

"I'm talking to you now, aren't I? And let's look on the bright side, shall we? At least it wasn't coppers doing the shooting."

Evans sipped his lager and then his eyes widened as a Chelsea player took a shot at goal that was tipped over the crossbar by the keeper.

"You a Chelsea fan, Dan?"

"Liverpool," said Evans. "My grandfather worked on the docks and my dad was a cop."

"So how did you end up in London?"

"We're never going to be bosom buddies, Jack, so you don't need my family history." He took another drink and then looked at Nightingale like an undertaker measuring him up for a coffin. "Look, what you did to the father of that little girl — you know, a lot of guys in the job think you did the right thing. She killed herself, you threw him out of his office window, and there're plenty out there would have done the same. But that was two years ago. Water under the bridge. Now you're a civilian, and a civilian who seems to be the catalyst for a hell of a lot of corpses."

"It's been an unlucky few weeks, that's certainly true."

"Unlucky? It's like you've got the plague, Jack. Everyone you talk to turns up dead."

"That's a bit of an exaggeration and you know it."

"Yeah? Well, a month ago you were a former cop scraping a living as a private eye and you weren't even on our radar. Now every time a body turns up Chalmers wants to know where you were."

"Chalmers has always had the hots for me," said Nightingale.

"I don't understand why you keep making a joke about it."

"What do you want me to do, Dan? Confess?"

"You see, you're doing it now. Your uncle and aunt are dead. He killed her and then topped himself."

"Murder-suicide," said Nightingale.

"And then you go and see the guy who killed Robbie."

"It was an RTA."

"It was a traffic accident when he died, but the guy took a flyer off his balcony while you were talking to him."

"He jumped, Dan."

"And then you go to Wales claiming that some woman was your sister and she hangs herself."

Nightingale shrugged and said nothing.

"You go to see the guy who used to drive Gosling around and he decapitates himself in front of you. Oh, and let's not forget the gamekeeper who blew his head off with a shotgun while he was talking to you."

"You're starting to sound like Chalmers."

"I've got to be honest, he's got a point. All this is going on around you and you're acting like it's no big thing."

"It's a huge bloody thing, but what can I do?"

"You can tell me what you think is going on."

Chelsea scored and the fans went wild, hugging each other and punching the air in triumph.

Nightingale sipped his drink while his mind raced. He liked Evans and he was a good detective, but there was no way he was ever going to believe what was really happening to Nightingale and the people around him. Evans lived in the real world, a world of criminals and victims, where crimes were solved by examining physical evidence and questioning suspects. Nightingale had come to realise that there was a separate world beyond the physical, a world where demons held the power and where magic and witchcraft were tools as effective as any DNA analysis or fingerprint records. In the car park of the police station he had opened the door to the truth but Evans hadn't even listened. Nightingale knew that if he really tried to explain what was going on, Evans would think that Nightingale was crazy. And he might well be right. "Dan, if I knew, I'd tell you."

"It's a series of coincidences, is that it?"

"What's the alternative? Someone's going around killing everyone close to me? Because if they are, you're going to have to watch yourself." Nightingale realised what he'd said and he closed his eyes. "Shit," he said.

"Yeah, like Robbie, you mean?"

Nightingale opened his eyes. The Chelsea fans were still celebrating even though the game had restarted and the Chelsea defence was under pressure. "Stupid thing to say, sorry."

"Forget it," said Evans. "You have a habit of firing from the hip; it's part of your charm."

"What happened to Robbie was so bloody stupid. Stepping in front of a cab the way he did." Nightingale shuddered. "Makes you realise just how precarious life is."

"Not getting all philosophical on me, are you?"

Nightingale sipped his Corona. "You know what I mean. You've seen how easily life can be snatched away. That's a big part of the job. Dealing with death."

"Amen to that."

"And the line between dead and not dead is such a fine one. If Robbie had just turned his head and seen the cab he'd be with us now."

"Nah," said Evans. "If Robbie was here it'd be him you'd be asking for help and not me."

Nightingale grinned. "Yeah, you're probably right." He clinked his bottle against Evans's glass. "That makes you my fallback position, I suppose."

"Don't bother sweet-talking me, Nightingale. Just tell me what it is you want."

"I need a vehicle registration checked. And then a name put to the vehicle."

"And this vehicle was involved in this morning's shooting?"

Nightingale nodded. "Black Range Rover, tinted windows. MAC-10s. Two shooters wearing Puffa jackets and ski masks. Drove off on Kawasaki trail bikes, one red, one black."

"And they were definitely shooting at you?"

"The black teenager was standing outside a shop. Wrong place, wrong time."

"And you got the registration number?"

"Of the Range Rover, yeah. But not the bikes. I was head down by the time they turned up." Nightingale took a piece of paper from his pocket and slipped it to the detective.

Evans put it away without looking at it. "Why didn't you just tell the cops at the scene?"

"Because I think I know who it was. Dwayne Robinson's gang. Someone must have told them what happened at the hospital."

Evans frowned. "Chalmers?"

"I'm not saying that he's got a direct line to Robinson's gang, but someone must have put the word out. That's what I want you to check, see if that car is connected to Robinson's people."

"And you saw the shooters?"

"I got a glimpse of the guy in the back and a pretty good look at the one in the front passenger seat. Show me pictures and I should be able to make an ID. But I can't say for sure who the shooters were because of the ski masks."

"I've got to ask you again, why didn't you just wait at the crime scene and talk to the responding officers?"

"What? Deal with a couple of box-ticking woodentops? Have you taken a look at the average beat cop these days?"

Evans chuckled. "Standards aren't what they were, that's for sure."

"Even when I was in the job they'd dropped the height and weight restrictions and now it seems they've dropped the requirement to have a brain."

"I hear what you're saying, but you could have spoken to the detectives on the case."

"And the first thing they'd have done is put my name into the PNC and I'm pretty damn sure that Chalmers has had me red-flagged."

Evans shrugged. "All roads lead to Rome," he said.

"At least this way I get to stay under the radar," said Nightingale. "If it was Robinson's men then I can ID them for you; if it wasn't, well, I don't want them knowing that I'm a witness because I'm in enough trouble as it is." He drank from his bottle, then moved closer to the detective and lowered his voice. "And we both know that the powers-that-be monitor all PNC checks these days. If I ask anyone else to run the number and it's been flagged then I'll be dropping them in the shit. But you're on the Dwayne Robinson investigation so you can just say that you saw the vehicle near the hospital or close to Robinson's place."

"You mean that in addition to breaching the Data Protection Act, I lie to my bosses and put my job on the line? Thanks, pal."

"It's a white lie. In the grand scheme of things, anyway."

Evans drained his glass and handed it to Nightingale. "Get me another lager while I think about it," he said. "And some crisps. Smoky bacon, if they've got them."

CHAPTER
THIRTEEN

Jenny was already at her desk when Nightingale arrived. He held out a brown paper bag. "Croissants and banana chocolate-chip muffins," he said. "The breakfast of champions."

Jenny's eyes narrowed as she looked up from her computer monitor. "What do you want?"

"You're so suspicious," he said, putting the bag down on her desk. "What makes you think I want anything?" He nodded over at the coffee-maker. "Want a coffee?"

"Now my spidey-sense is definitely tingling, but I've never been one to look a gift horse in the mouth, so yes, please. Milky with one sugar."

Nightingale busied himself at the coffee-maker. "Did you drive in today?" he asked.

Jenny sighed. "Your car's stopped working again, hasn't it?"

"Battery's dead," said Nightingale. "Must be a short somewhere."

"And you want a lift?"

"Your Audi is a lovely car," said Nightingale, stirring in a spoonful of sugar. "If I didn't like classic cars so much I'd probably go for an A4 myself."

"There's a world of difference between a classic car and an old banger," said Jenny, opening the brown paper bag. She smiled as she took out a muffin. "These are my favourites," she said.

"I know that," said Nightingale, taking two coffees over to her desk. He gave her one of the mugs and sipped from the other.

"Where do you need to go, Jack?"

"Gosling Manor. I promised to meet a building guy. He's going to give me an estimate for the repairs."

"How much damage did the fire do?"

"The upstairs hall is gutted but the fire brigade were there before the structure was damaged."

"It was insured, wasn't it? I mean, it was arson so it wasn't as if it was your fault or anything."

"I haven't checked. I hope so."

"Jack! Are you serious? How can you not have checked already?"

"I've had a lot on my plate. Anyway, there's a huge mortgage on the place and they usually come with insurance."

"You should check, and soon."

"To be honest, I'm more worried about water damage. The firemen used a hell of a lot of water and I haven't looked down in the basement yet. Water and books aren't a good mix."

"When do you want to go?"

Nightingale looked at his watch. "You've got time for your breakfast and I've got time for a fag and a quick read of the *Sun*." He grinned. "Now that is the breakfast of champions."

CHAPTER
FOURTEEN

Jenny brought her Audi to a stop in front of Gosling Manor. It was a sunny day but bitterly cold and Nightingale turned up the collar of his raincoat after he climbed out of the car to open the gates. Jenny drove through and he pulled them closed, then realised that the builder would be arriving shortly so he left them open and got back into the passenger seat.

"You still haven't done anything about a gardener, have you?" said Jenny as she drove slowly along the driveway to the house.

"It's winter. You don't cut grass in the winter," said Nightingale.

"There're always things need doing in a garden, and you've got acres here."

"I'll get it sorted once the builders are out," said Nightingale.

Jenny parked next to a massive stone fountain where a tousle-haired stone mermaid was surrounded by leaping fish and dolphins. They got out of the car and looked up at the two-storey mansion. The lower floor was built of stone, the upper floor of weathered bricks, and the roof was tiled, with four massive chimney stacks that gave it the look of an ocean-going liner.

"Every time I look at this house, it seems to cry out for a family. You know what I mean?" said Jenny. "It just seems so wrong that your father lived here alone. And now it's yours and . . ." She shrugged.

"And I'm a sad lonely bastard too — is that what you were going to say?"

Jenny laughed. "That's not what I meant at all," she said. "But this is a family home, Jack. No offence, but it's wasted on you."

They walked together towards the ivy-covered entrance. Nightingale had been the owner of Gosling Manor for almost three months but it didn't feel like it was his house. He'd inherited it from his father, Ainsley Gosling. Gosling was Nightingale's biological father, who'd given him away at birth, and Nightingale felt as little attachment to the man as he did to the house. He pulled his keys from his pocket. The oak door was massive but it moved easily on well-oiled hinges and opened onto the wood-panelled hall.

Jenny wrinkled her nose at the smell of smoke and then groaned when she saw the state of the hall. The marble floor was half an inch deep in mud and the wooden staircase was scorched. The massive multi-layered chandelier that looked like an upside-down crystal wedding cake was now caked in a thick layer of ash. "Oh Jack," she said.

"It's worse upstairs," said Nightingale. "The arsonist spread petrol all along the upstairs hall so the fire did far more damage up there. I don't want to go up until the builder's here. I don't know if there's been any structural damage or not."

"And you were upstairs when it happened?"

Nightingale nodded. "Yeah, it was pretty hairy. But the fire brigade got here quickly." He walked carefully across the mud to the section of the wooden panelling that concealed the entrance to the basement library. The wood was still damp from where the firemen had been spraying water, and as he pulled the panel open it pushed back a layer of thick black mud. There was a light switch just inside the panel and he flicked it, half expecting the electricity to be off but the fluorescent lights below flickered into life. Jenny tiptoed through the mud towards him, her face screwed up in disgust.

"It's not that bad, kid," said Nightingale.

"You're a smoker," she said, putting her hand over her mouth. "Trust me, it's bad."

Nightingale went down the stairs and Jenny followed him, holding on to the brass banister with her left hand as she kept her right cupped over her mouth.

The basement ran the full length of the house and was lined with laden bookshelves. Down the centre of the basement were two parallel lines of tall display cases which were packed with items that Ainsley Gosling had collected during a lifetime of devil-worship. At the bottom of the stairway were two overstuffed red leather Chesterfield sofas, one on either side of a claw-footed teak coffee table that was piled high with books.

A smile spread across Nightingale's face as he realised that there was no major water damage. The ceiling was stained in places and water had trickled down the wall by the stairs but other than that the basement was in exactly the same condition as when he'd last been there. "Finally, some good news," he said. "I half expected it to be flooded."

Jenny took her hand away from her mouth and sniffed the air cautiously. "No smoke down here either. The panel must be a tight fit."

Nightingale took off his raincoat and tossed it on the back of one of the sofas. He looked at his watch. "Shouldn't be long. I'd offer you coffee but I haven't got anything in the fridge."

"Well, it's not like you live here, is it?" said Jenny, sitting on one of the sofas. "Seriously, what are you going to do with this place?"

"I haven't decided," said Nightingale, sitting on the other sofa.

"You can't live here, can you? What would you do if you needed milk? Or bread?"

"Or duck noodles?"

"You know what I mean. Where's the nearest shop? How do you get a newspaper? It'd take a paperboy half an hour just to get down the drive."

"Now you're exaggerating."

"And could you put up with a commute like that every day?"

"We could work from here. There's plenty of room."

"So I'd be the one commuting? Every day from Chelsea?"

"That's the beauty of having an Audi A4."

"You're not seriously considering it, are you? How would clients get here?"

Nightingale grinned. "I'm joking," he said. "Of course we can't work from here. But there's something about the place that pulls me here, you know. It's like I belong."

"That's a freaky thing to say, Jack, considering that it's where your father killed himself. Doesn't that worry you?"

"Why should it?"

Jenny shrugged. "It sort of taints it, don't you think?"

"Are you worried about ghosts? Is that it?"

"It's not about ghosts. It's just knowing that in that room upstairs he put a shotgun under his chin and pulled the trigger. Doesn't that give you the willies?"

"I hadn't thought about it," he said.

"Could you sleep in that room, knowing that happened?" She shuddered. "I couldn't."

The doorbell rang and she jumped, then sighed and patted her chest. "I nearly gave myself a heart attack then."

"That'll be the builder," said Nightingale. "Do you want stay down here or do you want to come upstairs with me?"

"I'm okay here," she said. "I'll keep looking for titles on the list of books that your pal Wainwright wants."

"He's hardly a pal. But yeah, he's keen to buy and it's not as if I need a Satanic library, is it?" He grinned over at her. "Not scared, being here on your own?" He made a ghostly moaning sound and waggled his fingers at her.

"Behave, Jack."

"I'm just saying . . . Satanic library, things that go bump in the night . . ."

"Me being a girl and all?" Jenny picked up a leather-bound book and threw it at him, missing his head by inches.

"That's no way to treat an antique," he said. "And before you say anything, I meant the book."

Jenny picked up a second book to throw at him but he ran up the stairs and back into the hall. The doorbell rang again as he closed the panel and carefully walked across the muddy floor.

He opened the front door. There was a man in his thirties standing on the steps. He had short blond hair and an impish smile and was wearing dusty blue overalls. He was holding a clipboard and he looked at it and then grinned up at Nightingale. "You Mr Nightingale?"

"Jack," said Nightingale. "Domino's Pizza? You're an hour late so we get them free, right?"

The man looked confused and then realised that he was joking. "Chris Garner. I'm here to give you a quote." He stuck out his hand and Nightingale shook it. "Nice place you've got here," he said.

"Yeah, well, wait until you see inside," said Nightingale, holding the door open. "It's a bit of a mess."

Garner walked across the threshold and whistled softly. "You're not joking," he said, taking a pen from the pocket of his overalls. "What happened? Leak?"

"Firemen," said Nightingale. "There was a fire. The firemen were enthusiastic."

"Yeah, that's the way they are," said Garner. "They do love their hoses." He looked down at the floor.

"That's marble, though. Should clean up okay. Where was the fire?"

"Upstairs," said Nightingale. "What about the clean-up? Can you handle that as well?"

Garner nodded. "Can do," he said. He looked up at the chandelier and pointed his pen at it. "That's a professional job, though. You don't want amateurs messing around with that. It needs to be taken down and done properly."

"Do you know somebody?"

"Let me ask around. So where was the fire?"

"Upstairs," said Nightingale. "Most of the damage on the ground floor is from the smoke and water."

Garner walked over to the panelling by the stairs and ran his finger along it, then tapped it. He was only a few feet from the panel that led down to the basement. He rapped the wood with his knuckles. "The wood's basically sound," he said. "But you'd be best sanding it all down and revarnishing." He made a note on his clipboard.

Nightingale headed up the stairs and the builder followed him, still scribbling on his clipboard. They stopped at the hallway, where the fire had started. The smell of smoke and burned wood was much stronger here. There were darker burn marks running down the centre of the hallway and scorch marks up the walls.

"How did this start?" asked Garner, kneeling down to examine the burned floorboards.

"About a gallon of petrol and a match."

"It was deliberate?"

"Oh yes."

"That's funny. If someone wanted to burn the house down, why pour the petrol up here? They'd have been better off setting the fire downstairs."

"Who knows what was going through his mind?" said Nightingale. Actually he knew exactly what the arsonist had been thinking. Nightingale had been in the master bedroom and if all had gone to plan he would have died in the fire.

"What about the bedrooms?"

"Smoke damage, mainly. And water. The water went everywhere."

Garner opened the nearest door and looked into the bedroom beyond it. "What happened to all the furniture?"

"The place was empty."

"That's lucky," said the builder, making a note on his clipboard. He went back to the hall and stamped down on the boards in several places. "All the boards are going to have to be replaced," he said. "Until we've taken them up we won't be able to see how much damage has been done to the joists. But the wood is so old that it's as hard as metal, so you should be all right. All the panelling's going to need replacing." He gestured at the ceiling. "All the plaster's going to have to come down. It's been soaked and even if you let it dry out it's never going to be right."

He took out an electronic tape measure and measured up the hallway, then nodded at Nightingale. "I'll tell you what I'll do, Mr Nightingale. I'll give you two estimates. I'll give you a basic one where I'll put it back in as-new condition. New panelling, new floorboards, new joists, whatever needs doing, but using new materials. And I'll give you a proper restoration estimate, where it'll be put back to the condition it was before the fire. As if the fire never happened, if you get my drift."

"Okay," said Nightingale. "But do you have a ballpark figure?"

The builder looked pained and scratched his ear with his pen. "Difficult to say off the cuff," he said. "There're a lot of materials to price. But for a basic repair job you won't be getting much change from twenty-five thousand pounds. That's assuming there's no major damage to the joists. And that we don't uncover anything else when we start pulling panels off."

"Like what?"

"Dry rot, wet rot, insect infestation. Panelling can hide a multitude of sins. But if we do find anything then we're best dealing with it there and then."

"And the restoration budget?"

Garner exhaled through pursed lips in the same way the mechanics did when they were about to give an estimate for work on Nightingale's MGB. "A hundred grand. More maybe. We need craftsmen carpenters and they're not cheap." He put away his pen. "You're insured, yeah?"

"I hope so."

"You don't know?"

"I'm assuming I am. I'll check." He handed the builder a business card. "Send the estimates to me at the office."

They walked together down the stairs, across the muddy hall and outside. The builder looked up at the house. "They don't build them like this any more," he said. "Did you just buy it?"

"My father left it to me."

"Are you going to live here? Or are you planning to sell it?"

Nightingale shrugged. "I've not decided."

"Let me know if you want to sell. I'm doing some work for a Russian who lives a few miles away who's always complaining about his place being too small. He keeps putting in plans to extend but the local council don't like him so he's not getting anywhere. He'd love this place."

"Let me think about it," said Nightingale. "I'll let you know once I've seen your estimates."

They shook hands, then Garner climbed into his van and drove off. Nightingale lit a cigarette and was just about to go inside when Jenny came out.

She shook her head when she saw that he was smoking. "How many do you smoke a day?" she asked.

"A pack. Two, sometimes."

"Even though you know the dangers?"

"Of smoking?"

"Of course of smoking. Is everything a joke to you, Jack?"

Nightingale blew smoke up at the sky. "Everybody dies," he said. "Life is a zero sum game. The best you can do is to enjoy yourself as you go along."

"But smoking shortens your life."

"Maybe. But it only takes the years from the end of your life. Not the beginning or the middle."

Jenny looked at him, confused. "I have absolutely no idea what you mean."

Nightingale took another drag on his cigarette before continuing. "Say I live until I'm seventy-five without smoking. And say I die at seventy if I do smoke. I lose five years. But really, Jenny, what am I going to be doing during those five years? Sitting in a bedsit somewhere watching the football, assuming I've enough of a pension to be able to afford Sky Sport?"

"That's how you envisage your final years, is it? What about grandchildren? What about family?"

Nightingale laughed. "To have grandkids I'd need kids and to have kids I'd need a wife or at least a steady girlfriend, and that doesn't look like it's going to happen any time soon. Here's the thing, Jenny. It's not about how long you live, it's about enjoying the life you have. And I'm happy smoking."

"You're mad."

"Maybe. It's like my car. My MGB."

"The car that you can't use because the battery's flat again?"

"It's a classic," said Nightingale.

"You keep saying that. But it's not. It's an old banger."

"It makes me happy. I enjoy driving it. It's got a history and I like the way it handles."

"On the few occasions that it's actually on the road, you mean?"

"I'm not saying that your Audi isn't a great car. But driving your Audi is a totally different experience to being at the wheel of a classic car. You feel connected to the road. You really feel the speed when you're in the MGB, even though the Audi is faster. Driving it could well shorten my life. There're no airbags, the seatbelts are crap, the brakes aren't smart like they are in the Audi, so if I get into a smash I'll probably come off worst. But does knowing that stop me driving it? No. Because I enjoy it. The pleasure outweighs the risks." He held up the cigarette. "Smoking makes me feel good. It relaxes me, it helps me concentrate . . ."

"It gives you something to do with your hands."

"What?"

"Everyone knows that cigarettes help people get through awkward social situations."

"Jenny, really, I just enjoy smoking."

Jenny threw her hands in the air. "I give up," she said. "So how did it go with Bob the Builder?"

"His name's Chris," said Nightingale. "He's going to send me an estimate."

"You're going to get more than one, right?"

"We'll see," said Nightingale. "First thing I've got to do is get some cash." He tossed his keys to her. "Can you lock up? I want to make a call."

As Jenny went up the steps to the front door, Nightingale took out his mobile phone and called the number of Joshua Wainwright. The American had bought several volumes from the basement library and if Nightingale was going to have any hope of paying the builder he was going to have to sell him quite a few more.

"Jack, my man, how the hell are you?" said Wainwright. Nightingale could hear the hum of engines and figured that the American was probably on his Gulfstream jet.

"All good," said Nightingale.

"How was your Christmas?"

"Quiet," lied Nightingale. He'd spent Christmas Day at Jenny's parents' house and the fact that one of the game-keepers had blown his head off with a shotgun had taken the gloss off the festive season, somewhat.

"Well, I hope you have one hell of a new year," said Wainwright.

"You too," said Nightingale. "Where are you?"

"Cruising at thirty-one thousand feet."

"Going anywhere nice?"

"Private island in the Caribbean, as it happens. You should drop by if you get the chance. There're some very interesting people on the guest list — a couple of former prime ministers, a vice-president, three Oscar winners. And a couple of Russian billionaires."

"I'll have to take a rain check on that," said Nightingale. "Hey, the reason I'm calling is to see if I can send you another list of books. We've inventoried another couple of hundred."

"Sure thing," said Wainwright. "Look, Jack, how many books do you have in this library of yours?"

"Thousands," said Nightingale. "I haven't counted but there're a lot."

"So why don't I call in one day and have a look-see? Be easier that way."

"Sure," said Nightingale. "When are you in the UK again?"

"I'll be with Richard for two or three days, then I'm heading over to China. I could stop off on the way. I'll call you and fix up a time."

"Perfect," said Nightingale. He ended the call as Jenny came back down the steps. "Wainwright's going to come and look at the books for himself. Save us from doing the inventory."

Jenny shuddered and looked back at the house.

"Are you okay, kid?"

"The house is beautiful," she said, looking up at the massive chimneys. "Like a picture from a box of chocolates. But down in the basement, on your own . . ." She shuddered again. "It feels a bit . . ."

"Spooky?" He laughed. "There's some pretty weird stuff down there, Jenny. The books. The artefacts. God knows what my father was involved with, or what he did down there." He put an arm around her. "But there's nothing down there that can hurt you. Or me."

She shivered. "Let's go." She handed him the door keys.

"I'll buy you dinner."

"I'm not hungry," she said as she walked with him to the Audi. "I promised I'd go to the gym with Barbara."

"Pilates?"

She pointed a finger at him. "Don't take the piss or you'll be walking home."

Nightingale mimed zipping his lips closed as she got into the car. He climbed in next to her. "You know, you're right. I should sell the house. The builder says he might have a buyer. I'll get him to put out some feelers."

Jenny started the engine. "Probably best," she said.

"Maybe I'll move to Chelsea," he said. "I could be your neighbour."

She flashed him a tight smile. "Please don't," she said. "We're having enough trouble with falling property prices as it is."

CHAPTER
FIFTEEN

Two days later Nightingale's mobile rang while he was sitting down with a plate of chicken tikka masala and pilau rice that he'd picked up from an Indian restaurant in Queensway. The caller had blocked their number so Nightingale hesitated before taking the call.

"Nightingale?"

"Yeah?"

"It's me."

Nightingale recognised the voice. Dan Evans. "Yeah?"

"Where are you?"

"In front of the TV."

"Can you meet me in the park, by the water?"

"It's Saturday. Since when did they start paying inspectors overtime?"

"Haven't you heard? The powers that be have stopped all overtime and they're making us work until we're sixty. It's a brave new world for us public servants. I tell you, if we could strike we would but as always we just have to bend over and take it up the arse."

"I hear your pain, Dan."

"Anyway, I figured it best that I do this on my day off. So can you meet or not?"

"When?"

"Twenty minutes. I'm on the other side of the park."

"No problem. I'll be wearing a red rose and carrying a copy of the *Financial Times*."

"Nobody likes a smart arse, Nightingale," said Evans, and he ended the call.

Nightingale got off the sofa, put his meal in the microwave, then picked up his raincoat and hurried out of his flat. He walked down Inverness Terrace towards Hyde Park, his breath feathering in the evening air. He lit a cigarette as he waited to cross Bayswater Road. He spotted a gap in the traffic and jogged across. Evans was standing by the Serpentine, watching two swans gliding across the water.

"Property of the Queen," said Nightingale, nodding at the birds.

"That's a myth," said Evans. "She only owns the unmarked mute swans on open water. Dates back to the twelfth century. It was to make sure the royals had enough swans for their banquets."

"Yeah? I'm told they taste like chicken." He flicked what was left of his cigarette into the water.

"That's littering," said Evans.

"You're not going to arrest me, are you?"

"Not if you give me one," said Evans. "A cigarette, I mean." Nightingale grinned, took out his pack of Marlboro and lit one for the detective, then another for himself. Evans inhaled deeply then let the smoke out

90

slowly. He smiled as he looked at the cigarette in his hand. "Just don't tell the wife," he said.

"I hope she's worth it."

"She is," said Evans. "But that doesn't mean I don't miss it." He reached inside his coat and took out a manila envelope. "That Range Rover was registered in the name of a Lydia Brown. She lives in Brixton."

"I'm pretty sure it wasn't a woman driving," said Nightingale, opening the envelope.

"Yeah, me too. But she's got three kids by a Jamaican called Perry Smith, and Smith is Dwayne Robinson's right-hand man." He nodded at the envelope. "Smith's picture is in there, along with mugshots of the rest of his crew."

Nightingale slid out a dozen photographs. Most of them were shots taken in custody suites but a few were surveillance photos taken with a long lens. All of the men were black, most of them with shaved heads and heavy gold chains around their necks. The ones who'd had their pictures taken in custody all had the same arrogant tilt to the chin and contempt-filled eyes, as if being arrested was no big thing. And of course, in the grand scheme of things, getting arrested was no big thing. Men like Robinson ruled by terror and witnesses to their crimes either refused to give evidence or were killed. The police, overstretched, under-financed, with the upper echelons more concerned about box-ticking and press conferences than they were about putting away villains, were just an occupational hazard.

Nightingale recognised one of the men immediately. He'd caught a glimpse of him sitting in the back of the

Range Rover. He handed the photograph to Evans. "This is one of the shooters. I'm pretty sure that he was in the back when they cruised by me in Inverness Terrace."

"You didn't say anything about them cruising by."

"I was on my way to a surveillance job. The car went by, windows half down. Then I saw the car again in Queensway. The two guys got out wearing ski masks and started shooting. Then they ran off and got onto two motorbikes."

Evans looked at the photograph. "Reggie Gayle. He's one of Robinson's foot soldiers. Trident reckon he's behind half a dozen killings in south London over the past two years." He narrowed his eyes as he looked at Nightingale. "You'll give evidence, right?"

"Sure, and I'll pop down to the station and wash and wax Chalmers's car while I'm at it. One, I didn't actually see the faces of the guys who were shooting at me, and two, how long do you think I'd last if they thought I was a witness?"

"You're already in the firing line, Nightingale."

"They won't try again," said Nightingale. "Not after you've explained to them that what happened to Robinson is nothing to do with me."

"What?"

"They came after me because they think I shot Robinson. You need to go and turn Smith and Gayle over. If you're lucky you'll find forensics in the car, maybe a gun. But even if you don't you can put them right about Robinson."

"You think they'll believe me?"

"I think either way they'll be warned off. If anyone else takes a potshot at me they'll know that their names are in the frame." He handed a second photograph to the detective, another custody picture. "This is Smith, right?" Evans nodded. "He was in the front passenger seat of the Range Rover."

"You're sure?"

"Not a hundred per cent. But it was a big guy, thick neck like he was on steroids, lots of rings on his fingers."

"We can look for CCTV of the car, and we'll pay him a visit."

"The guns are what you need," said Nightingale. "You know how it works; they'll have passed them onto junior members of the gang, kids who can't be prosecuted for possession."

"I know the drill," said Evans, taking the remaining photographs back from Nightingale and putting them into the envelope.

"Sorry," said Nightingale. "Didn't mean to teach you how to suck eggs. What about the guy that got hit?"

"He's okay. Turns out he's hooked up with a gang in north London so the shooting's being looked at as a turf war. Which is good news for you."

"And what about Robinson? Best way of getting his gang off my back is to catch the guy who did shoot him."

"Yeah, well, like Chalmers said, it was a white guy so Trident aren't interested."

"That's bollocks. They're the ones with all the intel."

"It has to be black on black for Trident to be involved, you know that."

"But the shooting had to be drug-related, and it had to be personal," said Nightingale.

"Yeah, but we've not exactly been inundated with witnesses coming forward and no one on Robinson's crew is talking." He smoked his cigarette. "I'll see what I can do."

"Cheers, Dan. I'll owe you one."

"Damn you right you will," said Evans, putting away the envelope. "But instead of owing me a favour, why don't you just tell me what the hell's going on? It's like you're walking around with a bloody bullseye on your back."

Nightingale blew smoke across the Serpentine and the swans paddled away, their heads down. "Dunno what you mean," he said.

"Do you want my help or not?"

"Showing me those pictures was help enough, Dan," said Nightingale. "And I appreciate you doing what you did. I know I'm not exactly flavour of the month at the moment."

"What you did to that paedophile earned you a lot of Brownie points, but goodwill only stretches so far," said Evans. "Look, if you've crossed somebody, if there's someone behind all this, maybe we can do something."

"I appreciate the offer, Dan. Really. But I don't think there's anything you can do. Anyway, you wouldn't believe it. Hell, I'm not sure if I believe it."

"Believe what? Look, I put my job on the line checking that number for you and showing you those photographs. The least you can do is to tell me what's going on." He pointed his finger at Nightingale. "And I deserve a straight answer. None of that devil-worship bollocks you gave me last time."

Nightingale blew a smoke ring over the water. It lasted less than a second before the wind ripped it apart. "Do you believe in God?" asked Nightingale quietly.

"Do I what?" said Evans, turning to face him.

"God," repeated Nightingale. "Do you believe in God?"

Evans laughed softly but his eyes were hard as he looked Nightingale up and down. "That depends on who's asking," he said.

Nightingale flicked ash into the water. "What do you mean?"

"I've got two daughters, twelve and fourteen. Where we live, you wouldn't send a dog to the local State school. There's a knifing every other month, half the kids don't speak English as even a second language and the teachers are all on antidepressants." Evans took a drag on his cigarette. "We went to see the school before the older girl was due to go and it scared me shitless. There was no way I was going to send my kids there, but on an inspector's salary private schools weren't an option. So my wife and I started looking around and we found a Church of England school about two miles away. Great exam results, motivated teaching staff, small classes. Just one drawback — the kids had to come from Christian families and me and the wife hadn't been inside a church since the day we were married." The detective turned back to look over the water. "So, we put her name down and started going to church, every Sunday." He chuckled. "Pretty much the entire congregation was made up of parents wanting to get their kids into the school. We all had to sign in and I swear they even checked to see that we were singing along with the hymns."

"And it worked?"

Evans nodded. "Both girls are in and doing really well. Best thing we ever did, becoming Christians."

"But you don't believe, right? You don't believe in God and Heaven and Hell?"

"Like I said, it depends on who's asking." He took a long pull on his cigarette and then dropped the butt onto the grass and trod on it. "If there was a God, Jack, and if he cared about us, why would he allow scum like Dwayne Robinson and his gang to run riot? Wouldn't he step in and do something? You were a cop, you know the score. Some people are just plain evil and that's got nothing to do with God or the Devil."

"Maybe it's the Devil working through men like Robinson. Maybe the earth is the battleground where Good and Evil battle it out."

Evans looked at Nightingale, his brow furrowed. "Are you on something, Jack?"

Nightingale raised an eyebrow. "Drugs? Do me a favour, Dan. Nicotine and alcohol are all the stimulants I need."

"Are you seeing someone?"

"Romantically, you mean? Or professionally?"

"You know what I mean. Post-traumatic stress disorder. You negotiators, you get to see a lot of shit that the average copper never gets near."

Nightingale snorted softly. "The average copper these days spends his whole shift sitting on his arse filling out forms," he said.

"But you were at the sharp end," said Evans. "A negotiator and a shooter. Either one of those roles comes with enough stress to push anyone over the edge."

"Over the edge?" repeated Nightingale. "Is that what you think?"

"Just the way you're talking, that's all. The battle between Good and Evil. Heaven and Hell. Don't tell me you've gone and got religion."

"Okay, I won't." He flicked his cigarette butt into the water and turned to leave.

"Jack, I'm serious. Tell me what's going on. Maybe I can help."

Nightingale shook his head, then pulled up his collar against the wind that was blowing across the Serpentine. "Truth be told, mate, I don't think anyone can help me," he said, and walked away without a backwards look.

CHAPTER
SIXTEEN

Nightingale woke up early on Sunday morning and went out to buy a couple of newspapers, a pint of milk, a loaf of bread and a pack of bacon. He was back in his flat making himself a bacon sandwich when his mobile rang. It was a landline calling and he didn't recognise the number. He took the call and tucked the phone between his chin and shoulder as he used a spatula to flick over the sizzling bacon slices.

"Mr Nightingale?" said a female voice.

"Yes?" said Nightingale hesitantly.

"I'm so sorry to bother you on a Sunday, Mr Nightingale. This is Elizabeth Fraser."

Nightingale frowned as he struggled to recall the name.

"Hillingdon Home," she said and Nightingale remembered immediately who she was. Mrs Fraser was the administrator at the nursing home where his mother had lived the last years of her life. His biological mother. Rebecca Keeley.

"Yes, Mrs Fraser. How can I help you?"

Mrs Fraser hesitated, then appeared to cover the receiver with her hand and talk to someone else before continuing. "Well, it's a little awkward, actually. I wondered if there was any way that you could come here today?"

"Is it about my mother?" he asked, turning off the cooker.

"Sort of," she said. "It would be a lot easier to explain if you were here."

Nightingale wondered why she was being so evasive, but it was a Sunday and his plan for the day consisted of a bacon sandwich followed by an afternoon in the pub reading the papers so he agreed to go around as soon as he'd finished his breakfast.

He'd had the MGB repaired on Saturday morning and the mechanic had given the car a clean bill of health but he still held his breath when he put the key in the ignition. The engine turned over immediately and he smiled. "Good girl," he said, patting the wooden steering wheel. "Who says you're not a classic?"

It was a cold day but he had the top down. He was regretting the decision by the time he pulled up in front of the nursing home. He'd driven fifty miles to the outskirts of Basingstoke and his hands were numb and his eyes were watering from the wind. He climbed out of the car and checked the sky. It didn't look like rain so he decided to risk leaving the top down while he went inside.

The building was a sixties-built concrete block with rusted metal-framed windows and doors covered with spray-painted graffiti. As he looked up he saw the smudges of faces staring out of some of the windows. They didn't seem to be looking down at him, just staring blankly off into the distance.

He pushed his way through the double doors to the reception area where a plump woman with tightly permed hair and spectacles on a chain around her neck flashed him a smile and held up her hand as she dealt with someone on the phone. As soon as she put the phone down she smiled again and asked him how she could help. After she'd checked with Mrs Fraser she pointed down the corridor that led to the administrator's office.

He knocked on the door and was told to go in. Mrs Fraser was in her early fifties, stick-thin with hair dyed the colour of a shiny conker. She had a pair of thick-lensed spectacles on the end of her nose but she took them off as she stood up and extended a bony hand. Nightingale shook it carefully. "I think it would be best if we talk as we walk," she said, guiding him out of the office and along the corridor. "Do you know a Mrs McFee? Mrs Fiona McFee?"

"I don't think so. Is she a resident?"

Mrs Fraser nodded. "Yes, she has been for almost ten years. She's one of our oldest residents."

"I don't know anyone here," said Nightingale. "I didn't even know that my mother was here until last year."

"It's all very strange," said Mrs Fraser. "So far as we know your mother never actually met Mrs McFee. In fact your mother didn't interact with anyone during her time here."

She pushed through a pair of fire doors and took him up a flight of stairs and along another corridor. Ahead of them was another set of doors with a sign that said

100

"Hospital Ward". At the end of the corridor was a nurse in a white uniform and Mrs Fraser smiled and waved. "We're just checking on Mrs McFee," she said and the nurse nodded and went back to her paperwork.

"Here we are," said the administrator, opening a door. There was a hospital bed in the room, occupied by a white-haired old lady with a feeding tube snaking from a plastic bag on a stand into her nose. Mrs Fraser closed the door gently. "Mrs McFee has been in a coma for the past week," she said. "There doesn't appear to be anything wrong with her, it's simply that she won't wake up. We have to give her water and nutrients through a tube but she doesn't require medication. There're no signs of a stroke or any physical damage."

"Shouldn't she be in a hospital?" asked Nightingale.

"Our doctor has examined her and we brought in a neurologist but everyone agrees that there's nothing that can be done in a hospital that we can't do here. So we keep her under observation and take care of her and wait. She's an old lady, of course. Almost ninety."

"But healthy?"

"Mentally, yes, she was very sharp. But she has had problems with her heart and her kidneys and she has diabetes." She shrugged. "Old age," she said. "The body wears out eventually, no matter how well you take care of yourself."

Nightingale smiled. "Yeah, I'm having the same problem with my car."

Mrs Fraser looked at him sternly. "That's hardly the same thing, Mr Nightingale." Nightingale opened his mouth to apologise but she was already looking back at the old woman. "She just didn't wake up one day. But every now and again she says something."

Nightingale felt the hairs stand up on the back of his neck. He knew what was coming next.

"She says your name, Mr Nightingale. Sometimes it's a whisper; sometimes she shouts it at the top of her voice."

"Without waking up?"

Mrs Fraser stroked the old woman's arm. "It's hard to tell. Sometimes her eyes are open but immediately afterwards she's back in this state."

"And why did you ask me to come here, Mrs Fraser?"

"Frankly, Mr Nightingale, I was hoping that you might know her. Mrs McFee is in a similar situation to that of your late mother when she was a resident here. We have no next of kin listed and she hasn't had a visitor in five years." She stepped to the side and waved him towards the bed. "Can you have a closer look and make sure that you don't know her?"

"Sure, but I don't know anyone called McFee."

"There has to be some reason that she's saying your name," said Mrs Fraser. "She never met your mother, and no one on the staff would have reason to mention your name to her. It's a mystery." She motioned for him to step forward. "Please, if you don't mind." Nightingale nodded but he found it difficult to move. Mrs Fraser smiled encouragingly. "Just have a closer look," she said. "She might be someone you met some time ago."

Nightingale shuffled towards the bed. The old lady was lying on her back, her mouth open, snoring softly. He could see the feeding tube at the back of her mouth. She had no teeth and her tongue was covered with a thick white fur. Her eyes were closed and her white hair was thinning so that her scalp was clearly visible. He flinched as he felt a touch on his arm but then realised it was Mrs Fraser. "She won't bite, Mr Nightingale."

Nightingale bent over the old woman. He could smell her bitter breath and underlying it was a sickly sweet stench of decay. He swallowed and almost gagged.

"Jack?" The old woman's bloodless lips had barely moved and her eyes were still closed.

Nightingale stared in horror at the old woman.

"Is that you, Jack?"

"She does seem to know you, Mr Nightingale."

Nightingale shook his head. "No," he said.

"Jack?"

"Please, Mr Nightingale, say something to her."

Nightingale swallowed. "Yes. It's me."

The old woman's eyes opened. "Please help me, Jack. You have to help me." Her voice was a low growl, barely human.

Nightingale took a step back, shaking his head.

"Mr Nightingale, where are you going?" asked Mrs Fraser, grabbing him by the arm.

Nightingale twisted out of her grip and pulled open the door. "I have to get out of here," he said. He dashed out and ran down the corridor, his coat flapping behind him. He didn't stop running until he was outside, where he pulled out his cigarettes and lit one with shaking hands. He kept looking at the main entrance, half expecting Mrs Fraser to come after him but the doors stayed resolutely closed.

He finished his cigarette before pulling up the soft top and fitting it into place. He got into the car and put the key in the ignition. He turned the key and something made a clunking sound under the bonnet. He groaned and tried again and this time there was no sound at all. He made three more attempts before giving up and taking out his mobile to call the AA.

CHAPTER
SEVENTEEN

Nightingale's MGB was in the garage having its electrical system overhauled on Monday morning so Nightingale caught a black cab in Bayswater and had it drop him in front of the Wicca Woman shop in Camden. It began to rain as he paid the driver and he jogged across the pavement to the shop, holding a Waitrose carrier bag against his chest.

He opened the door but then had to stand back as two girls in matching Afghan coats and multicoloured Tibetan hats pushed by him. There was only one sales assistant, a chunky teenager with a spider web tattoo across her neck and short hair that had been dyed a fluorescent green. She was wearing a slashed T-shirt and camouflage cargo pants with zipped pockets.

"Is Mrs Steadman in?" he asked as he closed the door.

"Are you Mr Nightingale, the one who rang?" asked the girl in an almost impenetrable Scots accent. She jerked a thumb at a beaded curtain behind the counter before he could answer. "She's expecting you."

Nightingale smiled his thanks and went through to the back room, where Mrs Steadman was sitting at a circular wooden table reading the *Guardian*. She took off a pair of blue-tinted pince-nez and smiled up at him. "Mr Nightingale, I was so happy to hear from you," she said. She was dressed in a black silk shirt buttoned up to the neck, around which was hanging a large silver crucifix on a delicate chain. She had a bird-like face with a sharp nose and she cocked her head to one side as she looked at him with inquisitive emerald-green eyes. Her grey hair was tied back in a ponytail and her wrinkled skin was almost translucent, but there was a youthful energy about her that made guessing her age difficult if not impossible. If Nightingale had been put on the spot he'd have guessed that Mrs Steadman was in her late sixties but he wouldn't have been surprised to learn that she was seventy or even eighty. "Would you care for some tea?"

"That would be lovely," said Nightingale.

He took off his raincoat and sat down as Mrs Steadman made a pot of tea. She put the pot, a milk jug and blue-and-white-striped mugs on the table. A gas fire was burning in a black-leaded fireplace casting flickering shadows over the walls.

He passed her the Waitrose carrier bag. "A small token of my appreciation," he said.

Mrs Steadman smiled like a child who had been given an early Christmas present and she opened the bag and took out two books. He'd selected them from the library in the basement at Gosling Manor. "Oh really, Mr Nightingale, you shouldn't do this," she said, her eyes sparkling with pleasure. "They're far too valuable to give away."

"I know you'll appreciate them, Mrs Steadman," he said.

"You've made my day," she said. She put the books down and poured the tea. "But I get the feeling that you didn't come all this way just to give me some books. As much as I do appreciate the gift."

Nightingale felt his cheeks redden, as though he was a naughty schoolboy who had been caught out in a lie. "I need some advice, Mrs Steadman."

She sipped her tea. "So it's not just a social visit?" She giggled girlishly. "I'm only teasing you, Mr Nightingale. "Of course I'll help you in any way that I can."

Nightingale stretched out his legs and stared at his Hush Puppies, still flecked from the rain outside. "Can you tell me how I can talk to the dead?"

Mrs Steadman shook her head sorrowfully. "There you go again, Mr Nightingale, wanting to mess with things that you really shouldn't be messing with."

"It's important, Mrs Steadman."

"I'm sure that it is. But it's a very dangerous area."

"It is possible, though?"

She sipped her tea again. "You know that you can use Tarot cards, don't you?"

Nightingale raised his eyebrows. "I thought they were for telling fortunes?"

"Oh they do that, of course, but in the hands of an expert they can be used for so much more."

"But you're not really talking to the dead, are you? You're getting messages through the cards."

"That's true. But often the dead find it easier to communicate that way. And it can be safer."

"Because ghosts are dangerous?"

"You're confusing spirits with ghosts, Mr Nightingale." She frowned as if she was getting the beginnings of a headache. "Really, I must counsel you to be careful, Mr Nightingale. You're very much an innocent abroad, you know. And it can be dangerous to meddle with things that you don't fully understand."

"I keep telling people that I'm on a pretty steep learning curve," said Nightingale. "But I'm going to need more than Tarot cards."

Mrs Steadman poured more tea into her mug. "There are Ouija boards, but frankly they're unreliable and dangerous."

Nightingale chuckled. "Been there, done that," he said.

Mrs Steadman put down the teapot. "You tried?"

"A couple of times."

"With whom?"

"My assistant. It didn't work out so well."

"I'm not surprised," she said. "Who were you trying to contact?"

"My former partner. Robbie Hoyle."

"How did Mr Hoyle pass away?"

"RTA," said Nightingale. He saw the look of confusion on the woman's face and waved his hand in apology. "Sorry, police-speak," he said. "Road traffic accident. He was hit by a taxi while he was crossing the road."

Mrs Steadman sighed. "In a violent unexpected death, any spirit is going to be confused and disorientated," she said. "And that's all you'd get through a Ouija board. Confusion. Anger. Resentment. Even an expert would have trouble controlling such a spirit."

"It was a bit hairy," admitted Nightingale.

"And is it this Robbie Hoyle that you want to contact?"

Nightingale shook his head. "No," he said. "It's a girl. A girl who killed herself."

Mrs Steadman pursed her lips and looked down her nose at him. "Another violent end," she said. "You have to be very careful interacting with spirits who pass over with violence," she said. "Often times the spirits aren't even aware of the situation they're in until someone contacts them, and there can be all sorts of repercussions."

"Such as?"

"That depends on the strength of the spirit concerned," said Mrs Steadman. "But you could have objects being moved, flashes of light, flames, even — or worse."

"Like a poltergeist?"

"Like a poltergeist, perhaps, but a poltergeist is something different. And the potential for damage isn't only there for the one who does the summoning. It can be dangerous for the spirit."

Nightingale frowned and ran a hand through his hair. "I'm confused," he said.

"I'm sure you are," said Mrs Steadman. "Tell me more about this girl."

"Her name is Sophie and she killed herself just over two years ago. Jumped from an apartment block in Chelsea Harbour. Her father had been abusing her and her mother didn't do anything about it."

"You were there when it happened?"

Nightingale nodded. "I told you I was a policeman. I was with CO19, the armed police. But I was also a negotiator, part of the team that talks to people in crisis. That could be a hostage situation or a self-harmer or a domestic. Any situation where someone might get hurt." His mouth felt suddenly dry and he took a sip of his tea. "When I got the call I didn't know it was a kid. She was up on the thirteenth floor, talking to her doll. She'd locked the door to the balcony and the au pair had called the police. I was the first negotiator on the scene."

"And this Sophie, why was she on the balcony?"

Nightingale leaned forward and put his head in his hands. "She wanted to die, Mrs Steadman. There was nothing I could do that was going to stop that. I know that now."

Mrs Steadman stood up and walked around to stand behind Nightingale. She put her hands on his shoulders. "I'm sorry," she said quietly.

"She was talking to me and then she just slipped under the railing and fell." Nightingale shuddered. "I don't know what I should have done differently. I've gone over it again and again but I can't think . . ." He shuddered again. "She was just a kid, Mrs Steadman. Her life hadn't even started, not really."

"Is that why you want to talk to her?" asked Mrs Steadman.

"She's the one who's been trying to contact me," said Nightingale.

Mrs Steadman let go of his shoulders and took a step back. "What do you mean?"

Nightingale explained what had happened at the hospital and at the nursing home.

Mrs Steadman sat down again and looked at Nightingale, clearly concerned. Nightingale folded his arms and shrugged. "I'm not imagining things," he said.

"I wasn't going to suggest that you were."

"I just feel that Sophie wants to talk to me and I want to make it easier for her, if that's possible."

"You have to be careful," said Mrs Steadman. "It could be something else pretending to be the girl, have you thought of that? It could be an evil spirit that wants to do you harm."

"Why go to the trouble of pretending to be Sophie?"

"So that you'll let your guard down. And by the time you realise what's happened, it'll be too late."

Nightingale rubbed the back of his neck. He wanted a cigarette, badly.

"I don't like to ask, but would you help me? Would you show me what to do?"

"I'm not a medium, Mr Nightingale. It's not my field." She tapped the handle of her mug thoughtfully. "You should try a spiritualist association. There are several very good ones in London. You'll meet experienced mediums there and you'll be in a safe environment. If Sophie does want to come through she'll be in the care of people who know what they're doing. You'll do the talking through the medium, so you'll be one step removed. The medium will act as a fuse in a plug, if you like. If there's a problem the medium will break contact and no damage is done."

"I thought that most mediums were charlatans? Con artists."

"Some are. But people aren't stupid, Mr Nightingale. If they are being conned they'll realise it sooner rather than later. And the true mediums don't ask for money."

"What about doing it myself?"

"You, Mr Nightingale?" She chuckled softly. "You can do it yourself, if you have the talent. There are summoning spells that are said to work, but they're not for amateurs."

"Have you ever done it?"

"Summoned a spirit? I have, yes."

"And it worked?"

Mrs Steadman smiled. "Magic works, Mr Nightingale. If it didn't my shop and website wouldn't be as popular as they are."

"Could I try? To summon a spirit?"

"I really don't think you're experienced enough," said Mrs Steadman. "And if you were to contact this girl, this spirit, you might do her harm, inadvertently. That would be my main concern." She sipped her tea. "It's an inexact science, Mr Nightingale. There are things you can do to increase your chances of success.

112

You can burn lavender, mastic, orris root and frankincense in a brass bowl and you can scatter jasmine flowers, lilies, gardenias and mimosa in the room to appease the spirits. But at the end of the day it's down to the strength and ability of the medium. And like the Ouija board, you can't always stop a rogue spirit coming through. You might set out to talk to Sophie and end up confronting a quite different spirit."

"A demon, you mean?"

She smiled like a teacher humouring a young child. "Demons don't need to come through a Ouija board," she said. "If it was a demon that wanted to talk to you, it would just appear. And I'm not sure you'd have much success if you tried to contact one through a Ouija board either. No, I'm talking about an evil spirit. Or a mischievous one." She leaned towards him across the table and took his hands in hers. They were warm and dry without a single blemish or mark. "Please, Mr Nightingale, promise you won't do anything stupid. If you're serious about wanting to contact the spirit of this girl, use a professional."

Nightingale nodded. "I will," he said.

She stared at him intently and he felt her small hands grip his own with a strength that was out of proportion to their size. "Promise me," she said.

Nightingale opened his mouth to say something funny but he could see from the look in her eyes that she was serious. "I promise, Mrs Steadman. Cross my heart."

A smile slowly spread across her face and she let go of his hands. He looked down and saw red marks where her fingers had been digging into his flesh. "You've got quite a grip there, Mrs Steadman," he said.

CHAPTER
EIGHTEEN

Nightingale walked into the office and found Jenny sitting at her desk looking very unhappy. He hung his raincoat on the rack and held up his hands in surrender. "I know, I'm sorry," he said. "I had to go and see Mrs Steadman in Camden."

Jenny shook her head and pointed towards Nightingale's office and he looked over to see Superintendent Chalmers and Inspector Evans standing by his desk. Chalmers was flicking through a file on Nightingale's desk. He was wearing a dark blue suit that looked as if it had been made to measure. Evans was wearing a sheepskin jacket over a cheap sports coat and trousers that had gone baggy around the knees.

"You can't touch anything without a warrant," said Nightingale, walking into the office and picking up the file.

"It was in plain view," said Chalmers.

"Well, it isn't now," said Nightingale, dropping it into one of the desk drawers. He didn't want to sit down so he moved to stand behind his chair. He looked over at Evans, wondering why the two detectives were in his office. The inspector avoided eye contact and looked out through the window at the street below.

Nightingale's mind whirled. Had Evans told Chalmers about Nightingale's involvement in the Bayswater shooting? "What's this about, Chalmers?"

"We need you to come down to the station."

"Are you arresting me?"

"Not unless we have to," said the superintendent. "But you're in big trouble and I'd suggest that you agree to cooperate with us."

Nightingale looked over at Evans again but he was still avoiding eye contact.

"You know, I'm getting fed up with you dragging me in for questioning every time you get a case you can't solve. If you want me to come in of my own accord then you're going to have to tell me what it's about."

Jenny came to stand in the doorway, her arms folded.

"Where were you yesterday?" asked Chalmers.

Nightingale felt relief wash over him. He'd seen Evans in the park on Saturday so it couldn't have anything to do with the Dwayne Robinson shooting. "At home."

"Just at home?"

Nightingale sighed in frustration. "I got a call from Hillingdon Home and I went down to Basingstoke to see the administrator there. Elizabeth Fraser. It's a nursing home."

"I know what it is. And while you were there you spoke to a woman by the name of Fiona McFee."

"Are you asking me or telling me?"

"We have a number of questions regarding Mrs McFee," said Chalmers.

"In what sense?"

"In the sense that she's dead," said Chalmers.

Evans turned away from the window and put his hands in the pockets of his sheepskin jacket.

"Chalmers, Fiona McFee was getting on for a hundred years old and she was in a coma when I went to see her."

"Eighty-nine years old, to be precise," said Chalmers. "But it wasn't old age that killed her."

"She was in a coma when I left," said Nightingale.

"That's as maybe," said Chalmers. "But not long after you left she managed to get up to the roof and jump to her death." He slammed his hand down hard on the desk and Nightingale flinched. "Now stop messing me about and get your coat."

CHAPTER
NINETEEN

Evans pressed "record" and nodded at Superintendent Chalmers. Chalmers noted the time and date and both officers said their names for the benefit of the tape. Chalmers looked expectantly at Nightingale.

"Jack Nightingale," he said. "Helping the police with their enquiries. Again."

"On Sunday you went to Hillingdon Home in Basingstoke?"

Nightingale nodded.

"For the tape, please."

"Yes. I was asked to go there by the administrator. Elizabeth Fraser."

"She wanted you to see a patient there?"

"They don't call them patients. They're residents."

"Her name was Fiona McFee?"

"Apparently. Yes. That was the first time I had laid eyes on her."

"So you don't know who she is?"

"At the risk of repeating myself, Sunday was the first time I had ever seen the lady."

"And she was in a coma."

"Apparently, yes."

"But despite being in a coma, she said your name."

Nightingale nodded again.

"For the tape, please," Chalmers repeated.

"Yes," said Nightingale.

"Do you have any explanation for that?"

Nightingale shook his head. "No."

"What time did you leave Hillingdon Home?"

"Just after eleven thirty."

"Are you aware that at seven o'clock on Sunday evening Mrs McFee went up to the roof and threw herself off?"

"I wasn't until you told me, no."

"Can you think of any reason why Mrs McFee would have wanted to kill herself after you went to see her?"

"You make it sound as if the two events are connected."

"Aren't they?" said Chalmers.

"I spent less than a minute in her room."

"During which time she said your name several times."

Nightingale sat back, yawned and stretched out his arms.

"Mr Nightingale is refusing to answer the question," said Chalmers.

"You didn't ask a question," said Nightingale. "You stated a fact."

"And isn't it also a fact that last year you visited your mother at Hillingdon Home and that shortly afterwards she took her own life?"

"My mother was disturbed," said Nightingale.

"But she hadn't shown any suicidal impulses until you visited her," said Chalmers. He tapped his slim gold pen on his notepad. "And while we're on the subject of suicides, isn't it the case that on November the thirtieth last year you were in the home of one Constance Miller in Abersoch minutes after she took her own life by hanging?"

"That was a coincidence," said Nightingale.

"It's one hell of a coincidence, isn't it? Three visits, three suicides. And it doesn't stop there, does it? There seem to be a lot of deaths around you these days. Your uncle and aunt. Robbie Hoyle. Barry O'Brien who was driving the cab that ran over Hoyle. And of course good old Simon Underwood, who took a flyer through his office window while you were talking to him."

Nightingale said nothing. Chalmers flashed Evans a quick smile, playing to the crowd. "Then there's Christmas Day. You were in the country. Shooting."

"Shooting pheasant," said Nightingale. "And I wasn't. I was watching. Never seen the fun in killing things."

Chalmers raised an eyebrow, opened his mouth to say something but then seemed to think better of it. He settled back in his seat. "One of the gamekeepers blew his head off with a shotgun."

"Yeah, pretty much."

"Lachie Kennedy. He'd been with the family for years."

"So I gather."

"And he was standing next to you when he decided to kill himself."

Nightingale folded his arms but didn't say anything.

120

"Bit strange that, don't you think?" pressed the superintendent.

Nightingale said nothing.

"Did you know that game shooting is illegal in England and Wales on Christmas Day?"

"I didn't, no."

"Well, it is. Across most of the country. But that house is one of the few places where it's allowed. Seems that Edward the Seventh went shooting there and so did George the Fifth. Because of the royal connection they got special dispensation and they're allowed to shoot on Sundays and Christmas Day, unlike the rest of the country."

"Like I said, I'm not a fan of shooting."

"That's a strange thing for a former member of CO19 to say."

"Just because I was in CO19 didn't mean that I went around shooting people. If a CO19 officer fires his weapon then he's failed to do his job. The job is about containing situations, not escalating them."

"I'll take your word for that," said Chalmers.

"I resent the implication of what you're saying. You're implying that I was somehow involved in the shooting of Lachie Kennedy, but it was clearly self-inflicted. There were plenty of witnesses."

"Now you're sounding defensive, Mr Nightingale. Why is that?"

"I was there when Lachie blew his head off. It's a touchy subject."

"And what about Dwayne Robinson? Were you there when he was shot in the head?"

121

Nightingale leaned forward and clasped his hands together so tightly that his knuckles whitened. "That was nothing to do with me. I wasn't in Brixton. You were in my office today. You saw my assistant. She would have confirmed that."

"Miss McLean? Yes, we did ask her about your whereabouts and she said that you were in a pub. With Robbie Hoyle, who sadly is no longer with us."

Nightingale's eyes hardened. "Tread very carefully, Chalmers," he said.

"Are you threatening me, Mr Nightingale?" asked Chalmers, glancing at the recorder.

"I was with Robbie Hoyle, but I've spoken with the landlord and he remembers us being in the pub at the time that Robinson was shot."

"That could be classed as interfering with a witness," said the superintendent.

"I was doing your job," said Nightingale. "Establishing my alibi." He sat back in his chair.

Chalmers said nothing for several seconds. "Why do you think she works for you?"

"Who?"

"You know who. Jenny McLean."

"I guess she likes the work."

"Her family's very well off."

"Are you asking me or telling me?"

Chalmers smiled thinly. "How did James McLean make his money? Out in Hong Kong, wasn't he? Must have done something right to afford a house like that. I hear that Prince Philip used to shoot there."

Nightingale nodded. "I heard that."

"The father's very close to an awful lot of movers and shakers."

"I only met him the once."

"Really? How unlucky is that? The first time you get to meet him and his gamekeeper kills himself? I bet that took the gloss off the Christmas celebrations."

"I'm glad you think it's funny," said Nightingale.

"Oh I'm not laughing, Nightingale." The superintendent looked at Evans. "Do I look as if I'm laughing, Inspector?"

"No, sir," said Evans.

"See, Nightingale, I'm definitely not laughing. I'd hate you to think that murder was a laughing matter."

"Lachie wasn't murdered," said Nightingale. "He killed himself."

"Well, we'll wait for the inquest, shall we? But we can put it down as yet another suicide, if you want." He looked down at his notepad. "Tell me again why you were at the McLeans' house?"

"Jenny asked me down for Christmas."

"That was nice of her," said Chalmers, his voice loaded with sarcasm. "And was it a coincidence that Marcus Fairchild was there?"

"In what way?"

"In the way that he was part of your sister's legal team. Don't play the innocent, Nightingale. You spend Christmas with your sister's lawyer and a few days later she escapes from Rampton Mental Hospital. That seems suspicious to me."

"That was the first time I'd met Marcus."

"And what did you do? Plan your sister's escape? Is that why you were there?"

Nightingale sat back in his chair but didn't reply.

"I'd like an answer to my question, Mr Nightingale."

"I was there for Christmas. Marcus Fairchild was also a guest."

"Did you discuss your sister?"

"She was mentioned in passing. That's all."

The door opened and a uniformed policewoman stepped aside so that a man in his late fifties could walk into the interview room. The paunch that stretched the waistcoat of his pinstriped suit and the pug nose flecked with broken blood vessels suggested a fondness for good food and drink, and the mane of grey hair combed back hinted that he might have had an eye for the ladies when he was younger.

Chalmers put down his gold pen. "Well, now, speak of the devil," he said.

Fairchild smiled, but it was a cold baring of the teeth without a shred of warmth in it.

"Has my client been charged?" he asked.

"Mr Nightingale is assisting us with our enquiries," said Chalmers.

"Not any more he isn't," said Fairchild. "My client has done all the assisting he's going to do."

Nightingale raised a hand. "Marcus, I don't want to appear ungrateful, but when did I become a client of yours?"

"Jenny called me," said the lawyer. "She asked me to put a stop to this." He adjusted his shirt cuffs and gold links glinted under the fluorescent lights. "Of course, if

124

you want to stay here all day answering their questions then that's up to you, but it's clear that Superintendent Chalmers here has his own agenda and he won't be happy until you're behind bars."

"Mr Nightingale is here of his own accord," said Chalmers frostily.

"No, he's here because you are in the process of carrying out a vendetta against my client, a vendetta which began when he was a serving officer with the Metropolitan Police. And if this carries on much longer you run the risk of a civil action and a claim for substantial damages."

Chalmers stood up, his cheeks reddening. "Mr Nightingale is the prime suspect in the murder of a south London drug dealer," he said.

"According to the information I have you don't have a shred of evidence against my client," said Fairchild.

"We have a deathbed statement," said Chalmers. "The victim named Nightingale as his attacker."

"That's crap," said Nightingale.

"Then charge him," said Fairchild. "But be aware that we will have no hesitation in suing you for wrongful arrest, and in view of comments you have made about my client we shall also be considering an action for slander." He looked at his watch and then flashed the superintendent a sarcastic smile. "Do you need a minute to think about it?"

Chalmers put his pen into his jacket pocket, picked up his notepad and walked out of the interview room. Dan Evans tried not to smile as he leaned over and switched off the recorder. "Looks like you're free to go," he said to Nightingale.

Nightingale grinned. "It does, doesn't it?"

CHAPTER
TWENTY

"We could crack open a bottle of champagne, if you want," said Fairchild, waving a fifty-pound note at a barmaid who was busy polishing glasses. They were in a wine bar a short walk from the police station. It had just opened and they were the only customers. There were terracotta tiles on the floor, vineyard scenes on the walls and the gantry behind the bar was filled with bottles of Italian wine. As Nightingale stood with his back to the glass doors overlooking the London traffic and dismal English winter weather he could almost imagine that he was in Tuscany.

"You don't have to buy me a drink, Marcus," said Nightingale.

"Nonsense. I told Jenny I'd look after you until she gets here and look after you I will," said Fairchild. The barmaid was steadfastly refusing to make eye contact with him. He waved his banknote again. "When you're ready, darling," he said.

"I should go," said Nightingale.

Fairchild put a hand on his arm. "I insist," he said. His fingers bit into Nightingale's flesh through the material of the raincoat, gripping like steel claws. Fairchild released his grip as the barmaid walked over, drying her hands on a towel. "A double Hennessy with ice," he said. "Jack?"

Nightingale sighed. He didn't want to drink with the lawyer but he couldn't see how he could continue to refuse without being deliberately rude. "Corona, please." The barmaid went off to get their drinks. "Why did Jenny call you?" asked Nightingale.

"She felt that the police were overstepping their authority and frankly I think she's right."

"I could have handled it."

"How? By sitting there and answering questions until the cows come home? You mustn't encourage them, Jack, my boy. The police are like any other bureaucrats; they'll always take the path of least resistance. If you don't stand up to them, they'll walk all over you."

The barmaid returned with their drinks and Fairchild gave her the fifty-pound note. "Keep the change, my love," he said. "Come on, Jack, there's a table over there."

Nightingale picked up his Corona and smiled at the barmaid, who was staring after Fairchild with a look of astonishment on her face. "He prints them himself," said Nightingale, and he winked at her before following Fairchild to the corner table. The seats were white-painted wrought iron with overstuffed cushions, and the table had a glass top allowing Nightingale to compare his scuffed Hush Puppies with the lawyer's gleaming black brogues.

"So the last time we spoke you were telling me about your sister," said Fairchild, swirling his brandy around the balloon glass.

"That's right," said Nightingale.

"And very shortly afterwards she escaped. Vanished, by all accounts."

Nightingale sipped his lager.

"Did you have anything to do with that, Jack?" asked Fairchild. "And before you answer, remember that everything you tell me is covered by lawyer-client privilege."

Nightingale stared at Fairchild, trying to work out whether or not he was serious.

Fairchild laughed and raised his glass. "I can see from the look on your face that you did," he said. He clinked his glass against Nightingale's Corona bottle. "Here's to crime."

"Crime?"

"Look, Jack, I'm a lawyer and you're a police officer turned private detective — where would either of us be without the lawbreakers?"

"I hadn't thought about that."

"Well, you should," said Fairchild. "If there were no criminals we'd both be out of a job." Fairchild sipped his brandy and then put the glass down. "Seriously, Jack, what do you think happened to your sister?"

"In what way?"

"You know exactly in what way," said Fairchild, and he chuckled dryly. "By all accounts she vanished from a locked room leaving behind Satanic symbols and paraphernalia. You know as well as I do that you don't just walk out of a place like Rampton. It's the most secure hospital in the country."

Nightingale stared at the lawyer but didn't say anything.

"Of course, if you'd rather not say . . ."

"Looks like I've gone from one interrogation to another," said Nightingale.

"Hardly," said Fairchild.

Nightingale leaned forward, both hands around his bottle of lager. "Let me ask you something, Marcus. Okay?"

"Go ahead," said the lawyer.

"Are you a member of the Order of Nine Angles?"

Nightingale resisted the urge to smile when he saw the look of surprise that flashed across the lawyer's face. Fairchild adjusted his cufflinks as he tried to regain his composure. "That's a strange question to ask," he said.

"And that's you being evasive," said Nightingale.

Fairchild's face had hardened and there was a coldness in his eyes. Not annoyance, not contempt, but something in between. Nightingale could imagine the lawyer using the baleful stare to good effect on opposing counsel in court, but it made no impression at all on Nightingale. As a cop he'd faced down some of the hardest criminals in London and it had been years since he'd been fazed by a nasty look. He stared back at the lawyer, determined not to be the first to blink.

"One of the things I picked up during thirty years of cross-examination in court is never to ask a question to which you don't know the answer," said Fairchild.

"That's pretty much how it works with cops too," said Nightingale.

"So you know already. Yes, I am a member of the Order. Have been for years. So let me ask you a question in return, Jack. The Order goes to a lot of trouble to maintain a low profile, so who told you about us?"

"A friend."

"An informant, you mean? I assume that your friend is an outsider. In the entire history of the Order no member has ever divulged any details of who we are or what we do."

"Child sacrifice, is what I heard," said Nightingale quietly.

Fairchild's eyes widened and his jaw dropped, then he quickly forced a smile to cover his discomfort. "Exactly what were you told about the Order of Nine Angles?" he asked.

Nightingale smiled. "There you go, asking a question that you don't know the answer to," he said.

A small vein began to pulse in Fairchild's left temple and Nightingale saw the lawyer's legs begin to tremble, signs of the tension the man was feeling.

"Are you a Freemason?" asked Fairchild.

"Never went for funny handshakes and rolling up my trouser leg," said Nightingale.

"A lot of police officers are, though."

"No argument there."

"Superintendent Chalmers, for instance. I'd be very surprised if he wasn't the member of a lodge."

"I dare say. But what's that got to do with the Nine Angles?"

"People who don't understand the Masons think that they get up to all sorts of shenanigans."

"I don't think anyone has ever accused the Masons of child sacrifice."

Fairchild shook his head. "You really believe that, Jack? You think that in this day and age people actually go around sacrificing children?"

Nightingale slowly sipped his lager. "Since I discovered that my father, my genetic father, was a Satanist, I've tried to keep an open mind on the whole black-magic thing."

"Now it's black magic, is it? You're accusing the Order of black magic, devil-worship and killing children?"

"If I was, what would your answer be?"

"Jack, you're being ridiculous. You know that, surely?"

"I know that whenever you're faced with a difficult question, you prevaricate."

Fairchild leaned forward and glared at Nightingale. "I can unequivocally say that the Order of Nine Angles has absolutely nothing to do with child sacrifice or devil-worship or any other nonsense of that nature. It's a charitable organisation that allows like-minded people to network. There are judges in the Order, politicians, members of the royal family, sportsmen. It's not very different from the Rotary Club. Or the Freemasons, come to that." He stared intently at Nightingale for several seconds, then smiled, picked up his glass and swirled his brandy again.

"And my sister?" said Nightingale.

"What about her?"

"Was Robyn a member of the Order?"

"Of course not," said Fairchild. "Why would you even think that?"

"Because she confessed to murdering five children."

"Jack, you're not listening to me. The Order of Nine Angles does not kill children. But your sister . . ." He sipped his brandy.

"My sister what, Marcus? My sister is a child-killer? Is that what you were going to say?"

"As you just said, she confessed."

"But you were on her defence team, weren't you? You were defending her."

"Innocent or guilty, a person is entitled to the best possible representation in court," said Fairchild. He sipped his brandy again.

"I know what you did, Marcus," said Nightingale quietly.

Fairchild stiffened. "What do you mean? What do you think I did, Jack?"

Nightingale opened his mouth to speak but before he could say anything he saw Jenny McLean walk into the bar. She waved at him and then hurried over to their table. The two men stood up. Jenny headed straight for Fairchild, hugged him and kissed him on both cheeks. "Thanks for rescuing him, Uncle Marcus."

"Always a pleasure to put the police in their place," said Fairchild. "What can I get you to drink?"

"White wine would be lovely, thank you," said Jenny. Fairchild went over to the bar as Jenny sat down next to Nightingale.

"Why did you call him?" whispered Nightingale.

"You're welcome," said Jenny. "He got you out, didn't he?"

"I'm serious, Jenny. He's dangerous."

"Look, Jack, Chalmers clearly has it in for you and if he throws enough mud at you some of it is going to stick."

"I can handle Chalmers," said Nightingale.

"No you can't because you're a civilian and he's got the Met behind him. Now that he knows that Uncle Marcus is in your corner he'll be less likely to give you a hard time."

"He's not your uncle. I don't know why you call him that."

"You're a fine one to talk. You know that you were adopted at birth but you still call them your parents, don't you?"

"That's different. That's totally different."

"Sometimes you can be an obstinate bastard, Jack," said Jenny. She folded her arms and glared at him.

"Something wrong?" asked Fairchild as he returned to the table with a glass of wine for Jenny. He put the glass on the table and sat down.

"I'm starting to think that Jack enjoys sparring with Chalmers," said Jenny.

"What I can't understand is where all the bad feeling has sprung from," said Fairchild, adjusting the creases of his trousers. "You've obviously done something to get under his skin."

"It's probably jealousy," said Jenny.

"What, of my good looks?" said Nightingale.

Jenny smiled sarcastically. "Yes, I'm sure that's it."

"What, then?"

"For a start you were a better cop than he ever was," said Jenny.

"Is that so?" asked Fairchild.

"That's what Jack always says."

"Chalmers is an idiot," said Nightingale. "Always has been, always will be. But he knows how to tick the right boxes and how to say the right things at interviews to climb the slippery pole."

"Plus, the fact that you have the house must really get up his nose."

"House?" said Fairchild.

"Jack inherited a huge house in the country," said Jenny. She sipped her wine.

"Did he now?" said Fairchild.

"Gosling Manor," said Nightingale. "From my biological father."

"What about Robyn? Did he leave anything to her?" said Fairchild.

"He didn't know where she was. He gave both of us away at birth and although he found me he had no idea what had happened to her. So no, she got nothing."

"And this house — are you going to live there?"

"I'm not sure," said Nightingale. "I'm still considering my options. I'll decide once the builders are out."

"You're doing the place up?" asked Fairchild.

"I wish," said Nightingale. "I had a visit from an arsonist."

"You're joking," said Fairchild.

"If I am, there's no punchline," said Nightingale. "I was in the house at the time."

"Did the police catch him?"

"Sort of," said Nightingale. "But he set fire to himself before they could put the cuffs on him."

"And why did he pick on you?" asked Fairchild.

"It was probably his winning personality," said Jenny. She raised her glass to Fairchild. "Thanks for riding to Jack's rescue," she said. "I'm grateful, even if he isn't."

CHAPTER
TWENTY-ONE

Nightingale got into Jenny's Audi with every intention of not mentioning Marcus Fairchild but she knew him well enough to realise that something was wrong. "You really are pissed off that I got Uncle Marcus to bail you out, aren't you?" she asked.

"Bail wasn't an issue. I was helping them with their enquiries." He stared out through the windscreen. There were roadworks ahead and the traffic was crawling along.

"You know what I mean. What's your problem with him?" Rain began to spatter on the windscreen and Jenny switched on her wipers.

Nightingale turned to look at her. "Are you serious? Have you forgotten what my sister said?"

"Your sister was under hypnosis. We don't know if what she said was true. It could have been a false memory."

"She said that he killed a child. Have you forgotten that?"

"Jack, I've known him for as long as I can remember. He knew my father at university."

Nightingale looked through the windscreen again. Proserpine was standing in the middle of the road, her

137

dog at her side, her long black coat blowing in the wind behind her. "Jenny, stop!" he shouted and she slammed on the brakes.

"What?" she said.

He looked across at her. "You nearly ran her over."

"Who?"

Nightingale looked back at the road. Ahead of them was only traffic. There was no sign of Proserpine or her dog. "She was there," said Nightingale. "I saw her."

"Who?"

"Proserpine."

"There's no one there, Jack."

The car behind them sounded its horn and Jenny waved an apology and moved off.

"She was there, Jenny."

"She couldn't have been. I was looking straight ahead."

They drove in silence for several minutes, then Nightingale folded his arms. "You heard what my sister said about Fairchild. He killed a kid and framed her. And he admitted that he was in the Order of Nine Angles."

"When?"

"Back in the wine bar near the cop shop. Before you arrived. He tried to tell me that it was some sort of charitable organisation."

"Maybe it is." A bus pulled up in front of them and Jenny braked.

"Have you Googled it? The Order of Nine Angles? Trust me, there's nothing charitable about them.

138

Human sacrifice plays a big part in what they do. They call it culling."

Jenny sighed. "Jack, even if there is such a thing as the Order of Nine Angles, you don't know for sure that he's involved with them."

Nightingale took out his cigarettes. "He's got to you," he muttered.

"Please don't smoke in my car," she said. "And what do you mean? How's he got to me?" The bus moved off and Jenny edged the Audi forward.

"You're not thinking straight and I don't understand why. It's like he's a blind spot so far as you're concerned."

"He's my uncle."

"No he's not, Jenny. He's a friend of your father's, that's all."

Jenny flashed him an angry look. "What are you getting at, Jack?"

Nightingale slipped his cigarettes back into his pocket. "I'm just saying that you don't seem to think straight when he's around."

"Why did you mention my father?"

"Because you keep saying that Fairchild is your uncle and he isn't. He's just a family friend."

"You think that Marcus is a child-killer. Are you now suggesting that my father is as well?"

"Of course not."

"That's what it sounded like to me," she said.

"Now you're the one being ridiculous," he said.

Jenny stamped on the brake. For a second time the driver of the car behind them pounded on his horn. "Get out," she said.

"Oh come on, Jenny."

"I'm serious. Get out."

"It's raining."

The driver behind them sounded his horn again and the car behind him joined in too. Jenny stared ahead through the windscreen, her lips clamped together and her chin raised defiantly.

Nightingale could see that there was no point in arguing with her. He climbed out of the car and slammed the door behind him. As Jenny drove off he took out his cigarettes. He lit one and looked around for a black cab.

CHAPTER
TWENTY-TWO

Nightingale opened the office door half expecting Jenny not to be there, but he smiled when he saw her at her desk. "Sorry," he said, placing a Starbucks bag and two coffees in front of her. Jenny's desk was always immaculate, in stark contrast to his own, which was usually hidden under stacks of newspapers, files, dirty coffee mugs and overflowing ashtrays.

"You should be." She turned away from him.

"I'm an idiot."

She steadfastly refused to look at him. "Yes. You are."

Nightingale moved one of the coffees closer to her. "Latte."

"Thanks," she said quietly.

Nightingale gestured at the bag.

"Banana choc-chip muffin. And a croissant. Breakfast of champions."

"Thanks," she repeated. She looked at her watch. "But it's six o'clock in the evening so it's a bit late for breakfast."

"I figured if I turned up with a pizza it wouldn't have been as cute," he said. "Come on, Jenny, at least give me a smile. I know I'm an insensitive prick sometimes."

"Sometimes?"

"Okay, most of the time. I was just wrong-footed when Fairchild turned up out of the blue. I shouldn't have laid into you. I'm sorry." He grinned. "Especially when you were giving me a lift. You really are heartless, aren't you?"

"You deserved it," she said. "Anyway, you weren't far from the Tube."

"I did deserve it. And yes, the Tube wasn't that far, though it was pissing down." He put up his hands. "But, again, it was my own fault so I've only myself to blame. To be honest, I didn't really expect you to be here."

"I had work to do."

"Then I saw the light on and thought the least I could do to make amends was to buy you a very late breakfast." He pushed the bag towards her.

"I had work to do," she repeated. "I thought you'd go straight home." Jenny turned away from her computer and opened the bag. She took out the muffin. "There's a bit missing," she said.

"I broke off a piece, just to check it was fresh."

Jenny raised an eyebrow. "You bought me a muffin and then ate it?"

"Checked it for freshness," said Nightingale, taking off his wet raincoat. He shook it then put it on the rack by the door.

"Did you try my coffee too?"

Nightingale went back to her desk and picked up his cup. "No. And I didn't touch the croissant either." He sipped his coffee and smacked his lips. "So what are you doing later this evening?"

"Why?" she asked suspiciously.

"I thought I'd buy you dinner. By way of apology."

"You don't have to." She held out the muffin. "This is enough. Even if you did nibble it."

"I want to. You can choose the restaurant."

Jenny grinned. "Money no object?"

"If that means you accept my apology, sure." He took another sip of his coffee. "Just one thing, can you make it near Marylebone?"

Jenny sighed. "Why?"

"I need to swing by a meeting there."

"What sort of meeting, Jack?"

"A spiritualist group." He walked away from her desk towards his office. "Mrs Steadman at the Wicca Woman shop in Camden recommended it. It'll be fun," he said. He stopped and looked at his watch. "We've got to be there by seven thirty."

"We? Now it's 'we', is it?'

"It always is," said Nightingale. He grinned. "You know I'd be lost without you."

CHAPTER
TWENTY-THREE

The Marylebone Spiritualist Association met in a community centre not far from Madame Tussauds waxwork museum. Three Asian youths in baggy jeans and hoodies were standing outside smoking and Nightingale caught a whiff of cannabis as he and Jenny walked past them. The double doors opened into a reception area where an elderly black man in a shabby blue suit was sitting at a desk. Near him there was an easel supporting a board on which white plastic letters had been stuck to announce "Marylebone Spiritualist Association — Guest Medium Neil Morgan. Starts 7.30p.m."

"We're here for the MSA meeting," Nightingale told the man.

"Five pounds each," he said and smiled, revealing a mouthful of broken and stained teeth. Nightingale handed him a ten-pound note. The man took it and pushed a clipboard towards him. Nightingale picked up a pen and added their names to the list, then the man nodded at a door to the left. As Nightingale and Jenny headed in that direction two middle-aged women in long coats and black hats came in from outside, deep in conversation. Nightingale opened the door and let Jenny go in first.

The room was kitted out for sports with a wooden floor, basketball hoops at either end and two table-tennis tables that had been pushed against one wall. Orange plastic chairs had been lined up in the middle of the room, ten rows wide and five rows deep, facing a wooden lectern. There were blue screens on either side of the lectern. There were no religious symbols to be seen, though there was a vase of plastic flowers on a small table in front of the lectern.

"I thought it would be more like a church," said Nightingale. "I thought there'd be crosses and stuff."

"Clearly not," said Jenny. "Anyway, I thought the Church frowned on things like this."

"Things like what?"

"Talking to the dead," whispered Jenny. "Because that's what we're here to do, aren't we?"

There were more than a dozen people sitting on the chairs, mostly pensioners by the look of them. Nightingale looked at his watch. It was seven twenty. "Front or back?" he asked.

"What?"

"I'm guessing at school you were always sitting at the front, right?"

"While you were at the back with the rest of the troublemakers?"

"Let's compromise and sit in the middle," he said.

"I thought the idea was to see if we could contact Sophie. Wouldn't it be better to sit at the front? Aren't you more likely to be noticed that way?"

"Excuse me," said a voice behind them. Nightingale and Jenny moved apart to allow a short man in a dark green anorak to squeeze between them. He sat in the back row.

"He'd be a troublemaker, then, would he?" Nightingale asked Jenny.

"Behave," said Jenny. She shuffled along the third row of seats and sat close to the middle.

An elderly woman in a fur coat came through the door, followed by two middle-aged men wearing suits. The men sat at the front, with an empty seat between them, while the woman went to stand at the lectern.

Over the next five minutes another couple of dozen people arrived, most of them elderly but there was a sprinkling of teenagers and also a young couple, the woman holding a baby that couldn't have been more than six months old.

At seven thirty the woman in the fur coat went outside and returned a few minutes later with a young man in his late twenties. He was wearing a green corduroy jacket, black trousers that were an inch too short and scuffed brown shoes. One of the men in suits picked up a chair and placed it next to the lectern and the young man sat down. He kept his head lowered and every few seconds flicked his hair away from his eyes. He had his hands clasped together but Nightingale could see that his nails were bitten to the quick.

There was a buzz of excitement among the audience, but it disappeared as the woman in the fur coat walked over to the lectern again. She had far too much make-up on, Nightingale realised, and her bright red lipstick had slipped over the outline of her lips. She smiled at the audience. There was a smear of lipstick across her left canine tooth. "We are very fortunate today to have one of England's most skilled mediums with us," she said. She had a soft, regal voice that made Nightingale think of cucumber sandwiches with the crusts cut off and croquet on the lawn. "Neil Morgan is from Leicester and has stopped off to address us on his way over to America, where he will be touring a dozen cities. We're very lucky to have him." She nodded at the man sitting on her left. He was staring at the floor by his feet. "Neil has told me that he is feeling a little tired this evening but nevertheless he is happy to give us the benefit of his talent."

The audience clapped politely. Jenny clapped along with them but Nightingale sat with his arms folded. Jenny flashed him a withering look and he reluctantly clapped his hands a few times.

The woman waited for the applause to die down, then said a short prayer. Everyone bowed their head and when she finished there were several "Amens" from the audience.

"So, with no further ado, I'll leave it to Neil," said the woman. She smiled at Morgan. He stood up, avoiding eye contact with her as she took her place at the front of the audience.

The medium took a deep breath, still staring at the floor. He hadn't looked up since he'd taken his place behind the lectern, and Nightingale was starting to wonder if he'd been struck dumb with stage fright, but then he suddenly shuddered and straightened up. He cocked his head on one side like an inquisitive budgerigar and then pointed at an elderly woman sitting on the left of the room with a large handbag perched on her lap. "I'm seeing a man. He's bald and he keeps rubbing his head as if he has a headache."

"My father — is it my father?" she asked. "He passed away from a stroke."

"A long time ago, yes?" said the medium.

The woman nodded. "Forty years ago." She frowned as she did the calculation in her head. "Forty-three years ago."

The medium nodded encouragingly. "Yes, he said he passed over a long time ago and that he's happy now with his wife. Your mother passed over too?"

Nightingale leaned towards Jenny. "If she didn't she'd be more than a hundred by now," he whispered.

Jenny frowned at him and pressed her finger to her lips.

The old lady was nodding.

"Your father says he loves you and he says he and your mother are watching over you. He says your health isn't good at the moment but you're not to worry about him." He smiled. "He says you need to eat more fresh fruit. Can you take that?"

The old lady smiled gratefully. "Yes, I can take that," she said.

"He says you've not been feeling well, that your energy levels are low, so eat fruit. Apples and oranges. Can you take that?"

The woman dabbed at her eyes with a handkerchief. "Bless you," she said.

148

Nightingale looked over at Jenny. "What does that mean? They keep saying 'take'. I don't get it."

She put her lips close to his ear. "I think the idea is that the spirit is giving you the information or advice. You either take it or you don't. I guess that's what it means."

Morgan looked across at the young couple holding the baby. "I see a woman looking at your baby. I think it's the baby's grandmother. Would that be right?"

"My mother," said the woman.

"She passed recently?" asked the medium.

"Two years ago," said the woman.

"That's right, before she even knew that you were pregnant," said the medium.

Nightingale leaned over to Jenny. "That's just maths," he said. "The baby's not even a year old so of course she died before the girl got pregnant."

"Jack, stop taking the piss, will you?" hissed Jenny. "You're the one who wanted to come."

"I didn't realise it was going to be a snake-oil salesman we were going to see," whispered Nightingale. "He's just telling them what they want to hear."

The medium finished talking to the young couple. The woman was crying and her husband put his arm around her and said something to her as she hugged the baby tightly.

The medium pointed at Jenny. "I'm seeing a man near you, an old man. With a beard."

Jenny swallowed nervously.

"Does he sound familiar to you?"

"Yes."

"He passed over recently, this man. And it was sudden."

Jenny nodded. She was staring at the medium, her fingers interlinked in her lap.

"He's saying his name is Larry. Would it be Larry?"

Jenny shook her head.

"No, not Larry," said the medium. "But something beginning with an L."

"Lachie," said Jenny and Nightingale winced. It was a big jump from Larry to Lachie.

The medium was smiling enthusiastically. "Lachie, yes, that's it. Would he be your father or grandfather?"

"No."

"But he knew your father?"

"Yes."

The medium smiled at Jenny. "He says he's okay and that you're not to worry about him. He's at peace now."

"Can I ask him a question?" asked Jenny.

Nightingale muttered under his breath that she was being conned but she didn't hear him.

"We can try," said the medium.

"Can you ask him why he did it?"

The medium suddenly cocked his head to one side, his eyes focused several feet to Jenny's right. Then he smiled and looked back at Jenny. "He was unhappy, he says. But he's happy now. Lachie doesn't want you to worry about him. He's with his loved ones and he's at peace." He rubbed his hands together as if he was feeling cold. "He took his own life, didn't he?"

Jenny nodded. "Yes."

150

"When a spirit has passed over under those circumstances there's sometimes a reluctance to discuss what happened," he said. "Can I ask you this: were you the one that found the body?"

Jenny looked over at Nightingale, and then back at the medium. "Sort of," she said.

"And the gentleman sitting next to you, he was with you?"

Jenny nodded again.

The medium cocked his head again and stared off to Jenny's right. He made several murmuring noises and then looked back at Jenny. "Lachie says that he's sorry for any distress he caused you, and he doesn't want you to feel any guilt about what happened. He takes full responsibility for what he did." He frowned, muttered to himself, then looked at Jack. "Lachie wants you to know that the problem you're facing will be resolved shortly. Does that make sense to you?"

Nightingale didn't answer. He felt that the medium was manipulating him, trying to get him to play a part, but he found himself wanting to agree with the man. Morgan was staring at him earnestly, nodding slowly. "I suppose so," said Nightingale reluctantly.

The medium opened his mouth to speak but before he could say anything the James Bond theme echoed around the room. People twisted in their seats to see where the noise was coming from. Nightingale reached into his raincoat and took out his mobile phone. "Sorry," he said, to no one in particular. He switched off the phone and put it back into his pocket.

"God bless," said the medium. He smiled benevolently at Nightingale, then looked over to the other side of his audience. "I'm seeing a woman with grey hair," he said. "She's wearing reading glasses." Three men in the audience raised their hands tentatively. "I'm getting the name Alice. Or Anne. Does that mean anything to anyone? Anne? Or Alice? Or Amy, perhaps. She's very faint."

One of the men lowered his hand and bit down on his lower lip.

"She says she has a message for David."

"That's me," said one of the men, waving his hand in the air. "I'm David. Alice was my wife. She died last year."

"She died unexpectedly?" said the medium.

The man frowned. "It was cancer," he said. "She had chemo and radiation therapy. She fought."

"But the end, when it came, was quick?"

The man forced a smile. "Yes. She was taken quickly."

"And you haven't thrown out her clothes, have you?"

The man shook his head.

"Alice has a message for you, David. She says it's time for you to clear out her things. It's time for you to let go. Do you understand?"

The man nodded and forced a smile. "Yes," he said. "I understand."

"Alice is happy and she wants you to be happy. You have to move on with your life and part of that process is to get rid of her things. In the wardrobe. Does that make sense to you?"

152

The man wiped his nose with the back of his hand. His eyes were welling up with tears. "Yes," he said, and sniffed.

"You know that was nonsense, don't you?" Nightingale whispered to Jenny.

"What do you mean?"

"He was reading you. Picking up on the cues you were giving him."

The woman in the fur coat turned around in her seat and flashed Nightingale a withering look. He smiled apologetically.

The medium was pointing at a middle-aged woman in a cheap cloth coat and asking her if she knew a man called George. She took out a handkerchief, wiped her eyes, and then said that yes, George was her husband. The medium rubbed his chest. "I feel something here," he said. "A dull ache."

"His heart," she said.

"Yes, his heart wasn't good," said the medium. "But he is feeling no pain and says that he is waiting for you. He says you're not to worry about him."

The medium continued for another thirty minutes, throwing out names and initials and offering comfort and advice. It was, Nightingale realised, a sham. He'd seen magicians do a far better job of cold reading without any pretence of talking to the dead. Eventually Morgan complained that he was tired and the woman in the fur coat joined him at the lectern. She thanked him, announced that the medium would be available for private consultations when he returned from the States, and then led the audience in another prayer.

The two men in suits escorted Morgan out of the room, followed by the woman in the fur coat.

Nightingale stood up and stretched. "Sorry," he said to Jenny.

Jenny stood up. "For what?"

"For bringing you here," he said.

"It was fascinating," she said.

"You don't believe it, do you?"

"That Lachie was trying to contact me?" She shrugged. "I don't know."

"Jenny, he didn't say Lachie. You did. Morgan said it was Larry."

"That's pretty close, don't you think? And he got the beard right."

"He was taking cues from you. He picked up from you that I was there when Lachie died. He was good, but he was still conning you."

"How can it be a con? He didn't want anything from us."

"Maybe he just likes to play God. Maybe he hopes you'll pay him for a private consultation. Who knows? But I know one thing for sure and that's that he wasn't talking to spirits."

Nightingale jumped as a hand touched his shoulder. He looked round and saw a short man standing behind him; he had dark curly hair and was wearing a green anorak. Nightingale recognised him from the audience.

"I'm sorry, I didn't mean to startle you," the man said. "But you came to contact somebody, didn't you?"

154

"Isn't that why people come to a meeting like this?" said Nightingale. The last members of the audience filed out of the room, leaving the three of them alone.

The man laughed softly. "I suppose that's so," he said. "Though some are curious to know what if anything lies beyond this life. Sorry, you are . . .?" He waited expectantly for Nightingale's name.

"We're just on our way home," said Nightingale. He started to walk to the door.

"Is your name Jack?"

Nightingale stopped and slowly turned to look at the man.

He held up his hands as if he feared that Nightingale was going to get aggressive. "I'm just interested, that's all. Are you Jack?"

"Yes," said Nightingale. He frowned. "Do you know me?"

"Did you come to see a girl? A young girl?"

"Who are you?" asked Nightingale, taking a step towards him.

The man reached inside his jacket. Nightingale grabbed him by his lapels and threw him up against the wall.

"Jack!" shouted Jenny.

The man's hand was still inside his jacket and Nightingale groped for whatever it was that he was reaching for.

"My wallet," gasped the man. "I just want to give you my card."

Jenny put a hand on Jack's arm. "What's wrong with you?" she hissed.

Nightingale released his grip on the man's jacket and stepped back. The man opened his wallet with trembling hands and took out a business card. He held it out to Nightingale. "My name's Graham Lord," he said.

Nightingale looked at the simple white card. Underneath the man's name were the words "Spiritual Connections — Private Readings Available" and a mobile phone number.

"What do you want from me?" said Nightingale. "How do you know my name?"

"You came to contact a young girl. With blonde hair? Long blonde hair?"

"What's your game?" asked Nightingale.

"She was standing behind you," said Lord. "I couldn't hear her but I could see her mouth moving and I thought she was saying 'Jack'."

Nightingale frowned. "You could see her?"

"That's what I do. I talk to spirits."

"Like the guy we came to see tonight? The medium?"

Lord sneered. "Neil Morgan? He's a charlatan. Cold reading, that's what he does. Picks up on physical and verbal cues and plays the percentages." He looked across at Jenny. "Larry, Lachie. Father, friend of father. Then you effectively told him that Lachie had killed himself."

Nightingale looked at Jenny. "Told you," he said.

"There are very few genuine mediums around and they don't tend to go to places like this. The real ones don't bother with shows like we've just seen."

"What about you, then, Graham? Why were you here?"

"Lordy," said Lord. "Everyone calls me Lordy."

"So answer my question, Lordy. Why were you here?"

Lord sighed. "Because, unlike Morgan, I'm the real thing. I come to places like this because I can see the spirits. There were spirits here tonight trying to communicate, but Morgan can't see them. He's too busy playing his games. Remember the young couple with the baby?"

"The woman whose mum had died? Sure."

"Her mum was standing next to Morgan. She was so angry at him because she knew that he was lying."

"You really saw her?" said Jenny.

"I see spirits all the time," said Lord. "It's harder for me to talk to them. To hear what they say. I do that best at home. But tonight I saw the little girl standing behind you. Holding a doll."

Nightingale felt his head spin.

"I think she was saying your name," said Lord. "'Jack' she said."

"And what was her name?" said Nightingale. "Do you know?"

Lord nodded earnestly. "Sophie," he said. "She said her name was Sophie."

Nightingale pressed Lord for more information but the man insisted that he could only help them at a private meeting.

Nightingale and Jenny left Lord in the community centre and walked to where she'd parked her car. As

157

Jenny took out her keys, Nightingale patted her on the shoulder. "Give me a minute. I need to call Joshua back."

"Joshua?"

"The American. The guy who keeps buying my books. That was him who phoned back there."

Jenny unlocked the Audi and climbed in and Nightingale fumbled in his pocket for his mobile. He returned Wainwright's call and the American answered.

"Where are you, Jack?" he asked.

"London," said Nightingale. "I'm not a world traveller like you. I'm rarely outside the M25."

"The M25? What's that?"

"The motorway that runs around London, a.k.a. the highway to Hell. I guess you'd call it a freeway. What about you? Where are you?"

"About two hours away from Stansted Airport," said the American. "I was calling to see if I could have a look at your father's book collection tomorrow."

"Sure," said Nightingale.

"Ten o'clock in the morning?"

"Perfect," said Nightingale. He looked over at Jenny and flashed her a thumbs up.

CHAPTER
TWENTY-FOUR

Nightingale climbed out of his MGB and opened the gates. He'd picked up the car that morning and paid the repair bill of two hundred pounds in cash. The mechanic had given him a knowing wink as he'd pocketed the money, wishing him well and saying that he'd see him again soon, which hadn't inspired Nightingale with confidence. He left the gates open and drove slowly down the driveway to Gosling Manor. He parked next to the fountain in front of the house and smoked a cigarette as he waited for Wainwright to arrive. He wondered whether Wainwright would arrive in a stretch limo or behind the wheel of an expensive sports car but his question was answered when he heard the far-off throbbing sound of a helicopter. Nightingale grinned when he saw the huge blue and white machine come swooping over the conifers at the edge of the property. It did a slow, lazy circle of the gardens, disappeared behind the house, then reappeared and touched down in the middle of the lawn.

The rotor draught whipped Nightingale's hair and he flicked the remains of his cigarette away. A door opened and Wainwright climbed out. He bent double under the still-turning rotors as he jogged away from the helicopter, then straightened up and waved at Nightingale. In his left hand he was holding a half-smoked foot-long Cuban cigar. "Nice spread you've got here, Jack," said the American in his Midwestern drawl. He was a big man, a shade over six feet tall, well-muscled and with skin the colour of strong Colombian coffee. He had on a blue New York Yankees baseball cap and a leather baseball jacket; around his neck was a large letter J that Nightingale figured was almost certainly solid gold. He was wearing cowboy boots that looked as if they were made from rattlesnake skin and there was a fanged head on the toe of each boot.

They shook hands, Wainwright's hand dwarfing Nightingale's. "Do you live here now?" asked Wainwright as they walked up the steps to the front door.

"I'm still in my London pied-à-terre," said Nightingale. "I'm not sure what to do with this place. It's too big for me."

"You get used to big places," said Wainwright. He held up his cigar as Nightingale opened the door. "Are you okay if I take this inside?"

"Sure, I'm a smoker, remember."

"I know, but these days you always have to ask." Wainwright followed Nightingale into the hall and looked at the burned staircase and muddy marble floor. "Hey, man, what the hell happened?"

"Had a fire."

"Not smoking in bed?"

Nightingale chuckled. "No, definitely not that. It was deliberate, as it happens. An arsonist set fire to the place while I was upstairs. I only just managed to get out."

"Winning friends and influencing people?"

"It's complicated."

"Yeah, the last time we spoke you wanted to talk to Lucifuge Rofocale." He waved his hand at the scorched stairway. "Is this anything to do with him?"

"Funnily enough, no. This was Proserpine's doing. One of her minions."

Wainwright laughed. "What have you done to get her so riled up? Of all the devils on Lucifer's payroll she's definitely the one that you don't want to mess with."

"We did a deal," said Nightingale. "I did the pentagram thing and I summoned her. I wanted some information and she wanted to . . ." He shrugged. "I'm not sure what she wanted, truth be told," he said. "It was like she was playing a game with me. Toying with me."

"Just because they're demons from Hell doesn't mean they don't have a sense of humour," said the American. He flicked ash onto the floor and then grinned apologetically. "Sorry," he said. "Just figured that with all the crap on the floor a bit of ash wouldn't matter."

"Go ahead," said Nightingale. "Hopefully you'll be paying for the clean-up, anyway."

Wainwright nodded. "If you've got the books I want, money's not going to be a problem," he said. "So tell me about the deal you did with Proserpine."

"I needed help finding my sister," said Nightingale. "So Proserpine said that she'd answer any questions I had. But the deal was that for every question she answered, she'd send one of her minions to kill me."

"Sweet," said Wainwright.

"Yeah," said Nightingale. "Two down, one still to go."

"Good luck with that," said Wainwright. "Just remember that any time you do a deal with the dark side, the cards are almost always stacked against you."

"Yeah, I'm starting to learn that."

"Did you ever try to summon Lucifuge Rofocale?"

"You told me not to, remember?"

"I had the feeling that you weren't listening to me. So despite what I said, you summoned him, right?"

Nightingale nodded. "Yeah."

"And how did it go?"

"The jury's still out on that," said Nightingale.

"Jack, I'm serious about this. Be very, very careful with him. With all of them, but especially with Lucifuge Rofocale. They've been around for a long, long time and generally in the end they get what they want."

"It's all done," said Nightingale. "All done and dusted."

"You think that, but he might have other ideas." He blew smoke up at the massive chandelier hanging from the ceiling and then grinned at Nightingale. "Still, you're here, so that's got to count for something, right?"

"Like I said, the jury's still out." He walked over to the secret panel that led down to the basement and pulled it open. "Down here," he said, switching on the lights.

"You're kidding me," said Wainwright. "A secret door? Your old man had a sense of the absurd, didn't he?"

"I think he just didn't want anyone to know that the books were down there."

Wainwright followed him down the stairs. He stood at the bottom and whistled softly as he saw how many books there were. "These are all on black magic?"

"Black magic, white magic, witchcraft, devil-worship, spells, theology, philosophy, mythology."

"I knew your father was a collector, but I didn't realise it was on this scale," said Wainwright. "I'm tempted to make you an offer for the lot."

"Have a look around and let me know what you think. They're no use to me."

Wainwright walked over to one of the bookshelves and drew on his cigar as he studied the titles.

"I've got another question for you," said Nightingale. He dropped down onto a sofa and swung his feet up onto the coffee table.

"Ask away," said Wainwright, taking down a leather-bound book and flicking through it.

"Talking to the dead," said Nightingale. "How easy is that?"

Wainwright chuckled. "Talking to the dead is easy; the trick is to get them to talk back."

"You know what I mean," said Nightingale, taking his cigarettes and lighter out of his coat pocket.

"You want to initiate a conversation with someone who's dead," said the American. "Yeah, I know what you mean. Anyone in particular?"

"Yeah."

Wainwright put the book back and took down another. "Have you tried the old faithful? The Ouija board?"

"Yeah, but it didn't work out too well."

"Someone always pushes," said Wainwright. "And even if they don't, you've no guarantee who's going to come through. There're a lot of mischievous spirits about just waiting for the opportunity of slipping into our world." He flicked through the book he was holding. "You could try a medium," said Wainwright. "An intermediary. Someone who knows what they're doing."

"I went to see one last night but it was a bit of a disappointment," said Nightingale. "Do you know of any decent ones?" He lit a cigarette.

"Not really my field," said Wainwright.

"No problem," said Nightingale.

Wainwright turned around and gestured with the book that he was holding. "I'll definitely buy this one."

"Take it with you, we can settle up later," said Nightingale.

"You're very trusting," said the American, putting the book down on the coffee table by Nightingale's feet.

"You've seen me all right in the past," said Nightingale. "And I get the feeling that money isn't a problem for you."

164

Wainwright looked down the rows of display cases. "He was one hell of a collector, old man Gosling," he said.

"Pretty much everything he had went on what you see down here."

"And the house, of course? This must have cost a few million."

Nightingale shook his head. "It's mortgaged to the hilt. That's why I'm selling the books."

"Why don't I buy the lot off you?" said Wainwright.

"How do we work out a price?" asked Nightingale.

The American sat down and leaned across to tap cigar ash into a crystal ashtray. "How much do you want?"

"That's a good question." Nightingale sighed as he looked around the basement. "But I've no idea what they're worth."

"They're difficult to value, that's for sure," said Wainwright. "To someone who doesn't know their significance, they're just books. But to someone like your father, or me, they're close to priceless." He swung his feet up onto the coffee table. "I could buy them by the yard."

"That might work," laughed Nightingale.

"The thing is, a single book could be worth hundreds of thousands or it could be worth nothing. The problem is going to be sorting the wheat from the chaff."

"Yeah, my assistant's been helping me catalogue them but it's slow going. And all we can do is make a note of the title and author."

"You said you've done a couple of hundred?" He leaned back and blew a cloud of smoke at the ceiling.

Nightingale nodded. "Yeah, there's a list somewhere." He pushed himself up off the sofa and went over to a roll-top desk. He picked up a yellow legal pad and gave it to the American.

Wainwright studied the list and nodded approvingly. "Lots of good stuff here," he said. He tapped his finger on one of the titles. "You were asking about communing with the departed."

"I was?"

"Talking to the dead. There's a book here that'll give you the basics. Written by a guy called Daniel Dunglas Home. He was a Scotch but he made his name in the States in the nineteenth century."

"Scottish," said Nightingale.

"Huh?"

"Scotch is the drink. The people are Scottish. Or Scots."

Wainwright laughed. "Sidewalk, pavement, lift, elevator, Scots, Scottish, it never ends, does it?" He tapped the list again. "He wrote a book shortly before he died. It was a very small print run so I've never seen a copy but I'm told it's packed full of info about séances and trance states. He was very well thought of, and they never caught him faking. Have a look at his book. It might answer your questions." He looked down at the list, then back at the rows of books. "You've done what, one per cent? It's going to take you forever to do the lot." He tossed the pad onto the coffee table as Nightingale sat down again.

166

"Yeah, it's a pain too. Most of them don't have titles on the spines. We have to take them down, copy the details, and put them back. And a lot of them aren't in English."

Wainwright leaned forward. "How about this?" he said. "You agree to sell me the lot. I'll send in some of my people to value them, people who know the real value of books like this. You'll have to trust me, but I can promise you that you won't be ripped off."

Nightingale nodded. "You've played fair with me so far, Joshua," he said. "I'm okay with that."

The American held out his hand and Nightingale shook it. "Pleasure doing business with you, Jack," he said. He sat back and spread his arms across the back of the sofa. "Might take a day or two; the people I'm thinking about are based in New Orleans. I'll send over my jet. Can they stay here while they're doing the inventory?"

"There're plenty of rooms but nothing in the way of furniture," said Nightingale. "But if they're okay to rough it I'll bring in a few camp beds and they can sleep down here. The kitchen's working and I can put some food in the fridge."

Wainwright waved his cigar at the lines of display cases that ran down the centre of the basement. "What about the rest of the stuff down here? What are you going to do with it?"

"To be honest, Joshua, I don't even know what half of it is. There are crystal balls, knives, vials, bones, relics. Weird stuff, but Gosling must have known what he was doing because he spent every penny he had on this collection."

"And you're not thinking of following in his footsteps?"

Nightingale laughed but it came out more as a harsh bark that echoed around the basement like a pistol shot. "Me taking up devil-worship? After everything I've been through?"

"You're not tempted?"

"Tempted to do what? To sell my soul for money and power?" He held up his cigarette. "Give me a pack of Marlboro, a bottle of Corona and a United game on TV and I'm a happy bunny."

"No doubt, but what if you could own United? And watch the game from the director's box? What if it gave you the freedom to do whatever you want, whenever you want?"

"Are you trying to tempt me, Joshua?" said Nightingale, narrowing his eyes. "Is that what's going on here?"

The American chuckled and shook his head. "You choose your own path, Jack. There has to be free will. I'm just saying, with all this at hand, you'd be a master of the dark arts in no time."

Nightingale raised an eyebrow. "The dark arts? Are you taking the piss?"

Wainwright waved his cigar above his head. "I just want you to be sure about what you're doing here. Your father spent a lifetime assembling this collection and I wouldn't want you regretting anything down the line."

168

"I just want to get back to my life," said Nightingale. "I was happy before I got this house and all this crap. Okay, I'm not exactly living the high life but I have enough to get by and enjoy my job."

"You enjoy being a gumshoe? Following two-timing husbands and going through trash cans?"

"There's more to it than that," said Nightingale. "But yeah, I enjoy doing what I do. I was happier being a cop, but as a private eye I still get to bring down the occasional bad guy."

"Is that what you're worried about? You think that being a Satanist means you can't be one of the good guys?"

Nightingale stubbed out his cigarette in the ashtray. "I kind of figured that was the case, yeah."

"It's not about choosing sides. It's about acquiring power. Power and knowledge. It's what you do with it that counts. And that's your choice. Free will, remember?"

"Yeah, someone else said something similar to me a while back. She said that there was no black magic or white magic, that it was all like electricity and it was up to you whether you used it for good or bad."

"She knew what she was talking about," said Wainwright.

"Yeah, but she wasn't talking about doing deals with devils," said Nightingale. "In fact, she was totally against that."

Wainwright waved at the books behind him. "The books you've got there aren't all about devils and

169

demons. That's only a small fraction of what the black arts are about."

"Joshua, can I ask you something?"

"Sure."

Nightingale leaned forward. "Have you done a deal? With a devil?"

Wainwright threw back his head and roared with laughter. Nightingale lit another cigarette as he waited for the American to stop laughing. "First of all, if I had done I couldn't tell you," said Wainwright eventually. "There's a little thing called a non-disclosure agreement that means my lips would be sealed. And second of all, it's none of your darn business."

Nightingale held up his hands. "No offence," he said.

Wainwright laughed again. "None taken," he said. "You're new to this so I'll cut you some slack. But asking who's done what deal with who just isn't done."

Nightingale took a long pull on his cigarette.

"So do you want to sell all the artefacts too?" asked Wainwright.

"Sure. They're no use to me."

"That's what I'm saying, Jack. Maybe it could be of use to you." He stood up and went over to one of the display cases. It was full of earthenware pots, each one with strange markings on it. Wainwright nodded at the pots. "Can I . . .?"

"Sure, knock yourself out," said Nightingale.

Wainwright opened the cabinet door and took out a dark brown urn. He eased off the top, sniffed it cautiously and then frowned.

"What is it?" asked Nightingale.

170

Wainwright studied the markings on the side of the urn. "No idea, but these are runes, so I'm guessing it's some herb used in Druid magic." He put the urn back and took out another one. "These pots are hundreds of years old, by the look of them." He sniffed the contents of the second urn and then put it back. He walked over to the next display case, which was full of crystal balls of different sizes and colours. Wainwright peered at the balls.

"Be careful with them," said Nightingale.

"They're only crystal balls," said Wainwright.

"Friend of mine looked in one and saw his own death."

Wainwright straightened up and looked over at Nightingale. "Which one?"

"It smashed," said Nightingale. "He saw himself being run over by a cab. He dropped it and it broke."

"They shouldn't smash. They're solid crystal."

"This one did. Smashed to smithereens, it was."

"And you're saying what? He saw his own death?"

"I'm pretty sure that's what happened."

"That's unusual," said the American, rubbing his chin.

"You're telling me."

"No, I mean that's not how crystals work. Not normally. They're tools for mediums or fortune tellers; if you don't have the skills you're just staring into glass."

"I'm just telling you what happened."

"He was a good friend?"

Nightingale nodded. "We were cops together. My best mate."

"I'm sorry, Jack. Is it him you want to talk to?"

"No. He was the one I tried the Ouija board with but that didn't work out. It's a young girl I want to talk to now. Actually, I think she's been trying to communicate with me but she can't quite manage it. I thought there was maybe something I could do that might make it easier for her."

Next to the cabinet containing the crystal balls was something that had been covered with a black velvet cloth. It was a few inches taller than the American. Wainwright pointed at it with his cigar. "Do you mind?"

"Go ahead. I've no idea what it is."

Wainwright pulled the cloth away. It was a mirror framed with old wood that had gone black with age. The frame was made up of dozens of carved animals, but animals the like of which Nightingale had never seen.

"Interesting," said Wainwright, peering around the back of the mirror. "Do you have any idea what this is, Jack?"

"A mirror?"

"Not just any mirror. A black mirror. Some call it a dark mirror. And this is a beauty." He draped the cloth over a cabinet then took a long drag on his cigar and blew a cloud of bluish smoke up at the ceiling.

Nightingale walked over to the American. "What's so special about it?"

172

Wainwright gripped the sides of the mirror. It was heavy and he grunted as he turned it around. The back of the mirror was a single piece of aged oak, held in place with brass screws. The American rapped the wood with his knuckles. "The difference is behind here," he said. "In a regular mirror, the back is silvered. But for a dark mirror you use black paint, or black tape. Either will do the job. But for a real Satanic dark mirror they use paint containing blood. Human blood."

"What?"

"In England they used to use the blood from a corpse taken from the gallows, the fresher the better." He rapped the back of the mirror again. "The age of this, I'd guess that's what was used here."

"A dead man's blood?"

"Not just any dead man, Jack. To work it has to be blood taken from a criminal who's been executed. And the worse the criminal, the better. Child-killers and serial rapists would be top of the list, pretty much."

"And what would you use it for?"

"A regular dark mirror is used for scrying."

"Scrying?"

Wainwright grinned. "I keep forgetting what an innocent you are in all this," he said. "Scrying is all about using your inner eye to perceive or to discern what's normally hidden." He laughed. "Sounds like mumbo-jumbo, but it's not. It's almost a science and anyone can do it with practice. Witches tend to use crystal balls or dark mirrors, Druids stare at pools of dark water, and I know of some Tibetan monks who stare at a wet fingernail."

Nightingale looked at the American, trying to work out if he was joking or not but he seemed to be serious.

"The thing you look at is almost irrelevant. Scrying is about opening up the inner eye. It's all about gazing without focusing. Allowing the inner eye to see."

"Like fortune telling?"

"You can look forward or back. See something that has already happened or predict the future. But a dark mirror like this is more for communing with spirits."

"The dead, you mean?"

"Spirits that have passed on. Sure." He ran his hand over the intricate carving. "How much do you want for this?"

Nightingale shrugged. "I've no idea. I suppose I could put it on eBay and see what the going rate is for a dark mirror."

"How about I give you fifty grand?"

"Dollars?"

"Is that you bargaining?"

Nightingale laughed. "Fifty grand is fine," he said. "I guess you don't want to take it with you?"

"I'll have it collected." He went over to a display case that was full of ceremonial knives, some of them with dried blood on the blades. Wainwright bent down and peered at the knives on one of the lower shelves. "He had an eye for quality, your father."

Nightingale stroked the carvings down the side of the mirror. There was a snake, a lizard, and something with six legs and menacing claws. The wood was cold to the touch, as if it was sucking the heat from his flesh. The mirror was as dark as a pool of oil, still wreathed in the smoke from Wainwright's cigar. As Nightingale stared into the mirror, he realised that the smoke was on the other side of the glass. He reached out and realised with a jolt that there was no reflection: he was just reaching towards darkness and smoke.

"Jack!"

Nightingale jumped as Wainwright's hand fell on his shoulder. Wainwright pulled him away from the mirror.

"What's your problem?" asked Nightingale.

"Don't go touching the surface."

"It's only a mirror."

Wainwright snorted. "It's more than that, Jack. And you don't go touching the glass."

"Because?"

"Because a dark mirror is a delicate balance of the past, the present and the future. The glass is the interface, and if you touch it you can ruin it." He picked up the cloth and carefully draped it over the mirror.

"How would I go about using it?"

"To do what, specifically?"

"What you said. Talk to the dead."

Wainwright's eyes narrowed. "This isn't a toy, Jack."

"I know it's not a toy. I was just thinking that maybe I could use it to contact that girl. The girl I was talking about."

"Scrying is one thing; contacting the dead is a whole different ball game."

"I'm a big boy, Joshua. I can take care of myself."

"Don't get cocky. Just because you've called up a couple of demons doesn't mean you're an expert in the black arts. A black mirror like this is more than just a scrying tool. Under the right circumstances it can be a portal."

"A portal?"

"Jack, this is way above your pay grade." He gestured at the mirror. "You don't want to be messing with it unless you know what you're doing."

"I'm just curious," said Nightingale. "You made it sound like something I could use."

"Not if you don't know what you're doing. It's like the Ouija board. In the right hands it's a useful tool, but treat it like a toy and you're asking for trouble."

"Been there, done that," said Nightingale.

"Yeah, well, the Ouija board is one thing; a dark mirror like this is way more dangerous. Spirits might be able to manifest themselves through a Ouija board and cause mischief, but if they can get to a dark mirror and the person using it doesn't know what he's doing, they can use it to gain access to this world."

"Pass through it, you mean?"

"It has been known. A mirror like this isn't for amateurs, Jack."

"So tell me about scrying."

Wainwright shook his head. "Don't even think about using it to scry," he said. He went back to the sofa and sat down. He stubbed out what was left of his cigar in the ashtray there.

Nightingale sat down on the other sofa. "When my friend picked up the crystal ball, he saw himself being hit by a car."

176

"That's plain weird," said Wainwright. "Like I said, that's not how crystal balls work. They don't push out information like that. They're a means to an end, that's all. A way of focusing your concentration." He grinned. "You want a master class in the crystal ball, do you?" He waved at the display cabinets. "Go and get one and I'll show you how it works."

Nightingale got up and went over to the cabinet containing the balls. He opened the door and took out a medium-sized one, about the size of a large apple. It was sitting on a silver filigree stand and he took the ball and the stand over to the seating area. He sat down and put the ball on its stand, then looked expectantly at Wainwright.

"Good choice," said Wainwright. He looked around the basement. "Is there any way of dimming the lights?"

Nightingale shook his head. "There's just the one switch. On or off."

"Okay, well, in an ideal world you'd dim the lights. Or light candles. Now the trick is to be totally relaxed. And you need to keep both feet on the ground. Then it's a matter of getting into the zone. Breathe slowly and evenly while you look into the crystal."

Nightingale took a deep breath as he stared at the glass ball.

"Once you're totally relaxed, you let your eyes look under the surface of the crystal, so that you're not looking at the outside, but focusing somewhere inside. Like when you're looking at those 3D pictures, the ones that suddenly jump out at you."

Nightingale tried to do as Wainwright said, but he couldn't focus on anything other than the surface of the ball.

"If you're doing it right, the crystal will start to look cloudy, or it will move in and out of focus. You'll find your natural reaction is to tense up as soon as you see anything, but the trick is to stay relaxed."

Nightingale stared at the crystal but nothing happened.

"Relax," said Wainwright. "You're breathing like a train."

"It's not easy, is it?" said Nightingale.

"Concentrate on your breathing. Slow it down. Look deep into the crystal and then try to pull your focus back, just a bit."

Nightingale cupped the ball with his fingers and tried to breathe slowly, but all he could see was the crystal. Eventually he sighed and sat back. "It's not working."

"It takes practice," said Wainwright.

"And you can talk to spirits?"

"You can see them, or that's what I'm told," said Wainwright. "It's not my forte." He looked at his watch. "I've got to go," he said, standing up. "I'll call you when I know the dates my people are available. But we have a deal, right?"

"Do you want me to sign in blood?"

The American laughed and patted Nightingale on the shoulder. "I trust you, Jack," he said.

Nightingale stood up. "I'll see you out."

"I'll be okay," said Wainwright, heading for the stairs. "You get in some practice with the crystal."

The American went up the stairs, waved goodbye and left through the panel. Nightingale went over to the table and picked up the yellow pad. He ran his finger down the list until he got to the book written by Daniel Dunglas Home. There was no title but it was close to the top of the list so Nightingale figured that the book would be on the shelves closest to the stairs, which was where Jenny had started the inventory. He went over to the bookcase and found it on the third shelf from the top, a green leather-bound book with the author's name in faded gilt on the spine. He pulled it out. It was a slim volume, just over a hundred pages, and it was well-thumbed; the cover was scuffed as if it had passed through many hands over the years.

There was an index at the back and he ran his finger down it, smiling when he found what he was looking for. "Dark Mirrors: Their Use And The Dangers Thereof."

CHAPTER
TWENTY-FIVE

Nightingale used his lighter to light the five candles that he'd placed around the mirror. They were all black and as thick as his arm, with greasy wicks. One by one the candles spluttered into life. The wicks burned with a smoky flame and Nightingale wrinkled his nose at the acrid smell that filled the air. He flashed back to the Met's firing range where he'd spent hours honing his skills on the Heckler & Koch carbine and the Glock semi-automatic pistol.

One of the candles flared up, there was a crackling sound and a shower of sparks rained down over the tiled floor. Nightingale slid the lighter into the pocket of his trousers, then took an urn of herbs and sprinkled the contents in a circle around the mirror and candles. The book had been specific about the types of herbs and the quantities that had to be used, but one of the cabinets contained dozens of pots of herbs and he had found everything that he'd needed. The candles came from a storage chest at the far end of the basement. Inside it were candles of every shape and colour but the book had been adamant that the candles surrounding the dark mirror had to be large and black.

Once the urn was empty he placed it on the coffee table and then went up the stairs and switched off the lights. He stood for several seconds, staring down at the mirror surrounded by the five candles. The rest of the basement was in total darkness and he couldn't even see the stairs leading down. He shivered. He knew that switching the lights off couldn't possibly have lowered the temperature in the basement, but he had definitely felt a chill as soon as he'd flicked the switch.

He felt his way slowly down the stairs, holding onto the brass banister with both hands. By the time he reached the bottom step his eyes were more accustomed to the gloom and he walked over to the mirror and stood in front of it. There was no reflection, only blackness. He swallowed and realised that his mouth was completely dry. He grimaced. It was too late now to go upstairs and get himself something to drink. He bent down and picked up the book. He'd left it open at the page he needed. It had the words of a spell that the writer claimed would summon a spirit, though it was written in what appeared to be Latin and he had no idea how to pronounce most of the words. He moved closer to the candle on his left and turned the pages towards the flame.

"Ego astrum in speculum," he began, but his voice croaked and he stopped and cleared his throat. He took a deep breath and started again, saying each word slowly and clearly even though he had no idea what he was saying. "Ego astrum in speculum," he said. "Vos ero tutus. Nusquam hic vadum vulnero vos. Deus vadum servo vos. Ego astrum procul speculum quod

181

volo video vidi visum vos." Something moved in the blackness of the mirror, a dark shape that rippled through the smoke. The candles flickered as if there was a breeze blowing down from the panel at the top of the stairs and he shivered. He looked up, half expecting to see the panel open and someone standing at the entrance to the basement, but it was shut and there was nobody there. He took another deep breath and continued to read. "Deus servo vos. Hic illic est tantum pacis quod diligo. Adeo mihi quod sermo. Adeo mihi iam. Deus est vigilo nos. Nusquam nocens can venio. Adeo mihi iam. Adveho." He finished reading and closed the book as he stared at the mirror.

There was still no reflection, just slowly swirling smoke. Then something moved. A shape.

Nightingale wasn't sure what to do. He squinted at the mirror. The smoke seemed thicker now, and it was becoming greyer, like a fog rolling in from the sea. The shape was moving forward, through the smoke. Nightingale gripped the book with both hands, so tightly that his fingers began to ache.

"Sophie?" he said. "Sophie, is that you?"

The smoke was darkening, black around the edges, grey in the middle. The shape stopped. It was a figure, but Nightingale had no sense of its size.

"Sophie, it's Jack," said Nightingale.

The figure began to move again, towards the glass. Nightingale could make out long blonde hair and pale skin, and he could see something hanging from the figure's hand. Even though he couldn't see it clearly, Nightingale knew what it was. A doll. A Barbie doll.

182

"Sophie, can you hear me?"

The figure took another small step towards the glass. Nightingale could make out her shoes. Silver trainers with blue stars on them.

"Sophie, it's Jack."

"Please help me, Jack."

The voice took Nightingale by surprise and the book tumbled to the floor. He stared at the mirror. Sophie was about three feet away on the other side of the glass, smoke swirling around her. He couldn't make out what she was standing on or what was behind her. There was just her, and the smoke. She was wearing the same white sweatshirt and blue cotton skirt that she'd had on when he'd seen her on the balcony. Before she fell to her death.

"I'm cold, Jack," she said. "I'm so cold." She had her head down so that he couldn't see her face. She sniffed and wiped her nose with the back of her hand.

"Where are you?" asked Nightingale.

She sniffed again. "I don't know."

Nightingale took a step closer to the mirror. Except it wasn't a mirror any more. There was no reflection. It was a window, a window into Sophie's world, wherever that was.

"Jack, please help me." Her voice was hoarse. Muffled.

"I want to, honey, but I don't know what to do."

Tears were running down Sophie's cheeks.

"What is it you want me to do, Sophie?"

"Help me." She clutched the Barbie doll to her chest and buried her face in its long blonde hair.

"You have to tell me what to do, honey."

"Can you hug me?"

"Hug you?"

Her body was trembling. "It's cold here. Can you hold me?"

Sophie shuffled closer. Her head was still down so that Nightingale couldn't see her eyes but tears were glistening on her pale skin. Nightingale reached out with his right hand and touched the glass. Even though his fingers were pressed against the mirror there was still no reflection. "Sophie, I don't know how."

She slowly raised her head and stared at him with tear-filled eyes. "You can hug me if you really want to," she said.

Her eyes were jet black. He'd never noticed that before. He frowned as he tried to remember that day when he'd seen her on the balcony at Chelsea Harbour. Had he seen her eyes? Were they black? He couldn't recall.

"Please, Jack," she said. "I'm so cold." She shivered, then hugged the doll to her chest.

Nightingale put his left hand against the glass, next to his right. He splayed out his fingers. "I can't, Sophie."

"You can, Jack, if you want to. But you really have to want to."

She dropped the Barbie doll. Nightingale felt suddenly dizzy as he flashed back to the moment when Sophie had slid off the balcony. Her hair had whipped around in the wind as she'd fallen to her death, still clutching her doll. And Nightingale's stomach lurched as he remembered the sound she'd made as she hit the ground: a dull wet thud followed by complete silence. Nightingale's frown deepened. Sophie had fallen thirteen storeys to her death, smashing every bone in her body. But the little girl in the mirror looked fine. There were dark patches under her eyes and her hair was streaked with dirt but she didn't appear to be injured.

Nightingale opened his mouth but before he could say anything Sophie took a step towards him and put her hands up against her side of the mirror. "Please, Jack, you have to help me."

Nightingale gasped as he felt the palms of her hands press against his. Her skin was warmer than the glass, but only just. Her hands moved slowly, her fingers pushing his fingers apart until they were fully interlinked.

"Please, Jack," she said. Her voice sounded more assertive, Nightingale realised. Harder. And deeper. She pulled his hands towards her.

Nightingale stared into Sophie's eyes. They were completely black. He couldn't see where the irises ended and the pupils began. They seemed bigger than when he'd first seen her. And narrower. Almost reptilian.

"Come to me, Jack," she said.

"Sophie," began Nightingale, as he tried to pull his hands back. She was too strong and she grinned as she pulled him towards her. Her teeth were sharp, like fangs, and her gums were dark blue. Nightingale pulled harder but her nails dug into his flesh and she grinned in triumph as she dragged him closer. She began to laugh, a deep, throaty roar that made the glass vibrate. Her mouth was bigger now, the teeth longer and sharper; her eyes were wider and her hair was moving around her face as if it had a life of its own. Nightingale opened his mouth to scream but before any sound could leave his mouth something flashed over his shoulder and smashed into the mirror, breaking it into a thousand shards. He fell back, arms flailing, and slammed into the floor as bits of glass rained around him.

CHAPTER
TWENTY-SIX

"You stupid prick!" shouted Wainwright, staring down at Nightingale, his eyes blazing. "Didn't you listen to anything I said?"

Nightingale looked up at him but had trouble focusing and he blinked several times.

"Do you have any idea of the risks you're taking?" shouted Wainwright. "How stupid are you, Nightingale?"

"I'm not feeling too bright at the moment, that's for sure," said Nightingale. He touched his face gingerly. "Am I bleeding?"

"Bleeding is the least of your worries," said Wainwright. "I told you: you can't mess around with these things. They're not toys." He saw the book by Nightingale's feet and he picked it up. He looked at the spine and wrinkled his nose in disgust. "What do you think magic is, Nightingale?" He held the book up. "This isn't a cook book, with recipes that you follow. It's a way of handing down knowledge from one generation of practitioners to the next. It's not a do-it-yourself guide for amateurs." He tossed the book onto the top of a display cabinet.

"It worked," said Nightingale. "I saw Sophie."

The American sneered. "You've no idea what just happened, have you?"

"You smashed a fifty-grand mirror," said Nightingale. "That much I know." He held up his hand. "Help me up, yeah?"

Wainwright shook his head, sighed, then grabbed Nightingale's wrist and hauled him to his feet. Bits of glass tinkled to the floor. Nightingale brushed his raincoat with his hands but winced as a splinter of glass speared his left thumb. He pulled it out and sucked on the wound.

"You're an idiot, you know that?" said Wainwright.

Nightingale stopped sucking his thumb. "What are you doing here?"

"I knew what you were going to do. I told the pilot to bring me back."

Nightingale looked down at the shards of glass on the tiled floor. Among the glass was a Nokia mobile phone. He bent down, picked up the phone and handed it to the American. "Why did you do that?" he said, nodding at the broken glass.

"You were being pulled into the mirror," said Wainwright, examining the phone. "And if you'd crossed over, there'd be no coming back."

"That's not what was happening. It was Sophie, the little girl. She wanted my help."

Wainwright held up the phone. "It's bust," he said. "You owe me for a new phone."

"It's your own fault. What were you thinking?"

"I saved your life, Jack," said Wainwright, slipping the phone into the back pocket of his jeans.

"In what universe? I was fine. I was talking to Sophie."

Wainwright took out a black leather cigar case and lit a large cigar. "Jack, whatever was trying to pull you into that mirror, it wasn't a young girl."

"It was Sophie. Sophie Underwood."

"And this Sophie is dead, right?"

"I saw her die. Two years ago. She jumped off a balcony."

"Jack, listen to me very carefully. It wasn't a young girl I saw pulling you into the mirror."

"How could you see anything?" Nightingale jabbed a finger at the stairs. "You were up there. You couldn't possibly have seen what was happening."

"I could see just fine," said Wainwright.

"So what did you see?"

Wainwright shook his head again. "It doesn't matter. What matters is that you didn't get pulled in." He bit off the end of his cigar, looked around and then spat it onto the broken glass.

"I wasn't being pulled in," said Nightingale. "She wanted my help."

"What help could you possibly be to her? Think about that, Jack. She's dead, and dead is dead. There's no coming back." He lit the cigar with a match.

"I don't know what she wanted, but she said that I was the only one who could help her."

"You were being pulled in, and if you had crossed over you'd never have come back. It was a trap."

"I summoned her. How could that be a trap?"

Wainwright puffed on the cigar before answering. "Because when you stand in front of a dark mirror you have to be in complete control. I told you how dangerous it was. But, as always, you weren't listening."

"How did you know?"

"Know what?"

"How did you know what I was doing? How did you know to come back?"

Wainwright chuckled. "Maybe your guardian angel was on your case," he said. "I don't know what happened, Jack. We were flying back to Stansted and I had one of those hair-standing-up-on-the-back-of-my-neck moments. I tried to ignore it but the feeling got stronger and stronger."

"So it was what, a premonition?"

"I knew you were in danger. Can we leave it at that?"

"How do I know you weren't sent back by someone who wanted to stop me helping Sophie?"

"Now you're sounding paranoid," said the American. He walked over to the seating area and sat down on one of the red leather sofas.

"I'm serious, Joshua," said Nightingale. He nudged a piece of broken glass with his foot and it scraped along the tiles. "With the best will in the world, I hardly know you. And you turn up just in time to smash the one chance I had of talking to Sophie."

"You think that's what happened? Proserpine or one of the other Fallen sent me to screw things up for you?"

"Why would you mention Proserpine?"

"Because she's your nemesis," said Wainwright. He put his feet up on the coffee table and stretched out.

"Did she? Did she send you back here?"

Wainwright took the cigar from his mouth. "I told you what happened, Jack. Don't start accusing me of lying."

Nightingale sat down opposite Wainwright and lit a cigarette. "Just because I'm paranoid doesn't mean that they're not out to get me," he said. "I don't know how I decide who to trust."

"Well, you can start by considering the fact that if you'd gone I'd probably be able to pick up your library for a song."

"What?"

"I'm just saying that, with you out of the way, I'd get this for next to nothing. So I had a vested interest in you being trapped in there."

"You keep saying that, but how do I know that would have happened? How do I know that I wouldn't have been able to bring Sophie back?"

"Sophie's dead. She can't come back."

"She's talking to me. She's asking me to help her. She couldn't be doing that if she was . . ." He tailed off, realising that he wasn't making any sense. Sophie was dead. He'd seen her fall to her death from the balcony at Chelsea Harbour; he'd seen her broken body lying on the tarmac. And Wainwright was right. Dead was dead. The dead didn't come back and there was nothing he could do to help her. He ran a hand through his hair and then down along the back of his neck. "This is doing my head in."

"I hear you," said Wainwright. "I'm not saying you can't communicate with spirits. But you can't take someone who's dead and bring them back to life. That's the prerogative of . . ." He shrugged and left the sentence unfinished.

"So if it wasn't Sophie, who was it? Who was I talking to? And what did they want?"

Wainwright took his feet off the coffee table and leaned forward, the cigar in his right hand. "It could have been anyone, Jack. But whoever it was didn't have your best interests at heart."

"What did you see, in the mirror?"

"I know what I didn't see. I didn't see a little girl."

"Why are you being so evasive?"

"Because at the end of the day I think you don't believe me. I came back here because I thought you were in trouble, and now you're making me out to be one of the bad guys."

Nightingale nodded slowly. "Okay, I'm sorry. I apologise. Put it down to shock. You did scare the hell out of me, smashing the mirror like that." He grinned at the American. "The mirror that you were going to pay me fifty grand for, remember?"

"Yeah, well, it's not worth that now, that's for sure."

"Because you smashed it."

Wainwright laughed. "I'll write you a cheque," he said. He took a pull on his cigar and then flicked ash into the ashtray. "It was a demon, Jack. Big. Scales. Wings. Claws. I couldn't see much but it was big."

"I was definitely looking at Sophie."

"They can take on any form they want; you know that by now. So it appeared to you as Sophie but it didn't know that I was there so I saw it as it really was.

Trust me, it was a demon and it was about to pull you into the mirror."

"Is that how it works? I'd have been trapped inside the glass?"

Wainwright shook his head. "The dark mirror is a portal. If used properly then it's a way of communicating with spirits. But if you should try to pass through it then you'd go to wherever they were. Or they could come through into this world."

"But if it was a devil, it could appear here anyway, right?"

"It's not as simple as that. Some can; some are limited in what they can and can't do."

"You think it was trying to pull me in because it couldn't get to me here?"

"That's possible. It could have been appearing as Sophie so that you'd lower your defences."

"And it would take me where? To Hell?"

"Possibly," said Wainwright. "But not all demons are in Hell."

"And what about Sophie?"

"What about her?"

"Where is she?"

Wainwright sighed. "Who knows? You say she's been trying to contact you. Maybe she has, but what if it's been a demon all the time?"

"You mean it was never Sophie? It was always something pretending to be her?"

"I can't answer that, Jack." He looked at his wristwatch, a gold Cartier. "Sorry, I've got to go." He stood up and flexed his shoulders. "Promise me you

won't mess around with things you don't understand."
He grinned. "At least until we've done a deal over the
stuff you've got down here."

"Cross my heart," said Nightingale.

Wainwright jabbed his cigar in Nightingale's
direction. "I'm serious, Jack. You've been lucky so far.
But you're messing with things that you barely
understand and if you carry on it's going to end in
tears."

"I hear what you're saying, Joshua. Message received
and understood." He stuck out his hand and the
American shook it firmly.

They went back up the stairs and Nightingale walked
Wainwright outside. His helicopter was back on the
lawn, its rotors turning slowly.

"I'll call you when my people are ready to inventory
the books and artefacts," said Wainwright. "But I'll
send you a deposit first. How does a million sound?"

"Like music to my ears," said Nightingale. "Pounds,
euros or dollars?"

"You choose," said Wainwright. "Call me with your
bank details." The helicopter turbines began to whine
and the rotors picked up speed, their wash pulling at
Nightingale's raincoat as Wainwright clapped him on
the back. "You be careful, you hear?"

"Always," said Nightingale. He watched Wainwright
jog towards the helicopter. The American turned and
waved before climbing in. Nightingale waved back as
the helicopter lifted off, circled above the trees at the
edge of the grounds and headed north.

194

CHAPTER
TWENTY-SEVEN

Later that evening Nightingale lay on his sofa, reading the book that he'd taken from the basement of Gosling Manor. It was a tough read. The English was stilted and there were a lot of words in it that he didn't know the meaning of, and Daniel Dunglas Home had a habit of slipping in Latin phrases as if he was keen to show his reader what a smart chap he was. Towards the end of the book there was a chapter titled "A Ritual For Communing With The Departed". He read it twice, then made himself a coffee and read it again, and then he picked up his mobile and called Colin Duggan.

"What do you want, Nightingale?" were the first words out of the detective's mouth.

"What makes you think I want anything?" asked Nightingale.

"Because you called me, and the only time you ever call me is when you want something."

"Colin, I'm hurt. Can't a guy ring his mate and ask him out for a drink?"

"I've stopped drinking, remember? Diabetes."

"Are you still on that?"

"On what? Diabetes doesn't just go away. I have to eat healthily for the rest of my life or I'll end up on medication."

"Can I buy you a salad, then? Or a carrot juice? Or whatever it is you eat for pleasure these days?"

"I'm not a bloody rabbit," said Duggan. "Where are you?"

"In the flat. Bayswater."

"I tell you what, the wife's gone out to see her mother and I'm a loose end, so you can buy me noodles in that place underneath your building."

Nightingale winced. "I'm not flavour of the month there at the moment," he said. "Anyway, there's a better place in Queensway, to the left of the Tube station. When can you get there?"

"Thirty minutes," said Duggan. "And you're buying, okay?"

The detective ended the call before Nightingale had the chance to reply. When it came time to leave, raindrops were splattering on his windows so he grabbed his raincoat before heading outside. He turned right outside the front door so that he didn't have to walk by Mrs Chan's restaurant. He knew that at some point he was going to have to bite the bullet and apologise to her, but for the life of him he couldn't think what to say that would explain away what had happened.

Duggan wasn't at the restaurant yet so Nightingale took a corner table and ordered a pot of jasmine tea. All the serving staff were elderly men in black pants and red Mao jackets; none of them ever smiled. His tea arrived just as Duggan walked in and looked around. He spotted Nightingale and walked over to his table, taking off a woollen beanie hat to reveal his totally bald head and elf-like ears. He hung his beige raincoat and Burberry scarf over the back of his chair before shaking hands with Nightingale and sitting down.

"What's the problem with the other place?" asked the detective. "Their duck noodles are the best in London you always say."

Nightingale shrugged. "It's complicated."

"Slept with a waitress?"

Nightingale laughed. "Chance would be a fine thing," he said. "No, it's more complicated than that." He sipped his tea. Actually, what had happened in the restaurant had a direct bearing on the favour he was about to ask, but there was no way that he could tell Duggan that. "Colin, you trust me, right?"

"That's an open-ended question, isn't it?"

"But I've never lied to you. Never let you down. Always had your back when we worked together."

"You were a good cop, Jack. Right up to the moment that you chucked that banker through the window of his office." He winked. "Allegedly." He nodded at the menu. "Can we order? I might as well get my food ordered before you put your hooks in."

Nightingale waved over a waiter. Duggan ordered duck with thin noodles and extra wontons and Nightingale had his regular thick noodles. "What are you drinking?" asked Duggan, pointing at Nightingale's teapot.

"Jasmine tea."

"Jasmine's a bloody flower, isn't it?" Duggan looked up at the waiter. "Have you got Diet Coke?"

"Just regular Coke," replied the waiter, stony-faced.

"Have you any idea how much sugar there is in Coke?" He sighed. "I hate this diet thing. Why is it that everything that tastes good is always bad for you?"

Nightingale figured the question was rhetorical so he didn't say anything.

Duggan sighed again. "I'll have water. From the tap."

The waiter nodded and shuffled away.

"The staff are a lot friendlier at the other place," said Duggan.

"I'm not sure that's true," said Nightingale.

"Can you tell me why bottled water is so damn expensive? It's water, right? How can it cost the same as beer?"

"I don't think it does, does it? Mind you, I can't remember the last time I drank water."

Duggan sat back in his chair and rubbed his stomach. "Yeah, well, keep on eating and drinking the way you do and you'll soon find out. Practically everyone I know has diabetes these days."

"Smoking helps," said Nightingale. "Keeps the weight off."

Duggan leaned forward. "That's true, is it? Smoking suppresses your appetite?"

"I don't see many fat smokers," said Nightingale.

"And I don't see many fat heroin addicts," said Duggan. "Not sure that either is a cure for diabetes." The waiter returned with Duggan's glass of water. He sipped it and grimaced. "I really want a beer," he said.

"Bloody hell, Colin, have one, then. One beer's not going to kill you."

Duggan crossed his index fingers and held them up in front of Nightingale. "Get thee behind me, Satan."

"One beer, Colin. If it makes you feel better I'll have one too."

"You bastard."

Nightingale grinned and waved at the nearest waiter. "Two beers," he mouthed. "Coronas."

"I don't want that Mexican shit," said Duggan. "I'll have a Tsingtao. Chinese restaurant, Chinese beer." The waiter scribbled in his notepad and hurried away. "So what can I do for you?" Duggan asked. "I'm assuming that the 'do you trust me' question means it's something heavy."

"You made a crack about the banker. Underwood."

"Yeah, that bastard deserved what he got. That day, when the little girl died . . ." Duggan shuddered. "You never said anything, after you came down. If you had, if you'd told me what that bastard had done to her, I'd have gone with you, Jack. No question. I'd have thrown him through that window myself."

"Allegedly," said Nightingale. "You remember the doll she had with her when she fell?"

Duggan nodded. "The Barbie doll."

Nightingale took a deep breath. "Can you get it for me?"

"The doll?"

"Yeah. The doll."

"What the hell are you playing at?"

The waiter returned with two bottles of beer and two glasses. He put them down on the table and walked away.

"Jack?"

"I just need to borrow the doll for a day or two. Then I'll return it."

"There's no live case, so what's your interest?"

Nightingale sighed. "It's just a thing I've got to do."

"Someone's paying you?"

Nightingale shook his head. "It's personal. Look, her death was a suicide, no doubt about that. Her father died that day, and her mother killed herself two weeks after they buried the little girl. So I'm pretty sure that her belongings are still going to be in the evidence room."

"That's what you want me to do? Get into the evidence room and steal the doll?"

"Borrow. You'll get it back."

"And you want me to do this without telling me why?"

"Yeah."

"You really are full of yourself, aren't you?"

"I know I'm asking a lot. And I'll owe you one."

"Since when did a cop need a favour from a private eye? Shit always rolls downhill, remember?"

"You never know what's going to happen down the line," said Nightingale. "I need this, Colin. I wouldn't be asking if it wasn't important."

A waiter brought over two bowls of noodles. Duggan waited until he'd walked away before speaking but even then he kept his voice low. "Just promise that this won't come back and bite me in the arse," he said.

Nightingale made the sign of the cross on his chest. "Cross my heart and hope to die," he said. He was joking but the second the words had passed his lips he shuddered.

"What?" said Duggan.

Nightingale waved away the question. "Just someone walking over my grave," he said. "Don't worry, mate, I won't let you down." He picked up a fork and grinned. "Go on, dig in."

They ate in silence for a while. "What's the story with you and Dwayne Robinson?" asked Duggan eventually.

"What have you heard?"

"That you shot him in the head and he made a deathbed statement naming you."

Nightingale swore and put down the fork. "That's not what happened," he said. "Who told you that?"

"Word on the grapevine," said Duggan.

"Specifically?"

The detective shook his head. "Like all the best chefs I'm reluctant to identify my source," he said.

"Yeah, well, Jamie Oliver you're not. Was it Dan Evans?"

"Haven't seen him for months," said Duggan. "Chalmers is using him as his runner these days, I heard."

"I thought everyone understood that I wasn't involved in the Robinson thing. I was nowhere near Brixton when it happened."

"Well, on the street your name's very much in the frame, Jack."

Nightingale swore again.

"Problem?" asked Duggan.

"Nothing I can't handle," said Nightingale, wishing that he felt as confident as he sounded.

They finished their noodles and Nightingale paid the bill, then they shook hands outside the restaurant and Duggan climbed into a black cab.

Nightingale phoned Evans on his mobile as soon as he got home. "What the hell's going on, Dan?" asked Nightingale the moment that the detective answered the call.

"Yeah, and good evening to you too, Nightingale."

"Don't screw me around, Dan. You said you'd put the word out that the Robinson shooting was nothing to do with me."

"I said I'd see what I could do."

"Yeah, well it looks now like every man and his dog believes that I pulled the trigger."

"Shit," said Evans.

"Yeah, shit," said Nightingale. "Why have I just been told that the cops think I'm the one who shot Dwayne Robinson?"

"That's down to Chalmers. He's still got your name in the frame."

"So you didn't let Robinson's gang know that it wasn't me who shot their boss? That's what we agreed, right? You were going to get them off my back."

"Jack, how could I do that? Chalmers watches me like a hawk. And if he found out that I was sabotaging his investigation he'd have my guts for garters."

"Sabotage? Since when has telling the truth been sabotage?"

"Jack, don't get on your high horse with me. I did you a favour giving you the details of the Range Rover, and there's the matter of you not reporting a major crime."

Nightingale bit down on his lower lip. He wanted to shout and swear at Evans but he knew that wouldn't get him anywhere. Evans was a cog in the machine, and a small cog at that.

"I'm sorry, Jack. Really. But my hands were tied," said Evans.

Nightingale took a deep breath, calming himself down. "Dan, I am in so much shit. You can see that, right? They've already tried to shoot me once; if they think I killed Robinson then what's to stop them trying again?"

"They know we're on the case. I don't think they'll be stupid enough to have another go."

"They're drug dealers, Dan, that's not generally a sign of a high IQ." He took another deep breath. "You checked the Range Rover, right?"

"Yes, and there were no guns."

"And Reggie Gayle's house?"

"No guns there either."

"And Perry Smith? The face I recognised?"

"That I don't know."

"What do you mean, you don't know? He's one of the guys who shot at me."

"Yeah, well, I couldn't tell Chalmers that without dropping you in it, could I? If I'd told him that Smith was one of the shooters he'd want to know how I knew. It was hard enough getting him to give Gayle a pull. But it's not all bad news; we interviewed Gayle about the shootings in Queensway so he knows he's on our radar and he'll tell Smith."

"CCTV footage?"

"There's plenty of the car but we can't ID the driver or any of the passengers. Gayle's saying it was his missus out shopping. There were no cameras covering the area where the shooters got out of the car, which was probably luck rather than deliberate. And there's nothing usable of the shooting itself, which is good news for you because if Chalmers knew you were there your feet wouldn't touch the ground."

"And what about GSR? Was Gayle checked? Or his car?"

"Chalmers didn't think it was worth looking for gunshot residue," said Evans. "Jack, I'm sorry. I did what I could."

"Okay, I know what a bastard Chalmers can be. But I need one more favour, Dan."

"Why does my heart always sink when I hear that?"

"Perry Smith. I want his address."

"Bloody hell, Nightingale, have you got a death wish?"

CHAPTER
TWENTY-EIGHT

Wednesday was a quiet day for Jack Nightingale Investigations. Nightingale gave Jenny two reports to write up but when midday came and the phone hadn't rung he suggested that they go to Camden and pay Mrs Steadman a visit.

"You're asking me because your car is playing up again, aren't you?" said Jenny suspiciously.

"My car is just fine," he said. "I'm asking you because you've never met her and she's a sweetheart. And you never know when you might need the services of a white witch."

"I take it she doesn't have a pointed hat and a broomstick?"

"You've read too much *Harry Potter*," he said. "She's a lovely lady. Trust me." He picked up his coat. "Come on, we'll go by cab and I'll buy you lunch before we go."

They locked up the office and went down to the street to hail a black cab. It dropped them off close to Camden Lock market. It was a cold, blustery day and there were very few shoppers around. They ate Caribbean food in the Mango Room restaurant — goat curry, rice, peas and fried sweet-potato fritters — before walking round to the Wicca Woman store.

Mrs Steadman was standing by the till and she looked up from a receipt when the tiny bell attached to the door tinkled. Her bird-like face broke into a smile when she saw Nightingale. "This is a nice surprise," she said. She beamed at Jenny. "And who is this delightful young lady?"

"This is Jenny. She works with me," said Nightingale. "I keep talking about you so I thought I'd bring her in to say hello."

Mrs Steadman extended a child-sized hand and Jenny shook it. "So nice to meet you, my dear," she said. She was wearing a black shirt over black jodhpurs and knee-length black boots. Around her tiny waist was a silver filigree belt with a butterfly design.

"I love your shop," said Jenny, looking around.

An incense stick was burning in a pewter holder next to the old-fashioned cash register but there were other smells too, including lemon grass, lavender and jasmine. There were shelves filled with bottles of herbs and spices, open baskets of mushrooms, twigs and leaves, displays of amulets and bangles, pyramids made of every conceivable material, and crystals of every imaginable hue. Jenny picked up a pale pink crystal and held it up to the light.

"Place that under your pillow and you will dream about your future husband," said Mrs Steadman.

"Really?" asked Jenny.

"We have a money-back guarantee," said Mrs Steadman.

"Then I have to have it," said Jenny, pulling her wallet from her Gucci shoulder bag.

"Don't be silly, my dear," said Mrs Steadman, holding up her hands. "Take it as a gift from me. Mr Nightingale has been more than generous to me over the past few weeks."

"Thank you," said Jenny. She rubbed the crystal against her cheek. "It feels so cold."

"It can help with aches and pains too, but a sapphire crystal is better for pain relief," said Mrs Steadman. She put a hand on Jenny's arm. "I always suggest that the day before you use a crystal you should bury it in the ground so that it is fully recharged. Wrapped in silk or cotton, of course."

"Of course," said Jenny.

"But if you can't do that then soaking it in sea salt also helps revitalise the crystal." She nodded at the multicoloured beaded curtain behind the counter. "Now would you both like a nice cup of tea?"

"That would be lovely," said Jenny.

Mrs Steadman pulled back the curtain and showed them into the small back room where the gas fire was flickering and hissing. There was a flight of stairs to the left and Mrs Steadman called upstairs, "Sweetie, can you take care of the shop? I'm entertaining guests."

"Yes, Mrs Steadman," shouted a girl from upstairs, and a few seconds later a punk girl clattered downstairs in boots with four-inch-thick soles, a tartan skirt and a studded motorcycle jacket. She was wearing leather fingerless gloves and she wagged her fingers at Mrs

Steadman before disappearing through the beaded curtain.

Mrs Steadman made them tea as Jenny and Nightingale sat down. "So how did you end up working for Mr Nightingale?" Mrs Steadman asked Jenny.

Jenny smiled. "Serendipity," she said. "One of those things."

"Ah, serendipity," said Mrs Steadman. "How boring life would be without it."

"I really was in the right place at the right time," Jenny said. "I was near New Bond Street, killing time while I waited to hear about a job that I'd been interviewed for. It was the perfect job, unlike the one I ended up with." She flashed Nightingale a smile to show that she was joking. "Anyway, I popped into Costa Coffee and got myself a latte. I'd just sat down by the window when the director of human resources rings me to say that I didn't get the job but he'd keep my name on file and all the rest of the rubbish that means you'll never hear from them again. I was so disappointed, I really was. Then I picked up a newspaper and it was open at the page with the crossword. Whoever had been doing it had made a pig's ear of it, but underneath the crossword was Jack's advert."

"That was the first day it was in the paper," said Nightingale. "And the last. I'd paid for three days but I pulled the advert as soon as I'd seen Jenny. And her CV."

"Which I don't think he ever read," said Jenny. "But you see what I mean about serendipity? If I'd got the job with the advertising agency that would have been the end of it. But at the exact moment I get the call saying that I didn't get the job, Jack's advert is in front of me. And it was circled, that was the weird thing. As if the person who'd been in the coffee shop before me had been thinking about applying for the job." She frowned and looked over at Nightingale. "I never thought about that before," she said. "Did anyone else apply?"

Nightingale laughed. "Are you fishing for compliments? You want me to tell you that you beat a hundred people for the job?"

"Idiot," she said. "But whoever had circled the advert must have been interested, right?"

Mrs Steadman carried over a tray with a brown teapot, three blue-and-white-striped mugs and a matching milk jug and sugar bowl.

"You were the first to phone," said Nightingale. "There were a couple of calls later in the day but by then I'd already hired you."

"But you can see how luck played a huge part in it. If whoever had circled the ad had phoned you first, maybe you'd have hired her. Or him. Or what if whoever it was had taken the paper with them, or tossed it into the bin? So many ifs, so many maybes."

"But it all worked out well in the end, didn't it?" said Nightingale.

"That's up for discussion, Jack."

"At least I wasn't wrong when I said it would never be boring."

"Yes, there is that," said Jenny.

Mrs Steadman poured tea into the mugs. "So what is it you want from me?" she asked Nightingale. Nightingale looked surprised and she smiled at him. "I'm sure you didn't come here just for my tea," she said.

"We tried one of the spiritualist associations that you mentioned. The one in Marylebone."

"And it didn't go well?"

"It just didn't feel right. It felt forced."

"You didn't get a message?"

"I didn't, but Jenny did. Sort of." He shrugged. "To be honest, it wasn't a success."

"I'm sorry about that," said Mrs Steadman, putting her hands around her mug of tea. "But there are no guarantees when it comes to spiritualism." Jenny held up the pink crystal but before she could say anything Mrs Steadman wagged a finger at her. "Crystals are different," she said. "Crystals I can guarantee, providing they are used correctly. Spiritualism depends on the medium. There are good mediums and bad mediums."

"And average mediums," said Nightingale.

"What?" said Jenny.

"Medium. Average. It was a joke."

Jenny shook her head. "No, Jack. It wasn't."

Nightingale ignored her. "The thing is, Mrs Steadman, when we were leaving we were approached by someone who said they could give us a personal viewing."

Mrs Steadman raised an eyebrow. "Tell me more."

"It was a man. He gave me his card." Nightingale took out his wallet and retrieved Graham Lord's business card. He handed it to Mrs Steadman. "He said that he might be able to help me get in touch with Sophie."

Mrs Steadman fished her blue-tinted pince-nez from her shirt pocket and perched them on the end of her nose. She still had to hold the card at arm's length to focus and her lips moved as she read the name. "Sophie was the little girl who died?"

Nightingale nodded. "Sophie Underwood." He gestured at the card. "Do you know him?"

Mrs Steadman shook her head and handed back the card. "I don't, but I'm not well acquainted with the spiritualists. The groups I told you about are well respected, but I don't tend to go myself."

Nightingale put the card back in his wallet. "Is that normal, to have someone approach you after a session?"

"It happens, I suppose," said Mrs Steadman. "Did this gentleman say that he had already made contact with Sophie?"

"That's why I was interested," he said. "He seemed very . . . confident."

"And had you mentioned her name during the session?"

"Definitely not," he said.

He looked across at Jenny, who nodded in agreement. "Jack was very careful not to use her name."

"And did he suggest payment?"

"He just offered me a private session," said Nightingale. "I was worried that he might be setting me up for a con."

"That certainly does happen," said Mrs Steadman. "There are a lot of charlatans around. I would say that the true mediums rarely accept payment. They tend to believe that the gift they have shouldn't be sullied with money. There might be a collection for expenses or to help towards the running of the association but it's quite unusual for a spiritualist to ask for money up front." She waved a languid hand towards the shop. "Of course, in a way I'm in a similar position. I am a true believer in the power of Wicca but that doesn't stop me running a business based on it."

"So what do you think, Mrs Steadman? Is he setting me up for a con?"

Mrs Steadman chuckled and reached for her tea. "I'm sure you're a better judge of that than me," she said. "You were the policeman."

"I guess," said Nightingale. "But how will I know if he's genuine or not?"

"Only you will be able to tell, Mr Nightingale."

"But here's what I don't understand, Mrs Steadman. I went to the meeting to talk to Sophie. I was totally open and receptive, but nothing happened. Why didn't Sophie contact me then?"

"It's not as simple as that," said Mrs Steadman. "You have to think of it in terms of frequencies."

"Frequencies?"

"Imagine a spirit is at one frequency and the living are at a different frequency, which is why most people can't see spirits. Mediums can tune themselves into the frequency of the spirits. But just because they can see one spirit doesn't mean they can see them all. It could be that the medium you saw simply couldn't hear Sophie's frequency but can hear the frequencies of other spirits." She shrugged apologetically. "I'm sorry if I'm not being much help. It's not really my field."

"So Sophie might have been there but just couldn't come through?"

Mrs Steadman nodded. "It might just be a case of trying another medium," she said.

"Okay, I will," said Nightingale. "What harm would it do?"

CHAPTER
TWENTY-NINE

Nightingale dropped Jenny outside her mews house in Chelsea. "I feel bad taking the afternoon off," she said as she opened the door of the black cab and climbed out.

"It's four o'clock," he said. "And it's not as if we're rushed off our feet." He grinned. "It's the cold weather: people prefer to commit adultery in the summer. See you tomorrow."

Jenny closed the door and waved goodbye, then disappeared into her house.

"Where to, mate?" asked the driver.

"Are you okay to go south of the river?"

"I have to take you anywhere within six miles of the square mile," said the cabbie. "That's the law."

"Clapham, then," said Nightingale. "Close to the station." He looked at his watch. He wanted to get to Perry Smith's house before dark but it didn't look as if he was going to make it.

The traffic was no heavier than normal for a winter Wednesday afternoon. Drivers were switching on their lights as they crossed the Thames and by the time they reached Clapham it was dark outside. Nightingale had the cabbie drop him about a hundred yards from Perry

Smith's house. Dan Evans had given him the address, along with a warning: Perry lived with at least three other gang members in a part of Clapham that the local police regarded as a no-go area, unless they were mob-handed and armed to the teeth. Nightingale paid the cabbie and turned up the collar of his raincoat. As the cab drove away Nightingale shivered and felt very much alone. It wasn't a part of London that he was familiar with and he was about to confront a man who had already tried to kill him with a hail of bullets. He looked up at the dark sky and shivered again. He took out his cigarettes and lit one.

A black hatchback prowled past, rap music blaring out at such a volume that he felt the vibration in his stomach. There were four black teenagers inside and they all turned to look at Nightingale as they drove by. Nightingale blew smoke and started to walk down the pavement towards Smith's house.

The houses were in a terrace, two storeys high and with railings around steps leading to a basement. Most of the houses had been split up into flats judging by the multiple bells next to the front doors. There was a big black man in a Puffa jacket standing outside the house, stamping his feet against the cold, his breath feathering around his mouth. He turned to look at Nightingale and stared with undisguised hostility as Nightingale walked towards him.

"How's it going?" asked Nightingale.

The man grunted and continued to glare at Nightingale as he slid a hand inside his Puffa jacket.

"I'm here to see Perry Smith," said Nightingale.

"We don't deal here," said the man.

"I'm not here to buy gear. I'm here to talk."

"About what?"

"I'm looking for tips on how to get my roses to grow," said Nightingale. "What bloody business is it of yours?"

The man took a step towards Nightingale, his upper lip curled back in a sneer.

Nightingale stood his ground. "What are you going to do, beat me to a pulp in the street?"

The man jabbed a finger at Nightingale. "We own this street. Ain't no one gonna be calling three nines."

Nightingale took a step back. "Okay, maybe we got off on the wrong foot," he said. "Tell Perry I'm the guy he tried to shoot in Queensway a while back. The name's Nightingale."

"Like the bird?"

"Yeah, like the bird. Jack Nightingale."

The man nodded slowly, then turned and unlocked the front door. He disappeared inside for a few minutes and then returned. He jerked a thumb. "In," he said. Nightingale stepped inside and as soon as he did the heavy slammed him against the wall, kicking the door closed with his heel. The hallway ran the full length of the house with a kitchen at the far end, purple doors leading off to the right and a flight of stairs, which had also been painted purple, leading upstairs. A pretty black girl with waist-length dreadlocks was sitting halfway up the stairs, inhaling from a large glass bong. She exhaled a cloud of sweetish smoke and waggled her fingers at Nightingale.

216

"Easy," said Nightingale. His hands had gone up against the wall instinctively and he kept them there as the heavy patted him down, looking for a weapon. He didn't resist and didn't say anything. Eventually the heavy was satisfied and he told Nightingale to turn around.

He took him down the hallway to the first room. The walls were painted a pale purple and there was a huge spherical white-paper lampshade hanging from the middle of the ceiling. There were three large sofas around a coffee table that was piled high with drugs paraphernalia including several bongs and a silver bowl filled with a white powder. Nightingale smiled and shook his head in disbelief. If Chalmers and Evans had turned up with a search warrant the drugs alone would have meant Smith going away for a long time. An episode of *The Simpsons* was playing on a large TV fixed to one of the walls but the room seemed to be empty.

The heavy shoved Nightingale against one of the sofas. "Hey!" shouted Nightingale, but before he could say anything else a man stepped from behind the door, grabbed Nightingale by the collar of his coat and pushed him towards the wall again. Something hard pressed under Nightingale's chin, forcing his head back.

"What the hell you doing here?" growled the man with the gun.

"It's a social call," said Nightingale, trying to sound as though having a gun jammed against his neck was no big thing. But it was a big thing. A very big thing.

Especially when the man holding the gun was a gangster like Perry Smith. "I just wanted a word."

"Fucking comedian, huh?" said Smith. He pulled Nightingale away from the wall but kept the gun pressed against his flesh. Nightingale could just see the handle of the weapon: a chrome semi-automatic. "The cops outside? Because if they are you're a dead man."

"If I was with the cops, I'd hardly have come in here on my own, would I?"

Smith glared at Nightingale, his nostrils flaring as he breathed slowly. Nightingale could feel his heart pounding but he was pretty sure that the gangster wasn't going to pull the trigger. Not one hundred per cent certain, but close enough that he managed to force a smile.

"I just want to talk, Perry."

Smith scowled but released his grip on Nightingale's coat and slowly took the gun away. He released the hammer with his thumb but kept the gun aimed at Nightingale's face. He was wearing a silver tracksuit and gold Nikes, with several large gold chains on both wrists.

"You do know who I am, then?" said Nightingale.

"What the fuck do you want?" asked Smith

"You do know me. Last time we met you were wearing a Puffa jacket and a ski mask and you had a MAC-10 in your hand," said Nightingale. "You couldn't fire the thing to save your life but you did manage to hit an innocent bystander and scare the shit out of a lot of shoppers."

"Bollocks," said Smith. "I don't know you."

"I came here to talk," said Nightingale. He gestured at one of the sofas. "Can I sit down?"

Smith nodded. As Nightingale sat down a big man in an LA Lakers shirt and baggy jeans came down the stairs and into the hall, holding a Glock against the side of his leg. He joined the first heavy at the door and they both glared contemptuously at Nightingale, who smiled and raised his hands. "Please don't rape me," he said.

Smith grinned and so did the man with the Glock. "He's funny, isn't he?" asked Smith, waving his gun at Nightingale.

"Yeah, funny as fuck," said the man. He tucked the gun in the waistband of his trousers.

Smith placed his weapon on the coffee table, then reached for the TV remote and muted the sound.

"You remember me now?" Nightingale said to Smith. The heavy in the Lakers shirt went to stand by the windows. They were covered with dark oak blinds and the heavy peered through the slats, checking the street outside.

Smith wiped his nose with the back of his hand. "You used to be Five-O, didn't you?" he said.

"In another life," said Nightingale. "I'm self-employed now."

Smith laughed, showing several gold teeth at the back of his mouth. "Ain't we all these days. What do you want, Birdman?"

Nightingale heard a soft footfall on the stairs and another heavy appeared, a big man with a shaved head. He was wearing a Nike tracksuit and a gold chain around his neck that was as thick as Nightingale's thumb. He dropped down on the third sofa, his head bobbing back and forth. He had earphones in and an iPod strapped to a bulging forearm.

"I want to talk to you about Dwayne and about what happened in Queensway," said Nightingale.

Smith's eyes narrowed. "You wearing a wire?"

"Why would I be wearing a wire?"

Smith nodded at the heavy on the sofa. "Take his clothes off," he told him.

"What?" said the man. Smith mimed taking out the headphones. The man did as he was told. "What?" he repeated.

Smith gestured at Nightingale. "Strip him."

Nightingale held up his hands. "Whoa!" he said. "I've already been patted down out there. You can pat me down again if you want. But it's a waste of time, I'm not wired."

"Technology they've got these days, you could have the mike up your arse and picking up everything we say. Your choice, Jack-Shit. Get naked or the boys will take you for a ride." He reached for his gun.

"Perry, I'm here to talk not to screw you over."

"If you want to talk I need to know that it's safe," said Smith. He gestured with his gun at Nightingale's trousers. "I'm not gonna bother counting to ten, just do it."

Nightingale sighed, then took off his raincoat. He held it out to the heavy with the iPod but the man just stared at him, stony-faced. Nightingale draped the coat over the back of the sofa, then unbuttoned his shirt. He turned to face Smith and held the shirt open.

220

"Take it all off, Jack-Shit."

Nightingale did as he was told, putting the shirt on top of the coat and then removing his shoes, socks and trousers.

Smith pointed his gun at Nightingale's shoes. "What are they, suede?"

"Yeah," said Nightingale. "Hush Puppies."

"They comfortable?"

"Sure."

"They'd have to be," laughed Smith. Nightingale held out his arms to the side. All he had left were his black Marks & Spencer boxer shorts. Smith waved his gun at the boxers. "The lot," he said. "Don't be shy."

Nightingale cursed under his breath and slid off his boxers. Smith and his heavies burst out laughing and Nightingale hid his private parts with his hands. "Look, it's bloody cold and I'm under a bit of pressure here."

"It's true what they say about white men," sneered Smith.

"What? That we can't jump? Look, are you happy now?"

"I'll be happy when you've turned around and spread your cheeks," said Smith.

"Oh for fuck's sake," said Nightingale. "What do you think, that I've got a Nokia up my back passage?"

"You've never been inside, have you?" said Smith. "You're lucky I don't make you squat and tense. Now just show me your arse and we can start chatting."

Nightingale muttered under his breath, turned around and bent forward. The three men roared with laughter. Smith told Nightingale to get dressed, then he grabbed a pack of cigarette papers, reached over for a ceramic jar decorated with a Chinese dragon pattern, and opened it to reveal a large amount of cannabis resin.

By the time Nightingale had put all his clothes back on, Smith was lighting his joint. He took a long drag on it, held the smoke deep in his lungs then blew it at the ceiling. He waved at the empty sofa. "Sit your lily-white arse back down, Jack-Shit," he said.

Nightingale sat down and waited while Smith took another long drag on his joint. The room was already full of sweet-smelling smoke and Nightingale figured that if he stayed there for more than a few minutes he'd be as high as Smith.

"Speak," said Smith.

"I want you to know that I didn't shoot Dwayne," he said.

"Okay, that's all right, then," said Smith. "Off you go. No hard feelings."

Nightingale narrowed his eyes. "I'm serious."

Smith pointed the gun at Nightingale's groin and sighted along the barrel. "So am I, Jack-Shit."

"Well, I hope your aim's better than it was in Queensway."

The heavy with the iPod reached for the cigarette papers and began to assemble a joint.

Smith lowered the gun. "You know that was me, yeah?"

"Yeah."

"So why aren't I banged up? Why are you sitting there sweating like a turkey at Christmas?"

"Because you were wearing a ski mask, remember?" He nodded at the joint that Smith was holding. "That stuff plays havoc with your short-term memory, you know."

Smith looked at the joint as if seeing it for the first time, then he grinned and took another long drag on it. He blew the smoke straight at Nightingale's face and Nightingale tried not to inhale.

Deep frown lines furrowed Smith's brow. "How do you know it was me, then?"

"Because I saw you in the car."

"So again, same question. If you know it was me, why aren't I banged up?"

Nightingale sighed. "To be honest, nothing would make me happier, but when you shot at me your face was hidden. So a good brief, even an average brief, is just going to ask me whether or not I saw your face and I've got to tell the truth. I didn't. I know it was you, you know it was you, but on oath and standing in the witness box I'd have to say that I couldn't see your face."

"You could lie."

"Yeah, I could lie. But one, I don't tell lies, at least not when I'm on oath, and two, plenty of other people saw you and your mate wearing masks."

Smith grinned. "So you can't tell a fib, can you?"

"Like I said, I don't lie under oath. It's one of the few things that the criminal justice system really frowns on. They send peers of the realm to prison for perjury; with me they'd throw away the key."

Smith jutted his chin out and nodded. "Bit of a dilemma, innit?"

"One I've been wrestling with," said Nightingale dryly.

"So why are you here?"

"I'm hoping to persuade you that I had nothing to do with Dwayne's shooting."

Smith shrugged. "The cops seem to think you did it."

"I was nowhere near Brixton when it happened. And I don't shoot people. Not any more."

Smith's eyes narrowed suspiciously. "What do you mean?"

"Can I smoke?"

"You can burst into flames for all I care," said Smith, and he threw back his head and laughed at his own joke.

Nightingale took out his pack of Marlboro.

Smith stiffened. "Check them fags," he yelled at the heavy nearest Nightingale. "Why did no one check his pockets?" He waved the gun around. "If there's a bug in there someone's gonna get their nuts shot off."

The girl from the stairs appeared in the doorway holding her bong. Her eyes were glassy and she was unsteady on her feet. Smith waved her away. "Upstairs, bitch," he said.

"I'm hungry," she said.

"There's food in the fridge."

"I want pizza."

"Later," said Smith. The girl pouted and walked carefully down the hallway.

The heavy ripped the pack from Nightingale's hands, tipped the cigarettes out onto the coffee table and crushed it. He tossed the pack into Nightingale's lap.

"Happy now?" Nightingale asked Smith as he leaned forward and slotted the cigarettes back into the pack one by one.

"Can never be too careful where Five-O are concerned," said Smith.

"I told you, I'm not with the cops any more. Haven't been for two years now."

"And that's why I'm supposed to believe you? You were a cop and cops don't lie?"

"You're supposed to believe me because I didn't do it. I can prove that I was north of the river when Dwayne was shot."

"Prove how?"

"I can get the phone company to show you my GPS position."

"That just shows where the phone was. Doesn't mean you were with it."

"True, but I called my assistant so she can verify that I was with the phone." Nightingale lit a cigarette.

"She can, can she?" Smith sneered at him. "Do I look like I was born yesterday?"

"Not really, no."

"Then let's leave your assistant out of the equation, shall we?"

Nightingale drew on his cigarette and blew smoke. "I was watching the footie," he said. "With a mate. A cop."

"Oh yeah, I'll believe a cop, of course. How old do you think I am? Five?" He shook his head in disgust.

"The friend can't back me up anyway. He's dead."

"So no alibi there, then."

"The landlord of the pub remembers me being there."

Smith shook his head. "You think I care what he says? I'm guessing he's white, right?"

"It's not about race, Perry."

"Everything's about race. The long and the short of it is that he'll say whatever it takes to get me off your back." He waved the gun at Nightingale. "Look, Jack-Shit, the way I hear it, Dwayne said you were the shooter."

"That's not what happened."

"Deathbed confession, and that's gold."

"He wasn't naming me as his killer. And it wasn't a confession."

"He's lying in intensive care and starts calling out your name. That's what I was told."

Smith smoked his joint while Nightingale took a long drag on his cigarette. They both blew smoke, watching each other carefully.

"You and Dwayne were tight, right?" asked Nightingale eventually.

"Tight as tight can be."

"As tight as he was with Reggie Gayle?"

"Horses for courses."

"What, Reggie's the brains and you're the muscle?" He held up his hands. "No offence. I just meant that on the day in Queensway he stayed in the car and you were at the sharp end with the MAC-10."

226

"I hear you. Let's just say that when Dwayne needed a problem fixing, he came to me."

"And up to the shooting, he never mentioned a problem?"

Smith shook his head and then took a long drag on his joint.

"So did he ever mention me to you? Ever talk about me? Did he tell you one single thing about me?"

Smith stared at Nightingale and blew a cloud of sweet-smelling smoke but didn't say anything.

"I'm guessing that means no. So why would someone he didn't know put a bullet in his head?"

"Maybe somebody paid you," said Smith.

"So I'm a hired killer now?"

"Poacher turned gamekeeper, maybe."

"Strictly speaking I'd be a gamekeeper turned poacher, but believe me, that's not a line of work I'd be interested in."

Smith took another long drag on his joint, held the smoke and then exhaled through clenched teeth so that his face was shrouded in smoke. "See right there is the problem," he said eventually. "I don't trust you."

"Yeah, I figured that's what you'd say. So I've got a deal for you."

"A deal?"

"Yeah. Let me do what I do best. Let me play detective."

Nightingale stubbed out the last of his cigarette in a glass ashtray.

"Here's what I don't get," said Smith. "Why do you think you can find the man who shot Dwayne when Scotland Yard's finest can't?"

"Because Scotland Yard's finest aren't on the case," said Nightingale. "Operation Trident aren't interested because the shooter wasn't black, and they're the experts when it comes to gang shootings. But they can't touch it because the witnesses all say that the man who shot him was white. That means that a superintendent by the name of Chalmers is running the case and he's a moron."

Smith grinned. "A moron who thinks you pulled the trigger?"

"Chalmers would do me for littering if he found a cigarette butt in the street," said Nightingale. "He doesn't care whether or not I did it, so long as I go down for it. That means he's not looking for anyone else. Or if he is, he's just going through the motions."

Smith managed to get one more drag from his joint then he stubbed it out in the ashtray that Nightingale had used.

"And why do I let you do your Sherlock Holmes bit?" asked Smith.

"Because you want to know who killed Dwayne. And I think that deep down you know it wasn't me. And if it wasn't me, which it wasn't, then maybe whoever it was that put the bullet in Dwayne's head has another bullet with your name on it." He stared at Smith with unblinking eyes and Smith stared back.

"You play poker, Jack-Shit?"

"I've been known to," said Nightingale.

"Are you good, because that's one hell of a poker face, innit?"

"It's a genuine offer, Perry. Let me ask around, see if I can get you a name."

"And then what?"

"Up to you. I'm not going to go running to the cops. I don't have a dog in this fight. I just want to be able to go on with my life without looking over my shoulder every time a car with tinted windows goes by."

Smith nodded slowly. "Do you want a drink?"

"Got any Corona?"

"That Mexican shit?"

"Yeah. That Mexican shit."

"I've got Budweiser."

"That American shit?"

Smith laughed and looked over at his heavies, giving them a thumbs up. "Hear that?" he said. "That's banter, innit? This here Jack-Shit's a funny man. A funny, funny man." He looked back at Nightingale and the smile vanished. "He's going to be laughing all the way to the grave."

"Okay, forget the beer," said Nightingale. "But shooting me here isn't really an option because my pretty young assistant knows where I am and that I came to see you, so if anything happens to me she'll tell the cops everything."

Smith chuckled and scratched his ear with the barrel of his gun. "Do you know how many eyewitnesses get amnesia after we pay them a visit?" he said.

"It's not about amnesia; it's about the letter I wrote for her." He looked at his watch. "If I don't see her by nine o'clock she'll be dialling three nines."

"You didn't bring no mobile with you."

"Yeah, I figured you'd be wary of phones, what with you having a thing about microphones up people's arses."

"Plus, I'm guessing that you figured I'd be checking your phone once you told me about your back-up plan," said Smith.

"You can read me like a book," said Nightingale. He leaned forward and clasped his hands together. "Look, Perry, you know who I am and you've already tried to kill me once. There's nothing much to stop you trying again and next time I might not be so lucky. Now I could tell you that I've got some pretty heavy friends that owe me a favour or two but I don't think you're the type that reacts well to threats, so why don't you just let me have a go at finding out who really did shoot Dwayne? If I can do that we can call it quits. If I don't, well, I'm no worse off, am I?"

"Seventy-two hours," said Smith. "And the clock has just started ticking."

Nightingale looked at his watch. "Deal," he said. "Sex, money, rage," he said.

"Say what?"

"The three most common motives for murder," said Nightingale, sitting back in his seat. "That's what it all comes down to more often than not. One, he was killed by a former lover or by someone who was connected to a former lover. Jealous boyfriend or husband. Two, he

230

was killed for money or by a business rival. Three, someone was really pissed off at him, which might or might not be connected with one or two. Let's work backwards. Can you think of anyone who would have wanted Dwayne dead?"

"You sell drugs, you tread on toes."

"Anyone in particular?"

Smith shrugged. "Two crews locally but they wouldn't have the balls to attack us."

"White?"

Smith threw back his head and laughed. "White?" He shook his head, still laughing. "A white crew in south London? They wouldn't last five minutes."

"What about Colombians?"

Smith frowned. "Colombians?"

"In the heat of the moment no one's going to be able to tell the difference between a Brit and a South American."

"That's right; your lot had trouble telling the difference between a Brazilian electrician and an Arab terrorist."

"I told you, they're not my lot."

"But you were a cop back then, right?" He reached for the pack of cigarette papers.

"It was my day off."

"What sort of cop were you? Drugs?"

Nightingale shook his head. "I was with CO19."

"An armed cop?"

"For my sins. And I was a negotiator. Hostage situations, people in crisis."

"But you've shot people, right?"

"I was armed but I never shot anyone, no. Most CO19 officers never get to fire their weapon in anger, never mind hit someone. Shooting someone is a last resort."

Smith chuckled. "Yeah, well, in my line of work it's the method of choice for sorting out disputes."

"That's why I'm asking about business rivals," said Nightingale.

"Like I said, we don't have no white rivals. And definitely no Colombians."

"What about a black gang who want to outsource their anger?"

Smith was rolling his second joint but he stopped and frowned. "What do you mean?"

"Anyone who wanted Dwayne dead enough to pay for someone to shoot him? You were quick enough to assume that I was a hired gun. Maybe that's what happened. Maybe it was a professional hit."

Smith jutted out his chin. "That's worth thinking about."

"Did it look like a professional hit?"

"You don't know what happened?"

"I keep telling you, Perry, I'm nothing to do with the cops any more. I'm more of a suspect than an investigator so far as they're concerned. Where did it happen? All I know was that it was in Brixton."

"He was coming out of a nightclub. The Flamingo. It's a salsa place."

"What, Dwayne was into salsa, was he?"

"Dunno. He wasn't much of a dancer."

"And he was there alone?"

"Yeah." He picked up a lighter and lit the joint, puffing on it carefully.

"Is that normal?" He gestured at the heavies. "You've got muscle all around you; did he usually go out alone?"

"Are you saying I'm chicken? Is that what you're saying, Jack-Shit?"

Nightingale held up his hands. "No, I'm just asking a question, the sort of question that the cops should have been asking if they were serious about finding Dwayne's killer."

"We won't talk to no cops. Grasses we ain't."

"Okay, I get it. But that night, he was out without you or your posse? Is that what you call them, a posse? What is the collective noun for a group of bodyguards?"

Smith's eyes narrowed and he glared at Nightingale through a cloud of smoke. "You keep taking the piss and that collective noun is going to take you somewhere and put a collective bullet in your collective fucking head." He took another pull on the joint and blew smoke towards Nightingale. Nightingale tried holding his breath, not wanting to inhale the marijuana fumes.

"Dwayne said he wanted to go out on his own."

"To the Flamingo?"

"Didn't know he knew that place. Not his thing. He just said he didn't want anyone with him."

"And that was unusual?"

Smith shrugged. "Sometimes he wanted his space. But if it was business, I'd have been there, for sure."

Nightingale rubbed his chin. "So he was, what, on a social visit? How was he fixed for women?"

"Dwayne? Had all the women he wanted. Lived the life."

"Could he have been at the Flamingo to meet a woman?"

Smith took another drag on his joint. "It's possible. Yeah. He went out wearing his Hugo Boss." He nodded thoughtfully. "And stinking of aftershave. You might have something there, Jack-Shit. What are you thinking? Boyfriend?"

"Maybe. Or a honey trap. It wouldn't be the first time that a pretty girl has set someone up for a killing."

"So what next? What's your plan?"

"I'm going to ask around. See what I can find out."

"This doesn't let you off the hook, Jack-Shit." Smith picked up the gun and lazily pointed it at Nightingale. "You try to screw me over and you'll be squealing like new tyres in a car park."

"I love the simile," said Nightingale.

"Simile, analogy, so long as you get my drift, okay?"

"I get it. But I've got seventy-two hours, right?"

"You've got it, Jack-Shit. But that's all you've got."

CHAPTER
THIRTY

Jenny put Nightingale's coffee down on the desk by his Hush Puppies. He was sitting back in his chair with his feet up on the desk and the keyboard to his computer on his lap. There was a photograph leaning against the monitor and Jenny picked it up. The two men in the photograph were standing in what looked like a nightclub, their arms around each other, grinning at the camera.

"Good-looking guys," said Jenny.

"Yeah, under other circumstances we'd all go out for dinner, but as it is the one on the left is dead and the one on the right still wants to kill me."

"Who are they?" she asked.

"Guy on the left is the guy I shot," he said. "Allegedly. Dwayne Robinson."

"The one who talked to you while he was brain dead?"

"Yeah. And the guy next to him is the guy who tried to shoot me in Queensway. Perry Smith."

"You're calling the police, right?" She put the picture back against the monitor.

"I'm Googling and then I'll put in a call," he said.

"Googling what?"

"Just seeing what's out there about Robinson." He sighed. "Not much, as it happens." He sat up and put the keyboard back on the desk.

"They'll arrest this Smith guy, will they?"

"It's not as simple as that," said Nightingale.

"What's going on, Jack?" said Jenny, sitting on the edge of his desk and folding her arms.

"He's sort of a client."

"Sort of?"

"Yeah, but it's an unusual fee structure. Basically, if I can find out who shot Robinson, Smith will leave me alone."

"You have to go to the police. You know that."

Nightingale shook his head. "The cops can't help me. There's no evidence and even if there was, putting Smith away still leaves his gang. I'll be a target for the rest of my life." He grinned. "It'll be okay. All I have to do is find out who shot Robinson and then I'm free and clear."

"Can I help?"

"We'll see. I've got a few ideas."

"If you need a place to stay, you can have my spare room. As long as you want."

"Nothing's going to happen for the next two days. Let's see how it goes." He could see the look of concern on her face and he felt suddenly guilty for worrying her. He reached for his phone.

As Jenny went back to her desk, Nightingale tapped out the number for Andrew Britton, a chief inspector that he'd worked alongside in CO19. They'd both joined on the Met's graduate entry scheme and two months before Nightingale left the force Britton had been promoted and transferred to the Operation Trident team.

Britton answered with a cautious "Yeah?"

"Andy? Jack. Can you talk?"

"Bloody hell, a blast from the past. Hang on, give me a minute." Nightingale heard muffled voices and then traffic. Britton had obviously taken his phone outside. "Where are you?" asked Britton.

"The office, why?"

"Thought you might be banged up and this was your one phone call," said Britton. "What's this I hear about you knocking off south London drug dealers? You haven't gone all vigilante on us now that you're in the private sector?"

"That's not funny," said Nightingale. "But, yeah, that's why I'm phoning."

"If you're calling me to confess let me switch on the recorder," said Britton.

"Have you looked at the case?" asked Nightingale, ignoring Britton's attempt at humour.

"It's not black on black," said Britton. "And your old mate Chalmers has grabbed the case."

"Yeah, tell me something I don't know. Had you been looking at Robinson's crew?"

"Sure, they're on our radar. They've been responsible for a dozen or so shootings across the capital but they've not killed anyone yet, not that we know of anyway. Drive-bys mainly, and they favour the MAC-10 so not much in the way of accuracy."

"And when you heard that Robinson had been hit did you have any thoughts, before you knew it was a white shooter?"

"Nothing sprang to mind. There was the usual rough and tumble but nothing that should have led to an execution."

"That's what it was, yeah? No gunfight at the OK Corral?"

"Guy in a hoodie walked up behind him and put a bullet in the back of his head. Nine mill. They got the casing."

"Just the one?"

"There were civilians on the street. Looks like he didn't want to hang around."

"Understood. But one nine mill, even in the head, is no guarantee of a kill, is it?"

"You mean that a pro would have shot him twice?"

"Once in the heart and once in the head. That's how I'd do it. Anything on the gun?"

"We got the round and the casing and nothing known on either."

"But he took the gun?"

"We assume so. Either that or he dropped it and someone else took it but that doesn't seem likely."

"Sounds like you've had a good look at the evidence."

Britton chuckled. "Once I heard your name was in the frame I had a look-see," he said.

"It's all nonsense," said Nightingale. "I was north of the river. Watching the footie with Robbie."

"Damn shame about Robbie. I couldn't get to the funeral; I was over in Jamaica on a case. How's Anna?"

"Bearing up," said Nightingale.

"Life sucks sometimes," said Britton.

"Yeah, no argument here," said Nightingale. He picked up the photograph and studied it. "What about someone in Robinson's own gang?"

"Last time I looked there weren't any white faces in the Robinson posse."

"Very funny," said Nightingale. "I was wondering if Smith or Gayle might have brought in some outside help. Pay a pro to do the dirty."

"Yeah, but a pro wouldn't have left him alive, would he?"

"So what do you think?"

Britton laughed. "I'm a policeman; I'm not paid to think. I'm paid to tick boxes. Besides, your mate Chalmers has the reins. What's your interest in this?"

"Are you kidding? If I don't find out who shot Robinson, no one else will."

"The thing is, if it had been another gang they wouldn't have brought in an outsider. It has to be *mano a mano* otherwise they lose all street cred. I think you need to find a white guy who wanted Robinson dead, someone who hated him but wasn't used to shooting people."

"A civilian with a grudge?"

"That would be my bet."

"And you've no intel on that?"

Britton smiled thinly. "We don't have any informers on their crew, if that's what you mean. But I'll keep my ear to the ground for you."

"Cheers, Andy."

"No sweat. And don't be a stranger. Do you want to swing by for a pint and a curry tonight?"

"I can't. I'm having a drink with an old mate."

"Anyone I know?"

"Yeah, but it's a private session," said Nightingale.

CHAPTER
THIRTY-ONE

Nightingale climbed out of his MGB, locked the door and lit a cigarette as he walked down the street. He had to park some distance away from the off-licence because it was late evening and the roadsides were lined with cars. A police van drove slowly by and three officers in stab vests stared at him with expressionless faces through the side windows as if they were considering arresting him for smoking. When it reached the end of the street its siren kicked into life and its tyres squealed as it accelerated and turned right. Nightingale walked by a row of shops. Half of them were charity shops, two were boarded up, and a clothing shop was offering seventy per cent off.

A figure was sitting cross-legged in the doorway of an Oxfam shop, dressed in black and holding a cardboard sign. Scrawled in black felt-tip were the words "I am hungry. Please help. God bless." And below the words there was a pentagram. The figure looked up. Black hair, thick mascara and black lipstick. Nightingale stopped, his mouth open in surprise.

"Proserpine?"

Something stirred next to her. The dog. A black and white collie. The dog sat up and stared at Nightingale with coal-black eyes, panting softly.

Proserpine smiled and ran a ring-encrusted hand through her spiky black hair. "How's it going, Nightingale?"

"What's wrong?" asked Nightingale.

She smiled up at him. "Why do you think anything's wrong?" She was wearing a silver choker from which hung an upside-down crucifix.

"Why are you here? What do you want?"

"You think I'm here for you?" She chuckled and stroked her dog's neck. The dog's tongue lolled out of the side of its mouth as it stared at Nightingale with dead eyes. "You're not the centre of my universe, Nightingale," said Proserpine. "You're not even the centre of your own universe."

"So it's a coincidence? Is that it?"

"A happystance," said Proserpine. "A pleasing serendipity. Two ships that pass in the night." She grinned. "Give my love to Robbie."

Nightingale's eyes narrowed. "Do you know everything I'm doing?"

"You're an open book, Nightingale. And not a particularly well-written one."

Nightingale blew smoke up at the night sky. The dog growled.

"Be careful with your smoke, Nightingale," said Proserpine quietly.

"I need to ask you something," said Nightingale.

242

"I told you before that I'm not your phone-a-friend. Remember what happened the last time you asked me something?"

"This is different," said Nightingale. "It's about Sophie."

"Ah. The little girl. That was sad, wasn't it?"

Nightingale looked at her, wondering whether or not she was joking.

"You wish you'd saved her, don't you?" said Proserpine.

"Sure."

"Maybe you'll get the chance."

"What? What do you mean?"

She shrugged. "You'll find out. Eventually."

Nightingale leaned towards her. "How can I save her? What do I have to do?"

The dog growled and she stroked the back of its head. "You're on a journey, Nightingale. A voyage of discovery. Now how boring would that be if you had a map that showed you every step of the way?"

"But you can see it? You know where I'm going and what's going to happen?"

"I see things differently to you," said Proserpine. "But trying to explain it to you would be like running quantum physics past a tapeworm."

"You don't believe in building a man's self-esteem, do you?" He inhaled smoke and held it deep in his lungs.

"You're so far beneath me that even the tapeworm analogy is lacking."

Nightingale blew out the smoke and smiled. "So why do you bother with me? And the rest of us?"

"It's your souls we want, Nightingale. It's like when you want a steak. Do you care about the cow?"

"I guess not," he said. "Where is Sophie?"

"Beyond your reach," she said.

"Heaven?"

"She killed herself. That's a mortal sin."

"She was a child being molested by her father. That has to count for something, right?"

"Why are you so concerned about her?"

"She died on my watch. I was there. If I'd done it differently, maybe . . ." He shook his head. "What happened to her was so damn unfair."

"Life's unfair, Nightingale. You'll find the journey easier if you just accept that fact." She waved a languid hand in the direction that he'd been walking. "You should go."

"Can you just tell me, is there anything I can do?"

"Go, Nightingale," she said, her voice harder and deeper. "If you stay, worlds are going to collide and you won't like that." Nightingale sighed and started to walk away. "Oh, and one other thing, Nightingale."

Nightingale stopped. "What?"

"Don't keep taking my name in vain."

"I don't follow you."

"Stop talking about me. You do it with the lovely Jenny McLean and you did it with Dan Evans. I don't mind you doing it with Robbie because he's dead, but if you carry on talking about me there'll be consequences."

"Consequences?"

"Let's leave it at that, shall we? I'd hate to spoil a wonderful relationship."

"Is that what we have, a wonderful relationship?"

She pointed down the road. "It's time for you to go, Nightingale. And don't do a Lot's wife on me."

Nightingale nodded and walked away. He had to fight the urge to look back but he reached the end of the street and turned left. In the distance he heard another siren and high overhead there was the sound of a helicopter heading in the same direction as the police van. He flicked what was left of his cigarette into the gutter and pushed open the door to the off-licence. A bell jangled and the shop assistant looked up from her copy of *Hello!* magazine. She had dyed-blonde hair with dark brown roots showing and slab-like teeth that appeared grey under the off-licence's fluorescent lights. Nightingale whistled softly to himself as he studied the rows of bottles. He'd never been a great wine drinker and the names on the labels meant nothing to him.

"Can I help you?" said the assistant, who had appeared at his shoulder. Her accent was East European, Polish maybe.

"I'm looking for something red and not too pricey," said Nightingale.

"Spain, France, Italy . . . what country you like?"

Nightingale shrugged. "I'm easy. Just something that tastes good and doesn't cost the earth."

The woman took a bottle and held it up so that he could see the label. "This is a Bordeaux, from France," she said. "Seven ninety-nine."

Nightingale looked pained. "Do you have something with a screw top?" he said. "I don't have a corkscrew."

"I can sell you a corkscrew," said the woman. "Cheap. One ninety-nine."

"A screw top would be better," said Nightingale.

The woman replaced the bottle and selected another. "This is Chianti, from Italy."

Nightingale looked at the screw top and nodded.

"Is it good?"

"It's okay." She squinted at the price label. "It's four ninety-nine."

"Perfect," he said.

Nightingale paid for it and she put it in a plastic bag for him. He walked back to where he'd left his MGB. The shop doorway where Proserpine had been sitting was now empty but the cardboard sign was there, shifting in the wind that was blowing down the street. He climbed into the car and drove away with the bottle of wine on the passenger seat. It took him less than half an hour to drive to the cemetery where Robbie Hoyle was buried. The clouds overhead were threatening rain and he buttoned up his raincoat after he'd parked the car.

He swung the carrier bag as he walked through the cemetery, humming quietly to himself. There were security lights around the church and they cast long shadows from the statues and headstones. The line of conifers behind Robbie's grave swished back and forth in the wind and Nightingale shivered. He heard a rustling sound to his left and he flinched but it was only a brown and white cat, crouched beside a statue of an angel. The cat stared back at Nightingale, its eyes seeming to glow as they reflected back the halogen light.

As he reached Robbie's grave he took the bottle from the bag. The wind whipped the bag from his hands and it blew across the grass towards the church. Nightingale unscrewed the top and then poured a good measure over the soil. "Cheers, mate," he said. "How're things?"

There was a simple wooden cross at the top of the grave giving Robbie's name and the date that he had died. Nightingale nodded at the cross. "Wonder what they'll say on the headstone when they finally put it up?" he said. "Loving husband, doting father, or dumb detective who forgot the Green Cross Code and stepped in front of a black cab?" He raised the bottle in salute, then took a long drink before wiping his mouth with his sleeve and nodding appreciatively. "Not bad," he said. "Not bad at all. Last time it was French, right?" He looked at the label. "You know, I think I might have had some of this at your house, the year before last. Anna's birthday. Remember?" He took another drink from the bottle and then shook his head. "I'm knackered, Robbie," he said. He sat down carefully and crossed his legs, then stuck the bottle in his lap and took out his cigarettes and lighter. Nightingale held up the pack of Marlboro. "You don't mind if I smoke, do you?" he said, then grinned. "A graveyard's just about the only place left where you can have a fag these days," he said. "I bet it's going to be a criminal offence before too long."

Nightingale lit a cigarette, took a long drag on it, and then poured a stream of wine over the grave.

"I'll go and see Anna and the girls soon," he said. "I'm sorry, mate; I haven't been around as often as I should. I just . . ." He shrugged, then took a drink from the bottle. "I never know what to say, Robbie. What the hell can I say? You're dead and they're alone and they miss you like hell." He shook his head and felt tears sting his eyes. "You bastard, Robbie. You stupid bastard." He drew on his cigarette, holding the smoke deep within his lungs for several seconds, before blowing a tight plume of smoke into the air. "People get sick and die; that's the way of the world. People get old and die. Planes crash. Shit happens. But how the hell do you manage to walk under a black cab, Robbie? Look right, look left, and look right again. How bloody hard is that?" He drank more wine and then poured a slug over the soil and watched as it bubbled away. "I wish there was some way I could go back, Robbie. Some way of telling you to watch what you're doing. But that's the bastard thing about time, isn't it? It only goes the one way. There's no going back. So you're dead and you're staying dead and I have to go back to Anna and the girls and make small talk."

Nightingale sighed and lay back on the grass. He stared up at the clouds high above as he took another long pull on his cigarette.

"Robbie, if I'm talking to myself here, let me know, will you? I'd hate to be making a fool of myself." He blew smoke up at the sky. Off in the distance an owl hooted twice and then fell silent.

"I was wondering if that's how it works," said Nightingale quietly. "Maybe you can hear me but I can't hear you. Maybe it's a one-way thing. Your soul is there, watching or doing whatever souls do, and I'm stuck here. I just wish I knew for sure, you know? It's the not knowing that screws with your mind. Until all this started I was a happy enough atheist, or maybe an agnostic. Not that I'm sure what the difference is. Now I really don't know what the hell's going on." Nightingale sat up, took a drink from the bottle, and then poured some more over the grave.

He blew smoke across the grave and then smiled ruefully. "Here's the thing, Robbie. I know you can't communicate with me. If you could've you would've, I'm sure of that. According to Mrs Steadman it's because we're not all on the same frequency. But maybe you can hear me, right? And if you're there listening to me, maybe you can do me a favour." He drank from the bottle and once again used his sleeve to wipe his mouth. "Remember the girl who died at Chelsea Harbour? Sophie Underwood. She's been trying to talk to me and not doing a very good job of it. She's a kid, Robbie. Nine years old when she died and I'm guessing that souls don't age, right?" Nightingale chuckled. "How would I know that? How would anyone know? Age, don't age . . . it's not as if there's a handbook for death and what comes after, is there?" He gestured at the church with the bottle. "And the vicars and priests are no bloody help, are they? Even the ones that aren't paedophiles don't exactly inspire confidence, do they? And the guys at the top seem to be more concerned with not offending the multicultural minority than spreading God's word. Does anyone really believe that God talks to the Archbishop of Canterbury? Because I damn well don't."

He shook his head and took a long pull on his cigarette. "Okay, so here's what I need you to do, Robbie. I need you to take care of Sophie. She doesn't have anyone — her father was a bastard and her mother looked the other way — and I'm guessing that she's lonely and scared, and you were always great with your girls." He poured the rest of the wine over the grave. "So if you're there, Robbie, and if Sophie's around, just take her under your wing, will you? Find out what she wants. And if there is anything I can do to help, I will. Tell her I will, I swear. If she wants me to apologise, then I will. If she blames me for what happened, then maybe she's right. Maybe I could have stopped her from jumping. Hell, I'm not even sure if she jumped. One second she was sitting on the edge of the balcony, the next she was over the edge. Maybe she fell. Maybe she didn't mean to do it." Nightingale put a hand over his eyes and sighed. "It's the first thing I think of when I wake up in the morning, Robbie. And the last thing I think about at night. So if she wants me to apologise, I'll do that."

The cigarette he was holding had almost burned down to the filter and he slotted it into the bottle where it spluttered in the dregs of the wine and went out. He got unsteadily to his feet and stood looking down at the wooden cross.

"I can't bear the thought of you down there, rotting," he said quietly. "Please, please, please, just let me know that there's more to it than that." He closed his eyes and rubbed the bridge of his nose. "If Sophie can try to get through to me, why can't you, Robbie? Why did my parents never try to get in touch after they died?" He took a deep breath and then opened his eyes and stared up at the sky. "Just listen to me, talking to myself again. What the hell is wrong with me?" He winked at the cross. "Catch you later, mate."

He walked back to his car, dropping the empty wine bottle into a rubbish bin on the way out of the churchyard.

CHAPTER
THIRTY-TWO

Nightingale drove from the graveyard to Brixton. He was reluctant to leave the MGB on the street but it was late and he couldn't find a multi-storey car park. He decided to leave it close to Brixton police station in the hope that the proximity of the boys in blue would be a deterrent to any would-be car thief. Just to make sure he took a printed sign out of the glove box and left it on the dashboard: "BATTERY DEAD — AA ON THE WAY."

It was a ten-minute walk to the Flamingo and on the way Nightingale was asked by three different black teenagers if he was looking to buy drugs. The third dealer couldn't have been more than fourteen years old and was riding a BMX bike. He was wearing a black Puffa jacket and gleaming white Nikes.

"Weed, crack, blow?" he said to Nightingale as he pulled up next to him.

"How old are you?"

"How old are you?" said the teenager.

"Old enough not to be buying drugs from someone I don't know," Nightingale said. "How do I know you're not an undercover cop?" He carried on walking and the teenager followed him on the bike.

252

"I'm a kid," he said. "They don't have kids as cops."

"How do I know that? Maybe they've got a special kids unit."

"Why would I be a cop and try to sell you drugs?"

"Entrapment," said Nightingale.

"You're fucking crazy," said the teenager.

Nightingale stopped and studied the boy. "You're really selling drugs?"

"Sure. What do you want?"

"But you're not carrying, right?"

"Course not. You give me the money." He nodded over at the other side of the road where another teenager in a blue Puffa jacket was sitting on a bike. "He'll give you what you want."

"Clever," said Nightingale.

"What are you, Five-O?" asked the teenager suspiciously.

"If I was a cop I'd have busted you already for dealing," said Nightingale. He took out his wallet, extracted a fifty-pound note and moved as if he was going to give it to the teenager. "You're out every night?"

The teenager grinned at the banknote. "Rain or snow." He reached for the note but Nightingale snatched it away.

"What about when that guy was shot last year?"

"This is Brixton," said the teenager, standing up on the pedals of his bike. "People get shot all the time."

"July the twentieth. Dwayne Robinson. Dealer from Clapham."

"Oh yeah, him," said the teenager. He mimed firing a gun at his own head. "He's not dead, though, right? I heard he was in a coma. Brain dead or summfink."

"That's changed," said Nightingale. "He's dead."

The teenager shrugged. "Shit happens," he said. He nodded at the fifty-pound note. "You gonna give me that or not?"

"Where were you when he was shot?"

"You think I did it? You're mad, man."

Nightingale chuckled. "I'm just asking if you know what happened. You're a smart kid and I bet you keep your ear to the ground."

The teenager nodded at the banknote. "You gonna give me that?"

"If you've got something to tell me, sure."

The teenager held out a gloved hand. "Cash up front."

"Info first."

The teenager shook his head. His eyes were hard and his jaw was clamped shut. Nightingale gave him the money. The teenager pocketed it and gripped his handle-bars as if he was about to take off. "The shooter was a white guy."

"Yeah, I know that. Did you see it?"

"Nah, but I heard the shot. It was around the corner from the Flamingo."

"Yeah, I know that too."

"Do you know the gun jammed?" Nightingale raised his eyebrows. "Yeah, he shot Dwayne in the head and then went to shoot him again but the gun jammed and he ran off."

"How do you know that?"

The teenager tapped the side of his nose. "I got my sources."

"But did your source see it or did he get it from someone else?"

The teenager shrugged. "Maybe he saw it; maybe he spoke to someone who saw it. But that's the word. One shot in the head and then he was gonna shoot him again but the gun didn't fire and he ran off and got picked up by a bike."

"A motorbike?"

"No, a BMX. What do you think, man?"

"Do you know what sort of bike?"

"A trail bike. That's what I was told. Leathers and a full-face helmet and off they went."

"And does anyone have any idea who did it? Turf war?"

The teenager pulled a face. "Dwayne never did nothing on our manor. He knew there'd be a war if he did."

"But there'd be no problems with him going to the Flamingo?"

"Business is business and social is social," said the teenager. "Providing he don't try to sell gear here no one's going to care where he drinks."

"Okay, thanks. What's your name?"

"Jason," said the teenager.

"You take care, Jason." He took out his wallet and gave him one of his business cards. "If you hear anything else, you give me a call. I've more fifties with your name on them."

Jason slipped the card in the pocket of his jacket, winked at Nightingale, and pedalled away.

CHAPTER
THIRTY-THREE

The Flamingo was on the first floor above a row of shops in a side road not far from Brixton Tube Station. There were two big black men wearing glossy black bomber jackets and black cargo pants standing at the entrance. Two young white guys in tight Versace jeans walked by them, holding hands, and headed up the stairs. The doormen both had earpieces and their IDs hanging on lanyards. They smiled professionally at Nightingale as he walked up. They were both well over six feet tall and looked as if they spent a lot of the time in the gym. Or swallowing steroids. Or possibly both.

"I thought this was a salsa club?" he asked.

"Salsa is Tuesday and Friday," said the first doorman. "Wednesday is swing night. Saturday is disco. Thursday is Gay Night."

"And today is Thursday," said Nightingale.

"Yes it is."

"Cool," said Nightingale.

"You gay?" asked the second doorman.

"Do I look gay?" asked Nightingale, taking out his cigarettes.

"That would be sexist, us making an assumption like that," said the first doorman. "Be like you assuming I'm black just by looking at me."

Nightingale chuckled and slipped a cigarette between his lips. Another gay couple arrived — a young blond man wearing mascara and a black man with a shaved head and a tight-fitting Everlast shirt — and Nightingale stepped aside to let them get by.

"Maybe you should try another night," said the second doorman. He had a large diamond in his right ear. "You might have fun on disco night. We get an older crowd."

"I like women so I guess for the purposes of tonight you can put me down as a lesbian," said Nightingale. He offered the pack to the doormen but they both shook their heads. "Were you guys here when Dwayne Robinson got shot?"

The two doormen looked at each other, then back at Nightingale. "You a cop?"

"Private," said Nightingale.

"We don't talk to cops."

"Well, actually, you do because if you don't then you lose your Security Industry Licence and then you lose your job. And while the few quid you get paid for standing here freezing your nuts off probably doesn't mean much I'm damn sure you wouldn't want to lose the kickbacks you get from the dealers you let in." The first doorman took a menacing step towards Nightingale but Nightingale smiled amiably. "Look, I'm not here to rock anybody's boat, I just want some guidance as to what happened to Dwayne, that's all."

"Who are you working for, if you're private? Someone's got to be footing your bill."

"Yeah, this time I'm working pro bono," said Nightingale.

"What, the U2 singer?" said the first doorman, straight-faced.

Nightingale was just about to explain what "pro bono" meant when the man started laughing and poked his colleague in the ribs. "Pro bono, get it?"

Nightingale grinned. "Nice one. Seriously, guys, I know you probably wouldn't want to tell the cops much but I'm just trying to get a handle on what happened." He pulled out his wallet and fished out two fifty-pound notes.

"You're not thinking of bribing us?" said the first doorman.

"That was the idea," said Nightingale.

"With fifty?"

"There's a hundred here."

"And there're two of us."

Nightingale raised his hands in surrender. "My bad," he said. He took out two more banknotes and gave the doormen a hundred pounds each. The money disappeared into their bomber jackets.

"Dwayne took a bullet in the head, that's what happened," said the first doorman.

"Here?"

"Down the road aways," said the second doorman, gesturing with his chin.

"Anyone see it happen?"

"He'd gone around the corner. We heard a shot but that's not that unusual around here. Bit later we heard an ambulance."

"Who called the ambulance, do you know?"

The second doorman shrugged his massive shoulders. "A neighbour maybe?"

"There were no screams? No shouting?"

"Down this way nobody bothers screaming when someone gets shot. You just go on your way. You don't want to be a witness because witnesses have a way of ending up as casualties."

Nightingale nodded. "Okay. And he was shot around the corner? See, if he was shot in the back of the head, doesn't that mean whoever shot Dwayne must have followed him around the corner?"

"We didn't see nothing," said the first doorman.

"Yeah, but you wouldn't know, would you? You wouldn't have seen the shot fired but you might have seen the killer walking down the street after him or at the cross-roads there." He pointed at the corner with his cigarette. "Guy follows Dwayne around the corner so if you'd been looking you'd have seen him."

"Wasn't looking," said the first doorman. "We're here to watch who's coming in. Don't much care about what goes on down the road."

"What about when he arrived? Was he here on his own?"

The first doorman frowned and put his head on one side. "Yeah, I think so."

"How did he get here? Car? Cab? Walk?"

The two doormen looked at each other and then they both shrugged. "It was six months ago," said the first doorman.

"Car, I think," said the second doorman. "Big and black. Tinted windows."

"That sums up the wheels of pretty much every dealer in London," said the first doorman.

"I'm just saying that I thought he came in a black four-wheel drive, that's all."

"You don't remember who was driving?" asked Nightingale.

The doorman shook his head. "I might not even be right about the car. It was six months ago."

"What about when he left? He was on his own, right?"

The first doorman nodded. "Yeah, he came out talking on his mobile. He was looking for a car."

"A cab?"

"No, he was carrying on because the car wasn't there. Then he walked off."

"So someone was supposed to have picked him up?"

"That's the gist, yeah," said the first doorman.

"And do you have any idea who he saw while he was inside?"

The second doorman stamped his feet to keep warm. "We work the doors. You need to talk to the guys inside."

A minicab pulled up and four young men piled out and rushed up the stairs, giggling. One of them blew the doormen a kiss as he went by.

Nightingale dropped his cigarette butt onto the ground. "Oh well," he said. "I suppose I'd better go in."

"It's a tenner," said the first doorman. "That gets you in and two drinks. You pay at the top of the stairs."

"Thanks, guys," said Nightingale.

"I still think you'd have more fun on disco night," said the second doorman.

"I'm not here for fun; I'm here to work," said Nightingale as he headed up the stairs.

"Good luck with that," said the first doorman, and the two men laughed.

CHAPTER
THIRTY-FOUR

The upstairs bar was hot and airless and the music was loud enough to be almost painful. There was a dance floor at the far end of the room above which a giant mirrored ball was slowly turning. There were several dozen men dancing together and Nightingale couldn't help but notice that they were all younger, better-looking and fitter than he was. Sweat was already beading on his forehead so he took off his raincoat and slung it over his shoulder. He pushed his way to the bar, which ran the full length of the room. Two young black men in tight white T-shirts and even tighter denim shorts were mixing cocktails as they swivelled their hips to the music and another was pulling glasses out of a dishwasher. Nightingale managed to catch the eye of an Asian barmaid with waist-length pigtails and mouthed "Corona". He took his drink and managed to find a space close to a fire exit. To the left of the dance floor was a female DJ, a young black girl with a shaved head and giant hooped earrings, who looked as if she was in the grip of a perpetual epileptic fit. Any idea of showing Robinson's photograph to the customers had gone out of the window. It was far too noisy to start

263

asking questions and he doubted that they were the same crowd that would turn up for salsa night.

As he sipped his lager a middle-aged man with receding hair and a ponytail appeared at his shoulder. He was wearing a pale blue V-neck sweater with damp stains under the arms and leather jeans. He was also holding a bottle of Corona and he held it up and smiled at Nightingale. "Snap," he said.

Nightingale nodded and raised his bottle. "Breakfast of champions," he said.

He looked across at the dance floor. In the middle was a young punk girl in black leather, her head lowered but her black eyes staring straight at him. Proserpine. Her black and white collie was sitting next to her, its tongue lolling out of the side of its mouth. Nightingale frowned. There was no way that a dog would have been allowed into the bar. Two men moved together to hug in front of her, and when they moved apart Proserpine and the dog had gone. Nightingale blinked, not sure if he'd really seen her or if he'd imagined it.

"Do you want to dance?" asked the man, moving his hips suggestively.

"Not really my thing," said Nightingale. The music seemed to increase in volume so he put his head closer to the man's ear. He caught a whiff of expensive aftershave. "Any idea where I can smoke?" he asked.

The man winked and slipped his arm around Nightingale's waist. "You don't waste any time, do you?" He nodded at the sign to the Gents. "We can do it in there," he said.

Nightingale frowned, then he laughed when he realised what the man meant. He fished out his pack of Marlboro and showed it to him and the man laughed too.

"Ah, wrong end of the stick," he said, releasing his grip on Nightingale. He pointed to a doorway on the other side of the bar. "There's a terrace upstairs."

Nightingale gave him a thumbs up then threaded his way to the door and up a flight of stairs leading to a small decked terrace that overlooked the alley at the rear of the building. There was a brick wall around the edge of the terrace and at each corner there was a large propane patio heater with orange flames flickering under black metal canopies.

In the middle of the terrace were a dozen or so smokers huddled around two waist-high tables. The smokers had split into sexes with four women standing around one table and the men at the other. Nightingale lit a cigarette. A blonde waitress dressed all in black came up the stairs carrying a tray and she began collecting empty glasses and bottles.

"Busy night?" he asked.

"Busy every night," she said. She had an East European accent.

They both looked up as they heard a helicopter fly overhead, playing a searchlight over the rooftops.

"Are you Polish?" he asked the waitress.

"Hungarian," she said.

"Sorry."

"Sorry I'm Hungarian? Why? You don't like Hungarians?"

"No, I meant I'm sorry I was wrong."

Her face broke into a grin, showing uneven greyish teeth. "I was joking with you."

"Okay," said Nightingale. "You got me. How long have you been working here?"

"A year," she said. "Daytime I study computers." She finished loading her tray and was about to head downstairs when he pulled out the photograph of Robinson and Smith and showed it to her.

He tapped Robinson's face. "This guy here, he was at the salsa night last July. He was shot outside."

She bit down on her lower lip as she studied the photograph. "I remember, yes."

A siren burst into life in the distance. An ambulance.

"You remember him? Or you remember him being shot?"

"Both," said the waitress. "Salsa night."

"Was he dancing?"

She shook her head. "He was up here."

"Smoking?"

She shook her head again. "That's why I remember. He was standing over there," she said and gestured at the far corner of the terrace where two middle-aged men in matching camouflage shirts and cargo pants were French kissing. "He asked for a bottle of champagne, Cristal, which is why I remember. And he gave me a big tip."

Nightingale put the picture away. "You told the police this?"

She nodded. "Yes, they spoke to all the staff. They wanted to know if he'd been with someone but he was here on his own."

266

"He didn't talk to anyone?"

"He chatted to two men for a while but they weren't with him. I saw them shaking hands and then they left."

"And you told the police that?"

She nodded again. "They showed me some photographs but I didn't know their names. They do drink here sometimes, though." She lowered her voice. "I think they sell drugs, you know."

"But they left first, right?"

"I'm not sure if they left or if they were just up here to smoke and then went downstairs."

"But after they went downstairs, Dwayne stayed here?"

"For a while. He kept looking at his watch."

"So he was waiting for someone?"

"I think so. That's what it looked like."

"And then he left and that's when he got shot?"

She shrugged. "I guess so. I was down in the main bar when he left. The bottle was still half-full. I remember leaving it there for an hour just in case he came back, but he didn't."

Nightingale thanked her and gave her a twenty-pound note. He finished his lager and cigarette and then left the nightclub and headed back to his car.

There was a young couple lying in sleeping bags in a shop doorway, their arms wrapped around each other. By their feet was a paper cup with loose change in it and a hand-written cardboard sign. Nightingale jumped as he saw what was written on the cardboard in capital letters: "PLEASE HELP ME, JACK." He took a step back and slipped off the pavement. A black cab missed him by inches, the slipstream tugging at his raincoat. Nightingale stepped back onto the pavement, his heart racing. He looked again at the piece of cardboard. It said: "HOMELESS — PLEASE HELP" and there was a smiley face.

The girl opened her eyes and sneered at him. "What are you looking at, pervert?"

"What?" said Nightingale. "Nothing." He put his hand into his pocket, pulled out a handful of change and dropped it into the paper cup. The girl closed her eyes and snuggled up to her boyfriend.

As Nightingale walked away he phoned Perry Smith and asked him for Dwayne Robinson's mobile phone number.

"What, that's your plan?" said Smith. "Phone up the dead guy and ask him who shot him? It's no wonder you stopped being a cop."

"Very funny," said Nightingale. "He made a call just before he was shot. I want to find out who he spoke to."

"You can do that?"

"Yeah, Perry, I can do that. Now give me the number and stop wasting my seventy-two hours."

"No can do," said Perry. "He used throwaways, and he made a big thing about it. He didn't just toss the Sim card; he'd dump the phone as well. He said that these days they can track a phone no matter what Sim card's in it."

"So you don't know the number of the phone he had that night?"

"That's what I just said, innit?"

"Shit," said Nightingale. The line went dead.

Nightingale waited until he was back in his Bayswater flat before phoning Dan Evans.

"Hell's bells, it's after midnight," groaned Evans.

"Were you asleep?"

"I'm on the school run tomorrow because the missus isn't feeling well. So yes, I was asleep."

"Sorry, mate, but I didn't want to call you in the office, me being persona non grata and all."

Evans sighed. "What do you want?"

"Dwayne Robinson had a mobile phone on him when he was killed."

"So?"

"It was a throwaway, a pay-as-you-go. I need the number."

"Why?"

"Don't ask and I won't tell," said Nightingale.

"Please don't tell me you're going to be playing fast and loose with the Data Protection Act."

"That's why I said not to ask. Have you got the number?"

"Not with me, no. I'll give you a bell tomorrow."

"You're a star, Dan. Sweet dreams."

CHAPTER
THIRTY-FIVE

Dan Evans was as good as his word and first thing on Friday morning he called Nightingale's office and gave him the number of the mobile phone that had been found on Dwayne Robinson's body. Nightingale had contacts at most of the large mobile phone companies. The first guy he called was able to tell him which firm handled Robinson's number and the second guy agreed to get a list of calls made to and from the phone for his normal fee of £250. Nightingale made coffee for himself and Jenny, read the *Sun* and *Private Eye*, smoked three cigarettes and then decided that he would go and see Anna Hoyle.

"If anything needs doing, give me a call," he told Jenny.

"Will you be back today or are you away for the weekend?"

"I probably won't be back today," said Nightingale. "You might as well knock off early yourself."

"Is everything okay, Jack?"

"Sure, why?"

"I don't know. You just seem . . ." She shrugged. "Unenthusiastic. Like you're bored with the business."

"I'm fine. I'm not sleeping well, that's all."

"What's wrong?"

"Nothing. Really."

"It's Sophie, isn't it? Are you still having dreams about her?"

"Nightmares, more like. It's okay. It'll pass."

"Can I help?"

He shook his head.

"I still think you should talk this through with someone."

"Like Barbara, you mean?"

"Barbara's a psychologist, though I'm sure she could help. But I was thinking of a therapist, maybe."

Nightingale laughed. "You are joking, right?"

"You're not sleeping. You keep talking about this Sophie. And you've had a very stressful few weeks."

"I'm a big boy, Jenny."

"That's the problem, right there. You've got this macho man thing going on. Like nothing affects you. But look what you've been through. You find out that your mum and dad weren't your real parents. Your biological father blows his head off with a shotgun. Then your uncle kills your aunt and then kills himself. Then your biological mother kills herself. And —"

Nightingale held up his hand to silence her. "I get it, I get it," he said.

"There you go again," she said. "You just don't want to talk about it. But that simply means you're burying it. If you don't talk about stuff like that it'll fester in your subconscious and come out in some other way."

"Where are you getting this from? The Discovery Channel?"

"And then you make a joke about it. But it's not funny."

"I know it's not funny."

"At some point you're going to have to deal with what happened."

"You think I've got PTSD, is that it? Post-traumatic stress disorder?"

"I'm not saying that, Jack. I'm just saying that maybe you should think about talking it through with someone. Someone who knows about stress."

"I'll think about it," he said.

"No you won't," she said. "You'll just go on your own sweet way."

CHAPTER
THIRTY-SIX

Nightingale walked around to the multi-storey car park where he'd left his MGB and drove south of the river. There were no spaces in the street outside Anna Hoyle's neat semi-detached house in Raynes Park and he had to park a good five-minute walk away. It started to rain as he walked up to the front door and he jogged the last few yards and pressed the doorbell.

Anna opened the door. Her blonde hair was clipped back and there were dark patches under her eyes as if she hadn't been sleeping well. She wasn't wearing make-up and he could see that she'd been biting her nails.

"Jack, lovely to see you," she said. "Come on in, out of the rain." She closed the door behind him and pecked him on the cheek. "It seems like ages since I've seen you."

Nightingale felt his cheeks redden. The last time he'd seen her had been at Robbie's funeral. "I'm sorry, I've been worked off my feet," he said, but he grimaced as he realised how lame that sounded. He took off his raincoat. "Are the kids around?" he asked.

"Sarah's at a sleepover with a couple of her friends and the twins are napping." She put a hand on his arm.

"Come on into the kitchen. Do you want coffee? Or wine? I was going to open a bottle of wine."

"Bit early for me, love, but coffee would be great," he said, hanging his coat on the back of the door. He did a double take as he saw Robbie's coat hanging there.

"I know," she said, catching his look. "I can't bring myself to throw it away. It's funny: when I come in and see it my heart always skips a beat, like he's back, then my stomach lurches as I remember . . ." She put a hand up to her face. "I'm sorry, Jack, you're only just in the door and look at me, the grieving widow."

She took him through to the kitchen and ushered him over to a chair. The washing machine was on, just about to go into the spin cycle. Anna switched on the kettle.

"How is everything?" asked Nightingale.

"There're good days and bad days," said Anna, spooning coffee into a cafetière. She forced a smile. "Mainly bad, actually."

"And the girls?"

"Sarah's just shut down. She doesn't cry, doesn't do anything really. It's as if a part of her died along with Robbie. I had to practically drag her into the car to get her to the sleepover."

Nightingale felt tears prick his eyes. He felt totally helpless knowing that there was nothing he could say or do that would come close to easing the pain she was going through.

"The twins are okay, but they just don't understand. They keep asking when Daddy's coming back and I tell them that Daddy's up in heaven, so then they say that

274

they want to go to see him there." She put her hands up to her face as if she was wiping away tears, but her eyes were dry.

Nightingale stood up and put his arms around her. She buried her face in his chest.

"I don't know how I can get through this, Jack. It's too much for me."

"One day at a time, love. That's all you can do."

"I don't want to live without him. I know that sounds selfish but I keep thinking we'd be better off if . . ." She tailed off and held him tightly.

"That's crazy talk, love," said Nightingale. "Robbie would be as mad as hell if he heard you talking like that."

"I miss him, Jack."

"We all do. But you know that Robbie would want you and the children to move on with your lives. You know that, don't you?" Anna nodded, and sniffed. Nightingale stroked the back of her head. "My parents died when I was a teenager," he said. "They died suddenly, too, and I never got the chance to say goodbye. One day they were there, the next they were gone. I thought I'd never get over it. But you do. Bit by bit. You never forget, you never stop missing them, but day by day it hurts a little less. Then one day you wake up and it doesn't hurt at all. It takes time. It takes a long time. But eventually . . ."

Anna shook her head. "This hurt is never going to go away, Jack," she said. She put her hands on his chest and gently pushed him back. "I'm sorry," she said. "I still get weepy." She forced a smile and wiped her eyes with a tea towel. "Go and sit down in the front room. I'll bring in your coffee."

Nightingale sat down and waited for her. There was a wedding photograph on the mantelpiece, and next to it a family photograph. Robbie, Anna and the three girls. Nightingale stared at the photograph and shook his head. "You stupid, stupid bastard," he whispered.

Anna came in with two mugs of coffee. She put them on the table in front of Nightingale then sat down next to him. "Sorry about that," she said.

"Anna, you don't have to apologise to me for anything." He picked up the mug and sipped his coffee. "How is everything? Money's come through all right?"

She nodded. "The Federation has been a great help, and Superintendent Chalmers has been around twice since the funeral." She smiled at the frown that flashed across Nightingale's face. "I know you and Chalmers have a history, but he's been really helpful and supportive. A real rock."

"I didn't think he had much time for Robbie. To be honest, I don't think Chalmers cares about anyone other than himself."

"Robbie never liked him, and certainly didn't respect him as a copper. But ever since the accident he's been a godsend. The last time he just sat on the sofa and drank tea and listened to me for more than an hour. At one point he was close to tears."

Nightingale wanted to say something sarcastic but he could see that Anna was serious. He wondered if he'd misjudged the superintendent. Maybe the problem that he had with the man was a total one-off, and to the rest of the world he was sweetness and light.

"Did he say anything about me?"

Anna shook her head in disbelief. "You really do think that the whole bloody world revolves around you, don't you?"

"What do you mean?"

"Because you don't like him and because he was here with me, you naturally assume that we'd be talking about you."

"Anna, that's not it, really."

"It's okay, Jack, I'm not upset. It's just funny. You've always been like that; it's your way. In your mind you're the centre of the universe and nothing is ever going to convince you otherwise. So the answer to your question is no, your name didn't come up."

"He's got it in for me, that's all."

"And you thought what? That he came round here with presents for the girls just to spite you?" She laughed. "Your face," she said.

"What?"

"You look so shocked. Don't worry, I'm not getting at you."

"I'm sorry, really I am. I didn't mean to sound petty. But he's trying to put me away for a murder I didn't commit."

Anna looked concerned. "Are you serious?"

"Some drug dealer got shot in the head last summer and he's convinced that I did it. He keeps hauling me in for questioning." He held up his hands. "But you're right. It's nothing to do with you. Sorry. And fair play to Chalmers, for doing the right thing."

"Is that what I am, Jack? The right thing?"

"That came out wrong," he said. "My foot just keeps going straight into my mouth these days. I'm sorry."

"I'm only teasing you," said Anna. "I've known you long enough to realise that your heart is in the right place." She nodded at his coffee. "Do you want a biscuit with that? I've got some Hobnobs in the kitchen."

"I'm fine, thanks." He sipped his coffee. "I went to Robbie's grave yesterday."

"Why did you do that?"

Nightingale smiled. "I took him a drink."

"You did what?"

"I took a bottle of wine. Shared it with him."

"You don't know anything about wine."

"I took advice. Chianti. It was okay."

Anna nodded appreciatively. "Robbie was always a big fan of Chianti," she said. "Good choice." She forced a smile. "Why did you go, Jack?"

"You'll think I'm crazy," he said.

"That's a given," she said. "It wasn't just to take him a bottle of wine, was it?"

"I wanted to talk to him, and that seemed to be the place to go."

"Talk to him? You mean literally have a conversation?"

"Not literally, no," said Nightingale. "It's difficult to explain."

"Try."

Nightingale shrugged. "I've been under a lot of pressure these last few weeks and in the old days, when I needed to talk something through, it was always Robbie I went to, you know. He was my father confessor."

"There's something you want to confess?"

"Figure of speech," said Nightingale. "I just wanted to talk."

"I can't bring myself to go," said Anna. "The thought of him lying there, in the ground . . ." She shuddered. "I'm not sure if I should take the girls either. There I am telling them that Daddy's in Heaven, then I go to show them a grave and tell them Daddy's six feet under the ground in a wooden box."

"I guess the two aren't mutually exclusive," said Nightingale. "The body's in the grave, the soul is in Heaven."

Anna sat back on the sofa, a look of surprise on her face. "Wow, I've never heard you talking about Heaven before. Do you believe that, Jack? Do you believe in Heaven?"

"I'm starting to," he said. "Though I guess I'm starting to realise that there might be a Hell and if there's a Hell then there has to be a Heaven. But I don't think that angels sit on clouds playing harps all day." He drank some coffee. "What about you?"

"Do I believe in Heaven?" She smiled ruefully and shook her head. "Of course not." She stopped smiling and looked at him seriously. "I wish I did, Jack. Of course I do. I tell the girls that Robbie's up in Heaven watching us and I can see how that makes them feel better, but in my heart I know it's not true. It's simply not possible. Robbie's dead and that's the end of it. We have to move on with our lives. That's easier said than done but that's the only choice we have. It's like you said: one day at a time."

"Can I ask you something? Something that might sound a bit stupid?"

"Since when has that stopped you before?" said Anna. She smiled again. "Go on. What?"

Nightingale took a deep breath before replying. "Have you ever felt Robbie's presence? You know, felt that he was here?"

"All the time," she said. "But that's different. That's just my subconscious trying to make me feel better. I dream about Robbie every night and it's always as if he is still here. And then for a few seconds when I wake up it's as if he's still in bed with me. And I told you about his coat. This is our home so he's always here, in spirit. That doesn't mean that I believe in ghosts."

"You don't? You don't think that your soul lives on after you die?"

"Jack, what the hell's happened to you? What's brought this on?"

Nightingale desperately wanted a cigarette but he knew that Anna didn't like him smoking in the house. "It sounds crazy."

"Yes, it does." She leaned forward, concern etched into her face. "Are you okay?"

"I'm fine."

"You don't sound fine. Is it because you went to Robbie's grave?"

"That's part of it." He shrugged. "I don't know, Anna. I remember at the funeral how I kept looking around to see where he was."

She shook her head sadly. "I was doing the same," she said.

"Everyone who loved him, everyone who worked with him, they were all there. The only one who wasn't there was Robbie. Except of course he was. In the coffin. But I kept wondering why he wasn't standing there with us. That doesn't make sense, does it?" He put his head in his hands. "I'm sorry, I'm rambling."

"No you're not; you're trying to sort out your feelings. I understand, Jack. I'm going through the same thing myself. It's how you deal with loss. I lost my husband; you lost your best friend." She sighed.

"And you're sure that Robbie's gone for ever? That dead means dead?"

"Don't you?"

Nightingale flopped back in his chair. "I just don't know."

"Jack, if Robbie was still out there somewhere, don't you think I'd know? Don't you think he'd at least let me and the girls know? You think he'd want us to hurt the way we're hurting? What about your parents? Did you ever feel that they came back?"

"No," he said, shaking his head.

"The dead don't come back because they can't. That's what being dead means."

"Maybe they're there but they can't let us know." He picked up his coffee mug. "Jenny said something about caterpillars."

"Caterpillars?"

"Yeah, she said that caterpillars turn into butterflies, but you never see the butterflies hanging out with the caterpillars, do you? Caterpillars turn into butterflies and they fly away. Maybe it's the same with us. We die, we change, and we move on. And we can't communicate with those we leave behind. Or maybe we just don't want to. Maybe we don't want to spoil the fun." He drank the rest of his coffee but he couldn't taste it. When he put down the mug, his hand was trembling.

"Jack, you're starting to worry me now," said Anna.

Nightingale forced a smile. "I'm sorry," he said. "Just thinking too much."

"No, it's more than that," she said. "Have you looked in a mirror recently? You look like you haven't slept for a month."

"I'm fine."

"Clearly you're not. What's going on? What's worrying you?"

Nightingale looked at her and tried to hide the turmoil he was going through. He couldn't tell her. He couldn't explain about Sophie, not without appearing to be totally crazy. Anna was right. Robbie was dead and the dead didn't come back, and if they did then surely Robbie would be first in line. His death had been sudden and unexpected so he'd never had the chance to say goodbye to the people he loved. "It's nothing," he lied. "I guess visiting Robbie's grave shook me up."

"Are you sure?"

She held his look and Nightingale felt that she was looking right through him. She'd have made a great interrogator. He tried to smile convincingly. "I'm sure."

She relaxed and Nightingale realised that she believed him. He felt a sudden stab of guilt. He'd lied to her and she'd believed him without hesitation. But he knew that he'd done the right thing. Anna had more than enough to worry about already.

"You know, living on your own isn't helping. When are you going to get serious about Jenny?"

"What?" said Nightingale. "She works for me."

"I know that. But she's the perfect girl for you, not least because she puts up with your nonsense. Ask her out and have done with it."

Nightingale laughed and shook his head. "I don't think she'd be interested anyway."

"You should go for it," said Anna. "Ask her."

"Jenny's a great assistant; the office would fall apart without her."

"You're assuming that it'll all go wrong. You might get a pleasant surprise. You're thirty-three years old and single. It's time for you to settle down."

Nightingale grinned. "Maybe," he said.

"I'm serious, Jack. You've been on your own for too long."

"I'm happy enough, Anna, really. And I'm not going to ask Jenny out just because she's available."

"And you've never asked yourself why she works for you? Because I'm damn sure it's not for the money."

"I pay okay," said Nightingale. "And I'm a good boss."

Anna laughed. "I've seen the two of you together. She's got a soft spot for you."

"Yeah, a patch of quicksand behind her dad's mansion," he said. He groaned in defeat. "Okay, I give up. I'll think about it."

"Well, don't leave it too long. A girl like Jenny's going to be snapped up sooner rather than later."

Nightingale held up his hands. "Okay, okay, I hear you."

They both laughed and Anna wiped a tear from her eye and then her laughs turned into sobs. She put her hands over her face as she cried and her whole body started to shake. Nightingale hurried over to her, put his arms around her and held her tightly.

"I miss him, Jack," she sobbed. "I miss him so much."

"I know," said Nightingale, as she buried her face in his chest. "So do I."

CHAPTER
THIRTY-SEVEN

Nightingale had left Graham Lord's card on the table by the phone. As he sat and watched Saturday afternoon racing from Sandown Park on Channel 4 he drank a bottle of Corona and kept looking over at the card. On the way to the kitchen to get a second bottle of beer he picked up the card, looked at it, then put it down. He drank the second bottle of beer lying on the sofa, then he picked up the card again and dialled the number.

"Mr Nightingale," said Lord before Nightingale had spoken. "I was waiting for you to call."

"How do you know my name?" said Nightingale. "I don't remember telling you my name."

"You didn't," said Lord. "You're calling to arrange an appointment?"

Nightingale didn't reply. The hairs on the back of his neck were standing up and he shivered. He felt as if he was being played, as if a trap was being set for him and he was being invited to step inside.

"Mr Nightingale? You want an appointment?"

"I guess so, yes," said Nightingale.

"What about tomorrow evening? Sunday is always a good day." He chuckled softly. "The Lord's Day, of course. Shall we say eight o'clock?"

"Okay," said Nightingale.

"My fee is two hundred pounds," said Lord. "I'm afraid that's my standard charge."

"What sort of guarantee is there that I'll talk to Sophie?" said Nightingale.

"There are no guarantees; but trust me, you'll have a much more satisfactory experience than you had at Marylebone."

"And how does it work? We just sit down and talk?"

Lord chuckled. "It's a bit more complicated than that," he said. "But don't worry, Mr Nightingale. I know what I'm doing. I'll see you tomorrow at eight. My address is on my card. And if you have anything that belongs to Sophie, please bring it with you."

CHAPTER
THIRTY-EIGHT

There were three baristas working behind the counter, all Polish, all female, and all with dyed-blonde hair, as if Starbucks had a factory that turned them out with the same efficiency that they produced their coffees and cookies. Nightingale ordered a cappuccino and carried it over to a table near the door that led to the toilets. He looked at his watch. He was early. The coffee shop was busy with Saturday shoppers boosting their caffeine levels before heading back into the fray. There was a copy of that day's *Daily Express* on the table next to his and he retrieved it and flicked through it as he waited. He was halfway through his coffee when he saw a black Lexus pull up on the other side of the road. Perry Smith climbed out of the back and stood on the pavement, looking around. He was wearing a black Puffa jacket over a dark blue tracksuit and white Nikes. A big man eased himself out of the car, slammed the door and joined Smith on the pavement. Smith pointed in the direction of the coffee shop and the two men crossed the road. Nightingale felt his heart begin to pound and he took a deep breath to steady himself.

The heavy walked into the coffee shop first, his eyes watchful. Smith followed, then grinned when he saw

Nightingale. He swaggered over, his arms swinging loosely at his sides. He sat down opposite Nightingale and unzipped his jacket. "You just made it," he said, looking at a chunky gold watch on his wrist. "Your seventy-two hours are almost up." The heavy stood behind Nightingale, his arms crossed.

"Yeah, it wasn't easy," said Nightingale. He nodded at the heavy. "I told you to come alone. Tyson here can wait outside."

"Anything you want to say to me you can say in front of T-Bone," said Smith.

Nightingale shook his head. "You've no idea what I'm going to say. I might be here to tell you that I know that you've been screwing T-Bone's wife and you wouldn't want him to know that."

The heavy stared impassively at Nightingale.

"T-Bone ain't married," said Smith.

"That was an example. Trust me, what I've got to tell you is for your ears only. You won't want it generally known." Smith looked around the coffee shop, rubbing the back of his neck. "You're not scared, are you?"

"I'm not scared of nothing," said Smith.

Nightingale held up his hands. "No offence," he said. "You just seem nervous. Do you want a coffee? Or a muffin?"

"No I don't want a fucking coffee or muffin and I don't want tea and fucking crumpets. Just tell me what you want."

"Okay," said Nightingale. "You know why I wanted to meet you here?"

Smith snarled at him. "You like coffee?"

288

"Nah, I like CCTV." He nodded at the camera in the ceiling that was covering the seating area. "With the eye in the sky looking at us you're not going to do anything crazy."

"I hear you."

"And if this doesn't go well and something bad happens to me down the line, the cops will come knocking on your door."

"I ain't scared of no cops, and I ain't scared of no CCTV. Now tell me what the fuck you want or I'm out of here."

Nightingale leaned forward. "I know what happened to Dwayne. The thing is, do you?"

Smith's forehead creased into a frown. "What the fuck do you mean?"

"Have you been blowing smoke all this time, making it look like you give a shit who shot Dwayne? Because if you have it's all going to backfire on you."

Smith's lips pressed together tightly and his hands clenched as if he was about to attack Nightingale, but then he relaxed and nodded slowly. "Tell me what you found out and we'll take it from there."

Nightingale took a folded sheet of paper from the inside pocket of his raincoat and slid it across the table. "The first number there is the throwaway mobile that Dwayne was using the night he was shot. Obviously he couldn't throw it away, him being dead and all. I was able to get the records for the phone the night he died. The second number is the number that he called about three minutes before he was shot."

Smith unfolded the sheet and looked at the numbers. "Who did he call?"

"I don't know," said Nightingale. "The number's dead now. I'm guessing it was a throwaway too. But I was able to get a list of calls that were made from the second phone. The bottom two numbers are the calls made from the second phone after Dwayne phoned."

Smith looked at the last two numbers and his eyebrows went skywards. "That last number is mine, innit?"

"That's right. I thought you always used throwaways."

"That phone's not for business." He reached into his pocket and pulled out an iPhone. He put it on the table. "Friends and family," he said.

Nightingale sat back in his chair. "You can see why I'd be worried, then."

"I don't see what the problem is," said Smith.

"The problem is that third number, the one that the second phone called before it called you. It's not a throw-away either. It belongs to a gangster down Bromley way, did a ten-stretch for armed robbery when he was in his twenties but hasn't been in trouble with the law since. But word on the street is that he's a hitman."

"Hitman?"

"I had his name run through the Police National Computer and there's plenty of intel on him but no hard evidence. Name of Ben Marshal. Reckoned to carry out murder for hire at fifty grand a pop. About ten minutes after Marshal gets the call, he sends back a text message. A smiley face."

"Say what?"

"A smiley face. A colon, a dash and a bracket." He drew the symbol on the table with his finger. "A smiley face."

"So what are you saying, Nightingale? Spell it out."

"Okay, here's what I think happened. Dwayne went to the Flamingo to meet someone. I don't know who and I don't know what the meeting was about. Might have been a girl, might have been a dealer. But whoever it was, they didn't turn up. But the who isn't the point. The point was to get him in Brixton, out of his comfort zone. When he came out of the club he was looking for someone but they weren't there. I'm thinking he was expecting a car to be there waiting for him. A black four-wheel drive, maybe. Anyway Dwayne calls the driver and the driver tells him to meet him around the corner. Then the driver phones Marshal and tells him that Dwayne is outside the club and heading to the side road. Marshal is close by and he goes up behind Dwayne and shoots him. The gun jams and he legs it. He gets picked up on a bike and off he goes. He sends a text to the driver. A smiley face. That means the job's done. Half an hour after that the driver phones you."

Smith cursed under his breath.

"So who phoned you on the night that Dwayne was shot? About an hour after it happened?"

"Bastard," said Smith under his breath.

"You know who it was?"

Smith nodded. "Reggie."

"Reggie Gayle? Dwayne's number two?"

Smith nodded again.

"There you go, then. That's why I'm getting a bit nervous because how do I know that you and Reggie aren't in this together?"

"Because of what I'm going to do to Reggie. And to this bastard Marshal. That's how you'll know." He shook his head. "Reggie bastard Gayle. I'll have his balls —"

"I don't want to know," interrupted Nightingale. "I just want to know that we're good."

Smith stared at him but said nothing.

"So we're good?" asked Nightingale.

"Good as gold," said Smith quietly.

Nightingale stood up. "Can I ask you a question, Perry?"

"You can ask, that don't mean I'll answer."

"Proserpine. Do you know her?"

Smith frowned. "Proserpine?"

"When you came after me, it was all about Dwayne?"

Smith's frown deepened. "What are you talking about, Birdy?"

"It doesn't matter," said Nightingale.

"You need to chill," said Smith.

"Yeah, you're probably right." Nightingale headed for the door.

CHAPTER
THIRTY-NINE

Graham Lord lived in an innocuous semi-detached house in Highgate, north London. Nightingale parked his MGB close to the driveway of the house and walked past a five-year-old Honda before pressing the doorbell. Lord opened the door and smiled. He was wearing a baggy denim shirt over brown corduroy trousers. He wore reading glasses and his hair was flecked with dandruff. He shook hands with Nightingale. Lord's hand was limp and lifeless, warm and slightly damp. "You're early," said Lord.

"But you knew I would be, right?" said Nightingale. "Being psychic and all."

Lord smiled without warmth. "That's an old joke, Mr Nightingale. Or can I call you Jack?"

"Jack's fine," said Nightingale, taking off his raincoat.

"First names it is, then," he said, adding, "I'm Lordy to my friends." Lord hung the coat on a wooden rack, then led Nightingale down a woodchip-papered hall and into the front room. The curtains, made of thick dark-blue velvet, were drawn and a small Tiffany lamp cast red, green and yellow blocks of light across the ceiling. There was a bookcase on the wall opposite the window; it was full of books on the supernatural, although, unlike Nightingale's own collection, they were mainly newish paperbacks.

The flooring was bare boards that had been sanded and polished and they gleamed in the multicoloured light. In the centre of the room was a circular rosewood table with four high-backed chairs around it. There was a small hi-fi on a table under the window, with a flickering candle on either side. New-age music was playing, soft strings with the tinkling of wind chimes.

"Have you come far?" asked Lord, waving Nightingale to the chair that had its back to the window.

"Don't you know?" said Nightingale, sitting down.

"You really are a cynic, aren't you?" said Lord. "I'm not a psychic; I'm a spiritualist."

"Actually, I've got an open mind," said Nightingale. "If I hadn't, I wouldn't be here."

Lord held out his hand. "That's why I ask for the fee up front," he said. "It shows your commitment better than words ever can."

Nightingale took an envelope from his jacket pocket and gave it to Lord. Lord left the room, presumably to count the cash and possibly hide the money. Nightingale wanted a cigarette but there was no ashtray around so he took out his pack of Marlboro and placed it on the table in front of him.

Lord spotted the cigarettes as soon as came back into the room. "I'm sorry, but I can't allow smoking in the house," he said. "It interferes with the process."

"Smoke's an impurity, is that it?" said Nightingale, putting the pack away.

Lord sat down. "I have asthma," he said. He placed his palms on the table and smiled at Nightingale. "Now, I need you to relax, and to open your mind. I don't work the way the spiritualists do at the centre you went to. I'm not doing a show and I'm not playing to the crowd. I'm acting as a conduit to the person you want to talk to."

"Will I see her?"

Lord shook his head. "It doesn't work like that. I'm not summoning her spirit so I won't see her and you certainly won't. It will talk through me. The spirit will pass into my body and talk with my voice."

"So I won't hear her either?"

Lord's eyes narrowed a fraction. "Yes, you'll hear her. But it'll be my voice. She will use my voice to talk to you. Assuming that she comes through."

"Sometimes they can't communicate?"

"There are no guarantees. How could there be? We're communicating with the spirit world, not making a Skype call. Is it the money you're worried about? Is that it?"

"Well, I have just given you two hundred quid up front."

"If we're not lucky this time, you can come back. And you can keep coming back until you're satisfied."

"So now you're telling me that luck plays a part in all this?"

Lord put his hands together and interlinked his fingers. He looked at Nightingale over the top of his reading glasses. "Can you imagine how many spirits there are out there, Jack? Many of them have unfinished business in this world. There are people they want to contact, things they want to say. People like me are in demand in this world, but we're also in demand in the spirit world. Once I make myself available there's often a rush as spirits pour into the room and I can't always choose who speaks through me." He nodded, as if encouraging Nightingale to agree with him. "But I do know what I'm doing, Jack. You simply have to have faith in me. Okay?"

Nightingale could feel that he was being manipulated but he couldn't stop himself nodding in agreement.

"Great," said Lord. "Let's get started." He put his palms back on the table.

"I have a question," said Nightingale. "How will I know if I'm talking to a spirit or you?"

"You'll be able to tell," said Lord. "Trust me."

"And can I ask questions?"

"Of course," said Lord. "That's the point of the exercise." He scratched the side of his nose. "Are you ready?"

Nightingale nodded again. "Let's do it," he said.

Lord took a deep breath, closed his eyes, and tilted his head back. He shuddered, then splayed out his fingers on the table. He exhaled slowly, the breath whistling between his teeth, then inhaled again. Nightingale sat and watched him, trying to ignore the nicotine craving that was back with a vengeance. Lord spent several minutes breathing in and out with his head tilted back, then he slowly lowered his chin until it was pressed against his chest. His hands began to tremble and then the fingertips started to beat a tattoo on the table. Nightingale folded his arms and waited. Lord froze, the heels of his hands pressed against the table, then he slowly raised his head and his eyes opened. He seemed to be staring over Nightingale's right shoulder. Lord's lips began to move, but there was no sound. Nightingale tried in vain to read the man's lips but then Lord took another deep breath and closed his eyes again.

"Jack?"

Nightingale jumped as if he'd been stung. The sound seemed to have come from deep in Lord's chest. He stared at the man's mouth.

"Jack?"

Lord's lips hadn't moved.

"Yes?" said Nightingale hesitantly.

"Jack Nightingale?"

"It's me," said Nightingale.

Lord took several more deep breaths, his eyes tightly closed. Then he began breathing shallowly and quickly.

"This is Jack," said Nightingale.

Lord's eyelids began to flutter. "Jack?"

"Yes. Who is this?"

"You know who it is, Jack. It's me. Sophie."

Nightingale leaned forward and stared intently at Lord's face. It was a blank mask. "How old are you, Sophie?"

"I'm nine. Did you forget already, Jack?"

Nightingale frowned. Sophie Underwood was nine years old when she died, but she had been born eleven years ago. If it was Sophie, did that mean that she had no sense that two years had passed since she fell from the balcony in Chelsea Harbour?

"Jack, can you hear me?"

"I can hear you," said Nightingale. "Where are you?"

"I don't know," she said. "It's dark here."

"Can you see me?"

"I can now. Sometimes I can, but sometimes I can't. I saw you at that place where you went before but the man who was talking couldn't see me."

"The spiritualist association, you mean?"

Lord nodded, his eyes still closed. "I wanted to talk to you there but I couldn't."

"You could see me?"

"Yes. You were with a blonde lady. Jenny."

"That's right."

"The man who was talking to you said that he could see us but really he couldn't."

"Us? What do you mean?"

"There are lots of us. We can't talk to each other but we can see each other a bit."

"I don't understand."

"It's like we're reflections in something. It feels strange, Jack. I don't like it."

"What do you want, Sophie?" asked Nightingale.

"I want you to understand that it wasn't your fault."

"What do you mean?"

"It wasn't your fault what happened. I don't want you to feel guilty."

"Okay," said Nightingale hesitantly.

"You couldn't have saved me. No one could. You tried your best, I know you did." Lord's hands began to beat on the table and his eyelids were fluttering crazily.

"Are you okay?" asked Nightingale. "What's happening?"

"It's like you're fading, Jack," she said. "I can see you and then I can't and it's like you're a long way away."

"What do you want from me, Sophie?"

"I don't want anything really. But I don't want you to feel guilty because I died. You do feel guilty, don't you? You think it was your fault?"

"I wish I'd saved you, yes. I keep wondering what I should have done differently."

"You couldn't do anything. But it was nice that you tried. You were the only person who wanted to help me, Jack."

Lord went suddenly still and his head dropped so that his chin was against his chest again. He started to breathe heavily, as if he was in a deep sleep. Nightingale sat back in his chair and waited. The deep breathing continued for several minutes and Nightingale wondered if he should say something or try to wake the man up. Then Lord stiffened and slowly raised his head. His eyes opened and he stared at Nightingale.

"I know what you did. Jack."

Nightingale stared back at Lord. The man's eyes were blank and lifeless.

"I know what you did to my father, Jack. I know what you did. But you mustn't feel bad about it because he was a bad man."

Nightingale felt a chill run down his spine.

"I'm glad that he's dead, Jack. My mother too. She knew what he was doing and she didn't stop him." Lord began to cry silently. Tears ran down his cheeks and plopped onto the table.

"Sophie?" said Nightingale.

Lord started to tremble and then his whole body went into spasm and he slumped forward. Nightingale stood up and hurried around the table. He grabbed Lord by the shoulders and pulled him back into a sitting position. Saliva was dribbling from one side of his mouth and as he sat up his head lolled back. Nightingale slapped him gently on the cheek.

"Lordy, are you okay?" asked Nightingale.

Lord groaned, then coughed. Nightingale stood back and looked down at him. The man coughed again, pulled off his glasses and rubbed his eyes with the palms of his hands. He sighed and gazed up at Nightingale, blinking his eyes as if trying to focus. "What happened?" he asked hoarsely. "Did she come through?"

"Don't you remember?"

Lord rubbed his eyes again and then wiped his mouth with the back of his hand. "I'm not normally aware of what happens when I'm channelling," he said. "She was here?"

Nightingale nodded. "Yes."

"And did you hear what you wanted to hear?"

"I'm not sure," said Nightingale. He took out his pack of cigarettes. "It was . . ." He shrugged without finishing the sentence. "I need a cigarette."

Lord tried to get up but the strength seemed to have gone from his legs and he sat down heavily.

"Are you okay?" asked Nightingale.

"It can be draining," said Lord. "The spirits seem to suck the energy from me while they're talking through me. The longer they channel through me, the worse it is." He forced a smile. "I sometimes think that if I do it too long I won't recover." He put his head in his hands. "Sorry."

"No problem," said Nightingale. He patted him on the shoulder. "I'm going to go."

Lord looked up. "Did you hear everything you needed to hear?"

"It was interesting."

"If you need to hear more we can try again another time. Generally I find that subsequent sessions are easier. You can call me."

Nightingale tapped a cigarette out of the pack and slipped it between his lips. "I'll do that," he said. He let himself out of the house and lit the cigarette as he walked towards his car. He reached the MGB and turned to look back at the house. "What a load of bollocks," he said, blowing smoke up at the clouds.

CHAPTER
FORTY

Nightingale was back in his Bayswater flat taking a bottle of Corona from the fridge when his mobile rang. It was Jenny.

"How did it go?" she asked.

"Complete waste of two hundred quid," he said.

"Did Sophie talk to you?"

"Couldn't shut her up," said Nightingale, flopping down onto his sofa and pressing "mute" on his TV remote control. "Except it wasn't Sophie." Off in the distance he heard the wail of a police siren.

"So he was cold reading? Telling you what you wanted to hear?"

"No, I was careful not to give him anything," said Nightingale. "But she told me not to feel guilty, that there was nothing I could have done to stop her falling, and that she was happy about what I did to her father."

"Jack, that's amazing!"

"Is it?"

"Come on, that's incredible. How did you get the messages? Was it like a Ouija board or a séance?"

"He was channelling. She spoke through him."

"But he couldn't have got all that from reading you, could he? Not if you weren't telling him anything."

"It was a con, Jenny."

"How?"

"There was nothing in what he said that he couldn't have got from Google," said Nightingale. "The papers reported what happened to Sophie, and to her father. And I was named in several of the reports. He knew my name. Soon as I rang him up. He was showing off, but the point is that once he had my name everything flowed from that."

"But he didn't know who you were. We met him by accident, remember? He couldn't have known he'd meet you in Marylebone."

"He was behind us at one point, and you mentioned Sophie. He could easily have overheard us talking."

"Okay, I might have said the name, but it's not an unusual one, Jack. How does he go from 'Sophie' to knowing who you are and what happened?"

"We signed in at the meeting hall," said Nightingale. "He could have got my name from that. Then it's just basic research. Put my name and Sophie's into any search engine and you're going to come up with what happened at Chelsea Harbour two years ago."

"That's awful. And he did all that for two hundred pounds?"

"It's a long con. He said he had to stop because he lost the contact and that I should try again in a few days. And I'm sure that once I was hooked the price would start to go up. True mediums don't charge for their services, that's what Mrs Steadman said."

"But you're a former cop, doesn't he realise that he's taking a risk?"

"I think the emphasis is on 'former'. Plus, I probably looked vulnerable. Why else would I have gone to Marylebone in the first place? Everyone in there was looking for something; all he has to do is to find out what it is and then to give it to them. And at the end of the day, how do we prove that he's conning us? He says there are no guarantees and he's right about that. How would anyone prove that he wasn't actually channelling a spirit?"

"You sound very relaxed for a man who's just been ripped off to the tune of two hundred pounds."

"What was I supposed to do? Take my cash back? I doubt that he would have given it to me and I don't want to add theft and assault to Chalmers's hit list. Plus, I have to say, he put on one hell of a performance."

"Are you okay, Jack?"

Nightingale lifted the bottle of Corona. "Hunky dory," he said.

"Not a phrase one hears a lot these days," she said. "Are you drinking?"

"Affirmative."

"Corona?"

"Oh yes."

"At least you're not on the brandy. How many bottles?"

"What are you, my mother?" He looked up at the ceiling. "Oh no, she's dead. In fact they're both dead, aren't they? My biological mother and my real mother. Shuffled off this mortal coil." He placed the bottom of the bottle against his forehead.

"How many bottles, Jack?"

Nightingale groaned, took the bottle off his head, rolled sideways and peered down the side of the sofa. There were several empty bottles there and he counted them one by one. "Five," he said. "I'm on my sixth. A baker's dozen."

"Thirteen is a baker's dozen. Six is half a dozen. Please tell me it's six."

"It's six. I can handle it."

"Do you need company?"

Nightingale sat up. "I'm okay."

"I can come round."

"I'm not drunk, Jenny."

"No, but you're not happy."

"Which one of the seven dwarves do you think I am, then?"

"I'd have to go for Grumpy. Or Moron."

"There wasn't a dwarf called Moron."

"That's what I thought. I'll settle for Grumpy, then. You'd be better off with coffee."

"I'll put the kettle on. Soon as I've finished my beer." He sighed. "I'm okay, Jenny. Really."

"Call me if you need me, all right?"

"Like the Samaritans?"

Jenny didn't say anything for several seconds, and when she did speak he could hear the concern in her voice. "Why would you say that, Jack?"

"It was a joke."

"Are you sure?"

"I'm not suicidal." He laughed but it came out half bark, half cough. "I'm just having a few beers and then

I'm going to bed, and I'll be in the office bright and early tomorrow."

"Sometimes you worry me."

"I'm sorry. But I really was joking." Jenny didn't say anything. "Jenny, I'm okay."

"It wasn't your fault; you know that, don't you?"

"Of course I do. Jenny, it's not about guilt. I'm sure of that."

"I know you, Jack. You're not one of life's sharers. You bottle things up. And as I've said before, that's not healthy."

"Okay, tomorrow I'll take you for a lunch and we'll have a heart to heart. I'll share."

"There you go again, making a joke of it. That's your defence mechanism as soon as anyone tries to get close to you."

"I just don't want you worrying about me," said Nightingale. "I can take care of myself. Trust me. I know what I'm doing."

"I wish I believed that," said Jenny, and she ended the call.

Nightingale stared at the phone thoughtfully for a few seconds, then set it to silent and tossed it on the sofa. He picked up the remote, turned on the sound and began flicking through the channels looking for football.

CHAPTER
FORTY-ONE

Nightingale lit a cigarette and blew smoke towards the Thames. The wind whipped it away.

"Cigarettes are bad for you," said Sophie.

"I know," said Nightingale. He looked over at her and smiled. "That's why they don't let children smoke."

Sophie held her Barbie doll close to her face and whispered to it. Then she held the doll near her ear and nodded seriously. She clasped the doll to her chest and swung her legs back and forth as they dangled over the edge of the balcony. "Jessica says you can get cancer," she said.

Nightingale tilted his head back and tried to blow two smoke rings but the wind was too strong. "Jessica's right," he said. A police boat was heading up river, fighting against the current.

"You know you're going to Hell?"

"So I've been told."

"Doesn't that scare you?"

Nightingale shrugged. "Scared or not scared, if it happens, it happens."

"You don't care?"

"Shit happens," Nightingale said, grinning.

"You shouldn't say 'shit', Jack. It's a bad word."

"What do you want, Sophie?"

Sophie whispered to her doll. Nightingale took a long drag on his cigarette.

"You're here to help me, aren't you?" Sophie asked.

"That's the plan."

"But you can't, can you?"

Nightingale rubbed the back of his neck and his hand came away wet with sweat. "I don't know, Sophie. I don't know what to do; I don't know what to say. Can you tell me?"

Sophie shook her head. "I don't know either."

Nightingale felt something cold run down the small of his back and he shivered.

"Jack?"

He looked over at her. "What?"

"Could I just go with you now? Could you take me inside? Will that fix it?"

Nightingale smiled. "I don't think it will. No."

"Because I'm dead?"

Nightingale nodded.

"I don't want to be dead, Jack."

"So what do you want, Sophie? Tell me what you want."

A single tear rolled down her cheek. "I want to be alive, Jack. I want to take back what I did. I thought I wanted to be dead but now I don't. And only you can help me. Only you."

"Sophie, I don't know how," said Nightingale.

"You said you could help me, remember? You said we could go inside and talk about it. You said that you could help me and you said 'cross your heart', do you remember?"

Nightingale smiled sadly. "I remember, Sophie."

"So help me now. Cross your heart and help me."

"It's too late. There's nothing I can do." He put the cigarette to his lips.

"No one can help me, then," said Sophie. She lifted her doll, kissed it gently on the top of its head, and then slid off the balcony without making a sound.

Sophie's skirt billowed up around her waist as she fell. He leaned forward and reached out with his right hand even though he knew there was nothing he could do. "Sophie!" he screamed. Her golden hair was whipping around in the wind as she dropped straight down, her arms still hugging the doll.

He closed his eyes at the last second so that he didn't have to see her hit the ground but he couldn't blot out the sound, the dull thump her body made as it slammed into the tarmac at terminal velocity. The cigarette fell from his nerveless fingers and he ran into the apartment.

There was an old couple sitting on the sofa, holding hands. Mr and Mrs Jackson. They stared up at him with blank faces. "Please help me, Jack," they said in identical flat, emotionless voices.

Nightingale hurried by them. There was a young uniformed constable standing at the doorway, his right hand touching the mic on his shoulder. The constable's radio crackled but as Nightingale drew level with him his eyes misted over. "Please help me, Jack," he said. Nightingale pushed him out of the way and rushed along the corridor to the emergency stairs. He hurtled down the stairway. The cop shouted something after him but Nightingale was already out of earshot, taking the stairs two at a time.

He burst into the reception area, where a dozen paramedics and uniformed officers were all talking into their radios. Nightingale pushed through them. One of the men, a heavyset bruiser in a fluorescent jacket, grabbed Nightingale by the arm. "Please help me, Jack," he said, his voice a deep growl as he stared at Nightingale with unseeing eyes. Nightingale shook him away and ran out of the building, turning left towards the river.

Two female paramedics crouched over the little girl's body. The younger of the two was crying. Four firemen in bulky fluorescent jackets were standing behind them. One was being sick, bent double and heaving, while another was wiping tears from his eyes with the back of his gloves.

Nightingale went over to the paramedics. The younger one looked up at him, her face glistening with tears. Her lower lip trembled, then her face froze and her eyes glazed over. "Please help me, Jack," she said, staring up at Nightingale, her voice a dull monotone. He elbowed her out of the way and knelt down beside Sophie. A pool of blood was spreading around her shattered skull. Her eyes were closed as if she was sleeping and the Barbie doll was still in her right hand. Nightingale reached out to stroke her hair but as he did so her eyes opened wide. "Please help me, Jack," she croaked, then she took a long slow breath that rattled in the back of her throat before she began to scream at the top of her voice. The scream turned into the ringing of his mobile phone and that's when he woke up.

CHAPTER
FORTY-TWO

Nightingale groped for his phone and took the call. "Jack?" It was an American voice. Joshua Wainwright.

"Joshua, how's it going?" It was still dark outside and Nightingale squinted at his wristwatch. It was half past five. He groaned.

"Sorry, man, did I wake you up?"

"Nah, I had to get up to answer the phone anyway."

"Say what?"

"English humour," said Nightingale, sitting up. "Where are you?"

"New York," said the American. "Shoot, what time is it there?"

"Half five in the morning."

"Man, I'm sorry. I lost track of the time with all the flying I've been doing."

"Not a problem, Joshua." He yawned and covered his mouth.

"Are you okay? You sound a bit tense. I can call back."

Nightingale rubbed his chin. "I'm okay. I just had a bad dream, that's all. What's up?"

"Is it that girl? The dream?"

"What makes you say that?"

"Because it's been on your mind, and problems have a way of making themselves known in your dreams."

Nightingale sighed. "Yeah, so my assistant keeps telling me."

"I might be able to help," said Joshua.

"Is that why you're phoning? You're not psychic, are you, Joshua?"

"You mentioned her when I was round at your house. Doesn't take much to put two and two together. No, I'm calling about the books. My team can be at your house today, if that's okay. Late afternoon."

"Today?"

"Yeah, I know it's short notice but they're heading back from Rome and they can stop off in the UK for a couple of days to work on the inventory."

"Okay, sure," said Nightingale. "Get them to call me on my mobile when they're about ninety minutes away and I'll be there to let them in. I haven't had time to get any camp beds in, though."

"They can find a hotel," said Wainwright. "Now this Sophie thing . . . how determined are you?"

"What do you mean?"

"How serious are you about contacting this girl?"

"I'm still trying," said Nightingale.

"That's what I thought," said the American. "I hope you're steering clear of dark mirrors."

"I tried a medium but he was a con artist."

"There're a lot of them about, Jack. It can be tough separating the wheat from the chaff. But I can put you in touch with a group who might be able to help."

"I'm listening," said Nightingale.

"The thing is, Jack, we're talking about the dark side. Not as bad as the Order of Nine Angles, but they're still on the side of the fallen."

"Devil-worshippers, you mean?"

"It's more complicated than that, but they do have a track record of dealing with the dead. It's up to you."

"What would I have to do?"

Wainwright chuckled. "You wouldn't have to sell your soul, if that's what you mean. I know one of the guys in a London group and I could put you in touch."

"And it's safe?"

"It's a hell of a lot safer than what you were trying to do in the basement," he said with a laugh. "I'll talk to them and get back to you with the details if they're cool about it."

Wainwright ended the call. Nightingale decided that there was no point in trying to get back to sleep so he shaved and showered and put on his second-best suit, a dark blue pinstripe. He had a meeting with a solicitor in Earl's Court and wanted to make a good impression. Solicitors were a good source of work and Nightingale was trying to get more legal firms on his books.

He was in the kitchen frying bacon, wearing a blue-and-white-striped apron over his suit, when he heard his phone beeping to let him know that he'd received a text message. It was from Wainwright, with a name, a mobile phone number and a brief message: "You can trust him."

"I hope that's true," muttered Nightingale, putting the phone on the coffee table and heading back to finish frying his bacon.

CHAPTER
FORTY-THREE

The meeting with the solicitor in Earl's Court went really well. He was a middle-aged Bangladeshi wearing what seemed to be a Savile Row made-to-measure suit that probably cost ten times as much as Nightingale's pinstripe, a gold Rolex wristwatch and handmade shoes that put Nightingale's Hush Puppies to shame. The solicitor did a lot of immigration work and needed a private detective to do the legwork on cases where failed asylum seekers were being threatened with deportation. Most of the work appeared to be computer-based and Nightingale was confident that Jenny would be able to handle it in her sleep, so after an hour he shook the man's expensively manicured hand and headed back to his MGB. He'd parked in a multi-storey car park not far from the Exhibition Centre.

He lit a cigarette, blew smoke, then put the key in the ignition and turned it. There was a dull clunking sound from under the bonnet, then silence. He cursed and tried again. This time there wasn't even a clunk. He got out of the car and phoned Jenny.

"Dial-A-Cab," she said when she answered.

"Is the whole world psychic?" he asked.

"You drove your MGB; it's an hour since your meeting started so I'm guessing you've just left the solicitor; I doubt that he's told you anything that merits an immediate phone call, so I'm guessing your car has died again."

"You should be a detective," said Nightingale.

"And you should buy yourself a decent car," said Jenny.

"I know, I know," said Nightingale. "I hang my head in shame. But I've got a problem."

"I know. You've to get to Gosling Manor."

"Can you pick me up?"

"I can. But Jack, you really can't keep using me as a taxi service. I've got a stack of accounts to deal with here and I was going to go to the bank to pay in those cheques that arrived today."

"Pretty please?"

"You're the one who's going to be paying my expenses, so you can do whatever you want. I just think that you could be making better use of my time, that's all."

"So you'll come and get me?"

"Yes, master."

"I'll be in the Starbucks close to the Exhibition Centre. Give me a bell when you're in the area and I'll bring you a coffee."

"Make it a mocha," she said. "I could do with giving my blood sugar a boost."

"And a muffin?"

"Banana choc-chip."

"You're a sweetheart."

Nightingale locked up the MGB and finished smoking his cigarette as he walked to Starbucks. Jenny phoned when she was ten minutes away and by the time she drove up in her Audi he was standing outside with a large mocha and a muffin in a paper bag.

"Did you call the AA?" she asked as he slotted her drink into a cup holder and put the muffin on the dashboard.

"What's my drink problem got to do with anything?"

She laughed as she pulled away from the kerb. "Idiot. The AA. For what you laughingly call a car."

"I'll do it tomorrow," he said. He nodded at the Starbucks bag. "Do you want that now?"

"I'll save it for later," she said. "How did it go with Mr Deepak?"

"Great. Nice guy, very professional. Says he can put a lot of work our way."

"Can I ask you something?"

Nightingale looked across at her, surprised by the question. "Sure."

"Wainwright's going to buy the library, right?"

"Fingers crossed."

"Probably for a lot of money?"

"Fingers and toes crossed, sure."

"He paid you a stack for those books you sold him last year. Two million euros."

"Which went straight to the bank, if you're thinking about a pay rise."

"What I'm thinking is that if he's going to buy the entire library from you, he's going to pay millions."

"That's the plan."

"So you'll be able to pay off the bank and have a small fortune left."

"Maybe a big fortune," said Nightingale.

"And then what?"

Nightingale frowned. "What do you mean?"

She sighed and shook her head. "Sometimes you can be so obtuse."

"What?" said Nightingale, genuinely confused.

"What happens to Jack Nightingale Investigations?"

"It'll take the pressure off," he said.

"Jack, you'll be a very wealthy man. You're not going to want to work, are you?"

"I'm not old enough for a pipe and slippers."

"No, but you'll be rich enough to buy a villa in Spain or a go-go bar in Bangkok, or pretty much anything you want."

Nightingale grinned. "A go-go bar? Where did that come from?"

"It's an example of what guys do when they come into money," she said. "And you're coming into a lot of money."

"And you think I'll just up sticks and run off to the sun?"

"I don't know what to think," said Jenny. "But if that's what you're going to do I'd appreciate some advance notice so that I can make plans."

"You don't want to help me run the go-go bar, then?"

Jenny flashed him an exasperated look. "I'm serious. I don't want to turn up for work one day to find you've done a runner."

318

"Is that what you think's going to happen?"

Jenny shrugged. "I've no idea what's going to happen other than the fact that you're about to come into a large sum of money."

They stopped at a set of traffic lights and she picked up her mocha and took a sip.

"I enjoy being a detective," said Nightingale. "I was a good cop and now I'm a good private eye. I know it sounds corny but I like the work. Even the seedy stuff, following errant husbands and the like. I don't see me stopping work just because I've got a bit of cash."

"But it's not going to be just a bit of cash, is it?" She put the cup back in the holder. "You'll be rich, Jack." The light turned green and she started driving again.

"I'm not planning to retire, Jenny. Cross my heart."

"Okay."

"Are you worried about losing your job? Is that it?"

She sighed. "Yes, Jack, I'm worried about my wonderful job," she said, her voice loaded with sarcasm.

"I tell you what, if Wainwright comes through, you're definitely getting a pay rise."

"That makes it all worthwhile, really."

"You're being ironic, right?"

"Not much gets by you, does it?"

Nightingale pointed at the bag on the dashboard. "Do you mind if I have a piece of your muffin?"

"Help yourself," she said.

CHAPTER
FORTY-FOUR

Jenny brought the Audi to a stop in front of the gates that guarded the driveway of Gosling Manor. Nightingale looked at his watch. "We're early," he said.

"That's the thing about German engineering," said Jenny. "It gets you to where you need to be."

"Is that a dig at my MGB?"

"More a dig at someone who thinks an old banger is a classic," she said. "Is there any of my muffin left?"

Nightingale handed her the Starbucks bag and she peered inside. "You took the top," she said.

"It's the best bit."

"You took the best bit of my muffin," she said.

"I was hungry."

She shook her head in mock disgust. "Why are we waiting here?"

"Because Wainwright's people haven't been here before so they might miss it."

Jenny nibbled a piece of the muffin and drank her mocha. Nightingale took his cigarettes out and Jenny glared at him. "No," she said.

"I'll smoke outside," he said, opening the door.

"Good idea," she said.

Nightingale climbed out and lit a cigarette. It was a cold afternoon and he shivered, then started pacing up and down behind the car as he smoked. From the gates there was no sign of the house, just the driveway winding off to the right between clumps of trees. He hadn't thought about the difference that Wainwright's money would make, but Jenny was right. Ainsley Gosling had spent a fortune on the books in the basement and Nightingale doubted that they would have gone down in value over the years. He had met Joshua Wainwright only a few times but he trusted the man and he was sure that he would pay him what they were worth. That could be tens of millions of pounds and maybe Jenny had a point: would he really want to do Mr Deepak's legwork if he had that sort of money to play with?

The sky overhead was covered in grey and white clouds with not a shred of blue to be seen. Over to his left was a line of half a dozen towering trees stripped of all their leaves, the bare branches revealing two large nests. Sitting next to one of the nests was a magpie that must have been two feet from its beak to the tip of its tail. It was staring at Nightingale. Nightingale looked around for a second magpie, acting from a habit he'd picked up from his mother. She'd taught him the rhyme when he was still a toddler — "one for sorrow, two for joy, three for a girl and four for a boy" — and always made him look for a second bird whenever they came across a single magpie. He was still looking when he heard a vehicle coming down the road. He blew smoke and turned towards the sound. It was a silver Mercedes people carrier.

The vehicle came to a halt behind Jenny's Audi. Nightingale dropped his cigarette butt, crushing it with the sole of his shoe, and went over to the Mercedes. The side door opened and a pretty Chinese girl stepped out. She had long black hair and round-lensed spectacles, and was wearing a blue parka over a green baggy polo-necked sweater and tight blue jeans.

"Are you with Joshua?" asked Nightingale.

The girl grinned. "Sure am," she said. "Are you Jack?" She had a soft American accent.

Nightingale nodded and shook hands with her. She was tiny, under five feet tall, and she had to jut her chin up to maintain eye contact with him.

"Amy Lee," she said.

She held open the door of the Mercedes and introduced her three colleagues sitting in the back: two middle-aged men in raincoats and a slight elderly woman who reminded Nightingale of Mrs Steadman in the Wicca Woman store in Camden. Nightingale shook hands with them and nodded at the driver, a grey-haired man in a dark suit.

"Do you want to follow me to the house?" said Nightingale.

"Cool," said Amy, and she climbed back into the people carrier.

Nightingale opened the gates, and joined Jenny in the Audi. "That's them," he said.

"They don't look like Satanists," she said, putting the car in gear and driving slowly towards the house.

"What do Satanists look like, pray tell? Cloaks, sharp teeth, bloodshot eyes? They're book experts, not devil-worshippers." He looked over his shoulder. The Mercedes was following them. "I guess. Actually, I didn't ask Joshua. He just said they'd be able to value the books."

"And you trust him?"

"What do you mean?"

"You met him only a few weeks ago, you don't know him from Adam. Wouldn't you be better off getting in your own experts?"

Nightingale looked across at her. "When did you get so suspicious?"

Jenny shrugged. The house was off to the right, expansive lawns to their left. "I'm just saying that there's a lot of money involved and you might be better off getting a second opinion."

"He's been fair so far."

"You don't know that, Jack. He gave you a stack of money but you don't know that someone else might not have given you more."

"Cash," said Nightingale. "Let's not forget it was cash."

"Yeah, that says more about you than credit cards ever can," she said. She parked next to the massive stone fountain, switched off the engine and turned to look at him. "You're not the best judge of character, that's all I'm saying. I've never met this Wainwright and it's none of my business but maybe he's just being a bit too keen."

"I hear you, kid. Let's see what they say. I don't have to accept his first offer." He got out of the Audi and waved at the driver of the people carrier to park on the other side of the fountain.

Jenny got out of the Audi and shook hands with Amy and the rest of the book experts. They were all carrying aluminium briefcases.

"Nice place," said Amy, looking up at the house.

"The inside isn't that great," said Nightingale. "We had a fire a few days ago. Watch your shoes because there's still a fair bit of mud around. The firemen used a lot of water." He unlocked the front door and showed them inside. The driver stayed at the wheel of the Mercedes.

"You weren't lying," said Amy, peering at the thick mud covering the hall tiles. "How did the fire start?"

"They're not sure," lied Nightingale.

Amy sniffed the air. "Ugh," she said.

"I know. Nightmare."

"Where are the books? They weren't damaged, were they?"

"Luckily no," said Nightingale. He went over to the hidden panel while Jenny closed the front door. Amy and the team followed him across the hall, stepping gingerly through the mud. Nightingale pulled open the panel and Amy giggled.

"Are you serious?" she asked. "A secret panel?"

"Don't blame me, it was my father's house," he said.

"Ainsley Gosling. I can't believe you're his son."

Nightingale turned to look at her. "You knew him?"

Amy shook her head. "I know of him, of course. Mr Wainwright and Mr Gosling were often after the same books and Mr Gosling had a way of always persuading the vendor to sell to him."

"By offering more money, you mean?"

Amy shrugged. "Sometimes, but sometimes a book would be withdrawn from sale and later we'd find out that Mr Gosling had acquired it."

"Yeah, it's one hell of a collection all right," said Nightingale. He reached for the light switch and flicked it on. "As you'll see."

He stepped through the panel and headed down the stairs. He got halfway down before he realised that the bookshelves were empty. He stopped and gripped the banister with both hands and stared down the full length of the basement. Every single book had gone. He rushed down the stairs and hurried to the far end of the basement where the CCTV monitors were. Before he reached the monitors he could see that the console had been smashed. Nightingale cursed.

"Is there a problem?" asked Amy.

Nightingale turned to look at her. She was standing next to one of the display cabinets and looking around, clearly confused.

"You could say that," said Nightingale. He took his pack of Marlboro out of his pocket and slid a cigarette between his lips.

"Where are the books, then?"

Nightingale lit his cigarette, inhaled, then blew a tight plume of smoke up at the ceiling. "That, Amy, is a very good question."

CHAPTER
FORTY-FIVE

Nightingale and Jenny stood and watched the people carrier drive back towards the gate. Nightingale waved. "Thanks for coming," he said. "Catch you later."

"They think you're mad, you know," said Jenny.

"They might be right."

"What the hell's happened, Jack?"

"I've been robbed," he said.

"But who knew the books were down there?"

Nightingale flicked ash onto the ground. "Just you and me. And Joshua."

"You don't think he stole them, do you?"

Nightingale looked at her. "Joshua?"

"Basic detection, right? Motive, means, opportunity."

Nightingale grinned. "You've been watching too much *CSI*."

"You think this is funny? You've no insurance, remember? And you need the money from those books to pay the bank."

"I don't think it's funny, no. But it can't have been Joshua. Why would he have sent his team if he'd already taken the books?"

"So that you wouldn't suspect him."

Nightingale nodded slowly. "Nice," he said. "But he's out of the country, so how's he going to arrange a robbery from the States?"

"He knows people. You said that. With the sort of money he's got he wouldn't have any trouble getting professionals to clean you out."

"It's certainly true that they were pros," said Nightingale. "No signs of entry, they took absolutely everything and they wrecked the surveillance equipment."

"Was the CCTV system on?"

"No," said Nightingale. "But I guess they figured better safe than sorry."

"They knew what they were after, that's for sure," said Jenny. "But no one else knew the basement was down there. The firemen, for example. There were lots of them tramping around but all they'd have seen was an empty house. Same with the cops. The only things of value in the house were in the basement and no one knew the basement was there."

"Except Joshua, is that what you're saying? That's just circumstantial."

"You took him down there. He saw what you had. How much were the books worth? We don't know, but millions, right? Tens of millions? Don't you think that he might have come to the conclusion that he'd be better off taking them rather than paying you?"

"He's not like that, Jenny," said Nightingale. He flicked away the remains of his cigarette. "He's okay."

"A trustworthy Satanist? Isn't that a contradiction in terms?"

"You haven't met him, kid. He's a good guy."

"A good guy who worships the Devil?"

Nightingale chuckled. "It's not like that. Mrs Steadman explained it to me some time ago. There's no black magic or white magic, just magic. Like electricity. You can use electricity to save lives in an ICU or kill people in an electric chair. The power's the same; it's what you do with it that matters."

"That's nonsense," said Jenny. "Mrs Steadman is a sweet old lady who uses herbs and crystals, and by your own admission Joshua Wainwright is a devil-worshipper."

"Satanist," corrected Nightingale.

"You're bisecting rabbits," said Jenny.

"What?"

Jenny grinned at him. "Splitting hairs. It's something my dad always says. A Satanist is a devil-worshipper, Jack. The clue is in the name."

"I can't explain it but Joshua's heart is in the right place. I trust him."

"I'm sure you do, but, as I keep telling you, you're a lousy judge of character." She sighed. "What are you going to do, Jack?"

"I don't know."

"You're going to have to call the cops."

"Chalmers would laugh in my face."

Jenny shook her head. "I can't understand why you're taking this so calmly."

"What do you want me to do? Break down and cry? At the moment, here and now, there's nothing I can do. Whoever took the books has got clear away. The cops won't help, so I'm just going to have to figure it out for myself. Plus, they're specialist books. It's not as if the thief can sell them on eBay. They can only have been stolen by another Satanist and they're a pretty small group." He buttoned up his raincoat. "I need a drink."

"Drink's not going to get the books back," said Jenny.

"No, but it'll make me feel better," said Nightingale. He walked over to the Audi. "Come on, let's find the nearest pub. I'm buying."

"I'm the designated driver, remember?"

"You can watch me drown my sorrows, then." He grinned. "I'm joking. Let's go back to London."

CHAPTER
FORTY-SIX

First thing on Tuesday morning Nightingale phoned the number that Wainwright had given him. The guy was called Adrian Miller and he lived in Milton Keynes. They arranged to meet later that afternoon. Miller asked Nightingale to bring with him any personal possessions that had belonged to the person they were trying to contact. As soon as the call was over, Nightingale phoned Colin Duggan and asked him if he'd had any luck getting Sophie's doll from the evidence room.

"Nag, nag, nag," said Duggan.

"I'm sorry, mate, but it's important."

"Yeah, well, softly softly catchee monkey as the Chinese say," said Duggan. "The guy who's on nights this week is a real stickler and there's no way I can get anything by him. I know where the box is but I can't get near it while he's around."

"That's annoying. What about the day shift?"

"I figured night would be easier because they're quiet," said Duggan. "I can give it a go during the day but I'm not taking any risks. Any chance of me being caught and I'm out of there."

"I understand, mate."

"Do you?" said Duggan. "I'm risking my job and my pension to steal a child's doll and you won't even tell me what's going on."

"I can't. I'm sorry. But it's not stealing because you'll have it back. I promise."

"I'll see what I can do," said the policeman, and he ended the call.

Nightingale rang Jenny and told her that he wouldn't be in the office.

"Car trouble?" she said.

"Oh ye of little faith," he said. "The car's fine now, I'm heading up to Milton Keynes."

"Home of the concrete cows," she said.

"What on earth are you talking about?"

"That's what Milton Keynes is famous for, isn't it? Concrete cows and roundabouts. Is it a job?"

"I'm going to see the guy that Joshua recommended."

"Are you sure that's a good idea?"

"I want to give it a try," said Nightingale.

"If you want my opinion, I think you'd be better off talking to a therapist rather than talking to these charlatans," said Jenny.

"Charlatans?"

"You know what I mean," she said. "Just be careful."

CHAPTER
FORTY-SEVEN

Nightingale didn't see any concrete cows when he got to Milton Keynes but he did have to go around half a dozen roundabouts before he pulled up in front of Adrian Miller's house. It was a small semi-detached with a tiny front garden behind a neatly clipped hedge. Two rose bushes were growing under a bay window. It definitely didn't look like the home of a devil-worshipper and Nightingale checked the text message with the address. He lit a cigarette and smoked it down to the butt before getting out of the car and walking over to the front door. He pressed the doorbell. It was answered by a man with a shaved head and tattoos down his left forearm. He was wearing a black shirt with the sleeves rolled up and black trousers. He grinned and offered his hand.

"Are you Jack?" Nightingale nodded and shook his hand, and Miller ushered him inside the house. "Come far?" asked Miller as he closed the front door.

"London."

"I'm just making a coffee — do you want one?"

"Terrific," said Nightingale, and he followed Miller through to a modern galley kitchen with gleaming white units and a fridge festooned with family photographs and school notices.

Miller saw Nightingale looking at the photographs. "Wife and kids are staying with her mother for the night," he said. "No one's going to walk in on us. Milk and sugar?"

"Just milk," said Nightingale.

Miller picked up a jar of Nescafé Gold Blend and made him a coffee. "How long have you known Joshua?" asked Miller.

"A while," said Nightingale. "He's a good guy."

"One of the best," said Miller, pouring in a splash of milk.

"He thinks very highly of you," said Nightingale.

Miller blushed and waved away the compliment like a schoolgirl who had just been told she was pretty. "And you haven't done anything like this before?" He handed the mug to Nightingale.

"I'm not sure exactly what it is that we'll be doing," said Nightingale.

"It's a ceremony," said Miller. "There'll be five of us. You, me and three others. The other three will be masked. They're wary of outsiders."

"No problem," said Nightingale. "You've done this before, right?"

"Loads of times," said Miller. "There're a lot of like-minded people here in Milton Keynes. Quite a little gathering." He smiled. "So tell me who it is you want to contact?"

"A nine-year-old girl," said Nightingale. "Her name's Sophie Underwood. I say nine, but she'd be eleven now."

"Time doesn't pass once you move into the spirit world."

"How would you know that?"

"We've called up spirits that passed over fifty, a hundred, years ago. If time passed they'd be skeletons, right?"

"So Sophie will never get any older now that she's a spirit?"

"Appearance-wise, no. Ageing is something that happens in this world, not the next." Miller finished his coffee and nodded at the door. "So, let me show you the room."

He took Nightingale along the corridor to the stairs and up to the first floor. There was a small bedroom at the back of the house with a hatch in the ceiling from which protruded an aluminium ladder. Miller motioned for Nightingale to go up. He climbed the rungs slowly. The attic ran the full length of the house, with beams overhead and bare floorboards. There were no windows and the only illumination came from a single bare bulb hanging in the middle of the roof space.

Nightingale walked away from the hatch and looked around as Miller climbed up. In the middle of the attic floor was a piece of purple cloth, about four paces square, on which a pentagram had been drawn with white chalk.

Nightingale nodded at the pentagram. "I thought that was just for summoning devils," he said. "To protect against them."

"The pentagram has a lot of uses," said Miller.

At the top of the pentagram was a small wooden altar on which there was another, smaller, pentagram with a silver chalice and a small brass bowl at its centre. There were several peeled cloves of garlic in the bowl and a small black candle at each of the points of the pentagram.

"Are we going to be summoning a spirit? Is that how it works?" asked Nightingale.

"There won't be any fire and brimstone, if that's what you mean," said Miller. "What we'll be doing is basically a ritual that allows a spirit to return to this world and to interact with the people here. There are spirits all around us, but usually they can't see or hear us and we can't see or hear them."

"Like ghosts?"

"Ghosts are different," said Miller. "Ghosts are tied to a particular place because of something that has happened there. You only ever see them in that one place." He smiled and shrugged. "You really are a novice, just like Joshua said."

"I'm new to this, yes," Nightingale said. He gestured at the pentagram. "But I've learned enough to know that you use the pentagram to protect yourself when you summon devils, and that they appear in physical form. So tell me, have you done that? Have you ever called up a devil?"

"Me? God, no. That's not why I'm into this. Summoning up devils is totally different to what we do."

"But you're Satanists, right? The same as Joshua."

"Yes, but saying we're the same is equivalent to saying that a guy who plays football with his local team is on a par with a guy who plays in the Premiership. Trust me, there's no one in our group that would even contemplate summoning one of the Fallen. We worship them, sure, and we source power from them, but I'm nowhere near strong enough to start summoning one."

"I get it," said Nightingale.

"And if you're considering it you need to be very careful. A friend of mine tried it a couple of years ago and she ended up in a mental hospital. She's a shell; her mind was totally destroyed."

"Were you there when it happened?"

Miller shook his head. "When you do a deal with one of the Fallen it has to be one-on-one. That's why it's so dangerous. Any sign of weakness, or you drop your guard for a second, and they'll rip out your soul. I can't stress that enough: you don't mess around with them. Someone like Joshua, okay, maybe, but the likes of me?" He shuddered. "I wouldn't even think about it."

"I hear you," said Nightingale.

Down below, the doorbell rang. "That'll be the rest of the group," said Miller. "By the way, did you bring something belonging to the deceased?"

"I couldn't get anything," said Nightingale. "I did try."

"It's not essential," said Miller. He went back down the ladder.

Nightingale walked around the purple cloth towards the far end of the attic. There were two old steamer trunks there, wooden with leather straps around them.

They weren't locked but the straps were held in place with brass buckles. Nightingale's curiosity got the better of him and he knelt down and undid the straps of the trunk closest to him. The lid groaned as he pulled it open. It was full of chalices, bottles, and objects wrapped in cloths of various colours. There was a strong smell of incense and something bitter and acrid that made his eyes start to water. He picked up one of the cloth-wrapped bundles. It was a brass knife covered with runes, the handle in the shape of a goat's foot, the blade serrated and with a sharp point. Nightingale re-wrapped the knife and put it back in the chest. On the left-hand side of the trunk were bundles of candles, mostly black.

He heard voices downstairs so he hurriedly closed the lid and fastened the buckles. He was standing by the small altar when Miller's head popped through the hatch. He had changed into a long black hooded robe. He was holding a Marks & Spencer carrier bag and he took out a robe and handed it to Nightingale. "We all wear these," he said. Nightingale took off his raincoat and draped it over one of the trunks. As he was putting on the robe a second man appeared; he was in his sixties with a goatee beard and a black mask over his eyes and nose.

"This is Martin," said Miller. Martin shook hands with Nightingale. "Martin is my second in command."

"His wing man," said Martin. He was wearing a large sovereign ring on his left hand and a bulky gold chain on his right wrist. Even the baggy hooded robe couldn't conceal his expanding waistline; he was clearly a man who enjoyed his food and drink.

"Hood up or down?" asked Nightingale.

"Up when we begin," said Miller. "Colour is a distraction so things have to be as dark as possible."

A blonde head appeared in the hatch. A woman's. Miller and Martin helped her up. She was in her forties and had dark eyebrows and a slash of red lipstick over lips that looked as if they'd been pumped full of fat from elsewhere in her body. She was plump and as she stepped into the attic her robe fell open, giving them all a glimpse of cleavage and of a small rose tattoo on her left breast.

"Jack, this is Joanne," said Miller.

She offered her right hand as she adjusted her mask with her left. Her hand was pasty and white and there was a silver ring on each finger. Her nails were the same scarlet as her lipstick, long and filed to points. Her handshake was twice as firm as Martin's and she maintained eye contact while she shook.

"Are you going to be joining our little group?" she asked.

"Jack's just here for a one-off," said Miller. He looked down the hatch. "Ronnie, are you okay?"

"Coming!" called a Scottish voice from downstairs. "Just using the bathroom."

"That's Ronnie," said Miller. He lowered his voice. "Bladder like a marble."

Nightingale adjusted the robe, which reached down to his ankles. It was made of a thick coarse material that scratched against his wrists, and around his neck there were small knotted cords that tied together to close it at the front.

Downstairs the toilet flushed and the final member of the group slowly climbed the ladder, grunting with each step. He was a big man with a mane of ginger hair. His mask barely covered his eyes and nose and there was a sprinkling of large freckles over all his exposed skin. He grinned at Nightingale and stuck out his hand. There were nicotine stains on his fingers and the nails were bitten to the quick. "You're the new boy," he growled. His hand enveloped Nightingale's but there was hardly any strength in the grip.

"Just visiting," said Nightingale, resisting the urge to wipe his hand on the robe. He'd heard the toilet flush but hadn't heard Ronnie wash his hands.

Miller went over to the trunk that Nightingale had opened. He bent down, unfastened the leather straps and took out a large black candle. He carried it over to the purple cloth and placed it in front of the altar. He said something in what sounded like Latin, and then pulled a lighter from inside his robe and lit the five candles at the points of the pentagram. He said something else in Latin, moved his left hand over the burning candles, then went over to the light switch and turned off the light. Light was still flooding up through the open hatch and he pulled up the ladder and closed it. With the only light coming from the five small candles and everyone dressed in black, all Nightingale could see was the smudge of faces and the white pentagram on the cloth.

"Right, everyone, let's prepare ourselves," Miller said, clasping his hands together as if about to say a prayer. He looked across at Nightingale. "Just follow my lead, Jack. Do as we do."

Nightingale nodded and clasped his hands together.

Miller closed his eyes and lowered his head. He began to hum, the sound appearing to come from deep down in his chest. The rest of the group followed his example, all making the same sound. Nightingale closed his eyes and joined in, though he had to change the pitch of his hum several times until it matched the group's. When he did get the pitch right he felt his stomach begin to vibrate with the sound and before long his whole body seemed to be tingling. The humming continued for several minutes and then as one they stopped. Nightingale opened his eyes but when he saw that everyone else still had theirs shut he closed them again.

Miller began to recite a Latin incantation. That went on for several minutes and then he began to hum again. This time the note seemed to be lower and Nightingale had trouble matching it.

"Right," said Miller eventually. Nightingale opened his eyes and Miller smiled at him. "We don't have anything belonging to the deceased, so I'm going to ask Jack to say a few words about her." He gestured at Nightingale and nodded encouragingly.

"Her name is Sophie," said Nightingale. "Sophie Underwood. She was nine years old when she died. Her father had been abusing her, and her mother knew what was going on but did nothing to stop what was happening. I was with her when she died. She was on a balcony outside her apartment and she fell." Nightingale took a deep breath to steady himself. "I think Sophie has been trying to contact me. I'm hoping that you can help her tell me what it is she wants from me."

"We'll do our best," said Miller. He slowly pulled the hood of his robe over his head and his face disappeared into the gloom. One by one the others did the same. With the hoods over their heads it was almost impossible to tell who was who.

Miller picked up the big black candle, lit it, and placed it carefully in the middle of the purple cloth. "Gather round, please," he said, and the group spaced themselves around the pentagram. Miller went over to the Marks & Spencer carrier bag and took out a piece of parchment and a pen. He carried them to the altar, where he wrote on the parchment, murmuring in Latin as he did so. When he held it in the air, Nightingale saw that he'd drawn an upside-down pentagram. Miller used his lighter to set fire to it over the brass bowl, holding it for as long as he could before dropping the ashes.

He walked slowly back to the carrier bag and took out a bottle of red wine. It had a screw top and as he reached the pentagram he unscrewed it and carefully poured wine into the chalice. He put the top back on the bottle and put the bottle on the floor by the wall, then he picked up the chalice and held it above his head. "Servo nos," he said. "Protect us." He sipped the wine and then passed the chalice to his left, to Joanne.

She held it high and said, "Servo nos. Protect us," then drank. She passed it to her left and everyone took it in turns to drink from the chalice. Finally Ronnie handed it to Nightingale. He held the chalice above his forehead, said the words in Latin and English, took a sip and then gave it to Miller.

Miller spoke in Latin again and then put the chalice next to the brass bowl on the altar. He used both hands to pick up the black candle and he placed it on the altar between the bowl and the chalice.

He turned back to the group and held out his hand. Joanne took it. He led her onto the purple cloth and into the centre of the pentagram and then helped her lie down, her head towards the altar. He nodded at Martin and Ronnie and they moved into the pentagram and knelt down on either side of the woman.

"Jack, please join Martin. Make sure that you remain inside the pentagram at all times."

Nightingale knelt down next to Martin.

Miller moved to stand by Joanne's head and he crouched down carefully. Joanne had closed her eyes and was breathing softly. Miller began to gently massage her temples. "Joanne, your eyes are getting heavy and you are going into a deep, deep sleep," he said quietly. Joanne breathed deeply and then went still. "You see in your mind Sophie Underwood and her mind is like an open book to you and we ask that you read it to us."

Miller nodded at Martin and Ronnie and they extended the first and second fingers of both hands and moved them under Joanne's body, one under her shoulder, one under her hip.

"Jack, use two fingers under each leg," whispered Miller. "See how they're doing it? First and second finger only."

Nightingale moved around so that he could put two fingers under each knee.

Miller put his hands under Joanne's neck and then he nodded again. They all lifted her into the air. She was surprisingly light, Nightingale realised, and with no effort they lifted her three feet off the floor.

"Sophie Underwood," said Miller.

"Sophie Underwood," repeated Martin.

Ronnie said her name and all three men looked at Nightingale. He swallowed. His mouth had gone so dry that it hurt. "Sophie Underwood," he croaked.

The men slowly lowered Joanne back onto the purple cloth. Miller stood over her, looking down at her face. "Sophie Underwood, can you hear me?" he said.

Joanne took a deep breath.

"Sophie. Are you there?"

"Where am I?" said Joanne. Nightingale froze as he realised that it wasn't the woman's voice. It was the voice of a young girl.

"Sophie?" he said. Miller flashed him a warning look.

"What are you doing, Jack? Where are you?"

"You are Sophie Underwood?" asked Miller.

"Who are you?" said Joanne. Nightingale was now sure that it was Sophie's voice.

"We're here to help you talk to Jack," said Miller.

Smoke from the candles was beginning to swirl around Miller and Nightingale was finding it hard to breathe.

"Jack, you don't know what you've done."

The smoke was thicker now and all the men were coughing. Martin wiped his eyes.

"Run, Jack," said Sophie, her voice shaking. "Run before it's too late."

Lightning flashed, even though Nightingale knew that was impossible because they were indoors. It was followed almost immediately by a crash of thunder that shook the house. Dust showered down from the roof. The candles were flickering and the smoke was now whirling around in a grey vortex.

"What's happening?" asked Ronnie. "What's going on?"

"I don't know," said Miller, his voice trembling.

"Jack, run!" screamed Sophie, and then Joanne arched her back and her whole body went into spasm.

There was another bolt of lightning and a loud crack and then something appeared in the vortex, something big, its skin glittering as if it was covered in scales. The figure took a step forward and the floor shuddered.

Martin was backing away, his mouth moving soundlessly. Miller had crouched down next to Joanne and was holding his hands over his face. The woman was still in spasm, her feet and hands drumming on the floor.

The creature, whatever it was, roared and the foul stench made Nightingale gag. Martin took another step back, his arms flailing.

344

"Stay in the pentagram!" shouted Nightingale but Martin wasn't listening.

Ronnie went down on his knees and buried his face in Joanne's lap.

Lightning flashed again. Martin stumbled backwards and stepped out of the pentagram. He managed to twist around and regain his footing and then he ran to the hatch. He threw himself to the floor, his hands grasping for the handle.

"Martin, no!" shouted Nightingale.

Miller was coughing and spluttering. Joanne's spasms had stopped and she had opened her eyes. Ronnie was murmuring the Lord's Prayer, his face still buried in Joanne's lap.

The smoke was so thick now that all Nightingale could see was a massive shape moving slowly towards Martin. Martin turned, his mouth wide open in panic.

"Martin, get back here now!" shouted Nightingale. "It can't cross the pentagram!"

Martin tried to get to his feet but then something flicked through the smoke and struck him across the throat. Blood sprayed across the attic wall and Martin fell back, hitting the floor hard.

"Stop!" screamed Nightingale. He pushed the hood back off his head and pointed at the massive shape, now just a dark blur in the choking fog that filled the attic.

There was a deafening roar from within the fog and a wall of heat washed over Nightingale. The floorboards creaked as it moved towards Nightingale and he caught a glimpse of glistening scales and a claw with curved talons.

Ronnie took a look over his shoulder and began to scream the Lord's Prayer at the top of his voice before burying his head in Joanne's lap again.

The air was so thick and acrid that every breath burned Nightingale's lungs and tears were running down his cheeks.

Hot foul-smelling air blasted across his face again and whatever it was roared so loudly that the sound seemed to push against his chest and force him back. His right foot caught against Joanne's hip and he struggled to regain his balance.

Nightingale took a deep breath and then screamed at the shape in the fog. "Reverto per pacis quod per totus festinatio ex unde venit!" The shape froze, then what passed for a head turned towards him. Nightingale felt another blast of heat across his face and he threw up his hands up to protect his eyes. The shape growled and moved closer to the pentagram. Nightingale pointed at the shape and screamed again. "Reverto per pacis quod per totus festinatio ex unde venit!"

The creature, or whatever it was, threw back its head and roared, then space folded in on itself and it was gone. Nightingale went down on one knee, gasping for breath. His ears were ringing and his eyes were filled with tears. His lungs were burning and he forced himself to breathe slowly and deeply. The smoke was already starting to clear.

Martin was lying against the wall near the hatch, his hands clutched to his throat. Blood was trickling

346

between his fingers. He tried to speak but frothy blood spewed down his chin. Nightingale hurried over to him and knelt down by his side.

Miller appeared at Nightingale's shoulder. "Get me a piece of cloth," Nightingale said to him as he gently pulled Martin's hands away from his neck. Blood immediately began to spurt and Nightingale pressed the hands back to stem the flow.

"Keep your hands there until we get a dressing," Nightingale said to him. Martin didn't appear to hear him but did as he was told.

Joanne got up on her hands and knees and began crawling towards them.

Nightingale knew that they needed an ambulance but his self-preservation instincts kicked in and he realised that it would be a bad idea to make the 999 call on his own mobile.

"Does anyone have a mobile?" he shouted.

"Downstairs," said Miller.

Nightingale turned around to talk to Joanne. "Joanne, are you okay?"

She nodded and pushed herself up, using the wall to steady herself.

"Get downstairs now and phone an ambulance. Tell them it's a throat wound with heavy bleeding."

Joanne hesitated and looked over at Miller.

"Joanne, go!" shouted Nightingale.

As she moved by them and pulled up the hatch, Miller ripped a piece from the bottom of his robe and thrust it at Nightingale. "Will this do?"

Nightingale took it and folded the material into a pad. He looked at Martin. "Listen to me, Martin. I'm going to need you to take your hands away, just for a second." He held the wad of material in front of the man's face. "Then I'm going to press this against the wound. It'll do a better job of stemming the blood flow."

Joanne pushed the ladder down and lowered herself out of the attic. Nightingale gave her a quick look. She was scared and she was in shock but she was in control of herself. The last thing he needed was for her to run out of the house without calling for an ambulance. She caught his look and flashed him a nervous smile and he realised she was okay.

Nightingale looked back at Martin. His eyes were glassy and he was breathing quickly and shallowly, like a cornered animal. His hands were drenched in blood and there was bloody froth pulsing from between his lips. "Swallow, Martin," said Nightingale. "Get the blood out of your mouth."

Martin did as he was told.

"Good man," said Nightingale. "Now, I'm going to count to three. When I get to three I need you to take your hands away. I'll press this dressing against the wound and then you can put your hands back and hold it. Do you understand?"

Martin nodded fearfully.

"Good man. One, two, three." When he said "three" Nightingale used his left hand to loosen Martin's grip, and as the hands moved away Nightingale slapped the wad of material against the wound. Martin's hands scrabbled to hold the cloth in place. "It's okay," said Nightingale. "Just stay calm."

Ronnie crawled over. "Is he okay?" He was breathing heavily and his face was florid.

"We think so," said Miller.

"Can I help?"

"Can you go down and make sure that Joanne's called the ambulance?" said Nightingale.

Ronnie grunted, crawled over to the hatch and climbed down the ladder.

Nightingale looked over at Miller. "That thing that appeared," he said. "Has that ever happened before?"

Miller shook his head. "Never."

"Any idea what it was?"

"A demon," said Miller. "No doubt about it. But it wasn't anything to do with what we did. We don't summon devils, we talk to spirits." He put his hand on Martin's shoulder. "He's going to be all right, isn't he?"

Nightingale could hear the desperation in Miller's voice. "He'll be fine," he said, hoping he sounded more confident than he felt. He looked at Martin. The man was in shock, his eyes wide and staring. Nightingale put his face closer to the injured man's. "Listen to me: you're going to be all right. If a major vessel had been cut you'd be dead already. Breathe slowly, swallow what blood you can and be calm. You can get through this. Don't try to speak, just blink twice if you understand."

The man blinked twice, a look of fear in his eyes.

"There's an ambulance on the way. Just don't panic. It looks and feels a lot worse than it is. That cloth is stemming the blood flow, so just concentrate on not choking and you'll be okay. Understand?"

Martin blinked twice.

"Make sure that he keeps the pressure on, firm but not too firm," Nightingale said to Miller. "The ambulance won't be long."

"You're sure he's going to be okay?"

"If you keep the pressure on, he'll be all right. He's lost a pint or so of blood, but he can spare that. I've seen worse."

Miller nodded but Nightingale could see that he didn't believe him.

"How did you do that?" asked Miller. "How did you get that thing to go away?"

"I've had some experience of dealing with them," said Nightingale. "The words I used are what you say to send back a devil that you've summoned, so I just hoped it would work for an unwanted visitor. I was lucky."

Miller nodded. "We all were." He shuddered.

The ladder rattled and Ronnie appeared. He'd taken off his mask and robe. "The ambulance is on its way," he said. He pulled himself up into the attic.

Nightingale stood up. "I'm off," he said.

"You're not staying?" said Miller.

"The cops and I aren't on good terms at the moment. It's best they don't know I was here." He clapped Miller on the shoulder. "Sorry about this."

"It wasn't your fault," said Miller.

Nightingale left them to it, knowing that Miller was wrong. It almost certainly was his fault. He lit a cigarette as he left the house and walked towards his MGB. As he climbed into the car he heard a siren, heading his way.

CHAPTER
FORTY-EIGHT

Nightingale drove back to Bayswater, parked his car in his lock-up and was heading back to his flat when he remembered that he didn't have any beer left in his fridge. He walked along to the Prince Alfred pub and ordered a Corona. The barmaid was just putting the bottle down in front of him when his mobile rang. It was Duggan.

"Colin, did you get it?" he asked before Duggan had the chance to speak.

"Yeah, I'm fine, thanks for asking," said the policeman. "Where are you?"

"In the gym, lifting weights."

"Are you serious?"

"Nah, I'm in the pub. The Prince Alfred in Queensway. Opposite Whiteleys."

"Don't go anywhere."

"You've got it?"

"Trust me, it won't be a social call."

"I'll have a pint waiting for you," said Nightingale.

"Yeah, make it a latte, skimmed milk if they've got it."

Duggan arrived half an hour later, as Nightingale was finishing his lager. He waved over at a pretty Australian barmaid who was wearing one of her national rugby team's shirts. "Another Corona and a milky coffee," he said.

"Latte," growled Duggan. "Skimmed milk." He was wearing a heavy overcoat and a red wool scarf, and both were flecked with rain. "Bloody weather." He took off his scarf, shook it, and undid the buttons of his coat. He frowned as he looked at Nightingale. "You look like shit, Jack. Seriously."

"Thanks, mate."

"If I didn't know you better I'd think you were using."

"Using? Drugs?"

"You've got the eyes of a smack-head. Really."

There was a mirror behind the gantry and Nightingale bent down and peered at his reflection. Duggan wasn't exaggerating. He looked as if he hadn't slept for a week.

"Yeah, much better," sneered Duggan.

The barmaid returned with their drinks. She looked expectantly at Duggan and he pointed at Nightingale. "He's paying."

Nightingale took a handful of coins from his pocket and paid her, then reached for his lager.

"So what's wrong?" asked Duggan, scratching his fleshy neck.

"I'm under a lot of pressure. And I'm not sleeping well." He shrugged. "I've had a few rough nights, that's all. And today hasn't been a bundle of laughs either."

"What happened?

"You really don't want to know," said Nightingale. He pushed the slice of lemon down the neck of the bottle, put his thumb on the top and then turned it upside down.

"Why do you do that?" asked Duggan.

"Mixes the lemon through the lager." He turned the bottle the right way up and drank.

"Has Sophie Underwood got anything to do with the way you're behaving?" Duggan leaned closer to Nightingale and lowered his voice. "It wasn't your fault. What happened two years ago, it would have happened no matter who'd turned up. It could have been anyone on that balcony with her."

"Yeah, well, it wasn't; it was me."

"Luck of the draw, Jack. And no one would have done anything any different." He didn't add sugar but he stirred his coffee anyway.

"You can't say that, Colin." Nightingale drank his lager. "I went out with no back-up and totally unprepared. I started talking with no game plan, no idea what I was going to say."

"She was getting ready to go; even if you hadn't gone out onto the balcony she would have jumped."

"Again, you don't know that. If I'd said the right thing, maybe I'd have turned it around."

"What's done is done," said Duggan, shrugging.

"Don't you dare say that there's no use crying over spilt milk," said Nightingale.

Duggan's face tightened. "A little girl died, I know that. I was there, remember? And what you seem to forget is that you left me to deal with the aftermath. You went off to see the father and I had to wait with the body."

Nightingale nodded slowly. "I'm sorry, mate. You're right. I'm behaving like a prick."

Duggan grinned. "Nothing new there, then." He reached into his coat pocket and pulled out a package wrapped in a Tesco carrier bag.

Nightingale took it and slipped it inside his coat. "I owe you, mate."

"Yes, you do," said Duggan. "Can't you at least tell me what it's for?"

Nightingale sighed. "Best you don't know," he said.

"When can I have it back? You can tell me that much." He sipped his coffee. It left him with a white milky moustache on his upper lip and he wiped it away with the back of his hand.

"A day or two," said Nightingale. "Did you have any grief getting it out?"

"I chose my moment, let's just say that," said Duggan. "No one knows it's missing and providing I get it back soonish then no one will."

"I won't let you down. Cross my heart."

"Yeah, well, that and twenty pence will get me a piss at Paddington Station," said Duggan. "If anything goes wrong and you get caught with it, you'd better not drop me in it."

"Not a problem."

"I'm serious, Jack. If anyone finds out that I took it from the evidence room then I'll be in so much shit you'll need a submarine to find me."

"Colin, I won't let you down." He watched Duggan drinking his coffee and grimacing. "You sure you don't want a whisky in that?" he asked.

"You really are the devil, aren't you?"

"You're off the booze because of diabetes; it's not as if you're an alcoholic."

"It's all about calories. And alcohol's full of calories."

"So have one less slice of toast tomorrow."

Duggan chuckled. "Toast? I wish. Muesli, with skimmed milk and a banana."

"Actually, that sounds okay. But to be fair, my coffee and a fag has fewer calories."

"Yeah, it's the cigarettes I miss the most but the doc said they had to go," Duggan said, smiling sadly.

"I've told you before, mate, the cigs help keep the weight off. I tell you what, why not just forget about the diabetes for one night, have a single malt and we'll go outside for a cigarette?"

Duggan looked at the coffee he was holding and pulled a face, then he grinned at Nightingale. "Sod it. Go on, get me a Laphroaig. And make it a double. In for a penny, in for a pound."

CHAPTER
FORTY-NINE

Duggan blew smoke across the street, a look of contentment on his face. He looked at the cigarette. "My wife'll kill me if she finds out I had a smoke." He moved aside to allow two men in paint-stained overalls to push through the door into the pub.

"One cigarette's not going to kill you, mate. And neither's one whisky. Everything in moderation."

They both looked to the left as a police siren started up and their heads swivelled as a car went by with two uniformed officers inside. The driver looked as if he was barely in his twenties and the officer in the passenger seat was borderline obese, with rolls of fat protruding from under his stab vest.

"How many a day are you on now?" asked Duggan. "You were two packs a day when you were in the job."

"It varies," said Nightingale. He shrugged. "Everybody dies, Colin. I'd rather die happy than die healthy."

Duggan laughed ruefully. "I like that. Die healthy."

"It's true. Lots of very healthy people die."

"Sophie's father, for one," said Duggan. He grinned. "He was in the prime of life when you threw him through his office window."

"Allegedly," said Nightingale. He took a long drag on his cigarette.

The two men stood in silence for a few minutes, people-watching. Queensway was always busy and was one of the most multicultural areas of London, and while they smoked they heard conversations in Chinese, Arabic, French, Italian, Japanese and half a dozen that Nightingale didn't recognise. There were students, tourists, workers heading home, couples heading out, mates on the way to the pub or a restaurant. He watched two African women walk by in brightly coloured long dresses with headdresses made from the same material, laughing loudly at something one of them said. The one closest to Nightingale saw that he was watching her and she flashed him a beaming smile. Nightingale grinned back and winked. As the two women walked away the one he'd winked at turned and gave him another smile.

"You seeing anyone these days?" asked Duggan.

"Nah," said Nightingale.

"Why not? You were a bit of a lad when you were in the job. There was that blonde sergeant over at Harrow Road. And the dog handler, the cute one. You put yourself about a bit, back in the day."

Nightingale laughed. "Yeah, that's true."

"You need to settle down, get yourself a wife. How old are you now?"

"Thirty-three."

"You're not getting any younger."

"Who is?" said Nightingale. He smoked his cigarette. "You ever think about death?" he asked quietly.

"I'm a cop. What do you think? How many bodies did you come across when you were in the job? As a bobby you'll see one a month. Accidents, suicides, murders. In my first year on the beat I saw half a dozen pensioners who'd swallowed all their sleeping tablets and as many junkies who'd overdosed. Death's part of the job, you know that."

"I meant your own death. Dying."

Duggan chuckled ruefully. "I didn't until this diabetes thing hit me," he said. "But the doc read me the riot act and didn't pull any punches."

"So what do you think happens to you after you die?"

Duggan turned to look at him. "Bloody hell, what's brought this on?"

"It's the biggest question of all time, isn't it? It's the only question that matters and yet it's the one question you never hear asked. Turn on the news and it's about the economy and politics and conflict, and the one thing that really matters is never mentioned. What happens to us when we die? Is this it? Is this all there is?"

"People don't talk about it because they're scared."

"You think?" said Nightingale.

"It's easier to sweat the small stuff, right? Keeps you from thinking about the big stuff because the big stuff is very, very scary."

Nightingale didn't say anything. He smoked his cigarette and stared at Whiteleys Shopping Centre on the other side of the road.

Duggan looked over at him, the cigarette on the way to his mouth. "Are you all right?"

"I'm fine."

"You sure?"

Nightingale laughed but he could hear the unease in his voice. He smoked his cigarette.

"I'm serious, Jack. You look a bit tightly wound, truth be told."

"I've a lot on my plate at the moment. Did you hear about the fire at my house?"

"I heard there was an arsonist trying to burn your place down while you were inside. And you're doing your old trick of changing the subject when anyone asks you an awkward question. So I'll ask you straight out — are you thinking about topping yourself?"

Nightingale's jaw dropped. "Am I what?"

Duggan turned to face him. "You're showing all the signs. You're under stress, you're drinking, you're talking about death and dying. And you're two years out of the job. A lot of former cops end up killing themselves, you know that."

"Come on . . ."

"I'm serious, Jack. You wanting that kid's doll, that's the last straw." He nodded at Nightingale's coat pocket. "That's irrational, that is."

"I swear, cross my heart and all that, I'm not planning to top myself." He shook his head. "I'm amazed you'd even think it."

"If you need anyone to talk to, you call me," said Duggan earnestly.

"Colin . . ."

Duggan gripped Nightingale's shoulder, tightly. "Listen to me, you stupid bastard. I don't know what's going through your mind but I've got a really bad feeling about this. Promise you'll call me."

"Hell's bells, Colin, I promise. But it's not going to happen. Topping myself is the absolute last thing on my mind."

Duggan's nails bit into Nightingale's shoulder, then he relaxed and took his hand away. He flicked ash on the pavement. "See what happens when you get me drinking and smoking again? I go and get all emotional." He took a final drag on his cigarette and dropped the butt onto the ground.

"One for the road?" asked Nightingale, doing the same with his cigarette.

Duggan snorted softly. "You really are the devil, aren't you?" he said.

CHAPTER
FIFTY

Nightingale parked by the mermaid fountain and climbed out of his MGB. It was already dark and there were thick clouds overhead. He took a torch from his glove compartment and flicked it on as he climbed out of the car. He was holding the Tesco carrier bag that Duggan had given him and he juggled the bag and the torch as he locked the car. Off in the distance a fox barked and a second or two later another answered from behind the house. Nightingale pointed the torch at the front door and walked up the steps. It was cold and his breath feathered in the beam of light as he fumbled for his keys and unlocked the door. He shivered and looked over his shoulder but there was nothing there, just the darkness. He pushed open the door and flicked the light switch. The two dozen bulbs in the huge chandelier in the centre of the hallway flickered into life, though their coating of ash muted the light.

It was cold inside, only a few degrees above zero. There was a huge oil-fired central heating system powered by a huge boiler off the kitchen but it cost a small fortune to run and Nightingale had turned the thermostat right down. He shivered again as walked over the muddy floor to the panel that hid the entrance to the basement. After flicking on the lights he was just about to head down into the basement when he heard a noise upstairs, a short scraping sound as if something was being dragged across the floor. He walked back into the hall and listened intently but whatever the sound was, it had stopped. He was about to call out but realised immediately that would be a waste of time. Animals couldn't speak and burglars wouldn't answer.

He went to the bottom of the stairs and listened again but he couldn't hear anything. Jenny had been right: the house was far too big for one person. He couldn't even remember how many bedrooms there were upstairs. And having heard a noise, what was he supposed to do? How long would it take to go through every room in the house, to check every possible hiding place? He'd never be sure that there wasn't an intruder somewhere in the house, especially now that the CCTV console had been smashed beyond repair. He stood stock still and listened as he stared at his mud-splattered Hush Puppies for a full minute, counting the seconds off in his head, then he went back to the panel and down into the basement. He went over to the trunk containing the candles and rooted through it to find two light blue candles, each about a foot long. He took two gold candleholders from a display case and carried them over to the coffee table.

From the carrier bag he took a framed photograph of Sophie. He'd found the picture on the internet. It was a school photograph that the *Evening Standard* had used to illustrate their story on her death. He'd bought the frame from a shop in Bayswater. It didn't say in Daniel Dunglas Home's book that the picture had to be in a frame but Nightingale had felt that a frame was somehow more appropriate.

He placed the frame between the two candles, face down, then took the Barbie doll out of the bag. He held it in his hands and felt tears well up in his eyes. It was the last thing Sophie had held before she died. He flashed back to the moment she'd slid off the balcony, the doll clutched to her chest. He brought the doll up to his face and sniffed it gently before placing it next to the photograph. Already on the table was the book that described the ritual he was about to attempt.

He went over to a display cabinet that was filled with vases and bowls and chose a small brass bowl with no markings. He took it over to the coffee table. The last item in the carrier bag was a small box of purified sea salt that he'd bought from Mrs Steadman's shop in Camden. He poured some of the salt into the bowl.

He switched on the torch and went back up the stairs to turn off the lights. Using the torch beam to guide his way he walked back to the coffee table and sat down. He lit the candles and then turned off the torch and put it on the floor. He took several slow, deep breaths, closed his eyes and tried to remember as much as he could about Sophie, her face, her hair, her clothes, her voice. His mind kept drifting to the moment that she'd fallen from the balcony but he tried to blot that image out. He remembered what they'd talked about on the balcony. Smoking. Birds. How to programme a video recorder. Nightingale had tried to keep her talking, to keep her focused on his voice rather than on the ground far below.

Nightingale opened his eyes, then licked the index finger of his right hand and dabbed it into the salt. He touched the salt to his tongue and without swallowing he turned over the framed photograph. He stared at the picture, then dabbed more salt onto his tongue. This time he swallowed and fought against the gag reflex.

"Sophie," he said. "Are you there? Sophie, it's Jack."

The candles flickered but only for a second and then the flames steadied. Nightingale placed his hands palm down on the table and took two deep breaths and then closed his eyes. Again he tried to visualise Sophie. Her pale white skin. Her long blonde hair. The tears in her eyes.

He opened his eyes, dabbed his wet finger on the salt and then touched it against his tongue again. "Sophie, can you hear me?"

Nothing happened. Nightingale picked up the book and opened it at the page that described the ritual. He read through it again to make sure that he hadn't forgotten anything.

"Sophie. This is Jack Nightingale. Can you hear me?"

The candles flickered again and he heard a creaking sound above his head. He looked up. There was a second, slightly longer creak, then silence.

"Sophie? Is that you?"

The panel at the top of the stairs rattled and Nightingale flinched. The light from the two candles illuminated only the seating area; the stairs were in darkness.

"Sophie?"

Nightingale felt a cold draught run along the back of his neck and he shivered. There were no windows in the basement and no ventilation ducts so draughts were a physical impossibility.

"Sophie?"

He heard a fluttering sound from the desk where he'd left the yellow legal pad on which Jenny had written the inventory. Nightingale peered into the gloom and could just about see that the pages were moving slowly, as if someone was flicking through them one by one.

"Sophie?"

The pages stopped moving. Nightingale dabbed more salt on his tongue. He wondered if saying a prayer would help, but there had been no mention of that in the book.

"Jack?"

Nightingale froze. He wasn't sure if he'd actually heard his name being spoken or if he'd imagined it, but it had been a little girl's voice. The draught was back and he shivered. He stared at the doll, lying on the coffee table. Its hair was moving slowly, curling around its head as if it had a life of its own. "Sophie, can you hear me?"

"Jack?"

There was no doubt the second time. It was Sophie's voice, but little more than a whisper. "Sophie? Can you hear me? Where are you?" asked Nightingale.

"I'm here, Jack."

Nightingale felt something brush against the back of his head and he flinched. He started to turn.

"No! Don't turn round," said Sophie.

Nightingale forced himself to keep looking forward. The doll's hair had stopped moving and was spread out like a golden halo around its head.

"If you see me, I'll go back," she said.

"Go back where?" asked Nightingale.

"I don't know," said Sophie. She sniffed. "It's cold. And dark."

"Sophie, honey, what do you want?"

"I want you to help me." She sniffed again. "I want to go home."

"I don't think you can go home, honey," said Nightingale, clasping his hands together.

Sophie began to cry softly. Nightingale started to turn. "No!" she said urgently. "You mustn't. I told you."

Nightingale turned back to look at the photograph. She looked so happy in the picture. It had been taken two years before she died, and she was wearing her school uniform and smiling as if she didn't have a care in the world. Nightingale wondered if her father had already started interfering with her and felt a wave of sadness wash over him. He had been a cop for too long to believe that there was any sort of fairness in life, but what had happened to Sophie was just plain wrong. "Sophie, I do want to help you, but you have to tell me what you want."

"I told you already. I want to go home."

"Honey, do you know what happened to your mother? And your father?"

"Yes."

"Really? You know?"

"They're dead," whispered Sophie.

Nightingale shivered. "Aren't they with you?"

"I'm alone, Jack." She began to sob quietly.

Tears pricked Nightingale's eyes. He wanted to help but felt completely powerless. Sophie was dead. Dead and buried. He stared at the doll and then slowly picked it up and stroked the hair softly.

"Jack?"

"Yes, honey."

"You have to come and get me."

Nightingale frowned. "How do I do that?"

She sniffed once again. A cold wind blew by Nightingale's left ear, ruffling his hair.

"You know how," she said.

That was when the candles blew out and Sophie screamed as if she was in pain.

CHAPTER
FIFTY-ONE

Nightingale groped for his torch. He found it and switched it on, then he ran the beam quickly around the basement and up the stairs, his heart pounding. The wicks of the candles were smouldering. He frowned as he stared at the candles. There were no draughts in the basement but something had blown them out.

He was heading for the stairs to switch on the lights when his phone burst into life. It was the American.

"Jack, are you okay?" asked Wainwright.

"Why do you ask?"

"Just a feeling. What are you doing?"

"I'm in the basement of Gosling Manor."

"That's why I'm calling. Amy told me what happened. What's going on?"

"I was robbed."

"Amy said they took everything."

"Just the books. They left the artefacts and stuff, but cleaned me out of every single book. Must have taken them ages. Sorry I wasted your time."

"Don't worry about that. But do you have any idea who might have done it?"

"Hardly anyone knew that the basement was there," said Nightingale. "You, me, my assistant. Her friend. That's about it, so far as I know."

"What about Marcus Fairchild?"

"What? What about him?"

"Did you ever take him down there, did you show him the books?"

"No."

"You're certain of that?"

"Of course. Why? What's going on?"

"Word on the grapevine is that Fairchild has come into some books. Some very old, very expensive volumes. And bearing in mind what happened at Gosling Manor, that's one hell of a coincidence, don't you think?"

"Are you sure?"

"Jack, I wouldn't be calling you if I wasn't sure."

Nightingale said nothing. He ran a hand through his hair. Marcus Fairchild? How had he discovered the hidden library? He knew about the mansion, but how could he have known about the books?

"Jack, are you there?"

"Yeah, I'm here, Joshua."

"What are you going to do?"

"Do? I guess I need to have a talk with him."

"Be careful," said Wainwright. "He's a dangerous man."

"I'll be okay. I've met some real hard bastards in my time."

"Not like Marcus Fairchild. He's off the Richter scale."

370

"Okay."

"I'm serious, Jack. Fairchild is pure evil. Don't even think about taking him on. He's got the whole Order of Nine Angles with him. You go up against one and you'll be facing them all."

CHAPTER
FIFTY-TWO

Jenny's three-bedroom mews house was just off the King's Road in Chelsea. There were two cars parked outside the house, Jenny's Audi and a white VW Golf that Nightingale knew belonged to her friend Barbara. He parked his MGB behind the VW and pressed Jenny's buzzer. He stood back so that she could see him on the video monitor.

"Jack?" Her voice was tinny through the speakerphone.

He held up the bottle of champagne he was carrying. "I come bearing gifts," he said.

"Jack, it's almost eleven o'clock."

"The night is young," he said.

"But you're not," she said. "Have you been drinking?"

He waggled the bottle. "That's what I've brought this for."

"Barbara's here," she said.

"You've got three glasses, haven't you?"

The speakerphone went dead and a few seconds later he heard footsteps clicking across a wooden floor and the door opened. Jenny was wearing baggy tracksuit bottoms and an Adidas top and had her hair tied back with a silver scrunchy. "We've just got back from the gym," she said.

"At night?"

"Best time: it's much quieter, no ogling men." She stepped to the side to let him in, then closed the door. "We're in the kitchen," she said.

Barbara was sitting at the breakfast bar with a glass of orange juice in front of her. Like Jenny she was wearing tracksuit bottoms and a sports top. He winked at her and held up the bottle of champagne. "I can turn that into a buck's fizz, Barbara," he said.

"Music to my ears," said Barbara.

Jenny took a glass from the cupboard and put it on the breakfast bar. She poured in orange juice while Nightingale popped the cork from the champagne bottle.

"How decadent is this?" said Barbara as Nightingale poured champagne into the three glasses.

Nightingale sat down on a stool and raised his glass. "To exercise," he said.

They clinked glasses and drank. "Do you work out, Jack?" asked Barbara.

"He was being ironic," said Jenny.

"I'm not a big fan of gyms," admitted Nightingale. "They always remind me of hamsters on wheels."

"It's good for you," said Barbara. "Good for your heart, your joints, your general well-being."

"So to what do we owe the pleasure, Jack?" asked Jenny. She looked over at Barbara. "I'll bet you a quid he wants something."

Nightingale raised his eyebrows. "What makes you think that I want anything?" he said. "How do you know I didn't just pop round for a social call?"

"Because Bayswater is on the other side of town, because champagne isn't your tipple, and because it's eleven o'clock at night. What's wrong?"

Nightingale put down his glass and raised his hands. "First, I want you to promise that you won't bite my head off."

Jenny's face tightened. "What's happened?"

"Do you want me to go?" asked Barbara.

"Might be better if you stayed," said Nightingale. "You can referee."

"Jack, what's going on?" said Jenny.

"I spoke to Joshua Wainwright this evening." He looked at Barbara. "He's an American who was going to buy the books from Gosling Manor. The ones in the basement."

"Which Jenny says were stolen," said Barbara.

"That's right," said Nightingale. "Someone got in and took away the lot. Every last book. Here's the thing, though. Hardly anyone knew that the books were down there." He frowned. "You didn't mention it to anyone, did you?"

"I didn't realise it was a secret," said Barbara. "But no, I didn't."

"You're sure?"

"Jack!" protested Jenny. "She answered your question. There's no need for the third degree."

"I'm sorry, kid," said Nightingale. "I just meant that sometimes you can say things without realising it. Just in general conversation. And Barbara's right: it wasn't a secret. My point is that hardly anyone knew that the books were down there. Even the firemen didn't know that the basement was there, and neither did the guy who came to quote for the repair work. In fact, the only people who know about the books are the three of us."

"Come on now, that's not true," said Jenny. "That American has been down there and you've been giving Mrs Steadman books."

"Mrs Steadman doesn't know about Gosling Manor. She knew I had the books but she didn't know where they came from. And I'm sure that Joshua didn't take them."

"Really?" said Jenny. "And just as he's about to start discussing the price, they get stolen. Doesn't that strike you as a bit of a coincidence?"

"If he was going to steal them, why would he send in his valuation team?" said Nightingale.

"I told you before, Jack. To throw you off the trail," said Jenny. "Sometimes you are so naive."

Nightingale laughed and raised his glass. "It's not often that I get called that," he said, and clinked his glass against Jenny's.

She looked at him suspiciously. "Why are you here, Jack? What did Joshua say to you?"

"I just need you to promise that you won't fly off the handle."

"Why?"

"Because you won't like what he said." He sipped his drink.

"Just tell me," said Jenny.

Nightingale took a deep breath. "He said that Marcus Fairchild has them."

Jenny's eyes hardened. "You bastard," she said quietly.

He put down his glass and held up his hands again. "Don't shoot the messenger," he said.

"Your uncle?" said Barbara, looking at Jenny.

"Jack's got a thing about him. Blames him for all the evil in the world, pretty much."

"Joshua said that Marcus has come into a collection of books, and he's pretty sure they're the ones from the basement of Gosling Manor."

"How would Uncle Marcus know the books were there?" asked Jenny.

"You tell me."

"What are you suggesting?"

"When was the last time you spoke to him?"

"When he got you out of the cop shop. You were there when I saw him, remember? In the wine bar?"

"And you've not spoken to him since?"

"There you go again. What are you suggesting, Jack? Why don't you just come out and say it? You think I told him about the books?"

"Jenny, who else could it have been?"

"I keep telling you. Your new best friend. That bloody American." She sighed in exasperation. "I don't get you, Jack, I really don't. It's like you're determined to prove that Uncle Marcus is behind what happened at Gosling Manor no matter what. Why are you so set against him?"

"Jenny, you heard what my sister said about Fairchild." He looked at Barbara. "You remember, you hypnotised her and she remembered him killing a child and framing her."

"And we talked about false memories," said Jenny. "I've known Marcus for ever, he's not a devil-worshipper, he's not evil, and he's certainly not a thief."

"Barbara?" said Nightingale, hoping that she would support him.

"I really don't want to get dragged into this," said Barbara.

"You're the one who got my sister to talk about Fairchild and what he did," said Nightingale.

"Your sister was in a mental hospital," said Jenny. "Let's not forget that."

"Accused of murders that she didn't commit," said Nightingale. "Murders that your uncle carried out."

"You've only got your sister's word for that and she's not around to back you up." She glared at him. "I don't know why you keep banging away at this. Your sister was deranged, probably still is."

"Barbara?" said Nightingale. "You were the one who did the regression thing."

Barbara shrugged. "It wasn't really hypnotic regression; she was in a deep trance and she talked through what she remembered."

"What she thought she remembered," said Jenny.

"So now you're saying that she was making it up?"

"I'm saying that your sister has a lot of problems. You too. You both found out that your real father was a Satanist who gave you up for adoption at birth and you're both having trouble dealing with that. Jack, you're talking about a man that I've known for as long as I can remember." She put a hand over her heart. "I swear to you, I'd trust Uncle Marcus with my life."

"I can see that," said Nightingale. "And I can see how quick you are to defend him."

"You don't know him. You've met him twice, that's all. I've known him for ever."

Nightingale nodded slowly. "Jenny, you're not going to like what I'm going to say, but I want you to listen to me very carefully. There are two possibilities here. It might be that I'm completely wrong. It might be that Marcus Fairchild is a great guy and that my sister is crazy and that everything she said under hypnosis was just plain wrong. I admit that's a possibility."

"Thank you," said Jenny.

"But there's the other possibility and I want you to just think about it. What if I'm right? What if he is something else? What if he's able to conceal his true self? What if he's able to control what people think about him? What if he really did manage to convince my sister that she killed those kids?"

"And what if pigs can fly?"

"Please, Jenny, just hear me out. Suppose he is evil. Suppose he can affect the way people see him. What if he can use hypnosis or mind control or something?"

"You should listen to yourself. Have you any idea how crazy you sound?"

"Can you at least consider the possibility that he might have done to you what he did to my sister?"

"What are you saying, Jack?"

378

Nightingale took a deep breath. He had no idea how Jenny was going to react to what he was about to say, but he was pretty sure that she wouldn't be happy. "I'm saying that maybe he's hypnotised you, the way that he hypnotised my sister. And that maybe you're the one who told him about the books in the basement."

Jenny looked at him coldly, picked up her glass, and threw her drink in his face.

CHAPTER
FIFTY-THREE

Nightingale wiped his face with the tea towel that Barbara had given him after Jenny stormed out of the kitchen and upstairs to her bedroom. "She didn't take that well, did she?" he said.

"What did you expect, Jack? You accused her of betraying you. That's not something you say lightly."

"I didn't mean that she did it deliberately," said Nightingale, dabbing at his soaked shirt. "I think Fairchild has conned her. Maybe even hypnotised her."

"Jack, she's known Marcus since she was a child. He's been a close friend of Jenny's father since before she was born. He's her godfather, for goodness sake. You can't go making vague accusations like that."

"I don't think I was that vague, actually." He dropped the tea towel onto the worktop. "I'm serious about this, Barbara. She told him that the police had taken me for questioning. Why would she do that?"

"He's a lawyer, and a bloody good one. She wanted to help you."

"But after what happened with my sister, she must have known that I'd want nothing to do with him. So why talk to him about me?"

Barbara shrugged. "I can't answer that. I don't know."

"And the first time I met him, at her parents' house over Christmas, he'd already talked to her about my sister."

"Well, he was on your sister's legal team."

"And you don't think that's a coincidence?"

Barbara frowned. "You've lost me, Jack."

"Fairchild was on my sister's legal team, but from what you got out of her under hypnosis it's clear that he was responsible for her conviction in the first place. He killed at least one of those children, maybe all of them."

"That's if you believe what your sister said. And that's a very big if, Jack."

"I heard the recording, and that seemed pretty definite."

"I'm sure that your sister believed what she told me, but that doesn't mean it's true."

"What do you think, Barbara? Do you think my sister's making it up? Or do you think that Marcus Fairchild framed her for murder?"

Barbara threw up her hands. "I don't know, Jack. I'm sorry."

Nightingale looked towards the stairs. "She's really pissed off, isn't she?"

"Do you blame her? Her dad's been best mates with Marcus Fairchild since the year dot. If you accuse him that's as good as accusing her dad."

"This is nothing to do with her dad. Barbara, there's something not right about that man, and I need you to help me prove it."

"Me? What can I do?"

"Same as you did before."

Barbara's mouth fell open. "Jenny's never going to agree to that," she said.

"She might," said Nightingale. "If you asked her."

CHAPTER
FIFTY-FOUR

Nightingale looked up as Barbara came down the stairs, He was about to say something when he realised that Jenny was behind her. Her eyes were red as if she'd been crying. "I'm sorry, kid," he said. "I didn't want to upset you."

Jenny pointed a finger at him. "I'll do this because Barbara asked me to, but once it's done I'm going to want an apology from you and a promise that you'll never, ever, mention my uncle again."

"It's a promise," said Nightingale, getting off his stool.

Jenny looked at Barbara. "This is crazy. It really is crazy."

"You have to go into this with an open mind," said Barbara. "It's not going to work if you're negative."

Jenny nodded. "Okay, I'll get myself into a more positive frame of mind." She walked over to the breakfast bar and poured champagne into her glass.

"I hope that's not for me," said Nightingale.

Jenny flashed him a tight smile, drank it all in one, then refilled her glass.

"Is she okay drinking?" Nightingale asked Barbara.

"What do you mean by that?" said Jenny. "I'm not the one with the drink problem." She drank half her champagne.

"I meant for the hypnosis. Doesn't drink affect the process?"

"In moderation it can actually help," said Barbara. "It's a relaxant."

"I'll drink to that," said Jenny. She toasted them with her glass and then drained it.

"You're going to relax yourself into a coma," said Nightingale.

Jenny smiled sarcastically. "Yeah? Pot. Kettle. Black." She poured the last of the champagne into her glass.

"Shall we get started?" asked Barbara.

"Let's," said Jenny. "Where do we do it?"

"The sofa in the sitting room should do the trick," said Barbara. "But anywhere you feel comfortable is fine."

"The sofa works for me," said Jenny. She finished her champagne and headed for the sitting room.

The television was on with the sound muted. Barbara picked up the remote and switched it off. "Take off your shoes," she said. "You'll probably be most relaxed if you lie down but sitting is okay." Jenny sat down on the sofa, slipped off her shoes and then lay back. She plumped up a cushion and slid it behind her head.

"What about me?" asked Nightingale.

"That's up to Jenny," said Barbara. She looked at her friend. "If it makes you uncomfortable then he should stay outside."

"It's okay," said Jenny. "Unless he hears it for himself he's not going to believe it anyway so he might as well stay."

Nightingale sat down in a winged easy chair by the fireplace.

Barbara picked up a chair from around the circular dining table by the window and carried it over to the sofa. She put it down so that she could sit at Jenny's shoulder.

"Are you sitting comfortably?" asked Jenny.

Barbara wagged her finger at Jenny. "You take this seriously, young lady," she said. "You're dealing with a professional, remember?"

"Yes, miss. Sorry, miss." Jenny took a deep breath and exhaled slowly.

"Okay, close your eyes and I want you to listen to your own breathing. Try to breathe as slowly as possible. Slow and even. The slower the better. Not too deep, not too shallow."

Jenny did as she was told. Nightingale crossed his ankles and sat back in his chair. Barbara began to speak in a slow, deep voice, barely more than a murmur, her mouth close to Jenny's ear. Nightingale couldn't make out what she was saying but the tone and rhythm were so soothing that he started to feel his eyelids getting heavy. He blinked and forced himself to concentrate but even then he had to struggle not to fall asleep.

Barbara continued to talk to Jenny for almost five minutes before sitting back in her chair and nodding over at Nightingale. "She's under," she mouthed.

385

Jenny's eyes were closed and her chest was rising and falling slowly. Nightingale could hear a slight wheeze as she breathed in and out.

"Jenny, can you hear me?" asked Barbara quietly.

"Yes," said Jenny, her voice a dull monotone.

"Everything's calm and peaceful. You're safe here, you're among friends. Do you understand?"

"Yes."

"I want you to go back in your mind to the last time that you spoke to your Uncle Marcus. Can you do that for me?"

"Yes," said Jenny.

"Did you talk to him on the phone? Or did you see him?"

"I saw him," said Jenny.

"Where?"

"He came here."

"Here? To your house?"

"Yes."

"When?"

"Three days ago. Saturday."

"That can't be right," said Nightingale.

Barbara silenced him with a warning look, then pressed a finger to her lips. "Shhh."

Nightingale nodded. He was leaning forward in his chair, his elbows resting on his knees.

"Jenny?"

"Yes?"

"I want you to go back to three days ago, when Uncle Marcus came to see you. Can you do that? Can you do that for me, Jenny?"

"Yes," she said.

"It's five minutes before he's due to arrive. What are you wearing?"

"Blue jeans. My Versace T-shirt. The one with the angel wings on the back."

"I need you to look at your watch, Jenny. What time is it?"

"Five to eight," said Jenny.

"And he said he'd come to see you at eight o'clock?"

"Yes. He phoned me before."

"And it's Saturday?"

"Yes. Saturday."

Nightingale frowned as he realised that Jenny had lied when she'd said that the last time she'd seen Fairchild was when he'd gone to the police station. But that didn't make any sense at all. Why would she lie to him?

"Now I want you to go forward until Marcus arrives. Did he knock at the door or ring the bell?"

"He rang the bell. The intercom."

"That's good, Jenny. Now I want you to go to the door and open it. Can you do that for me?"

"Sure," said Jenny.

"So open the door and tell me what you see."

"It's Uncle Marcus."

"What's he wearing, Jenny?"

"A dark blue suit. A pink shirt with a white collar. A dark blue tie."

"And what happened then, Jenny? Did you let him into the house?"

Jenny said nothing.

"Jenny, can you hear me?"

"Yes."

"Marcus is there, standing at the door, right?"

"Yes."

"Good, now I want you to let him in the house. Can you do that?"

Jenny said nothing.

"Jenny? Can you hear me?"

There was no response. Barbara looked over at Nightingale and shrugged. Nightingale made a circling movement with his hand. "Move her forward," he mouthed.

Barbara nodded and turned back to Jenny. "Jenny, I want you to go forward an hour, it's now nine o'clock. Can you do that?"

"Yes," said Jenny.

"Where are you?"

"I'm showering."

"You're in the shower?"

"Yes."

"And where is Uncle Marcus?"

"I don't know."

"Okay, Jenny. I want you to finish showering. What do you do then?"

"I go downstairs."

"Is Uncle Marcus there?"

"No."

Barbara looked over at Nightingale. He made another circular motion with his hand and mouthed, "Take her back."

"Jenny, I want you to go back to eight o'clock. Can you do that for me?"

"Yes," said Jenny.

"Look at your watch, Jenny. Tell me what time you see."

"Eight o'clock."

"That's good. Now I want you to wait until you hear the intercom buzz."

"Yes," said Jenny quietly. She lay on the sofa, breathing softly.

Barbara looked at Nightingale, frowning. He could see that she was worried and he shared her concern. He tried to flash her a reassuring smile but he knew that he wasn't fooling anyone. Something had happened on Saturday evening and he feared the worst.

"There he is," said Jenny. "The intercom is buzzing."

"That's good. Now open the door."

"Okay."

Barbara waited a few seconds. "Have you done that? Have you opened the door?"

"Yes," said Jenny.

"And what do you see, Jenny?"

"It's Uncle Marcus."

"That's good. Now tell me what he's wearing."

"A blue suit and a dark blue tie and a pink shirt."

"Does he say anything?"

"No. He's just smiling."

"That's good. Now let him inside the house."

Jenny continued to breathe softly but didn't say anything.

"Jenny, can you hear me?"

Jenny said nothing but her chest continued to rise and fall slowly.

"Jenny?"

Nightingale stood up and went over to the sofa. He looked down at Jenny, then put a hand on Barbara's shoulder. "What's happening?" he whispered.

"Nothing," said Barbara. "That's the problem. She should be able to tell me what she says and hears but that's not happening." She reached out and stroked Jenny's hand. "Can you hear me, Jenny?"

Jenny didn't react.

"How about taking her back to before he arrives, then move her ahead half an hour?"

Barbara nodded. "Okay, I can try," she said. She took a deep breath, then began to talk in a low hushed voice, her mouth just a few inches from Jenny's ear. "Now, Jenny, I want you to go back to five minutes to eight. Can you do that for me?"

"Yes," said Jenny.

"That's good. And now I want you to look at your watch. Can you tell me what time it says?"

"Five minutes to eight," she said.

"And what are you doing?"

"I'm in the kitchen. Drinking wine and reading."

"What are you reading?"

"A Jodi Picoult book. The new one."

"That's good. Now listen to me very carefully. It's five to eight now. I'm going to ask you to move ahead to half past eight. Are you able to do that for me?"

"Yes," she said.

390

"That's good. So I want you to do that now. Move forward to half past eight. Do it now."

Jenny sighed, and then went still.

"Jenny, can you hear me?" asked Barbara.

There was no reaction. Barbara looked up at Nightingale. "It's just not working."

"Why not? What's the problem?"

"I don't know, Jack. It's as if that hour just doesn't exist for her. She can tell us what happens before he arrives, then she's in the shower afterwards. But there's nothing in between."

Nightingale nodded. "Okay, move her forward until after he's gone."

Barbara turned back to Jenny. "Listen to me, Jenny. I need you to move forward to nine o'clock. Can you do that for me?"

There was no response.

"Jenny, can you hear me?" Barbara stroked Jenny's hand. "Tell me you can hear me." Jenny didn't respond. "Jenny, can you hear me?" Barbara repeated.

"What's wrong?" asked Nightingale, but Barbara ignored him.

She patted the back of Jenny's hand. "Come on, love, I need you to go back. Go back to before he came to the house. Go back to five to eight. Do it now. Come on."

Nightingale could hear the fear in Barbara's voice and he knelt down by the side of the sofa. Jenny wasn't moving and her eyes were closed.

"Jenny, talk to me," said Barbara. "Can you hear me?"

Nightingale's stomach lurched as he realised that Jenny had stopped breathing. "Jenny!" he shouted.

"You mustn't wake her, not like that," said Barbara, still rubbing Jenny's hand.

"She's not breathing, Barbara!" said Nightingale, his heart racing.

"What?"

"Look!" said Nightingale, pointing at Jenny's chest.

Barbara put a hand on Jenny's cheek. "Jenny, it's time to wake up," she said.

Jenny lay completely still.

"Barbara, you're going to have to wake her up now."

"I'm trying," she said. "Nothing like this has ever happened before."

"Jenny!" shouted Nightingale.

Barbara seized Jenny's shoulders and shook her. "Come on, Jenny, wake up!"

Jenny's mouth dropped open but her eyes stayed closed. Nightingale pushed Barbara to the side and pulled Jenny upright. Her head lolled to the side. He shook her hard, then slapped her across the face but she didn't react.

"Shall I call an ambulance?" asked Barbara, her voice trembling.

"No time," said Nightingale. He placed his fingers against Jenny's neck and found a pulse. Her heart was beating but she'd stopped breathing. That made no sense at all. He bent down and grabbed her around the waist, then straightened up with a grunt and carried her out of the sitting room to the stairs.

"Jack, where are you going?" screamed Barbara.

"We've got to snap her out of this, now," said Nightingale. He carried Jenny upstairs, using the banister to pull himself up. The bathroom was at the back of the house, next to the spare bedroom. He rushed in, pulled open the glass door of the shower and carried her inside. He twisted the temperature control to cold and then turned the water on full, gasping as the jet of freezing water washed over them both. He twisted around so that the water sprayed over Jenny's face. Within seconds she began coughing and spluttering, thrashing her head from side to side.

Nightingale lowered her so that her feet were on the floor, and Jenny put out a hand against the tiled wall to steady herself. She shook her head as the freezing water poured down her face, still coughing and fighting for breath.

Barbara followed them into the bathroom and grabbed a white towel.

Nightingale put his hands on either side of Jenny's face and looked into her eyes. "Are you okay?" he asked.

"What the hell are you doing, Jack?"

"How do you feel?"

"Soaking wet and bloody freezing," she said. "How do you think I feel?" She saw Barbara standing at the door clutching the towel. "What's going on, Barbara?"

"The regression went wrong," she said.

Nightingale turned off the shower and tried to help Jenny out but she shrugged him away. "Leave me alone," she snapped.

Barbara wrapped the towel around Jenny.

"Is this because I threw champagne over you?" she asked Nightingale. "Is that what this is about?"

Nightingale shook his head. Water was pouring from his soaking wet clothes and pooling around his shoes. "We need to talk," he said.

CHAPTER
FIFTY-FIVE

Nightingale walked into the sitting room with three mugs of coffee on a tray. He put it down on the table in front of Jenny and Barbara. Jenny had taken off her wet clothes and put on a pink bathrobe. She was on the sofa with her legs curled up underneath her. Nightingale had dried himself off as best he could but he was still wet and he was shivering.

"There's another robe in the airing cupboard," said Jenny. She picked up her mug. "You'll catch your death."

"I'm okay," he said.

"You're not okay," said Barbara. "Jenny's right. You'll end up with pneumonia."

Nightingale shivered and nodded. He headed for the stairs.

"Leave your clothes on the rail in the bathroom," Jenny called after him. "It's heated."

Nightingale went upstairs, took a white robe from the airing cupboard and stripped off his wet clothes in the bathroom. He patted himself down with a towel, put on the robe and hung his clothes on the towel rail to dry.

Jenny and Barbara were sipping coffee when he got back downstairs.

"Did you tell Jenny what happened?" he asked Barbara as he sat down.

"I was waiting for you," she said.

"What happened?" said Jenny.

"What do you remember?" asked Nightingale. He realised that the robe had ridden up his legs and he pulled it down.

"Lying on the sofa. Hearing Barbara telling me to relax. Then the next thing I remember is being in the shower."

The robe rode up Nightingale's thighs again. He pulled it down and then grabbed a cushion and placed it on his lap. He caught Barbara grinning at him but he ignored her. "Jenny, you stopped breathing."

"What?"

"You stopped breathing. Your heart was still going but, trust me, you weren't breathing. We tried to wake you up but you weren't having it. That's why I took you into the shower. I figured cold water was the only way to get a reaction."

"Yeah, well, that worked a treat."

"And you don't remember anything before that? You don't remember what you said to Barbara?"

Jenny shook her head. Nightingale looked over at Barbara. She motioned with her hand for him to continue, and he understood why she didn't want to be the one who told Jenny what had happened. He grimaced, then sipped his coffee, realising that he was playing for time; but he was all too well aware that

Jenny wasn't going to be happy with what he was about to tell her. He put down his coffee mug.

"Okay, here's the thing," he said. "You told us that Marcus Fairchild came around here on Saturday night. Two days before the books vanished."

Jenny's mouth fell open in astonishment. "Rubbish." She looked over at Barbara but Barbara was nodding in agreement. "I already told you that I haven't seen Uncle Marcus since he got you out of the police station."

"While you were under, Barbara asked you when you'd last seen him and you said Saturday evening. And you were quite specific that he came at eight o'clock."

Jenny grabbed a cushion and clutched it to her stomach. "That's impossible."

"Where were you on Saturday evening?" asked Nightingale.

"Here," said Jenny. "But I was alone."

"Reading a Jodi Picoult book?"

"How did you know that?"

"Because you told us," said Nightingale. "You said you were in the kitchen drinking wine and reading a Jodi Picoult book. Wearing blue jeans and a Versace T-shirt."

Jenny hugged the cushion. The blood had drained from her face.

"Are you okay?" Barbara asked her.

Jenny shook her head. "No, of course I'm not okay. He's doing this to play with my head, isn't he?" She ran a hand through her hair. "That's what I said? Really?"

"Word for word," said Barbara. "You were waiting for him to come at eight."

"I have absolutely no recollection of that," said Jenny.

"He buzzed and you opened the door," Nightingale continued. "He was wearing a dark blue suit and a pink shirt, you said. And you let him in."

He stopped speaking and looked across at Barbara.

"Then what?" asked Jenny quickly. "What happened?"

"We don't know," said Barbara. "Something went wrong when we tried to move it forward."

"What do you mean? What went wrong?"

"You saw him at the door. But when we tried to find out what happened when he was in the house, you wouldn't say anything."

"Wouldn't or couldn't," said Nightingale.

"You're scaring me now," said Jenny.

Barbara put a hand on Jenny's arm. "Regression doesn't always work," she said. "Not everyone's susceptible."

"That's not the problem," said Nightingale. "And you know it."

"We don't know what the problem was," said Barbara.

"Jenny nearly died. She stopped breathing. And it happened because you tried to get her to talk about what was happening. You know what the problem was. Marcus bloody Fairchild."

"What?" said Jenny, resting her chin on the cushion. "What do you mean?"

"He did something to your head," said Nightingale. "Same as he did with my sister."

"You don't know that for sure, Jack," said Barbara.

Jenny looked at Barbara. "But it's possible, is that what you're saying?"

"I've never come across anything even remotely like it," said Barbara.

"That's not what I'm asking, Barbara. Is it possible?"

Barbara sighed. "Yes. I suppose so."

"You remembered everything that happened up to the moment you opened the door to him," said Nightingale. "Then it's a blank. But your memory starts again after he'd gone and you're in the shower."

"Why was I in the shower?" asked Jenny.

Nightingale shrugged but didn't say anything.

"My God," said Jenny. She sat back and groaned. "This can't be happening to me."

"Jenny, it's all supposition," said Barbara. "We don't know for sure what happened."

"We tried to move you forward half an hour, to when he was in the house," said Nightingale. "That's when you stopped breathing."

"What are you saying, Jack?" said Jenny. "What do you think happened?"

Nightingale leaned forward. "You want to know what I think? I think Fairchild played the same trick on you that he did on my sister. He made her believe that she killed those kids. How? By hypnosis or black magic, I don't know. But whatever he did to her he did to you. He came round here on Saturday night and got inside your head and removed all memory of whatever he said or did. I think that was when you told him about the basement and the books."

Jenny put her hands over her eyes. "No," she said.

"It's the only explanation, Jenny. It's the only thing that makes sense. And I think you told him about my sister and how Barbara had helped get to the truth. So he decided to ensure that if Barbara did the same with you, you'd die. That's why you stopped breathing. He wanted you dead."

"That's one hell of a leap," said Barbara.

"What other explanation is there?" said Nightingale. "You saw how Jenny reacted when she was under. She wouldn't tell us what was happening and she stopped breathing. If we hadn't dumped her in the shower she'd never have woken up."

Tears were running down Jenny's face.

Barbara put her arm around her. "It's okay, everything's okay now."

Jenny shuddered and shook her head. "No, it's not okay. How can it be okay?" She looked up at Barbara, blinking away her tears. "Why was I in the shower? What did he do to me, Barbara? Why did I have to shower?"

Barbara's mobile rang from inside her bag, which was on the floor by the side of the sofa. "I'm sorry," she said, patting Jenny on the back before grabbing her bag and hurrying to the kitchen to take the call.

Nightingale went to sit next to Jenny. "I'm sorry," he said.

"Why? It's not your fault."

"Because I pushed you into this. It was my idea."

She shook her head. "If you hadn't, I'd never have known." She wiped her eyes with the back of her hands. "I've known him for ever, Jack. How could he have done this to me?"

"I don't know."

She started to cry again and Nightingale put his arm around her. He didn't know what to say to make her feel better; all he could do was to show that he cared. He gave her a hug and then kissed her on the top of the head.

Barbara came back into the room, looking strained. "My bathroom's sprung a leak," she said. "That was Mrs Simmonds, who lives in the flat below me. There's water pouring in and she says if I don't get it fixed now she's going to call the fire brigade."

"Are you serious?"

"Mrs Simmonds is in her eighties and has bad arthritis so doesn't have much of a sense of humour, Jack. I've got to go. She says the water's flooding into her bedroom."

"It's okay, I'll stay with Jenny," said Nightingale.

"Jenny, I'm sorry," said Barbara. "I'll get an emergency plumber in and I'll be right back."

Jenny looked up, wiped away a tear and forced a smile. "I'll be fine," she said. "I'll be going to bed soon anyway."

"Seriously, Barbara, I'll stay with her," said Nightingale.

Barbara nodded. "Okay." She fished her car keys out of her bag. "If you need me later, call me," she said to Jenny.

"Stop worrying about me," said Jenny. She sniffed and wiped her nose. "I'm fine."

Nightingale got up and showed Barbara out.

"I'm serious, Jack," she said. "If you think she needs me, you call me."

"She's had a shock, but she's tough."

"What are you going to do?" she asked. "About Fairchild?"

"I'm not sure," said Nightingale, but even before the words had left his mouth he knew that was a lie. He knew exactly what he was going to do about Marcus Fairchild.

CHAPTER
FIFTY-SIX

"You haven't finished your coffee," said Nightingale, dropping down on the sofa next to Jenny.

"I'm not sure that I need caffeine right now," she said. "You know what I would like?"

"A chocolate muffin?"

Jenny laughed. "I was going to say a drop of brandy but if you've got a banana choc-chip muffin hidden away that would do the trick."

"No muffin, I'm afraid, and Starbucks is shut at this time of night. Where's the brandy?"

"Kitchen," she said. "Cupboard over the fridge."

"Funny place to store the booze."

"I cook with it," she said.

"What a waste."

He patted her on the leg and pushed himself up off the sofa. In the kitchen he found the bottle and two brandy glasses and took them back into the sitting room. He poured two large measures and sat down next to her. They clinked glasses and she gulped hers down before he could say anything. "Hey, careful," he said.

"What do you mean?" she asked, reaching for the bottle.

He grabbed it and held it out of reach. "You're an amateur when it comes to booze," he said. "You should leave the hard drinking to the professionals."

"You, you mean? You drink that poncy Mexican stuff. Now give me that bloody bottle before I break it over your head."

"See? It's already making you aggressive." He laughed and poured brandy into her glass, a smaller measure this time. "Try to savour it and appreciate the bouquet. Don't just throw it down your neck."

"I hear and obey," she said, taking a sip.

"Are you okay?"

She shook her head tearfully. "It's going to be a while before I'm okay," she said.

Nightingale swirled his brandy around his glass. "I'm sorry."

"Stop saying that," said Jenny. "It's not your fault." She sipped her brandy again. "Why do you think he did it?"

"He was getting information from you, about the books. Gosling was well known for buying up every Satanic book he could find, so when he died Fairchild must have figured that, as Gosling's son, the books would have passed to me. So he hypnotised you to find out where they were."

"You think that's all there was?"

Nightingale took a sip of his brandy. It slid down his throat and he felt the warmth spread across his chest.

"You're not answering my question, Jack."

"I don't know," said Nightingale. "How can we know? He erased your memory so we might never know. And I don't see him telling us, do you?"

"Do you think he . . ." She shuddered and didn't finish the sentence.

She hadn't said the words but Nightingale knew what she meant. "Don't think about that, kid."

"How can I not think about it, Jack? There's an hour missing from my life. And I was showering. Why the hell was I in the shower?"

"I don't know, and I'm not sure it's worth guessing."

"That's easy for you to say, Jack."

"I'll take care of it, Jenny. I swear."

"Take care of it? How?"

He put his arm around her. "Don't worry about it."

"What are you going to do, Jack?"

Nightingale took a deep breath and exhaled slowly. "Can't you just leave it, kid?"

"I have a right to know, don't I?" She wiped her damp cheeks with her hands. Nightingale got up off the sofa and went to get her a roll of kitchen towel.

When he got back she was refilling her glass with brandy. He sat down, tore off a couple of pieces of paper towel and gave them to her. She smiled gratefully and dabbed at her face.

"You didn't answer my question," she said. "What are you going to do?"

Nightingale took another sip of brandy. "Marcus Fairchild framed my sister for murders she didn't commit. I'm pretty sure he stole the books from the basement. And he's done God alone knows what to you. He's not going to get away with that."

"So you'll go to the police?"

Nightingale shook his head. "The police won't help. And even if they did, Fairchild's a Satanist. He's got access to all sorts of powers. I'm sure that the police won't be able to touch him."

"So what will you do?"

"I'll take care of it. That's all you need to know. I'll do whatever it takes."

"Promise me one thing?"

"If I can," he said.

"Ask him what he did to me. And why. Will you do that?"

"Don't worry. There're a lot of questions I want answers to."

Jenny nodded and reached for her glass again. Nightingale took her hand. "Please don't," he said.

"It helps," she said.

"How does it help?"

"It numbs me and that's what I need now. I need to stop thinking."

"Alcohol never helps."

"You think I should try smoking instead?"

Nightingale laughed. Jenny slipped her hand around the back of his neck and before he could react she had pulled him down towards her and was kissing him. For a second he kissed her back but then he pushed her away.

"What?" she said.

"What are you doing?"

406

"What do you think I'm doing?" She pulled him back towards her but he resisted.

"This isn't a good idea," he said.

"Why?"

"Because you're vulnerable. Because you're in shock. Because you've been drinking."

"What, you're worried that I'll accuse you of date rape?"

"Don't be daft."

"It won't be rape, Jack. It's what I want. It's what I've wanted for a long time." She kissed him again and this time he found it harder to resist. Her tongue probed between his lips and he found himself kissing her back, but again he pushed her away.

"Jenny . . ." he said, his heart pounding.

"You don't want to?"

"No. I mean yes. Yes, I want to. Of course I want to." He felt his cheeks redden. "This isn't a good time."

"For me? Or for you?"

"For either of us."

"I want you, Jack. And that's got nothing to do with what's happened today or because I've been drinking."

Nightingale smiled. "And what about tomorrow? What happens then?"

"Can we cross that bridge when we get to it?"

"Are you sure?"

"Jack?"

"Yes?"

"Shut up and kiss me."

Nightingale did as he was told.

CHAPTER
FIFTY-SEVEN

Nightingale opened his eyes and frowned at the unfamiliar ceiling. He looked at the window. Blinds and not curtains. It wasn't his bedroom. Then the bed moved and he realised with a start that he wasn't alone. Immediately he remembered where he was and who he was with.

Jenny had turned on her side with her back to him. He looked at his watch. It was just after ten.

"If you want to do a runner I'll pretend I'm asleep," she murmured.

Nightingale laughed and rolled over so that he could put his arms around her. "Idiot," he said.

"I'm sorry, I . . ." She didn't finish the sentence.

"Jenny, I'm here because I want to be here."

"You don't have to say that, Jack. I was vulnerable last night and I needed somebody to be with me."

"I hope you don't mean that you were just using me."

She pushed her backside against him. "Now who's the idiot?" she said.

He held her tighter and pushed his face against her hair. "I guess this is going to make things harder in the office."

"Feels like it's making things hard now," she said, pushing against him again.

"Are you okay?"

"In what way?"

"You and me."

"More than okay."

"You're sure?"

"Jack, you're going to talk this to death if you're not careful."

"Talk what to death?"

Jenny twisted around and rolled on top of him. She kissed him on the lips, her hair falling over his face. "This," she whispered and slipped him inside her.

CHAPTER
FIFTY-EIGHT

Nightingale carefully carried a tray into the room and placed it on the bedside table. He sat down on the bed and gently stroked Jenny's hair. She opened her eyes sleepily and smiled up at him.

"What time is it?" she murmured.

"Eleven," he said.

Jenny ran a hand through her hair. "Shit, I'm late for work," she said. "And my boss is an absolute bastard."

Nightingale grinned. "I'm sure you can twist him around your little finger." He nodded at the tray. "Coffee, and I warmed a croissant for you."

Jenny looked at the tray and frowned. "Where's yours?"

"I've got to go out."

Jenny rubbed her eyes. "Where are you going?"

"I've got to take care of something."

"What?"

He stroked her hair again. "Don't you worry about it," he said.

Jenny sat up and pulled the quilt around her breasts. "You're not going to do something stupid, are you?"

Nightingale smiled. "Do I ever?"

"Frequently."

"I'll be okay," he said.

"Let's just tell the police. Let them handle it."

"Our word against Fairchild's? What good would that do? He's a top lawyer, he plays golf with the Deputy Commissioner, he's probably a Freemason as well as a Satanist. And what evidence do we have? And you can only half remember what happened even when you're under hypnosis."

"So what are you going to do?"

"I'm going to take care of it."

"Can't you just forget it?"

Nightingale took her hand. "Can you?"

Jenny forced a smile. "If I've got you, maybe I can."

"You've got me, kid. But I need to sort this out once and for all."

"Sort out what? Your books? Your sister? Me?"

"All of the above," said Nightingale. "Yes, I want to know what he's done with my books. But I need to know what he did to you and why. And you need to know too."

"And then what?"

"What do you mean?"

"When you know everything, what will you do then?"

"We'll see." He squeezed her hand. "Don't worry."

"You can't tell me not to worry, not when I don't know what you're planning to do."

"I'll be back this evening, okay? I'll fill you in then. I promise."

She grinned. "Fill me in?"

"You know what I mean." He leaned forward and kissed her. She slipped her hand around his neck and tried to pull him back into bed but he slipped out of her grasp.

"Stay here, Jack," she said. "Let's just hang out here, have lunch, fool around."

"I need to get this done first, kid," he said, standing up. "Don't go into the office today. Stay here. Okay?"

Jenny nodded. "You'll come back? Today?"

"Of course." He bent down and kissed her. "I promise."

"Be careful, Jack."

"Always. I just need one thing from you."

"What's that?"

"Fairchild's address."

CHAPTER
FIFTY-NINE

Nightingale put his mobile on hands-free as he drove over Lambeth Bridge and into south London. He called Eddie Morris.

"What do you want, Nightingale?" asked Morris as soon as he took the call.

"What makes you think I want anything, Eddie?"

Eddie Morris was an old-school villain who had put a lot of work Nightingale's way during the two years he'd been a private detective, mainly standing up alibis to keep him out of prison. His speciality was breaking into country houses but he wasn't averse to burgling city centre apartments if the pickings were right. He was the ultimate gamekeeper turned poacher as he'd once worked for one of London's top security companies, and there was nothing he didn't know about burglar alarms and safes.

"Because I only hear from you when you want something."

"I've been hearing that a lot lately," said Nightingale. "I need to update my Christmas card list."

"No, you need to start thinking about other people and not just yourself," said Morris. "It's time you started sharing."

"Bloody hell, Eddie, since when did you go all touchy-feely?"

"I've been watching a lot of daytime television," said Morris. "Jeremy Kyle, Oprah, all that crap. So what do you want?"

"Where are you?"

"Now? Betting shop."

"Can I persuade you to come to Epping with me? I've a job needs doing. Near the forest."

"What sort of job?"

"The sort you're good at. Country house. I assume with all the whistles and bells."

Morris sighed. "Jack, one of these days you're going to drop me in it, you really are."

"I just need you to get me inside. I'll do the rest. If you get caught you can just say you're a squatter. The way the world is, squatters have more rights than owners these days."

"I'll need a monkey."

"To help with the locks?"

"Tosser. Five hundred quid. To help with my expenses."

"How about we take five hundred quid off my next bill?"

"How do you know there'll be a next bill?"

"Because I know you, Eddie. You'll be needing my services again. Look, I'm south of the river, can you meet me there? In Epping?"

"Hang on, you just said you wanted me to go with you."

"I meant to the house. I want you to get me in and then leave me to it. If you've got your own transport then you can drive yourself back to London."

"You'll pay for the petrol?"

"Yes, I'll pay for the bloody petrol. Just make sure you've got your tools with you."

"You're a hard taskmaster, Jack."

"I'll text you the address." Nightingale ended the call. So far so good.

CHAPTER
SIXTY

Nightingale didn't recognise the two heavies standing at the door to Smith's house but he knew the type: big men who spent a lot of time in the gym and who'd probably been behind bars at least once. They were both wearing Oakley shades and heavy leather coats, and their hands were festooned with chunky gold rings. They stared at him as he parked the MGB and climbed out. Nightingale lit a cigarette before walking over to them. From a distance he hadn't realised just how massive the two men were; up close he had to crane his neck to look at them. "I'm here to see Perry," he said.

"He expecting you?" growled the bigger of the two heavies, who was a good six inches taller than Nightingale. He had a gold canine.

"No, but I'm an old friend."

"You don't look like no friend of Perry's," said the other. He had a thick scar across his left cheek that missed his eye by millimetres.

"Yeah, well, we used to be lovers," said Nightingale, flicking ash from his cigarette. "Just tell him Jack Nightingale's here."

"Wait there," said the one with the gold tooth and he walked inside, turning sideways so that his massive

416

shoulders could fit through the door frame. Nightingale had smoked the cigarette halfway down by the time the heavy returned. "I'm gonna have to pat you down," he said.

"Be gentle with me," said Nightingale. He dropped his cigarette onto the pavement, stubbed it out with his shoe, and raised his hands.

"You know they give you cancer," said the heavy as he began to pat Nightingale down. He worked his way along both his arms, then ran his hands over Nightingale's back and chest.

"What do?"

"Cigarettes," said the heavy. His probing fingers found Nightingale's mobile phone in his jacket pocket. He took it out and examined it. "They still make these?" he said, holding up the Nokia to show his colleague. The other man chuckled.

"It's a classic," said Nightingale, taking the phone from him and putting it back in his pocket. "Like the car. Quality never dates."

"Can't take video, can it?"

"It's a phone," said Nightingale. "If I want a video I use a camera. Did Perry ask you to search me or grill me on my use of technology?"

The heavy knelt down and patted Nightingale around the groin and between his legs.

"While you're down there . . ." said Nightingale.

"Don't even think about finishing that sentence," growled the heavy, starting on Nightingale's legs. He checked both legs all the way down to Nightingale's Hush Puppies then straightened up with a grunt.

"Happy?" asked Nightingale, lowering his arms.

"You a cop?"

"Used to be," said Nightingale.

"Yeah, you've got that cocky thing going, haven't you?"

"That's more my natural exuberance," said Nightingale.

"Yeah, well, you wanna watch that your natural exuberance doesn't get you your legs broken," said the heavy. He turned and knocked on the door and it was opened by another heavy. "T-Bone will look after you. You can try your natural exuberance on him."

T-Bone was the heavy who had accompanied Smith to the coffee shop, but he showed no signs of recognising Nightingale. He was wearing a dark blue tracksuit and had a fist-sized gold medallion hanging on a thick gold chain around his neck. He turned and walked down the hallway. Loud rap music was blaring out of the back room, something about shooting a cop in the face and stealing a car.

Smith was sprawled on his sofa, his feet up on the coffee table. He was playing a video game, shooting at soldiers with a sub-machine gun. Sprawled on either side of Smith were pretty blonde girls in short skirts and low halter-neck tops. They were staring with vacant eyes at the screen and rubbing Smith's thighs. "Give me a minute, Nightingale," said Smith, before shooting a soldier in the face and then blasting a group of four soldiers with a single hand grenade. He ducked behind a crate, reloaded, popped up again and let loose a burst that cut down three soldiers; then he tossed a grenade into a Jeep, killing another four men. Smith grinned, paused the game and put the controller on the coffee table. "You an X-box man or a PlayStation man?"

Nightingale shrugged. "To be honest, Perry, I've never seen the attraction of shooting people for fun."

"It's a game, man." He picked up a joint from an ashtray next to the video game console and lit it.

"I guess," said Nightingale. "But you do it enough in a game and maybe the lines get blurred and people start to think that killing's fun and that you always get a new life. And we both know that you don't. You get killed and that's that. There's no reset button." He gestured at the girls. "I need to ask you something. Are you okay for them to be here?"

"Off you go, girls," said Smith, patting the girls on the legs. "Wait for me in the bedroom. If I'm not up in ten minutes, start without me."

One of the girls whispered in his ear and he grinned. He waved T-Bone over. "Give them a couple of wraps," he said.

The girls uncurled themselves from around Smith and left the room with T-Bone. In the hallway he gave them two wraps of crack cocaine and they went upstairs, giggling.

"Fit, huh?" said Smith.

"Yeah, they say gentlemen prefer blondes. What are they? Russians?"

"Latvians. And they'll do anything for crack. Now, to what do I owe the pleasure, Nightingale? I thought you and I were old news."

"You sorted out the Reggie thing?"

Smith grinned. "Reggie who?" He looked over at T-Bone. "You know anyone called Reggie?"

T-Bone shook his head. "Name don't ring a bell."

Smith stretched his arms out along the back of the sofa. "Looks like the Reggie thing, whatever it was, got sorted," he said. "So what do you want?"

"Bit of business, actually," said Nightingale.

Smith blew a cloud of sweet-smelling smoke at him. "Not sure I wanna do business with a former cop," said Smith. T-Bone stood behind the sofa, his arms folded across his massive chest.

Nightingale reached inside his raincoat and pulled out a manila envelope. He tossed it onto the table in front of Smith. Smith leaned forward and picked it up, the joint clamped between his teeth. He opened the envelope and rifled through a thick wad of fifty-pound notes. He nodded and sat back, looking expectantly at Nightingale.

"I need a gun," said Nightingale.

Smith grinned. "A gun?"

"Yeah. A bloody big one."

"What's your game, Nightingale?"

"No game. I want to buy a gun."

Smith's nostrils flared as if he'd smelled something bad in the room.

"My money's good," said Nightingale. "I left the stuff I printed back at home."

"Do I need to get you to strip down again, Nightingale?" His eyes hardened.

"What, you think I'd wear a wire to get you on a gun charge?"

"Last time I checked having a gun gets you a ten stretch."

Nightingale sighed, opened his raincoat and began to unbutton his shirt. Smith took his joint out of his mouth and waved for him to stop.

"I don't want to see your raggedy arse again," he growled. He scratched his chin and then nodded. "Okay, this is how it's going to work. You pick up that money and put it back in your pocket." He gestured with his joint at the heavy standing by the door. "T-Bone there is going to take you for a ride and show you what we've got. You're going to give him the money and all's well that ends well."

"Cool," said Nightingale, reaching for the envelope.

Smith lashed out with his foot and slammed his shoe down on the envelope, missing Nightingale's hand by a fraction of an inch. "Just so we're clear," said Smith. "If anything happens to T-Bone, if he so much as gets a parking ticket today, then I'll come looking for you again and this time I won't miss. Clear?"

"Like glass," said Nightingale.

Smith moved his foot. Nightingale took the envelope and put it in his pocket. "Thanks," he said.

"This ain't nothing to do with me. This is between you and T-Bone." He grinned. "But you're welcome."

CHAPTER
SIXTY-ONE

Nightingale followed T-Bone out of the house and along the road. The heavy was now wearing a Puffa jacket over his tracksuit, and black leather gloves.

"Where you parked?" growled the heavy. Nightingale pointed at the MGB. "That works?" said T-Bone. "What is it, clockwork?"

"It's a classic," said Nightingale.

"That's rust around the wheel arch, innit?"

"A bit. When you're that age you'll probably be a little rusty around the edges."

T-Bone chuckled. "You're a funny man, Nightingale."

"I have my moments," said Nightingale. He took out his cigarettes and offered the pack to T-Bone, who shook his head. Nightingale lit a cigarette and blew smoke up at the sky, careful to keep it away from the other man. "So how did you get a nickname like T-Bone?" he asked. "You got a bit of an appetite?"

T-Bone shook his head. "Nearly killed a guy with a stake once."

"What? A piece of meat?"

"Broken bit of wood. Like doing a vampire. He had a machete; I had a stake."

"And how do you get from impaling to T-Bone?"

"It's ironic, innit?" he said. "You never have a nickname?" He grinned, showing two gold front teeth.

"They called me Birdy at school."

"Nice," said T-Bone. He nodded at the MGB. "You get in your toy car and follow me. We're going to a lock-up in Streatham."

"Streatham? That's not far; why don't we go in the same car?"

"Because I'm not riding in your piece of shit and you're as sure as hell not riding in my motor. If we get stopped I want deniability."

"We won't get stopped."

"You don't know that. Black man in an expensive car, he's got a target on his back. So you follow me." He jerked a thumb at the MGB. "How fast will that thing go?"

"I'll keep up with you. I'll pedal real fast."

T-Bone laughed and clapped Nightingale on the back. "I like you," he said. The smile vanished and he gripped Nightingale's shoulder. "What Perry said back there is only half the story," he said. "Anything happens to me you'd better hope I don't get bail because I'll personally be tearing off your balls and shoving them down your throat. Hear?"

Nightingale nodded. "I just want a gun," he said.

"I know. A big one. Don't worry about that; we've got big guns coming out of our arses."

"Nice image," said Nightingale. He blew smoke. "Let's go. I've got things to do, rivers to cross, mountains to climb."

"What?"

Nightingale grinned. "My clock's ticking." He dropped the cigarette onto the pavement and stamped it out.

T-Bone went over to a black Porsche SUV and climbed in. He waited until Nightingale was in the MGB and then pulled away from the kerb and headed south. Nightingale kept close behind. T-Bone slowed down when they reached Streatham and after they'd driven along the High Road he made a right turn and then a left and then drove down an alley between two rows of houses. They came to a block of six brick-built lock-up garages with metal doors and corrugated iron roofs. There was a black Lexus there, its engine running. T-Bone parked facing it. Nightingale pulled in behind the Porsche and parked. As he climbed out, T-Bone was hugging two big black men who had got out of the Lexus. Nightingale recognised one of them from the photographs that Dan Evans had shown him by the Serpentine.

T-Bone said something and they all laughed, then T-Bone pulled out a set of keys, unlocked the door of one of the lock-ups and pushed it up. The other two went back and leaned against the bonnet of their Lexus, their hands deep in the pockets of their overcoats. As Nightingale walked over to the lock-up, one of the men pulled something black and metallic from his pocket. Nightingale's heart began to race but then he realised it was a Magnalite torch. The man chuckled as he switched on the torch as if he knew what Nightingale had been thinking.

T-Bone waved for Nightingale to join him and disappeared inside the lock-up. The man with the torch pushed himself off the Lexus and followed T-Bone. There was an old Jaguar there, its boot facing outwards. T-Bone pulled the door down behind them. "Don't want anybody looking in," he explained. He used another key to open the boot, then stood to the side to allow Nightingale to see into it. The other man used his torch to illuminate a dozen or so sackcloth-wrapped packages.

Nightingale picked up one of the packages and unwrapped it. It was a Glock, similar to the one he'd used when he was with CO19. He rewrapped it and put it back in the boot.

"Too small?" said T-Bone. A larger package contained a sawn-off shotgun with a stubby single barrel and a pistol-grip butt. "Takes five shells," said T-Bone. "Untraceable. It'll blow off everything above the waist from six feet away. Bang!"

"Maybe not quite as big as that," said Nightingale. "You know what I'd really like? An MP5."

T-Bone sneered as he rewrapped the shotgun. "Nine mills don't do no damage," he said. "Like the Glock. Nice gun, but most guys I know could take a couple of nine-mill slugs and keep on walking. You get shot in the face with this and you ain't going nowhere." He put the package back in the boot. "Are you going to fire it?"

"Am I what?"

"The gun. You gonna fire it or just wave it around? Horses for courses, innit?"

"I'm going to be playing it by ear."

"Here's the thing. If you don't fire it you can sell it back to us at fifty pence in the pound. You buy for five hundred and we'll take it back for two-fifty. But if it's been fired it's on you because then it's traceable."

"Unless it's the sawn-off?"

"You can fire that all day long and it'll never be traced," said T-Bone. "But if you're gonna be letting rip then you don't want the Glock or the MP5 or the MAC-10 because you're gonna be spitting out shells all over the place."

"Yeah, well, when Perry came after me I seem to remember the tinkle of casings hitting the pavement."

T-Bone chuckled. "That was Reggie's idea," he said. "He wasn't concerned about getting his money back. They were brand new and he was planning to sell them on to a gang north of the river so that they'd take the heat for your hit."

"Nice," said Nightingale.

"He was clever like that, all right," said T-Bone. "Too clever for his own good as it turned out. But if you're planning to let fly you'd be better off with a revolver. Keep your casings."

"Fewer shots, though."

"See, you being a cop and all I'd be thinking you'd make every shot count," said T-Bone.

Nightingale smiled at the irony of a former member of a Metropolitan Police armed response unit being given firearms advice by a south London gangster, but everything that T-Bone said was right. Nightingale didn't know how the evening was going to play out but if he did have to fire the weapon he didn't want to be

426

leaving evidence around. "So what do you have in the way of revolvers?"

"I can do you a nice Smith & Wesson," said T-Bone, reaching for a second parcel.

Inside were two stainless-steel guns with black rubberised handgrips that looked very similar but Nightingale recognised one as the Model 627, a .357 Magnum that took eight rounds while the other was a Model 629, a .44 Magnum that held six rounds. The 627 had a four-inch barrel and the 629's was more than an inch shorter.

"Nice," said Nightingale, reaching for the 627. He checked the action and nodded approvingly.

"You wouldn't want to be firing at any distance," said T-Bone. "But with eight in the cylinder you've got more of a margin for error."

"How much?" said Nightingale.

"Twelve hundred quid."

"What? I only want the one."

"List price in the States for them both is about a thousand dollars. And we have to get them over here."

"Do I have 'idiot' written on my forehead?"

"I can't see in this light," said T-Bone. "Maybe. But for a new gun that's the price, innit?" He took the 627 off Nightingale and wrapped it up. "How close do you think you're getting to the target?"

"Not sure," said Nightingale. "Why?"

"The Smith & Wessons have both got short barrels. I've got something a bit longer." He rooted among the packages and pulled out the one that he was looking for. "It's a Taurus 627," he said, handing the gun to

Nightingale. "The barrel's eight and a half inches so you can be accurate up to fifty feet without too much trouble, seventy-five feet if you're lucky. Holds seven rounds, not too much of a kick, but again you know what you're doing so that shouldn't be a problem."

Nightingale nodded, then looked along the barrel.

"It's a bit front-heavy so two hands are better than one," said T-Bone. "The grip's a bit small but you're not a big man."

"I've had no complaints," said Nightingale.

T-Bone wagged a gloved finger at him. "Funny man," he said.

"How much?" asked Nightingale.

"It goes for about five hundred bucks in the States so you can have it for seven hundred and fifty."

"Dollars?"

"You should do stand-up, Birdman," said T-Bone. "Quid. But I'll throw in a box of rounds."

Nightingale took out the envelope of cash, then turned his back on T-Bone while he counted out the notes. He heard T-Bone chuckling behind him but he ignored him. He turned round again and gave him the money.

T-Bone shoved it into his coat pocket without counting it, handed Nightingale the gun and then pulled a box of cartridges from the boot. He gave them to Nightingale. "Pleasure doing business with you," he said. He raised the door and daylight flooded in. "Like I said, return it unfired and I'll give you half the cash back."

428

"That's not going to happen," said Nightingale. "Whatever happens, I'll dispose of it."

"Pity," said T-Bone. "It's a nice bit of kit." He pulled the door down and locked it. As he straightened up he stopped smiling and looked at Nightingale with dead eyes. "If anything happens to this stash any time soon, your life won't be worth living. You know that, right?"

"I hear you," said Nightingale.

T-Bone took a step closer and glowered down at him. "Don't let my pleasant disposition lull you into a false sense of security," he said. "Just because you were a cop doesn't mean you can't be hurt. And hurt bad. And if you fuck with us, I'll be the one doing the hurting. Clear?"

"Crystal," said Nightingale. He winked. "Be lucky, T-Bone."

"Yeah. You too, Birdman."

Nightingale shoved the gun into his pocket as he walked back to the MGB.

CHAPTER
SIXTY-TWO

Nightingale called Morris on his mobile when he was a few miles away from Fairchild's house. "Are you ready, Eddie?"

"I'm in the pub, about half a mile past the house," said Morris.

"You're not drinking, are you?"

"You're not my mother, Nightingale. And I'm the one doing the favour here."

"For a monkey. Let's not forget the five hundred quid in my pocket. See you in a bit."

Nightingale ended the call. He slowed the car once he got near the house, getting a good look at it as he drove past. It was a stone barn conversion with a steep roof that looked brand new and a dovecote at one end. There was a sweeping driveway leading from the main road and a two-car garage running at a right angle to the main house. Nightingale had phoned Fairchild's Mayfair office and confirmed that the lawyer was in London, and a check of the electoral roll had shown that he lived alone in the house.

Nightingale parked at the side of the pub and found Morris at the bar drinking a bitter lemon. Nightingale ordered a coffee from the landlord. "I'm pretty sure the house is empty," he said. "There's an alarm box on the side wall. That means there's probably not a link to the cops, right?"

"Sometimes they have both," said Morris. "But the nearest cop shop with twenty-four hour cover is thirty miles away so there's not much point in a phone link. But I'll be able to deal with it no matter what the system."

"It's that easy, is it?"

Morris tapped the side of his nose. "It is if you know what you're doing. I used to install them, and nine times out of ten the factory setting is still there. Even if it's not . . ." He shrugged.

Nightingale's coffee arrived.

"By the way, have you got my cash?" asked Morris.

Nightingale sighed, took out his envelope of cash and counted out ten fifty-pound notes.

"Petrol?" said Morris.

Shaking his head, Nightingale sighed again and then handed over another fifty-pound note.

Morris grinned and pocketed the money. "You're a prince among men," he said. "Right, how are we going to do this?"

"I'll leave my car here," said Nightingale. "We take your car to the house, you get me in, then you shove off back to London."

"You're staying?"

"That's the plan. And when I'm done I'll come back here and pick up my car."

"What are you up to, Jack?"

"It's complicated," said Nightingale.

"You're not robbing the place, I hope."

"If anything it's the opposite. He's stolen from me."

"So we're on the side of law and order?"

"Not exactly," said Nightingale. He finished his coffee and patted Morris on the back. "Let's go."

Morris had parked his Saab behind the pub. "I need to get something from my car," said Nightingale. He went around to the MGB and retrieved the Taurus and the box of ammunition from the glove compartment. He put the gun in his right coat pocket and the cartridges in the left. They were so heavy that they pulled the coat down, so he took it off, rolled it up and carried it. He figured that Morris wouldn't be as amenable if he knew that Nightingale was carrying a gun.

The Saab pulled up next to the MGB and Nightingale climbed into the passenger seat then sat with the coat on his lap. "Not cold?" asked Morris.

"Adrenaline," said Nightingale. He felt the gun shift and held the coat tighter.

"Do you want me to park on the road or what?"

"Let's just drive straight up to the house," said Nightingale. "I know the guy so just in case there's somebody inside I'll ring the bell. If there is someone there I'll spin them a line and we'll get the hell out of Dodge."

"You said the place was empty."

"I said the guy isn't there. He's in London. And as far as I know he lives alone. But there's a chance he has a housekeeper or something."

"And if he has, then what?"

"Then we have a rethink. But there's no point in counting chickens."

Morris turned off the road and pulled up in front of the house. He stayed in the car while Nightingale got out. Nightingale kept a tight hold on his coat as he walked up to the front door. He pressed the doorbell twice but no one answered. He turned and gave Morris a thumbs up.

Morris joined him at the front door, carrying a black gym bag with a Nike swoosh across the side.

"How do you want to play this?" asked Nightingale.

"I'll go in through the back," said Morris. He lifted the bag. "I've got the gear to get through most locks here but if all else fails I'll go through a window. You'll hear the alarm start to beep inside once the sensors kick off but I'll get straight to the console and get it sorted."

"Go for it," said Nightingale. "If there's a problem I'll call you."

Morris nodded and walked around the side of the house. Nightingale unrolled his coat, put it on, then lit a cigarette. He was halfway through it when he heard a beeping sound from the hallway. Then he heard footsteps hurrying across a wooden floor. The beeping continued and Nightingale pulled a face as he anticipated the burglar alarm bursting into life. There was a muffled curse from the other side of the door and then the sound of something metallic hitting the floor, another curse followed and then the beeping stopped. Nightingale flicked what was left of his cigarette across the lawn. The front door opened and Morris stood aside to let Nightingale in.

"Any problems?" he asked.

Morris gestured at a control panel on the wall by the stairs. The panel had been opened to expose the circuitry. "They'd removed the factory settings so it took me a bit longer than usual, but all good. In fact I've added another code so you can come back whenever you want. Just key in four nines and Robert's your father's brother." He went over to the console and began to reattach the cover.

"I doubt that I'll be back," said Nightingale. "But thanks." To the right was a huge open-plan room with exposed beams high overhead and a brick fireplace. "How did you get in?"

"Kitchen door. It wasn't bolted and I didn't damage the lock. You can lock it from the inside and leave by the front door and no one will be the wiser. Or are you planning on staying until he gets here?"

"Why do you say that?"

Morris finished fixing the burglar alarm console and picked up his holdall. "Let's just say that either you're very pleased to see me or that's a gun in your pocket."

Nightingale's hand went instinctively to his pocket. The gun was weighing down his coat on that side. "Thanks for getting me in, Eddie. You can head off now."

"What's going on, Jack?"

"Just go, Eddie."

"I've known you a long time. Since you were a copper, remember? I know that you're not a cop any

434

more but you've always played by the rules. That's why I put business your way. People trust you because they know you're a straight shooter." He grinned. "Now isn't that an unfortunate choice of words?"

"This is personal, Eddie, and you don't know the background."

"I know that guns don't solve anything."

"I think the army might beg to differ."

"Yeah, but you're not in the army. And you're not a cop. You're Joe Soap, just like the rest of us. And just carrying a firearm will get you ten years. And you pull the trigger in anger and they'll throw away the key."

"I can't believe you're lecturing me on the law," said Nightingale. "It seems to be my day for receiving advice." He nodded at the door. "I know what I'm doing, Eddie. I'll be fine."

Morris shrugged, clearly not convinced. He forced a smile and headed out of the door. Nightingale closed it and waited until he heard the Saab drive away before taking out the gun and clicking the safety off.

CHAPTER
SIXTY-THREE

Nightingale walked up the stairs, the gun in his hand. At the top of the stairs was a hallway off which there were four doors. One was to a wet room, all grey marble, stainless steel and glass. Next to it was a bedroom with a Japanese theme; it contained a futon bed, black lacquered chests with brightly coloured birds on the sides, and a framed kimono on one wall. The door next to the Japanese bedroom was locked. Nightingale bent down and squinted through the keyhole but the room beyond was in darkness. He straightened up then stiffened as he heard a car horn. He hurried back into the Japanese room and carefully peered through the slatted wooden blinds, but the driveway was empty. The horn sounded again and he saw a white van in the road trying to overtake a Volvo towing a caravan.

Nightingale reached for his cigarettes but then realised that smoking in the house wouldn't be a good idea. Fairchild was a cigar smoker but even so he'd probably smell the cigarette smoke as soon as he opened the front door. He went back to the landing. The final door led through to the master bedroom. This room had thick beams running overhead, a large picture window looking over the garden and a small orchard, a big-screen plasma television on one wall and a king-size bed with leopard-print duvet and pillows. To the right was a door leading to another bathroom; this one had a large roll-top bath with clawed feet. One wall was mirrored and Nightingale stared at his reflection. His hair was unkempt and his face looked strained. He tried smiling but it felt more like a snarl. "Are you looking at me?" he said to his reflection in a passable attempt at a Robert de Niro impersonation, and took aim with the gun. "Because I don't see anyone else standing here." He grinned and winced as he realised that he appeared even more manic.

He went back into the main bedroom. There were black wooden cabinets on either side of the bed, and standing on the top of each one was a modern chrome lamp. He went over to the cabinet on the right side and pulled open a drawer. Inside were several packs of Viagra and a bottle of massage oil. Nightingale chuckled and closed the drawer.

He went back downstairs feeling less apprehensive now that he was more familiar with the layout of the house. He walked through the sitting room, which was an interesting mix of old and modern. The furniture was Italian — low, white leather sofas and black leather and chrome chairs — and there was a huge plasma screen on one wall with a state-of-the-art sound system. The bare floorboards had been polished like glass, but overhead were old blackened beams dotted with woodworm holes, and there were various rusting agricultural implements on the walls, including a ploughshare and an enormous scythe. The walls were criss-crossed with more original beams, blackened with age. In one wall was a huge brick fireplace that was big enough to walk into and there was a metal grate piled high with logs.

As he stood in the middle of the room he realised that there was nothing of a personal nature to be seen. No photographs, no souvenirs, no books or magazines. It was as if he was standing in a show house that had yet to be occupied. The sensation was so strong that he went back upstairs and slid open the wardrobe door. There were suits and shirts lined up on hangers and a rack of ties; in the drawers there were socks and underwear. He closed the door, satisfied that Fairchild did actually live there.

Downstairs again he found that opposite the sitting room was a door that opened into a study. It had a low ceiling, with half a dozen parallel beams, and a small fireplace with ashes in the grate that suggested it had been used recently. Dark wooden bookshelves lined the walls, and in front of the old desk was a captain's chair. For the first time since he'd set foot in the house Nightingale saw personal items: framed certificates for educational and professional qualifications on the wall behind the desk, a humidor on a table. He opened the humidor and inhaled the heady aroma of top-quality cigars. There was a green-leather winged armchair next to the fireplace and on the mahogany table by the side of it was a crystal ashtray containing a couple of cigar butts.

Nightingale ran his finger along a line of books. They were mainly concerned with criminal law, psychology and politics. He checked all the shelves but couldn't find any volumes about witchcraft or devil-worship.

He went back to the hallway and along to the kitchen. There were more beams across the ceiling but the appliances and units were all of stainless steel and the worktops of black marble. There was a door leading to the rear garden, and another one next to the large double-fronted fridge. Nightingale frowned as he wondered where the second door led, then realised that it could only open into the double garage. He tried to open it but it was locked. Glancing around the kitchen he saw a row of keys on a rack close to the back door. There were several that looked as if they might fit the lock to the garage door so he took them and tried them one by one. The third one that he tried worked. He put the keys down on a worktop and pushed the door open.

The double garage had been filled with metal trunks, dozens and dozens of them, and Nightingale knew immediately what they contained. He went over to the nearest trunk and saw it had catches on either side of the lid and a lock in the middle. Selecting a hammer from the rows of tools hanging on one of the walls, he used it to smash the lock, then he undid the catches. He pulled open the lid to find the trunk filled with leather-bound books. The first one he picked up and opened had a woodcut of a devil holding a pitchfork and standing in front of a woman with long hair; above it was the title *Spells To Repel A Curse And Other Magiks*. Nightingale flicked through the book. It had

439

been handwritten in copperplate script, the ink fading in places. Nightingale put the book back into the trunk. "Got you, you bastard," he muttered under his breath.

He jumped as his phone rang. It was Jenny.

"Where are you?" she asked.

"Fairchild's house," he said. "The books are here. All of them. In dozens of metal trunks. He must have had a small army helping him."

"What are you going to do? Call the police?"

"The police won't do anything, kid. I can't even prove that the books are mine and anyway I'd have to explain how I got into the house."

"Did you break in?"

"No, he left a key under the mat." He laughed. "Of course I broke in."

"So are you coming back now?"

"Soon," he said. "Are you okay?"

"I'm tired," she said. "I'm going to lie down. Don't be too late."

Nightingale ended the call and went back to the sitting room. He put the gun on the coffee table and sat down on one of the chrome and leather chairs. It wasn't comfortable but that was a good thing because he didn't want to fall asleep.

CHAPTER
SIXTY-FOUR

Jenny woke up to the sound of buzzing and she groped for her alarm clock. As she fumbled for the off switch she realised that it wasn't her clock; it was the door intercom, buzzing in the kitchen. She blinked as she stared at the clock. It was just after nine. She pulled on her robe and hurried downstairs. As she reached the bottom she remembered that she hadn't checked the intercom. She turned to go back upstairs but then the buzzer rang again, longer this time. It was probably Nightingale. "Okay, okay," she said, hurrying across the hall to the front door. She opened it but froze when she saw who was standing on her doorstep. It was Marcus Fairchild. He was wearing a double-breasted blazer, beige slacks and shiny brown shoes. He smiled and his eyes sparkled.

"Good evening, darling," he said. "I didn't realise you went to bed so early."

Jenny took a step back, clutching her robe around her neck. "What do you want?" she asked.

His smile broadened. "Don't worry, darling," he said, stepping towards her. "There's absolutely nothing to worry about." Jenny backed down the

441

hallway. She could feel the strength draining from her legs. "Now listen to me, darling, listen to me very carefully."

CHAPTER
SIXTY-FIVE

Nightingale groaned and stretched and slapped his right cheek a couple of times, trying to wake himself up. He was sitting on one of Fairchild's sofas, his feet on a glass coffee table that was balanced on three large marble spheres. At just after ten o'clock he'd raided the fridge and found some cheese, tomatoes and celery and he'd eaten them with a couple of slices of bread and butter, and a can of Carlsberg. By his feet was a crystal ashtray with half a dozen cigarette butts in it. Once he'd found all the books in the trunks in Fairchild's garage he'd decided that there was no point in keeping a low profile. One way or another it would all be over by morning, so he'd sat and he'd smoked and he'd waited.

Every book from the basement of Gosling Manor had been packed into the trunks and transported to Epping. It would have needed a huge truck and quite a bit of manpower. Nightingale hadn't even considered calling the police. He wasn't sitting there in the dark because he wanted to talk to Fairchild about stolen books. He wanted to talk to Fairchild, that much was true. But Nightingale wanted to know exactly what the man had done to Jenny, and why. And he was sure that

Fairchild would tell him, not because of the gun that Nightingale would be pointing at his chest but because the lawyer was arrogant, one of life's boasters. He'd want to tell Nightingale everything, to revel in his superiority. Nightingale would listen to Fairchild, he'd hear everything that the man had to say, and then he'd pull the trigger.

He reached for his pack of Marlboro. There were only three cigarettes left. He cursed under his breath. Why hadn't Fairchild come home? When ten o'clock had come and gone Nightingale had assumed that Fairchild had gone for dinner in London, but now it was starting to look as if he wasn't coming home at all.

Standing up, he paced around the room as he smoked, then he stood at the window and looked out over the garden towards the road. He looked at his watch. It was just after midnight. He had no choice now: he had to wait until Fairchild came home because when he did he'd smell the smoke and he'd notice the missing food and he'd realise that someone had been in the house.

Nightingale flinched as his mobile burst into life. He went over to the coffee table, picked up the phone and looked at the screen. It was Jenny. He pressed the green button to take the call. "Hi, kid, are you okay? I thought you were going to sleep."

"Where are you, Jack?"

"I'm still in Epping. Fairchild hasn't come back yet."

"Jack, I want you to come back. Now."

"I want to wait until Fairchild comes home."

"And then what?"

"Best you don't know, kid. But I'll take care of it. He'll never hurt you again; I'll make sure of that."

Jenny sniffed. "Please come back, Jack."

"What's wrong?"

"I'm scared. I need you."

"Jenny, just a few more hours."

"Please, Jack." She began to cry.

"Jenny, honey, let me do this and then I'll be straight back."

Jenny said nothing but he could hear her sobs.

"What's wrong, Jenny?"

"I don't want to be on my own. I'm scared."

"Did something happen?"

"I just need you here. Now."

The line went dead.

CHAPTER
SIXTY-SIX

Nightingale parked outside Jenny's house. He climbed out of the MGB and pressed the buzzer on the intercom. There was a chill in the air and his breath feathered around his mouth as he stamped his feet to warm them up. He pressed the buzzer a second time. He stood back and looked up at the upper windows of the mews house. There was a light on in the front bedroom. He reached out to knock on the door but realised that it was ajar. He pushed it open. The light was on in the kitchen at the end of the hallway. Nightingale looked back at the MGB. He'd left the gun in the glove compartment because he knew that if Jenny saw it she wouldn't be happy.

"Jack, is that you?"

Nightingale peered down the hallway. "Jenny? The door's open." There was no answer. "Jenny, are you okay?"

"I'm in the kitchen."

Nightingale stepped inside the hall and closed the door. "How are you feeling?" he called. There was still no answer. "Jenny?"

He heard what sounded like a sob and he hurried down the hallway. She was sitting at the kitchen table wearing her pink bathrobe. He walked towards her.

446

"Jenny?" he said.

She was trembling and then she looked to her left and Marcus Fairchild stepped from behind the kitchen door. He was holding a carving knife.

Nightingale froze.

"Don't be shy, Jack," said Fairchild. "Come and join us."

Nightingale took out his mobile phone.

"Don't even think about making a call," said Fairchild, walking behind Jenny and thrusting the knife against her neck. He grabbed her hair with his left hand and pulled her head back, exposing her neck.

"There's no need for that, Marcus," said Nightingale. He put the phone away and raised his hands. "We can sort this out. There's no need for anyone to get hurt."

Fairchild laughed harshly. "You think you can negotiate with me, Jack? Big mistake." He pressed the knife harder against Jenny's throat. Jenny stared at Nightingale, her eyes wide with fear but she didn't put up any resistance.

"What is it you want, Marcus? The books? You can have the books. All of them. Just leave Jenny alone."

"This isn't about the books, Jack. It's not about Jenny either."

"What, then? What's the point of all this?"

Fairchild laughed again. "Don't you get it, Jack? You're the point. It always has been you."

Nightingale started to walk towards the kitchen, keeping his hands up. "We can sort this out, Marcus. It doesn't have to end badly."

As he passed the door that led to the garage, it opened. Nightingale began to turn but he stopped when something hard pressed against the small of his back. It was the barrel of a gun. The gun was being held by a short man with rat-like eyes and a receding chin. His hair was slicked back with oil that glistened in the overhead lights.

"Just keep walking, nice and slowly," said Marcus. "It'll soon be over."

CHAPTER
SIXTY-SEVEN

Nightingale held up his hands as he walked into the kitchen. The gunman was close behind him, keeping the barrel pressed into the small of Nightingale's back. That was a mistake, Nightingale knew. If he turned quickly enough there was a good chance that he'd be able to push the weapon to the side before the man could pull the trigger. But it wasn't the man with the gun that Nightingale was worried about; it was Marcus Fairchild and the knife that he was holding to Jenny's neck.

"What do you want?" asked Nightingale. "Whatever you want, you can have it, Marcus. Just let Jenny go."

"What I want? This isn't about what I want."

Nightingale frowned. "What do you mean?"

"You really are stupid, aren't you? Have you forgotten what you did? You cheated Proserpine out of your soul. Then you cheated Lucifuge Rofocale. You think you can play around with the Fallen without there being repercussions?"

"I didn't cheat anybody. I did deals. I gave Proserpine what she wanted and Lucifuge Rofocale did what he had to do to keep the peace."

Fairchild sneered at Nightingale and pressed the knife harder against Jenny's throat. "They don't see it that way, Nightingale, and now it's time for you to pay the piper."

"Okay, but this has nothing to do with Jenny. Let her go, Marcus. Let her go and you can do whatever you want to me. You've won. Okay? Just let her go."

"This isn't about me. This isn't about what I want."

"Just let Jenny go. Please. I'm begging you."

Fairchild shook his head. "That's not going to happen," he said. "That's not how this is going to play out. That's not what they want."

"What do they want, Marcus? Tell me."

"They want you to suffer, Nightingale. They want you to suffer in this world and the next. And that suffering starts here."

"What have they told you to do?"

Fairchild sneered at him. "They want you to kill her."

"What?" A chill ran down Nightingale's spine.

"They want her dead and you to take the blame. They want you behind bars. Locked away. For the rest of your life."

"Marcus, this is crazy talk. You know that."

"You had sex with her. Your sperm is inside her. They'll find you with the knife in your hands and her blood all over you. You were a cop, Nightingale. You know how they can put two and two together." He chuckled. "That's pretty much all they can do. But it's enough. Your sperm. Your prints on the knife. Your options are pretty limited."

"I haven't touched the knife."

"Not yet," said Fairchild.

Nightingale realised that Fairchild was wearing black leather gloves. "Don't do this, Marcus. Please."

Fairchild laughed out loud. "Is that the best you can do? You were a police negotiator, right? And that's your best shot? To say 'please'? That's it?"

"She's your god-daughter," said Nightingale. "She's loved you her whole life."

"You think I care? She's nothing to me. A quick shag when I wanted one, that's all."

Nightingale stared at Fairchild in horror.

"Hadn't you worked that out already? I've been fucking her since she was ten years old."

"No . . ." Jenny gasped, and for the first time she began to struggle. Fairchild yanked her hair savagely and she grunted in pain.

"Lost a lot of attraction once she was legal, but I'd revisit her every few months, just for old time's sake. She doesn't remember a thing, of course. But she enjoys it, Nightingale. She could screw for England, this one."

Nightingale took a step towards him but Fairchild pushed the knife harder against Jenny's throat. "Don't even think about it. You take one more step and she's dead."

"Uncle Marcus," moaned Jenny.

"Shut up, whore!" he hissed. "This is nothing to do with you." He glared at Nightingale. "You still haven't worked it out, have you? Last night, she was doing what I told her to do. What I programmed her to do.

Everything the two of you did, last night and this morning, was down to me, Nightingale. She screwed you because I told her to screw you." He laughed. "How does that make you feel, Nightingale? Angry? Angry enough to kill?"

"You bastard."

"Yes, I am a bastard. An evil bastard. Now do you know how this ends? Have you worked it out yet?"

"Don't do this," said Nightingale.

"Do what? This?" Fairchild drew the knife across Jenny's throat and her blood sprayed across the floor.

Nightingale opened his mouth to scream but then the butt of the gun slammed against his temple and he fell to his knees. He saw blood pumping from the gaping wound in Jenny's neck. She was still alive, just, and he could see the fear and panic in her eyes and then everything went black and he slumped to the floor.

CHAPTER
SIXTY-EIGHT

"Jack, you have to get up." Nightingale groaned. "Jack, come on. Wake up." Nightingale's eyes fluttered open. He was lying on his front, his face turned towards the oven. "Jack!"

"Jenny?" he moaned.

"Wake up, Jack."

He pushed himself up onto his knees, struggling to clear his head. "Jenny?"

"Jenny's dead, Jack. You know that."

Nightingale felt something hard in his right hand and he looked down. He was holding the carving knife. The blade was glistening with blood and it was all over his hand. He turned and looked over his shoulder. Jenny was lying on the floor by the table, blood pooling around her head like a scarlet halo.

"She's dead, Jack. Now get up and finish this. You know what you have to do."

Nightingale threw the knife away and got to his feet. The room began to swim around him and he fought to stay conscious. There was blood all over the front of his coat and splattered up his right sleeve.

"Jack. You have to go. Hurry."

He turned towards the voice. Sophie was standing in front of the refrigerator, her Barbie doll dangling from her right hand. Her hair was loose around her face and she looked as if she was about to cry.

"Sophie?"

"You can do it, Jack. You can do what needs to be done." She pointed down the hallway. "Go, Jack. Go now."

Nightingale staggered down the hallway. He tripped and slammed against the wall before pushing himself upright, and as he took his hand away he saw he'd left a bloody handprint. A car screeched to a halt outside and he ran to the door and out into the street. Fairchild was pulling open the rear door of a large grey Jaguar. He looked over at Nightingale and grinned, then climbed into the back.

Roaring like an animal in pain, Nightingale hurried towards the MGB. As Fairchild slammed the door shut, Nightingale leaned into his car, opened the glove compartment and pulled out his gun.

The Jaguar drove off as Nightingale stepped away from the MGB, flicked off the safety and brought up the gun with both hands. He squeezed the trigger. The first shot slammed into the front wing, the second blew apart the front tyre. The Jaguar accelerated but veered to the right. It straightened up but then the driver lost control and it hit a concrete tub filled with ivy and span around, the engine revving uncontrollably. A cloud of steam billowed out from under the bonnet.

Lights were going on in houses all along the mews.

The rear passenger door opened and Fairchild staggered out of the car. His eyes were wide and staring and he bent low, trying to use the door as cover, but Nightingale knew that the thin steel would be no better than cardboard at stopping the next bullet. He squeezed off another shot but Fairchild had already started to turn and the bullet missed him by inches.

That was the third bullet. Four rounds left.

Fairchild was running as fast as he could but his feet were slipping on the cobbles and his arms flailed out for balance. Nightingale took two quick steps to the side, steadied the gun and fired. The bullet hit Fairchild in the left shoulder and he pitched forward and fell to his knees. Nightingale's ears were ringing from the explosions and the cordite was stinging his eyes.

Fairchild crawled down the street on his knees and right hand, his left arm dangling uselessly.

Nightingale walked past the Jaguar. The driver was pitched forward against the airbag, blood streaming from his nose. The heavy in the front passenger seat was also trapped against his airbag but he was conscious and groped for his gun when he saw Nightingale. Nightingale caught a glimpse of metal in the man's hand and he shot him through the window. The glass exploded and the heavy's face folded into a bloody mess.

Fairchild managed to get to his feet and began to lurch along the street, blood streaming from the wound in his shoulder. Nightingale walked after him. He fired one-handed and the bullet slammed into Fairchild's back. The lawyer took two more steps and then fell face down onto the cobbles.

As Nightingale walked up, Fairchild rolled onto his back. He coughed and bloody froth spewed from between his lips. "I'll see you in Hell, Nightingale," he said. He coughed again and thick blackish blood trickled out of his mouth and down his neck.

"You can bank on it," said Nightingale. He pointed the gun at Fairchild's chest, just above the heart, and pulled the trigger.

Fairchild's entire body convulsed and his bloody lips curled back in a snarl but then he went still and the life faded from his eyes.

Nightingale turned and walked back to Jenny's house. More lights were coming on, and he saw a young woman standing in the window of the house opposite, staring at him in horror. He pushed open the door and then hesitated. He knew there was nothing he could do to help Jenny. She was dead. He stopped, unable to cross the threshold into the house. Realisation hit him like a punch to the solar plexus. Sophie was right. He did know what he had to do. And he had to do it now.

He turned on his heels and walked back to the MGB. He threw his gun onto the back seat and started the engine. As he drove away he saw the young woman pointing a phone at him, taking a photograph or a video, he couldn't tell which. It didn't matter. Nothing mattered any more.

CHAPTER
SIXTY-NINE

Nightingale screeched to a stop next to the fountain in the driveway of Gosling Manor. He switched off the engine and ran up the stairs to the front door, fumbling in his coat pocket for the key. He unlocked the door and let himself in, then relocked the door and slid across two heavy brass bolts. He rushed across the hallway, pulled open the secret panel that led to the basement, closed the panel behind him and hurried down the stairs. Taking off his coat he tossed it onto one of the leather sofas, then he looked down at his bloodstained shirt and cursed. He was supposed to be spotless when he entered the pentagram, any impurity would weaken the magic circle. He looked at his watch and tried to work out how much time he had. He doubted that the police would be too far behind him. The woman in the window opposite Jenny's house would have got the registration number of the MGB and as soon as the police went looking for his car they'd see that he had been red-flagged, and then Chalmers would be called and he would tell them about Gosling Manor.

He went over to the large oak desk and pulled open a drawer. Inside was a plastic bag containing several sheets of parchment that he'd bought from Mrs Steadman. The parchment was special, prepared from the skin of a virgin goat, and on it Nightingale had to draw the special symbol that belonged to Lucifuge Rofocale.

He sat down at the desk. Lying on the blotter was a quill that he'd made from a swan's feather the last time that he'd summoned Lucifuge Rofocale. There was dried blood on the nib. Nightingale's blood. He wiped it on his shirt sleeve. Also on the blotter was the razor blade that he'd used to nick himself. He picked it up and made a second incision on his left index finger, half an inch away from the last cut. Blood trickled down his finger and he dabbed at it with the nib of the quill, then began to draw the symbol from memory. He worked quickly but carefully. If the symbol wasn't perfect, it would be useless.

When he'd finished he blew on it to dry it, then carefully rolled it up and slid it into the pocket of his trousers. There were seven black candles in a Wicca Woman carrier bag, along with plastic bags of herbs and spices. He picked up the bag and took it upstairs.

CHAPTER
SEVENTY

"Can't we go any bloody faster?" asked Superintendent Chalmers. He pointed at the disappearing lights of the armed response vehicle ahead of them. "If they can do seventy, why can't we?"

The driver pressed his foot down but the country roads were narrow and winding and even at sixty miles an hour he had trouble maintaining control of the vehicle. Chalmers took several deep breaths. His heart was racing, not because of the high-speed drive through the Surrey countryside but because he was finally going to see Jack Nightingale where he belonged: behind bars.

This time there was no way that Nightingale could escape justice. Three eyewitnesses had seen him shoot a man dead in cold blood as he lay in the street, and then drive off in his MGB. There had been another man shot at close range in the front of a car, and Nightingale's assistant had been found in the kitchen of her home with her throat ripped open.

Chalmers was holding his iPhone and he stared at the screen. It showed a map of the area and a dot marked the position of the car he was in. When he'd visited Gosling Manor he'd marked the GPS position on his phone and now he was able to use it to follow his progress in the dark.

"We're coming up to the gate," he said. "About half a mile on the left."

CHAPTER
SEVENTY-ONE

Nightingale finished drying himself and tossed the towel into the bath. He'd used a nailbrush to clean his hands, feet and under his nails, and he'd used mouthwash and brushed his teeth thoroughly. His bloodstained clothes were draped over the toilet. Jenny's blood. Nightingale shivered, but it wasn't from the cold. "I'm sorry, kid," he muttered to himself. "But I'll make it right. I promise."

He padded naked into the bedroom. The pentagram was already prepared, with large black candles at the five points, and the herbs he needed were in a brass crucible in the centre, along with the parchment.

He took a deep breath and stepped into the magic circle. He picked up his cigarette lighter and began to light the candles, moving anti-clockwise around the circle.

CHAPTER
SEVENTY-TWO

The armed response vehicle came to a halt between the MGB and the stone fountain and the four cops piled out. Three already had their MP5s at the ready and they rushed up to the front door. The first to reach the door was a sergeant. He tried the handle but the door was locked and bolted. The driver hurried around to the boot, opened it and pulled out the orange metal battering ram that they called "the enforcer".

Chalmers arrived just as the driver was running up the steps to the door. He got out of the car and walked over to the MGB, still holding his iPhone. He pulled open the driver's door and peered inside. "Sergeant, over here!" he shouted. He put away his phone and pulled on a pair of purple latex gloves. He picked the gun off the back seat and took it out just as the sergeant ran up. He sniffed the weapon and wrinkled his nose at the acrid tang of cordite. Chalmers held out the revolver so that the sergeant could see it. "If this is his only gun then he's in there unarmed," said Chalmers.

"Understood, sir," said the sergeant.

Chalmers looked up at the upper floor as the driver began to batter the enforcer against the lock. There was a light in one of the upstairs bedrooms. It was flickering.

Chalmers pointed up at the window. "See that, sergeant? Candlelight. That's where he is."

The sergeant stepped back, looked at where Chalmers was pointing, and nodded.

"Go right up there, soon as you're inside," said Chalmers.

"Sir, procedure is to clear the lower floor first."

"Screw procedure. He's upstairs. I know it."

The sergeant nodded and jogged over to the door. It was made from solid oak but on the fifth strike the wood began to splinter around the lock.

CHAPTER
SEVENTY-THREE

Nightingale took a deep breath and began to read from the paper. "Osurmy delmausan atalsloym charusihoa," he said. Then he took another deep breath and continued to read the rest of the words, taking care not to make any mistakes. When he finished he held the parchment over the north-facing candle. As it burned he spoke again, his voice louder this time. "Come, Lucifuge Rofocale," he said. "I summon you."

The burning parchment singed his fingers but he ignored the pain. It had to burn completely while he held it. If he dropped it the spell would be broken. Grey smoke began to fill the room, far more than could have been produced by the parchment alone. It began to whirl around in a tight vortex and as Nightingale stared at it he felt himself begin to fall so he quickly closed his eyes and steadied himself. "Come, Lucifuge Rofocale!" he shouted. "I command you to appear!"

When he opened his eyes again what was left of the parchment had crumbled to ash between his fingers and thumb and he rubbed his hands together, blackening them. The room was full of smoke and he could barely make out the walls and ceiling. The vortex was spinning faster and faster and the centre of it had turned black. Nightingale held up his hands. "Appear before me, I command you!" he screamed.

There was a loud crack as if a tree had split down the middle and a flash of light that was so bright he could feel it burn his flesh. For a few seconds he was blinded and there were tears in his eyes when he blinked. As he put the palms of his hands over his eyes he heard a roar so deep that his stomach vibrated. Nightingale took his hands away from his eyes. There was a large figure standing in the smoke, something reptilian with grey scales and yellow eyes and a forked tongue that flicked out from between razor-sharp teeth. "You are Lucifuge Rofocale and I command that you speak the truth!" shouted Nightingale.

Grey, leathery wings spread out from its back and waved to and fro, disturbing the smoke, then it threw back its head and roared. Nightingale took a step backwards and almost tripped. The floor began to shake violently and then there was another loud crack and the figure rippled and morphed into a dwarf wearing a red jacket with gold buttons and gleaming black boots. The dwarf waddled towards the pentagram on bow legs, his silver spurs jangling with each step. In his right hand he was carrying a riding crop and he ran his left hand through unkempt curly black hair as he glared up at Nightingale.

"How dare you!" screamed the dwarf. "I'm not some underling to be summoned on a whim!" He lashed out with his riding crop but Nightingale didn't flinch. The crop swished back and forth but it didn't cross over the pentagram. So long as he stayed inside it, Nightingale knew that he couldn't be harmed. "You've no idea what I can do to you, Nightingale! The pain I can put you through!"

"I have a deal for you," said Nightingale.

The dwarf snorted contemptuously. "You've nothing I want or need."

"My soul," said Nightingale. "I'm offering you my soul."

The dwarf's eyes narrowed suspiciously. "Do you take me for a fool?"

"That's the last thing I'd take you for," said Nightingale.

"I don't believe you," said the dwarf.

"That's why I've summoned you."

"You've done nothing but fight to keep your sad little soul," said the dwarf. "Why are you so keen to surrender it now?"

"Because . . ." Downstairs there was a loud thump, the sound of an enforcer being slammed against the front door. The door was solid oak and it would hold for a while. "Because there's something I want more than my soul," he finished.

There was another loud thump and the dwarf turned towards the bedroom door. "What is that?" he asked.

"The police," said Nightingale.

The dwarf turned back to look at him. "You think they can help you? Against me?"

Nightingale shook his head. "They're not here to help; they're here to arrest me."

"For what?"

"Murder."

The dwarf chuckled. "So who did you kill, Nightingale?"

There were two more loud thumps from the enforcer.

"It's a long story and we don't really have time for it now." His eyes were watering from all the smoke and a tear rolled down his cheek. "Do you want my soul, or not?"

"That depends on what you want in exchange."

There was a much louder thump followed by the sound of splintering wood.

The dwarf chuckled. "You want to escape, is that it? Like your sister?"

Nightingale shrugged. "Sort of," he said.

"That's the deal, then? I get you out of whatever predicament you've got yourself into, and in return I get your soul?"

"I want more than that," said Nightingale.

There was another loud bang downstairs followed by shouts outside and the crackle of radios. And in the distance, the siren of an ambulance. The police were anticipating casualties, Nightingale realised.

"I'm listening," said Lucifuge Rofocale.

"I want to go back."

"Back where?"

"Back to that day when Sophie died. Everything that's happened to me stems from that day. If Sophie hadn't died then I'd still be a cop and Jenny would still be alive."

"And you think you can change that?"

"I can try."

The dwarf laughed again, then looked at Nightingale with narrowed eyes. "That's your deal? You go back to that day and I get your soul?"

"That's what I want."

The dwarf jutted his chin up. "Then it is agreed," he said. "The deal is done." He grinned triumphantly and folded his arms.

Nightingale stared at him in silence for several seconds. "You planned this, didn't you? Right from the start."

The dwarf tilted back his oversized head and laughed. The walls of the room vibrated and dust showered down from the ceiling.

"This has been all your doing, hasn't it? You've been letting Sophie contact me because you wanted my soul. You were using her to get to me."

"You're flattering yourself, Nightingale. You think I care about you? You think you occupy my thoughts for even one millisecond?"

Nightingale nodded slowly. "I think you're a vindictive, nasty little shit. I think you did whatever you had to do to get one over on me. You wanted my soul and you didn't care who you had to destroy to get it."

The dwarf grinned. "Maybe you're not as stupid as you look," he said.

"You used Fairchild, didn't you? Maybe it was Proserpine who pulled his strings but she works for you. And everything that happened was to get me here, wasn't it? So that you could get my soul?"

"And now I have it," said the dwarf. He pointed at Nightingale with his right index finger. The nail was long and yellow and as sharp as a knife. "I have a special place for you in Hell, Nightingale. Ready and waiting."

CHAPTER
SEVENTY-FOUR

"For God's sake put your back into it!" shouted Chalmers. "If you can't put some weight behind it then give it to someone who can."

The man with the enforcer turned to glare at the superintendent. "With the greatest of respect, sir, this isn't some jerry-built council house. This door is a couple of inches thick and built to last."

Chalmers pointed his finger at the officer. "Don't bloody stop, man!" he shouted.

An ambulance turned into the driveway, its siren blaring.

The officer began to pound the enforcer against the door again. Each time he hit it the wood around the lock splintered a little more, and after half a dozen more blows the lock gave way.

"Finally," said Chalmers.

"Sir, you need to stay outside until we've secured the house," said the sergeant.

"Just get upstairs and get the bastard," said Chalmers.

The ambulance pulled up behind the armed response vehicle and Chalmers turned and flashed them a cut-throat gesture, telling them to kill the siren.

With one final blow from the enforcer the door crashed open and the three armed officers piled into the mud-splattered hallway, led by the sergeant. Chalmers followed them inside and watched as they moved carefully up the charred stairs, their MP5s against their shoulders.

The sergeant took them to the door of the room where they'd seen the candlelight. He pointed at the door, then gingerly tried the handle. "Locked," he mouthed. The door was fire-damaged but in one piece.

Chalmers came down the landing and the sergeant motioned for him to go back but the superintendent ignored him.

The officer with the enforcer pushed past Chalmers and joined the sergeant. The armed cops had their MP5s pointing at the door. The officer swung the enforcer and he grunted as it made contact. The door was nowhere near as strong as the one at the entrance to the house; it buckled with the first blow and sagged on its hinges with the second. The sergeant kicked the door out of the way and stormed into the bedroom. "Armed police! Drop your weapon!" he shouted.

The two other armed officers followed him inside, one moving to the right, the other to the left, both shouting at the top of their voices. "Armed police! Armed police!"

Then there was just silence. Chalmers walked quickly into the room but stopped when he saw the three officers standing around a pentagram drawn in chalk on the floor. There were five black candles burning, one at each of the points of the pentagram.

"Where is he?" said Chalmers, looking around.

"There's no one here, sir," said the sergeant.

"Nonsense. The room was locked from the inside. We all saw that."

The sergeant shrugged.

"You checked the bathroom?"

"Sir, there's no one here," said the sergeant testily.

"If there's no one here then who lit the candles?" asked Chalmers.

The sergeant looked away and didn't answer.

Chalmers snorted and stormed into the bathroom. There was a white towel hanging on a chrome rail and he grabbed it. It was wet. And so was the bath. He threw the towel into the tub and picked up the shirt left on the toilet. It was soaked in blood, as was the raincoat underneath it. Chalmers went back into the bedroom. The four policemen were looking around the room, trying to avoid eye contact with the superintendent.

"Find him," shouted Chalmers. "Tear this bloody house apart. He has to be hiding somewhere."

CHAPTER
SEVENTY-FIVE

Nightingale kept his foot down hard on the accelerator and he pounded on his horn as he ran a red light, swerving around the back of a bus and narrowly missing a black cab. His mobile rang and he fished it out of his pocket. It was the coordinator of the Metropolitan Police's negotiating team.

"I'll be there in ten minutes," said Nightingale. "What about Robbie? Have you reached him?"

"He's not answering his phone."

"Keep trying. I need him there."

"I've got other officers on the way, Jack. We're covered."

"I need Robbie Hoyle. No one else will do." He braked to avoid a woman who had pushed a buggy into the road and was glaring at him as if daring him to run her and the child over. "Are you stupid?" he screamed at her. She swore at him and gave him the finger, her face contorted with hatred.

"What's up with you, Jack?" asked the coordinator.

"I'm sorry, that wasn't at you," said Nightingale. "Look, Robbie will make it, but you just have to tell him to get a move on, okay?"

"Okay, Jack. And you drive carefully, do you hear?"

"Driving's the least of my worries," said Nightingale, and he ended the call. He put the phone back into his pocket and concentrated on the road ahead.

His heart was racing and he took slow, deep breaths as he tried to calm himself down. There was no point in rushing, he told himself. Nothing would happen until he reached Sophie. And he wouldn't be doing anything until Robbie Hoyle had arrived.

A set of lights ahead turned red and he pulled up next to a bus. He took out his cigarettes and lit one. As he blew smoke he looked up to see a young schoolgirl staring at him from the bus. She was in a green uniform with a beret and couldn't have been more than six years old; she had curly red hair and a sprinkling of freckles across her snub nose. Nightingale smiled at her and waggled his eyebrows but she looked at him with unseeing eyes. Nightingale took another long drag on his cigarette.

The girl's mother was sitting next to her, talking on a BlackBerry. The mother, in her thirties, with similar hair and freckles, turned to look at her daughter, then glared through the window at Nightingale. Nightingale smiled, but neither of them reacted. Then their lips began to move. He couldn't hear what they were saying but it was easy enough to read their lips: "You are going to Hell, Jack Nightingale."

Nightingale flinched and the cigarette fell from his hand into his lap. He cursed and grabbed for it and when he looked up again the mother and daughter were talking to each other. A horn blared and Nightingale realised that the traffic light had turned green. He put the MGB in gear and drove off.

His mobile rang as he drove along the King's Road. It was the coordinator. Nightingale fumbled for his phone and pressed the button to take the call.

"Robbie's on his way. He was in the area so he should get there about the same time as you."

"I'll wait for him," said Nightingale.

"I don't have any details yet, just that it's a person in crisis," said the coordinator.

"That's okay; I know who it is," said Nightingale. He ended the call and tossed the phone onto the passenger seat.

The traffic ahead had slowed to a crawl and he tapped his fingers impatiently on the steering wheel. On the far side of the road a West Indian traffic warden was writing out a ticket for a white BMW sports car. A blonde woman with half a dozen carrier bags came out of a boutique and began pleading with him. Nightingale smiled to himself, but the smile froze when the woman and the traffic warden both turned to look at him. "You're going to Hell, Jack Nightingale," they mouthed, sending a shudder down Nightingale's spine.

A young woman pushing a pram stopped behind the traffic warden, and so did two pensioners, women with headscarves and matching overcoats. They all turned to stare at Nightingale, their eyes blank and their faces impassive. Then their mouths began to work in unison. "You are going to Hell, Jack Nightingale."

The traffic started to move and Nightingale accelerated down the road. He glanced in the rear-view mirror and saw more than a dozen people standing still on the pavement, staring after him.

He drove into Chelsea Harbour. Ahead of him he could see the tower block. Sophie was on the far side, he knew. Sitting on the balcony. With her doll.

There was a police car pulled across the road to stop traffic and two Community Support Officers in police-type uniforms and yellow fluorescent jackets held up their hands, telling him to stop. One of them was about to tell Nightingale to turn his car around but he wound down the window and showed them his warrant card.

"Inspector Nightingale," he said. "I'm the negotiator."

"Sorry, sir," said the CSO. He pointed over at a parked ambulance but Nightingale had already put the car in gear and was driving towards it. The two CSOs jumped out of the way.

As Nightingale climbed out of the MGB, Colin Duggan hurried over. He was wearing his inspector's uniform and holding a transceiver.

"Robbie's on his way," said Nightingale.

"Yeah, he'll be here in five minutes," said Duggan. "He just called."

Nightingale took his pack of Marlboro from his pocket and held it out to Duggan. The inspector took a cigarette and Nightingale lit it for him, then lit one for himself.

"It's a kid, Jack," said Duggan, scratching his fleshy neck.

"I know," said Nightingale. "Nine years old."

"Her name's Sophie. She's locked herself on the thirteenth-floor balcony and she's sitting there talking to her doll. Father's at work, mother's shopping, and the girl was left in the care of the au pair." Duggan gestured with his cigarette at an anorexic blonde who was sitting on a bench, sobbing, as a uniformed WPC tried to comfort her. "Polish girl. She was ironing, then saw Sophie on the balcony. She banged on the window but Sophie had locked it from the outside." Duggan frowned. "How do you know how old she is?"

Nightingale looked at his watch. "Where the hell is Robbie?" he muttered.

"I told you, five minutes," said Duggan. "He'll be here. Do you want to talk to her? The au pair?"

"No need," said Nightingale.

"The girl's talking to her doll, won't look at anyone. We sent up two WPCs but she won't talk to them."

"You're supposed to wait for me, Colin," said Nightingale. He dropped his cigarette onto the ground and crushed it with his heel. "Amateurs only complicate matters, you know that."

"She's a kid on a balcony," said Duggan. "We couldn't just wait."

"There's time," he said. "Just don't do anything to spook her. Maybe you should call Robbie."

Duggan was reaching for his phone when they heard a siren in the distance. He put the phone away.

"She's sitting on the edge, Jack. A gust of wind and she could blow right off. We're trying to get an airbag brought out but no one seems to know where to get one."

"We don't need an airbag, Colin."

The siren was getting louder.

"You could talk to her through the balcony window," said Duggan.

"That won't work."

"How do you know? You've only just got here."

"I know," said Nightingale flatly. He looked at his watch. There was time.

"The way I see it, there are two possibilities," said Duggan. "She's too high up for you to use a ladder, so we can either lower you down from the roof or we can get you into the flat next door."

"Robbie and I'll handle it," said Nightingale.

A patrol car with its blue light flashing and siren wailing appeared at the entrance to Chelsea Harbour. It screeched to a halt. The rear door opened and Robbie Hoyle rushed out. He had a North Face fleece over his suit and was holding his mobile phone.

"Better late than never," said Nightingale.

"What's the story?" asked Hoyle.

"Girl on the thirteenth floor, threatening to jump," said Duggan.

"Her name's Sophie Underwood, and her father's been fiddling with her," said Nightingale.

"What?" said Duggan, stunned.

"Her father's been fiddling with her and the mother knows about it."

"How the hell do you know that?" asked Duggan.

"I just know," said Nightingale. He put a hand on Duggan's shoulder. "Listen to me, Colin. Robbie and I are going to handle this but afterwards you need to get

Sophie to a hospital and get her examined. There's a bruise on her leg; the father did it. And there'll be other signs. You arrest him and put him away. And the wife too. No matter what she says, she knew what that bastard was doing." He nodded at the au pair. "She's got his business card. He works for a big bank in Canary Wharf."

"Jack, what's going on?" asked Duggan.

"Just do what I say, Colin," said Nightingale. "As soon as you examine the girl you'll know that I'm right." He turned to Hoyle. "Let's go, Robbie."

"I've got a PC who can take you up," said Duggan.

"I know where we're going," said Nightingale. "Come on, Robbie," he said, and they hurried towards the apartment block.

"Why aren't you up there, getting her down?" shouted a bald man holding a metal toolbox. He pointed at Nightingale. "You should do something instead of pissing about down here."

Nightingale walked over to the man and punched him in the face. The cartilage splintered and the man fell on his back, blood pouring down his chin.

"Jack!" yelled Hoyle, pulling Nightingale away.

"He asked for it," said Nightingale. "He just wants to see her jump." He jabbed his finger at the man on the ground. "She's not dying today, you ignorant bastard!"

"Jack, what the hell's wrong with you?" said Hoyle. "You'll be thrown out of the job for that. You can't go around thumping civilians." He tugged at Nightingale's arm and the two of them began jogging to the entrance of the block.

The reception area was plush with overstuffed sofas and a large coffee table covered with glossy magazines. A doorman in a green uniform was talking to two uniformed officers.

"Where're the stairs?" shouted Hoyle.

The doorman pointed to three lift doors. "The lifts are there, sir," he said.

"We need the stairs," said Hoyle.

"It's okay, Robbie," said Nightingale. "We can take the lift."

Hoyle stared at him in amazement. "You never use lifts."

"It's okay."

"How many years have I known you? You've never once stepped inside a lift."

Nightingale stabbed at the call button. "Yeah, well, today's the day, the first day of the rest of my life."

The doors to one of the lifts opened and Nightingale strode in. Hoyle followed him. Nightingale pressed the button for the fourteenth floor.

"It's the thirteenth," said Hoyle.

"There is no thirteen. It goes from twelve to fourteen."

"Why?"

Nightingale scowled. "Because the developer thought that thirteen was unlucky. And in this case he was probably right."

The lift doors closed. "Are you okay, Jack?"

"I need you to listen to me and to do everything that I tell you, do you understand?"

"I'm not retarded, mate."

"Everything," insisted Nightingale. "No matter how . . . unorthodox it seems."

"Unorthodox?"

"The girl is in Fourteen C. On the balcony. Actually, it's more like a terrace. Next door, in Fourteen D, are a Mr and Mrs Jackson. Nice couple, in their sixties. They'll let you out onto their terrace. Make sure that they stay well back, okay?"

"Okay," said Hoyle hesitatingly.

"Go out and talk to her. Her name's Sophie. She's holding a doll. The doll's name is Jessica Lovely."

"What's going on, Jack?"

"Just listen to me. Sophie wants to jump, Robbie. She wants to end it. Her father's been abusing her and her mother isn't doing a blind thing. There's a bruise on her leg and God only knows what else. When she jumps she'll just jump. There'll be no shouting or screaming, she'll just go. She's sitting on the edge with her legs hanging over so all she has to do is slide under the railing and she's gone."

"How do you know all this? Do you know her?"

"You have to keep her talking, Robbie. Get her attention. Talk about the doll. Talk about the sky. Talk about birds."

"Birds?"

"Whatever it takes to distract her. You can jump over to her but the way she's sitting that'll just spook her and she'll go over the side."

"Where will you be?"

"I'm going up to Fifteen C. I'll get onto the balcony above her." He took out a cigarette and lit it.

"And then what?"

"Then I'll drop down. I'll drop and I'll push her away from the railing. And at the same time you jump across and grab her."

"Bollocks you will," said Hoyle.

"It's the only way," said Nightingale. "She wants to jump and if she thinks you're trying to stop her, she'll do it."

"Jack, you're not the bloody SAS. We don't do jumping off balconies."

"Keep your phone switched on, but set to vibrate. I'll call you when I'm in position. When your phone vibrates you get ready, and as soon as I drop you jump across. I'll push her back, you catch her."

"And then what? What about you?"

"I'll be okay. I'm dropping one floor. I'll grab the railing and pull myself up. You keep hold of Sophie."

"Have you cleared this with Chalmers?"

"This has nothing to do with Chalmers."

"What's got into you?"

The lift arrived at the fourteenth floor and the doors rattled apart. Nightingale pressed the button for the fifteenth floor and then held the doors open for Hoyle. "Just go, Robbie. Keep her sweet and wait for my call. I drop, you jump, we save her life. Deviate from that and she'll be dead. Robbie, I swear to God she'll jump. Just do exactly what I say and we'll save her."

Hoyle opened his mouth to argue but then he sighed. "Okay," he said.

"One more thing," said Nightingale. "Every time you cross the road, you bloody well look both ways, do you hear me?"

"What?"

"The Green Cross Code. Just look and keep looking every time you cross the road. Any road."

"Okay."

"Swear."

"What?"

"Swear," said Nightingale. "Swear on the life of your kids that you'll look both ways every time you cross a road."

"What's going on, Jack?"

"Swear, you bastard," hissed Nightingale.

"Okay, okay, I swear. Cross my heart." Hoyle made the sign of the cross on his chest.

"On the life of your kids."

Hoyle's eyes narrowed. "This isn't funny, Jack."

"Swear," repeated Nightingale. He took a drag on his cigarette.

"On the life of my kids," said Hoyle quietly.

Nightingale smiled. "One day you'll thank me," he said.

"When this is over, you and I need to talk," said Hoyle. He stepped out of the lift.

"Phone on vibrate, remember? And when I drop, you jump across."

Hoyle nodded.

Nightingale moved away from the doors to allow them to close.

"And watch out for black cabs!" shouted Nightingale through the gap.

The lift started up and Nightingale took a final pull on his cigarette and then dropped the butt onto the floor. At the fifteenth floor, the lift doors opened and Nightingale stepped into the corridor. He took a deep breath, then walked over to Fifteen C and rang the bell.

CHAPTER
SEVENTY-SIX

Hoyle walked over to the window that overlooked the terrace. He gestured at the door. "That's unlocked?"

Mr Jackson nodded. He was in his early sixties with grey hair that was only a few years from being completely white. He had a stoop and he had to twist awkwardly to look Hoyle in the eye.

"What's going to happen?" asked Mrs Jackson anxiously. She was sitting on a floral-print sofa, her hands in her lap.

"Mr Jackson, could you sit down with your wife while I go outside? The fewer people that Sophie sees, the better."

Mr Jackson nodded and went to sit next to his wife. She reached for his hand.

"Do you know Sophie?" Hoyle asked them.

They both nodded.

"And her parents? Are they good people?"

Mr and Mrs Jackson looked at each other. "Six years, and I can count on the fingers of one hand the number of times I've seen her with her mother or father," said Mr Jackson. "It's always an au pair she's with, and they seem to change them every six months or so." He looked at his wife again and she nodded in agreement.

"The thing is," he continued, "one doesn't like to talk out of school but they didn't seem to be the most attentive of parents."

"Okay," said Hoyle. "Now please just stay there while I go out and talk to her." He walked over to the glass door that led to the terrace. There was a small circular white-metal table and four chairs, and several pots of flowering shrubs. Around the edge was a waist-high wall which was topped by a metal railing.

Hoyle opened the door and stepped out onto the terracotta tiles. He could hear the buzz of traffic in the distance and down below the crackle of police radios.

Sophie was sitting on the wall of the balcony next door, her legs under the metal rail, her arms on top of it. She was wearing a white sweatshirt with a blue cotton skirt and silver trainers with blue stars on them. She didn't look over at him even though he was sure she must have heard him open the door. She had porcelain-white skin and shoulder-length blonde hair that she'd tucked behind her ears, and she was bent over a Barbie doll.

Hoyle coughed but the girl didn't react.

"Hi, Sophie," he said.

The girl stiffened but didn't say anything.

"My name's Robbie. Are you okay?"

"Go away," she said, but she didn't look at him.

Robbie stayed close to the door. He had a clear view to the River Thames and far off to his left was the London Eye. There was a gap of about six feet between his terrace and the one that Sophie was on. It would be easy enough to jump across but Nightingale had been right: she could easily fall before he reached her.

"How old are you, Sophie?"

She didn't answer.

"I've got a daughter called Sarah," said Hoyle. "She's eight."

"I'm nine," said Sophie, looking out over the river.

"Yes, you look a bit older than Sarah," said Hoyle.

CHAPTER
SEVENTY-SEVEN

Nightingale pressed the bell for the third time but he already knew that there was no one in. He took a step back and kicked the door hard, just below the lock. It shuddered but didn't give. Taking another step back he kicked harder this time, putting all his weight behind it, and he heard wood splinter. The third kick left the door hanging on one hinge and it hit the floor with the fourth.

He walked over the door and down the hallway. The flat was the same layout as the one directly below: a kitchen diner and two bedrooms on the left, a bathroom and one bedroom on the right, and a large sitting room with a terrace overlooking the Thames. The sitting room windows ran from floor to ceiling and to the left was a door that led out to the terrace.

There were abstract canvases on the walls, a huge glass coffee table covered with fashion magazines, and a baby grand piano at the far end that was covered with family photographs.

Nightingale strode over to the door. There was a key in the lock and he turned it and stepped out onto the terrace. There was a wooden bench there and a bird table that had a mesh bag of peanuts hanging from it.

He wanted a cigarette but knew that he didn't have time. He took off his coat and tossed it onto the bench, then leaned over the railing and looked down.

Sophie was sitting with her feet hanging over the edge of the balcony, the doll clutched to her chest. She had turned towards Robbie and was listening to him. Nightingale smiled. Robbie Hoyle could talk the hind legs off a donkey. He retrieved his mobile from his coat and took a deep breath.

CHAPTER
SEVENTY-EIGHT

A helicopter flew along the Thames, heading towards Battersea heliport. "Have you ever been in a helicopter, Sophie?" asked Hoyle.

She shook her head but didn't say anything.

Hoyle knew that he had to keep the little girl talking. So long as she was talking she couldn't be thinking about jumping.

"What about a plane? Have you been in a plane?"

"We went to Italy last year," she said.

"Yeah? I've never been to Italy. Was it fun?"

Sophie didn't reply. She kissed her doll on the top of the head. "Don't worry, Jessica, everything's going to be okay."

"What do you like to eat, Sophie?" asked Hoyle, trying to get her attention. He took a step towards her.

She looked over at him as if she'd forgotten that he was there. "Excuse me?"

He stopped moving. "What's your favourite food?"

"Pizza. Inga always lets me order pizza."

"Who's Inga?"

"My au pair." She forced a smile. "The au pair at the moment. We change au pairs a lot."

"But you like Inga?"

"She's okay."

Hoyle felt his phone vibrate in his pocket. He wanted to take the call, to tell Nightingale that everything was all right and that he was getting through to the girl, but he knew that it was important to stay focused. Nightingale had been right. The girl wasn't scared, she wasn't seeking attention; it was as if she had made up her mind what she was going to do and was just waiting for the right moment.

"Why don't we go inside and I'll order us a pizza?" said Hoyle. He moved closer to the side of the terrace. There were several potted plants and if he judged it right he'd be able to spring off one and jump over to the terrace where she was. Six feet. Seven at most. Then another four feet to get to her.

"I'm not hungry," she said.

"What about a drink? Do you like Coke? Or Pepsi?"

"Coke, of course," she said scornfully.

And that was when Nightingale dropped from the sky.

CHAPTER
SEVENTY-NINE

Nightingale let go of the railing. For a moment he seemed to be frozen in time and then gravity got to work and pulled him down. He twisted around, his hair whipping in the wind, ignoring the fear and focusing every fibre of his being on Sophie and what he had to do.

The bricks of the terrace wall flashed by his face and then he was looking down at Sophie, her face turned to the left, the doll in her hands clutched to her chest.

He saw Hoyle, one foot on a plant pot, the other over the railing, his right hand outstretched as he jumped.

The doll slipped from Sophie's fingers and it span through the air.

Nightingale's stomach lurched and he grunted as his hands flailed towards the girl.

Hoyle opened his mouth to scream but all Nightingale could hear was the wind rushing past his ears.

CHAPTER
EIGHTY

The doll tumbled over the side of the balcony but Sophie didn't seem to have noticed. She was staring at Hoyle with wide eyes but she wasn't moving and she hadn't seen Nightingale dropping from the balcony above her. Hoyle cleared the railing and scrambled across the terrace just as Nightingale reached Sophie.

Sophie screamed as Nightingale pushed her in the chest and she fell backwards.

Hoyle threw himself forward and caught Sophie under the arms. She slammed into his chest, knocking the breath out of him, and as he gasped he locked eyes with Nightingale.

CHAPTER
EIGHTY-ONE

Sophie fell backwards into Hoyle's arms, her mouth open in surprise, as Nightingale's chest thudded against the railing. His right arm was outstretched towards Sophie but he managed to catch hold of the railing with his left hand. He fell but jerked to a halt and the momentum almost wrenched his arm from its socket. He felt the skin scrape from his palm but there was barely any pain because of the adrenaline that was coursing through his body.

He heard screams from far below and one man's shout sounded like he was telling people to keep back, but all Nightingale could think about was that Sophie was okay.

He smiled and then reached up with his right hand, gasping for breath. He managed to grab the railing and he tried to haul himself up but he didn't have the strength so he just hung there, his face pressed against the balcony wall, breathing heavily.

CHAPTER
EIGHTY-TWO

"Jack!" screamed Hoyle. He had turned Sophie round so that her face was pressed against his chest; now, keeping a firm grip of her with his left hand, he reached out with his right. He didn't want to let go of the girl but he couldn't let his friend fall. His fingers touched the back of Nightingale's left hand and he took another step forward, grabbing Nightingale's wrist. "Hold on, Jack!" he shouted.

Sophie was crying, her tears soaking into Hoyle's shirt.

He felt Nightingale's hand start to slip from the railing.

"Jack, hold on!" Hoyle yelled.

Sophie wrapped her arms around Hoyle's waist. "I'm sorry," she said, sobbing.

Hoyle reached out with his left hand, trying to grab Nightingale's other wrist, but Sophie was in the way.

"Jack, hold on, man!" he screamed. He pushed Sophie down onto the terrace with his left hand. "Stay down, honey, just for a moment, please."

CHAPTER
EIGHTY-THREE

"Robbie, it's okay," said Nightingale. He forced a smile. "It was always going to end this way."

"I've got you. I've got you," said Hoyle. As he grabbed at Nightingale's right hand both Nightingale's hands slipped from the railing. Hoyle grunted as he took all of his friend's weight.

"No, you haven't, mate," said Nightingale. He could feel his wrists slipping through Hoyle's fingers.

"Jack!" shouted Hoyle.

"It's okay, Robbie. Really. It's okay." And Nightingale meant it because it really was okay.

"No!" Hoyle screamed.

Nightingale felt his left hand slip from Hoyle's grip and then his right hand was free and he was falling backwards, away from the balcony.

He heard Hoyle scream and then all he could hear was the wind rushing past his ears. His arms and legs were pointing upwards and he suddenly realised how beautiful it was: pure blue sky and high overhead the white trails of jets flying to far-off places.

There'd be no pain, he knew that. When he hit the ground he'd be travelling at a hundred and twenty miles an hour and it would be over in a fraction of a second. He thought about counting or praying but he did neither; all he did was think about Sophie and Jenny and smile because by dying he was saving them and that was all that mattered.

He was right.

There was no pain.

He hit the ground and it was over in an instant.

CHAPTER
EIGHTY-FOUR

There was nothing.

Time seemed to have stopped and yet not stopped.

Nightingale was there but not there.

He wasn't even sure if he was Nightingale.

There was nothing to see, nothing to hear; he was just there and yet not there.

All his thoughts were there, and all his memories. But there was no emotion. No feeling.

Time passed.

Or maybe it didn't.

He had no way of telling.

CHAPTER
EIGHTY-FIVE

"Nightingale?" A voice, but not a voice. He didn't hear it but someone had spoken. Not spoken, exactly. There weren't words. More like feelings. Vibrations.

"Who is that?" said Nightingale, except that he didn't say it. There were no words.

"How quickly they forget." It was Proserpine.

"Where are you?"

"There is no where," she said.

"Why can't I see you?"

"Because there is nothing to see."

"Where am I?"

"No where. And no when."

"I don't understand."

"There is nothing to understand."

"Am I dead?"

"Yes. And no."

"That doesn't make sense."

"Because you don't understand. Alive and dead supposes that there is change. And that supposes time, and there is no time. You are alive and dead, born and not born."

"So I'm imagining this?"

Proserpine laughed. "Would it help if you could see?"

"I don't know. Yes. Maybe."

There was a flicker and then everything was white, but not the white of a snow-covered mountain or a cloud in the sky; it was the white of a television screen that was only showing static. There was no up and no down, no feeling of depth or height or any perspective. Nightingale couldn't see anything, just white. Then she was there in front of him. Except there was no him. Just her. And her dog, on a leash.

She smiled. She was wearing a long black leather coat that hung straight down past knee-length black boots with stiletto heels. She was wearing black lipstick and black nail varnish and silver upside-down crucifixes dangled from her ears. The dog looked up at Nightingale, its tongue lolling from the side of its mouth. But they weren't standing on anything. They were just there.

"Where am I?"

She waved a languid hand. "I told you. Nowhere. Nowhen. Outside time. Outside space."

"Once before you talked about the Elsewhere. You said that's where you went."

"This isn't the Elsewhere," she said. "This isn't any place."

"Limbo? Is that it?"

"It has been called that."

"And how long do I stay here?"

"There is no long, there is no short; there's nothing. There's no you. There's just . . ." She shrugged.

500

"Why are you here?"

"I'm not. But you said it would be easier if you could see me. So you can."

"What's happening?"

"Nothing is happening. Everything just is. Or isn't."

"So why are you here?"

She laughed. "I told you. I'm not."

"What do you want?"

"To see how you are."

"I don't know how I am. I don't know anything. I remember falling. I remember hitting the ground."

"No you don't," she said. "You don't remember anything. Remembering suggests that there is a past and a present, but there is neither in the Nowhen. There is nothing to remember because there is no passing of time."

"But I fell."

"You are still falling. You are still getting ready to jump. And you are dead on the ground. You are all those things, Nightingale. Before, you saw them in an order. You got ready to jump. You fell. You hit the ground. But in the Nowhen there is no sequence. There just is . . ." She smiled sadly. "You will never understand."

"Do I stay here for ever?"

"You are already here for ever, Nightingale. Time does not exist here. I could go away and come back in ten thousand years but there would be no sense of time passing. How long do you think you have been . . ." She shrugged. ". . . here?" she finished. "For want of a better word."

"I don't know."

"An hour? A day? A year? A hundred years?"

Nightingale tried to remember. But she was right. There had been no sense of time passing.

"Do you understand?"

"No," said Nightingale. "So what happens now?"

"In the Nowhen nothing happens. The question is, do you stay here or do you go back or do you move on?"

"Move on to where?"

She laughed again. "Nightingale, if you can't fathom the Nowhen, there's no way you will ever understand what lies ahead of it." Her dog growled and she bent down and rubbed it behind the ear. "I know you don't like it here, but we'll go soon," she said.

"You said there was no soon," said Nightingale.

"For you there isn't," she said. "But I follow my own rules."

"Why can't I see myself?"

"Because there is nothing to see. We're going round in circles."

"This is all your fault," said Nightingale.

"Fault? You want to blame someone for this?"

"You sent Marcus Fairchild after me, didn't you?"

"I told you there would be three. He was one of the three."

"So why did he kill Jenny? What had she ever done to you?"

"That wasn't my doing, Nightingale. That was Lucifuge Rofocale."

"So Fairchild went behind your back?"

"Lucifuge Rofocale sits on the left hand of Satan. He does what he wants to do." She chuckled. "Though you have given him a problem."

"What do you mean?"

"You sold your soul. You promised it to the Darkness. And then you gave your life to save another. An innocent. Which made it even worse."

"Sophie?"

"Yes, Sophie."

"Is she okay?"

Proserpine nodded. "She's fine. Your partner caught her. All's well with the world."

"That's something."

"Yes, that's something. A very big thing, as it happens. You saved her by sacrificing your life, so how can they allow you to spend eternity in Hell?"

"They?"

"The Light."

"God?"

"Don't go there, Nightingale. Think of it as the opposite of the Darkness. Good rather than Evil, if you like, but those labels never work, not in the grand scheme of things. But you were promised to us and now there's doubt."

"Doubt?"

"No one is sure what to do with you, Nightingale. And until a decision is reached, you stay here." She smiled. "Except there is no here. And no when." The dog growled. "Catch you later," she said, and disappeared. Then the whiteness vanished and there was nothing.

CHAPTER
EIGHTY-SIX

"Mr Nightingale?" A woman's voice. A voice that Nightingale recognised but couldn't place. "Mr Nightingale? It's me."

There was no remembering because Nightingale had no memory. There was nothing to remember because everything was. Or is. He was in the Nowhen, which meant there was no past and no present so there was nothing to remember. But he knew who it was. Alice Steadman.

"Are you there, Mr Nightingale?"

"I'm here. But I don't know where here is."

"Are you okay?"

"I don't know. How long have I been here?"

"No time at all, really," said Mrs Steadman.

"It feels like for ever."

"It is. In the Nowhen everything is for ever."

"What's happening to me?"

"Nothing. Nothing can happen in the Nowhen."

"I don't understand any of this. Am I dead?"

"Would you like a cup of tea?"

"What?"

Reality, or what passed for reality in the Nowhen, flickered. Nightingale was sitting at a table and Mrs Steadman sat across from him, holding a teapot.

"Would you like some tea?" She was dressed in black: a glossy silk shirt over black knitted tights and a string of black pearls around her neck. She smiled at him and nodded like a pecking bird. "It's still hot. The tea."

"Thank you," said Nightingale. He looked around. They were in the room behind her shop in Camden. Except he knew that was impossible.

"This isn't real, is it?" he said.

Mrs Steadman smiled benignly. "Is anything real?" she said.

"Where am I? Where is this place?"

"You're asking me to describe something that can't be described," she said. "You don't have the terms of reference."

"But I'm dead?"

"There is no dead, Mr Nightingale. When you hit the ground, you died. Then. But you are still alive before you fell."

"I didn't fall. I jumped."

She smiled. "That's right. You jumped."

"And now I'm — what? A ghost?"

"No. You're not a ghost."

"I'm not really here, am I?"

Mrs Steadman looked around the room. "Here? No, you're not here. But I am. I just thought this might be easier for you."

"What's happening, Mrs Steadman?"

"What's happening? Well, your future is being discussed. Of course in the Nowhen there is no future as there is no past and no present, so the choice is either to leave you where you are or to come to a mutually acceptable decision. You see, you're an anomaly, Mr Nightingale, and the universe really doesn't like anomalies."

"How am I an anomaly?"

"Because you sold your soul, Mr Nightingale. Even though I warned you about getting involved with the Darkness, you went and sold your soul." She wagged an admonishing finger at him. "You should have listened to me."

"Why are you talking to me? Who sent you?"

"Someone has to explain to you what's happening, and it was felt that any explanation was better coming from someone you know. And hopefully someone you can trust."

"And who decides what happens to me?"

"Negotiations are taking place," she said.

"Between who?"

"Between those who want you to burn in Hell for eternity, and those who think you deserve a second chance."

"And is that possible? A second chance?"

She smiled and nodded. "It has happened before, yes."

"And when will I know?"

Mrs Steadman shrugged. "You'll know when I know," she said.

Reality, or what passed for reality in the Nowhen, flickered again.

Nightingale was alone.

Time passed.

Or didn't.

He had no way of telling.

CHAPTER
EIGHTY-SEVEN

"Are you happy now, Nightingale? Is that what you wanted? An eternity of nothingness?"

Nightingale didn't recognise the voice, but then strictly speaking there was no voice to recognise. He didn't actually hear the words; they were simply there.

"Who is that?" said Nightingale, except that he didn't say anything. It wasn't even a thought, truth be told. Just a feeling, a vibration in the nothingness that was the Nowhen.

There was a flash of light and then he was standing on a windswept cliff looking out over an ocean; the waves were flecked with white froth and dark storm clouds were gathering overhead.

"Your soul was supposed to be mine, Nightingale. Mine to do with as I want."

Nightingale turned round. It was Lucifuge Rofocale, wearing his crimson jacket with gold buttons and gleaming black jodhpurs. He was holding a black riding crop and he swished it from side to side as he glared up at Nightingale with blood-red eyes.

"I know that," said Nightingale. "We had a deal. This has nothing to do with me."

"You never said you were going to kill yourself for the girl."

"That's not what happened," said Nightingale. "I wanted to save her. And I did."

Lucifuge Rofocale stamped his foot. "You sacrificed yourself for her and now look what's happened." He raised the riding crop as if he was about to strike Nightingale across the face and sneered when he saw Nightingale flinch.

Nightingale raised his hands to protect his face. "It wasn't planned," he said.

"Planned or not you've screwed everything up."

"So take my soul and have done with it," said Nightingale. "I don't care any more."

"Don't you understand? It's not my decision any longer. It's out of my hands."

"This isn't my fault," said Nightingale. "We had a deal. You kept your end of the bargain and I did what I had to do. I had no idea it was going to end up like this." He looked out across the sea. "Whatever 'this' is. I still don't understand what's happening."

Lucifuge Rofocale glared at Nightingale. "This was what you intended all along," he growled. "You tricked me."

"I didn't," said Nightingale.

"You knew that if you went back and died to save the girl then all bets would be off."

"I'm not as smart as that. I just did what I had to do." He patted his pockets, looking for his pack of Marlboro.

Lucifuge Rofocale cackled and waved his crop, and a lit cigarette appeared between the index and second fingers of Nightingale's right hand.

Nightingale stared at the cigarette in disbelief, then raised it to his mouth and inhaled gratefully.

"I don't know what's going to happen, Nightingale. I don't know who's going to get your soul. But I know one thing as surely as if it was carved in stone. I will make your life, or what passes for your life, a misery for all eternity."

Nightingale blew smoke. "Sticks and stones," he said.

Lucifuge Rofocale roared and shimmered and there was a loud crack and a rancid stench, then something huge and scaly loomed over Nightingale. A massive claw whipped out, just missing his stomach but ripping through his sleeve. The monster's jaws opened and Nightingale saw rows of sharp teeth and a forked tongue covered in purple scales, and then a wave of foul-smelling smoke washed over him.

"Like I said, sticks and stones," said Nightingale. "This place doesn't exist. I'm in the Nowhen. Neither here nor there. So there's nothing you can do to hurt me." He stared up at the monster, his eyes watering from its sulphurous breath. "If I'm wrong, do whatever you want and do it now because I'm past caring."

The monster roared and a cloud of yellow smoke engulfed Nightingale. The giant claw lashed out again, missing his face by inches, but Nightingale grinned because he knew he was right.

"Screw you," he said, and turned his back on Lucifuge Rofocale. "I'll see you in Hell. Or not."

Everything went white again and Nightingale was alone.

Time passed.

Or didn't.

CHAPTER
EIGHTY-EIGHT

"Mr Nightingale?"

"Yes?"

There was nothing to see. Just white. Or an absence of white. Then Mrs Steadman was standing in front of him, smiling benignly and dressed in black.

"A decision has been reached."

"Yes?"

"You are to go back."

"Back where?"

"To where you were before."

"And then what happens?"

"That's up to you."

"And who has my soul?"

"You do." She smiled. "Take better care of it this time."

"Mrs Steadman?"

"Yes?"

"Thank you."

"There's no need to thank me, Mr Nightingale. Goodbye."

"Goodbye, Mrs Steadman."

CHAPTER
EIGHTY-NINE

Nightingale was falling. The wind whipped at his hair and roared past his ears and he saw Sophie and he saw Hoyle, one foot on a large plant pot, just about to launch himself from the next-door terrace. Time seemed to have stopped. Hoyle's eyes were wide and staring, his right hand stretched out in front of him, his fingers splayed. Directly below Nightingale, Sophie was kissing the top of her doll's head, her legs sticking under the balcony railing.

He twisted in the air and reached out with his right hand.

Hoyle scrambled across the terrace, his arms outstretched.

Nightingale pushed Sophie back with his right hand just as Hoyle reached her and she fell backwards into his arms.

Nightingale hit the railing so hard that it knocked the breath from his lungs but he managed to hang on with both hands.

Hoyle put Sophie on the ground and rushed over to the railing. He reached down, grabbed Nightingale's collar and hauled him up. Nightingale's Hush Puppies scraped against the wall and then he fell over the railing and collapsed onto the terrace, gasping for breath.

Sophie was sitting with her back to the wall. "I'm sorry," she said.

"Don't worry," croaked Nightingale. "You've got nothing to be sorry about."

"Bloody hell, Jack, don't ever try a stunt like that again," said Hoyle.

"It was a one-off," said Nightingale, rolling onto his back. He ruffled Sophie's hair. "Are you all right, Sophie?"

Sophie nodded but didn't say anything. She began to sob quietly.

"It's okay now," said Nightingale.

Hoyle picked her up and hugged her.

"No," she sobbed into Hoyle's chest. "It's not okay."

Nightingale got to his feet and brushed himself down. Hoyle looked at him over the top of Sophie's head. "Social Services," mouthed Nightingale, and Hoyle nodded.

While Hoyle took care of Sophie, Nightingale took the stairs down to the ground floor. He lit a cigarette as soon as he was outside.

Colin Duggan was standing by a patrol car talking into his radio. He finished the call as Nightingale walked over. "Please tell me that wasn't you playing Batman up there," he said.

Nightingale offered him his pack of Marlboro and Duggan took one. "All's well that ends well," said Nightingale, lighting the cigarette for him.

"The girl's okay?"

Nightingale shook his head. "No, she's not. Robbie's going to take her to Social Services."

"What about the father?"

"You should pick him up now. The mother too."

Duggan nodded. "That was Chalmers on the radio. He wants you in the office."

"Screw Chalmers."

"You'd better go, Jack."

"Yeah, I know."

Duggan blew smoke. "What's going on, Jack? Do you know this family?"

Nightingale shrugged. "I just know what's been going on, that's all."

"If that's the case, why didn't you do something before?"

"This is the first chance I've had," said Nightingale. "Be lucky, Colin." He walked over to his car.

CHAPTER
NINETY

"You're finished, Nightingale. And not before time."
Superintendent Chalmers held out his hand. "Warrant
card," he said.

"What?"

"I want your warrant card. Then you can report to
Professional Standards."

"I didn't do anything to Underwood," said
Nightingale.

"Who?"

"Simon Underwood. The father. I haven't been near
him."

"What the hell are you talking about? Who is Simon
Underwood?"

"Sophie's father. He's been having sex with her. The
mother knows what's going on. She's either scared of
him or doesn't want to lose him."

"The girl in Chelsea Harbour?"

Nightingale nodded. "She wanted to end it all
because of what her father was doing to her."

"But she's not at risk now."

"Not now, no. She's with Social Services. But she
was serious about wanting to die. She's going to need a
lot of therapy."

"Look, Nightingale, this isn't about the girl. This is about you assaulting a member of the public."

"What?"

"I'm told that on the way into the building you thumped a plumber in the face. Broke his nose and chipped a tooth, as it happens. His lawyer's already been on to us and he's looking for six figures. Which, considering the number of people who saw you attack him for no reason, he'll probably get. And apparently there was a photographer from the *Daily Mail* there, so expect to see yourself on the front page tomorrow morning."

"He was a rubber-necker; he only wanted to see her die," said Nightingale.

"You walked up to him and belted him without provocation."

"Yeah, well, you had to be there, and of course you never are, are you?"

"Just watch your lip, Nightingale," said Chalmers, pointing a finger at him. "You hit a civilian, which means you're out. You can resign or you can wait to be sacked, but either way you'll be out by the end of the month." He tapped the desk. "Warrant card. Now. Then you can get yourself over to Professional Standards to make a statement. If you want to take your federation rep with you, fine, but it won't do you any good."

Nightingale took his warrant card out and threw it down, then he took out his cigarettes and lit one.

Chalmers glared at him. "What the hell do you think you're doing? You can't smoke in here!"

"What are you going to do, Chalmers?" asked Nightingale. "You've already sacked me, right? What else can you do? Arrest me for smoking?" He blew smoke up at the ceiling. "You are full of shit."

"Yeah? Well, you're a crap copper. But I'll be keeping my job and my pension and you'll be out on your arse."

"You've no idea what happened. You've no idea why I did what I did."

"Get out, Nightingale."

Nightingale took a long pull on his cigarette and blew smoke as he stared at Chalmers through narrowed eyes. "Okay, I'm going," he said. "Screw you and screw the job. But you need to look at Underwood. He's a banker, over at Canary Wharf. You need to get a doctor to examine Sophie, run a rape kit too. With the right sort of handling Sophie will talk and I'm pretty sure the mother will give evidence against him once he's taken away from the family. Okay?"

Chalmers nodded. "Okay," he said. "Now get the hell out of my office."

CHAPTER
NINETY-ONE

SIX MONTHS LATER

Nightingale sipped his coffee and looked out of the window at the wealthy housewives walking by with their designer bags and coats that cost more than he earned in a month. He filled in another crossword answer but realised that left him with a word ending in "J" so he figured that he'd made yet another mistake. He'd never been good at crosswords but he was even worse at Sudoku.

He saw Jenny walking down New Bond Street. She was carrying a leather attaché case and looking at her watch. Nightingale knew that she was expecting a call from an advertising agency that had interviewed her. She wasn't going to get the job. The director of human resources would be calling to tell her just that.

Underneath the *Evening Standard* crossword were classified adverts including the one that he'd paid for: "Private Investigator seeks bright assistant with a good telephone manner and Microsoft Office skills for a job that will never be boring." Nightingale wasn't sure whether in modern Britain he was allowed to advertise for someone bright, as that presumably discriminated against all the stupid people in the nation's capital, but the wording had been accepted without comment by the woman who'd taken his advert over the phone.

Jenny walked into the Costa Coffee and ordered a latte. She was wearing a blue suit under a long raincoat with the collar turned up, and she had clipped up her hair at the back. He'd never seen her with her hair done that way before and it suited her. He smiled to himself. Strictly speaking, of course, he'd never laid eyes on her before. They'd never met or spoken. That was all in the future.

Nightingale took out his pen and circled the advert, then dropped the paper down on the table. He stood up just as Jenny was collecting her coffee. She smiled when she saw that there was an empty seat but Nightingale turned away so that she couldn't see his face. As he walked by her he caught the scent of her perfume.

As he left the coffee shop she was sitting down and putting her attaché case on the table, next to the newspaper. He stopped, lit a cigarette and watched through the window as she sipped her coffee. "Catch you later, kid," he whispered, and walked away.

Also available in ISIS Large Print:

Fair Game

Stephen Leather

Spider Shepherd is up against the most violent enemies he's ever encountered. Somali pirates have kidnapped the crew of a yacht in a brutal attack, and are demanding a huge ransom in return for the hostages.

The pirates have chilling terrorist ambitions in the UK, and are making terrible plans to change the London skyline forever. Thousands of lives are on the line.

Spider is sent to sea on an undercover mission to stop the pirates. But time is running out.

ISBN 978-0-7531-8918-4 (hb)
ISBN 978-0-7531-8919-1 (pb)

Midnight

Stephen Leather

Jack Nightingale found it hard enough to save lives when he was a cop. Now he needs to save a soul — his sister's. But to save her he has to find her and they've been separated since birth.

When everyone Jack talks to about his sister dies horribly, he realises that someone, or something, is determined to keep them apart.

If he's going to save his sister, he's going to have to do what he does best — negotiate. But any negotiation with the forces of darkness comes at a terrible price. And first Jack must ask himself the question: is every soul worth saving?

ISBN 978-0-7531-8852-1 (hb)
ISBN 978-0-7531-8853-8 (pb)

Rough Justice

Stephen Leather

Villains across London are being beaten and killed by vigilante cops. Crime rates are falling, but the powers that be want Dan "Spider" Shepherd to bring the wave of rough justice to an end.

Shepherd is never comfortable investigating cops, but working for the Serious Organised Crime Agency means he has no choice. He goes undercover with an elite group of officers at the sharp end of policing, risking their lives daily on the worst streets in the Capital.

And he has more hard decisions to make when his family is in the firing line . . .

ISBN 978-0-7531-8720-3 (hb)
ISBN 978-0-7531-8721-0 (pb)

Nightfall

Stephen Leather

"You're going to hell, Jack Nightingale": They are words that ended his career as a police negotiator. Now Jack's a struggling private detective — and the chilling words come back to haunt him.

Nightingale's life is turned upside down the day that he inherits a mansion with a priceless library; it comes from a man who claims to be his father, and it comes with a warning. That Nightingale's soul was sold at birth and a devil will come to claim it on his 33rd birthday — just three weeks away.

Jack doesn't believe in Hell, probably doesn't believe in Heaven either. But when people close to him start to die horribly, he is led to the inescapable conclusion that real evil may be at work. And that if he doesn't find a way out he'll be damned in hell for eternity.

ISBN 978-0-7531-8624-4 (hb)
ISBN 978-0-7531-8625-1 (pb)